CONCERNING LILY

'A painful, acutely observed novel about self-deception and
the break-up of longstanding relationships.
The novel specialises in beautifully choreographed
tension, the narrowly avoided row, the tiff where
nothing is openly said. Her unhappy dialogues have
an achingly familiar rhythm'
Evening Standard

'Sally Brampton's latest novel is a brilliant easy-reading
version of Iris Murdoch. What Brampton does
particularly well is spin out the agony . . . the build-up is
delicious. This is an amorality tale – and it's a real
achievement that Brampton makes Lily interesting,
if not sympathetic'
Sunday Times

'Pithy and pertinent'
She

Praise for Sally Brampton's previous novels:

'Completely absorbing and painfully accurate'
Fay Weldon

'Sally Brampton is an excellent writer'
Literary Review

Also by Sally Brampton

Good Grief
Lovesick

SALLY BRAMPTON was born in 1955 in Brunei and spent her childhood in the Middle East and Africa. She studied fashion at Central St Martin's School of Art before joining *Vogue*. Four years later she went on to become the fashion editor for the *Observer* and in 1985 she launched British *Elle*, which she edited for four years. She has written two previous novels, *Good Grief* and *Lovesick*. She lives with her husband and their daughter in London.

SALLY BRAMPTON

CONCERNING LILY

ARROW

Published in the United Kingdom in 1998 by
Arrow Books

3 5 7 9 10 8 6 4 2

Copyright © Sally Brampton 1998

The right of Sally Brampton to be identified as the author of this
work has been asserted by her in accordance with the
Copyright, Designs and Patents Act, 1988

First published in the United Kingdom in 1998
by William Heinemann

Arrow Books Limited
Random House UK Limited
20 Vauxhall Bridge Road, London SW1V 2SA

Random House Australia (Pty) Limited
20 Alfred Street, Milsons Point, Sydney
New South Wales 2061, Australia

Random House New Zealand Limited
18 Poland Road, Glenfield, Auckland 10, New Zealand

Random House South Africa (Pty) Limited
Endulini, 5a Jubilee Road, Parktown 2193, South Africa

Random House UK Limited Reg. No. 954009

A CIP catalogue record for this book
is available from the British Library

Papers used by Random House UK Limited
are natural, recyclable products made from wood grown in
sustainable forests. The manufacturing processes conform to
the environmental regulations of the country of origin

Printed and bound in Great Britain by
The Guernsey Press Co. Ltd., Vale, Guernsey, Channel Islands

ISBN 0 7493 2302 7

For Sarah

One

Elisabeth Delaware felt in an obscure way that life had let her down. This, despite everything surrounding her, which conspired to make her as happy as she could be.

As she manoeuvred the heavy car through a tangle of streets in North London, she considered this, deciding that it was not so much that she was unhappy as that she was not as happy as her friends seemed to think she had a duty to be. She thought, they tick off my blessings like items on a shopping list.

First, Charles. One lovely husband. He adored her. Everybody said so. They said it so often that it was as if his adoration had become a part of her character, like her blue eyes or blonde hair. They didn't, of course, ask her how she felt. Well, you don't ask a person whether they are happy with the colour of their hair. Not, that is, unless they go out and change it. And she adored Charles too, of course she did. Those occasional snagged threads of irritation were just part of the fabric of marriage, particularly a marriage of seventeen years' standing.

You don't, in particular, ask a woman who is loved if she is happy. Doubtless, she is happy. Not to be so would be ungrateful and there is nothing so uncomfortable to other people as ingratitude. Or truth, Elisabeth thought, peering out of the snug womb of the Volvo estate at the dark, wet March afternoon, remembering an interview in the *Guardian* with a man, quite famous (although she couldn't, as usual, remember his name), who admitted that it had taken him twenty years of therapy to say out loud

1

that he didn't like his mother. He calculated that those five words had cost him ten thousand pounds – and still he couldn't bring himself to use the word hate. Later, Elisabeth stood in the middle of her quiet, shining kitchen and tried saying it too. 'I hate my mother.' Trouble was, it wasn't true. She had adored her mother, missed her daily. So she said instead, very loudly, 'I am not happy.'

The walls responded blankly, as walls do.

She slid the car into the nearside lane, preparing to turn left into Kentish Town High Road. Just as she was creeping towards the front of the queue, the lights changed to red. Sighing, she glanced down at the newspaper that lay next to her on the passenger seat, checking the street name that she had scrawled across the top of the page. Orchard Road. It had started to rain. She turned on the windscreen wipers and waited patiently for the lights, watching the neon shop signs smearing silver and gold across the wet glass. It seemed impossible that once there had been orchards here, that trees had ever lived in this jostling mass of brick, although she knew that they once had, that centuries ago this area had been open country, a tangle of leaf and bramble and birdsong now crushed under the weight of urban development. She imagined the roots writhing, starved and white, beneath the grey concrete pavements, crushed flat under the weight of a million busy lives, and felt a sudden, sharp stab of sympathy. She sometimes felt crushed too, squashed by the weight of her blessings until she felt as flat and featureless as the paper dolls that her children used to cut out at nursery school.

Ah yes, her children, James and Lucy. Two more blessings. Why then, did she think of them more often than not with alarm, wondering how those small, sticky creatures had metamorphosed into the bony, elegant strangers who greeted her with a faintly surprised air, cool blue stares piercing her as she rushed to embrace them on their increasingly rare visits home from boarding school. They were good kids – everybody said so – sensible and clever; had been dutiful even as children, contriving to be born in just the right order, James first and then Lucy, with the requisite twenty months' difference in age. They had been punctilious, too, in their share of the usual childish illnesses; not so severe as to be worrying but thorough enough to ensure that the right number of antibodies surged through their pink-cheeked, healthy bodies. And they were popular too, always being asked away to weekends in the country; a party, supervised of course, followed by a sleep-over in some nice, safe comfortable Gloucestershire home; invitations to the ballet and opera in smart London theatres extended by other parents, grateful for their cool, undemanding presence, their calming influence on their own boisterous offspring. 'Such a pleasure . . .' they breathed over the telephone, 'always a pleasure.'

She missed them, of course, but no longer as bitterly as she had their first year away, when their absence had caused her actual physical pain. They had gone off to school two years ago (was it really so long?), when James was thirteen and Lucy eleven; both to the same liberal, co-educational establishment. It was Charles's idea that they should go together – dear Charles, always so conscious of fair play – and Elisabeth who had fought against it. He had been right, of course, as he so often was. Too right, she thought, thinking of James's and Lucy's unfamiliar new habits, their silent conspiratorial exchanges.

Just as he had been right about the pain, which had diminished to an ache and then to a lingering, although not pressing consciousness of the empty space where they should have been. Perhaps that's what this feeling is, Elisabeth thought, as she swung the car into Orchard Road and slowed down, peering at the dim numbers on the houses, searching for number 59. Perhaps I am suffering

3

neither the absence of happiness nor the presence of unhappiness. Perhaps all that I am feeling is the emptiness of space.

Finding the house, she eased the car into a parking space and peered out at the dark, wet, unfamiliar street. And perhaps that's why I am embarked on this ridiculous errand, a woman in search of a wedding dress that I do not want or need.

The absurdity of her situation struck her suddenly and she sat motionless in the car, staring at the forlorn terrace house opposite, its once gracious Georgian lines blurred by neglect, its sagging windows and porticoes wrinkled with age. She wondered about the woman in the house, the one she had come to see and she asked herself, once again, why she was there.

Elisabeth was not a reckless woman. But just lately, her not-happiness had begun to inspire in her feelings of quivering impulsiveness. It was those feelings that had led her to make the telephone call that morning, dialling the number with trembling fingers even as her rational self stood at her side demanding, quite loudly, what on earth she thought she was up to. Still, she could not help herself, not after she'd seen the small ad in the local paper, buried among the Mothercare strollers and pine bunk beds; 'Wedding dress. Never Worn. £250 only.' She had sat for a moment, stunned by pity, her hand hovering over the cup of coffee cooling by her side. Never worn. The words reverberated in her head as she pictured a woman sitting alone, a dark head bent over a froth of lace and white satin, a silk skirt soaking up bitter tears. Elisabeth picked up the cup of coffee, took a gulp of the tepid liquid, stared around at her large, beautiful kitchen and heard only silence. Awful, she thought, awful, and her eyes strayed upwards, to the floors of her house hovering above her, the large but cosy bed that she and Charles shared on the second floor, the pretty white bathroom leading off it, two dressing-gowns hanging comfortably side by side on twin hooks. Awful to be so suddenly, so brutally denied the comforts of marriage. She must do something. But what? A drink, perhaps, a cup of coffee, a sympathetic ear. Before she knew it, her hand was on the telephone, dialling the number, and she heard her own voice saying, 'I'm calling about the wedding dress.'

'I've come about the wedding dress,' Elisabeth said, staring uncertainly at a pale face peering through the half-opened door. The door swung slowly open to reveal a slender young woman with large, dark, unblinking eyes and a mass of slithery dark hair, pulled back and knotted in an awkward pony-tail. As Elisabeth stepped forward into the weak light thrown by the single bulb hanging in the shabby hallway, she saw that the woman was younger than she had first thought, looked scarcely more than a girl in her loose tracksuit trousers and baggy, misshapen jumper. She wore old leather moccasins, trodden down at the heel as though she had thrust her feet clumsily into them in a hurry. Plastering a bright, encouraging smile on her face, Elisabeth moved forward and extended her hand in greeting. 'Elisabeth Delaware,' she said.

The girl's eyes flickered dismissively towards the hand. 'All right?' she said in a harsh, toneless voice, then turned on her heel and moved across the hallway. 'I'm Lily, by the way,' she threw over her shoulder, 'Lily Clifton.'

Elisabeth followed obediently, her eyes taking in the shabby wallpaper and chipped paint, her ears registering the muffled boom of a television playing somewhere in the house. Lily was silent save for the slap of her shoes on the worn lino as she moved to the narrow staircase. She stopped at the foot of the stairs, stared blankly at Elisabeth for a moment before gesturing to her to follow. Catching a glimpse of her face under the full glare of the light hanging above the stairs, Elisabeth could see that there was something appealing about the broad, heart-shaped face and large, dark eyes. They reminded Elisabeth of the sweet, faintly bruised appeal of a pansy. Why, how silly of them, she thought suddenly, to choose the wrong flower.

The girl stopped outside a door, fumbling at the lock with a shiny gold key. 'It sticks,' she explained, jiggling the key in the lock, pushing the door with a thin shoulder and easing it open.

It was the emptiest room Elisabeth had ever been in; bare save for a bed, a chair, a narrow wardrobe and a basin on which stood a solitary toothbrush.

'Horrible, isn't it?' Lily said, following her gaze.

Elisabeth smiled uncertainly. 'It's OK,' she said, pity making her voice brisk.

The girl's eyes flickered over Elisabeth's face. 'Don't be daft,' she said good-naturedly. 'Be all right, though, once I've got myself sorted. Want a coffee?'

'That would be nice,' Elisabeth said doubtfully, looking around for any evidence of a kettle, but the girl suddenly swept back a thin curtain to reveal a set of shelves and a makeshift kitchen. 'Black do?' she said, clattering instant coffee into two mugs. 'Didn't have time to get down to the shops for milk, what with waiting for you and that.' She switched the kettle on and waited for it to boil, subsiding into silence as she slouched against the wall, thin shoulders drooping. She seemed to have forgotten entirely about the wedding dress and about Elisabeth, who was marooned awkwardly in the space between the bed and the wardrobe. Elisabeth gazed at the limp, patterned curtains and then at a fluffy dog, pale pink and solitary, propped neatly on the narrow bed. She felt a sudden, overwhelming rush of sympathy for the bleak room, and the thin, silent girl. 'Do you mind if I sit down?' she asked.

Lily looked up, her blank gaze coming into slow focus. 'Forget my own head next,' she said, a smile glimmering on her pale face. 'Take the bed, it's more comfortable than that chair. Springs have gone, or something. Look, and here's the kettle ready,' she continued, as a thin spiral of steam erupted from the spout of the ancient, juddering electric kettle. 'Soon have some coffee ready. Warm you up a bit.'

'I'm fine,' Elisabeth said, lowering herself cautiously onto the bed, her eyes fixed on Lily's thin white wrists protruding from the lumpy jumper, a scabbed blister glowing red on a bare heel. From the back she looked scarcely older than Lucy. Elisabeth's throat closed with a clamp of maternal tenderness and she wondered where this girl's mother was, if she knew her daughter was living in this bleak, cold place. 'Is it your first time in London?' she asked.

Lily smiled. 'Yeah,' she said briefly. 'Big, isn't it?'

It was that, Elisabeth thought later, that decided her. Those few pathetic words and the girl's evident courage, her cheerful fortitude. 'Not a trace of self-pity,' she exclaimed the next day to her friends Bella and Daisy. The idea slowly formed as she drank the coffee, grew in strength as she exclaimed over the wedding dress – a cheap, commonplace design of cream polyester silk trimmed with drooping machine-made roses – and said, regretfully, that no, it wasn't quite what she had in mind for her daughter, after all. By the time Lily said, her shoulders drooping with disappointment but a smile set bravely on her thin, pale face, that it couldn't matter a bit – well, by then the idea was so bursting with vigour and importance that Elisabeth exclaimed, without preamble, 'Why don't you come and have supper?'

Lily blinked slowly. 'Supper?' she echoed.

'Just a few friends,' Elisabeth said, watching her anxiously, 'nothing grand or frightening.'

'Well, I'm not sure –'

'It'll give you a chance to meet a few people in London,' Elisabeth said eagerly, 'get you out of this place for an

7

evening.' The idea was so fixed in her mind that she was determined not to let it go. 'Do say you'll come,' she pleaded. 'Charles – my husband – will be thrilled. It'll just be a few close friends, Bella and Tom, Daisy and Alex,' she went on, as if they were all known to Lily and that the mere mention of their names would determine her acceptance.

'All right,' Lily said eventually, and her blank eyes took on a curious, brilliant shine.

Elisabeth swept out, glowing and triumphant, into the dark March night. It was only when she was in her car, driving home, that she realised that she had forgotten to ask Lily the thing she had so longed to know that morning; what it was that had caused her to sell her wedding dress in the first place.

Charles trudged home through the wet, dark evening, sunk in thought, his eyes fixed on the pavement. He was a solid, rumpled man in his late forties with a stiff, closed look about his face and tired smudges under his eyes that contrasted violently with a thick, lively thatch of dark hair. He was ambling a little, distracted by a case he was working on: a messy, bitter divorce following a thirty-year marriage. He had thought, that afternoon, that the year-long negotiation was finally over but his client, the wife, had suddenly insisted on the return of a book she claimed her husband had taken from the family home. When Charles had pointed out that the book, a £5.99 paperback, was easily replaceable, she had looked at him oddly and said, 'But it's mine. It's got my name in it.'

Charles, reflecting that the settlement was half a million pounds, grinned wryly, causing a woman out walking her dog to glance at him with sudden interest, for the sweetness of his smile lent his tired face a dishevelled, kindly glamour. Her heart twisted briefly – recalling a time and a place, some distant happiness buried deep in her memory – and she glanced at him again but the smile had gone and the glamour with it; his face fading into the sullen repose of a tired, middle-aged commuter.

As he turned the corner of his street, Charles quickened his pace, his eyes straining in the yellow glare of the street lights to pick out the familiar, graceful lines of his house, its pale pink face and sleepy, shuttered windows gazing benevolently over the street, its garden spread out like a skirt, rolling gently down a slight incline, lapping the pavement with a low picket fence over which spilled a hem of roses. The rose hedge was dormant now, of course, a tangle of bare branch and thorn, but its barbed-wire silhouette still held a graceful savagery. Charles loved that house, just as he had loved it the first time he saw it fifteen years ago and had determined to buy it. Five years later, he had put their names – his and Elisabeth's – to a piece of paper and it was theirs, to live in happily ever after.

Well, and so it had seemed until a few years ago, Charles thought, experiencing the slight sinking feeling he had started to feel recently when he was about to confront his wife. She had been so strained of late, fretful and impatient with him, but he ascribed her mood to the children's leaving to go to school. He knew she was frustrated – she told him often enough – and bored now that the children had gone and she had nothing to devote her considerable energies to. He had tried to talk to her about it, made suggestions, had even brought home various leaflets that he felt might interest her – a course in decorative arts at the V&A, a series of lectures at the Chelsea Physic Garden – but she greeted all his attempts with a contemptuous indifference and so he had long since given up. He knew he wasn't much help, was too tired by the time he got home to do much more than eat supper before going off to his study to do a few hours' more work. Charles considered the sudden fashionability of his firm – of which he was a founder and senior partner – following a couple of celebrity divorces, a mixed blessing but what with two children away at an expensive boarding school and a large house to maintain, it was one he contemplated most often with gratitude.

Turning into the darkened garden, he struggled with the stiff latch on the black wrought-iron gate and walked up to his front door. Squaring his shoulders, he took a deep breath and stepped inside.

Elisabeth offered him her cheek. He noticed how she did that these days, her face turning from him as he approached to present a cool, impersonal expanse of flesh. Once, she used to kiss him on the mouth. He felt her soft, pliant skin under his lips, smelled wine and raw onions on her breath.

'Good day?' she said, turning back to the chopping board.

'Middling,' he said evenly, 'a half-a-million-pound settlement held up by a dispute over a £5.99 paperback.'

She shook her head. 'Aren't people strange,' she said, but her voice was vague, her interest merely dutiful.

'Aren't they,' Charles agreed, going to the fridge to pull out a bottle of wine, replenishing her glass, filling one for himself. 'Anything happen today?' he asked, sitting down at the table, stretching out his tired legs. He lifted the glass to his mouth to take a gulp of wine and as he did so, caught the flash of her face turning to him and away again, saw a glimpse of concentrated anger in her eyes. What now? he thought wearily, contemplating her stiffened back, her hand savagely pumping over a pile of chopped onion. He waited for her to speak but she said nothing so after a while he enquired mildly, 'Everything all right, darling?'

'Fine,' she said abruptly, without turning round, and he wondered again what it was that he had said to offend her.

'Things do *happen* here,' she exclaimed suddenly. 'I

mean, it's not as if I sit in this house all day long, doing nothing.'

'Darling, I didn't mean –'

'And, amazing as it may seem to you, something did happen today. I invited somebody for supper –' Elisabeth turned to him, her gaze challenging, two spots of colour burning in her cheeks. 'A woman who was selling her wedding dress.'

Charles stared at her, mystified. 'Wedding dress? Do we need a wedding dress?'

Elisabeth giggled suddenly. 'Not for us, silly. Because I felt sorry for her.'

'Why?'

The smile faded, to be replaced by the closed, irritable look she had worn of late. 'Oh, never mind,' she said, turning back to her preparations for supper.

'Smells good,' he said after a while.

'Roast chicken with garlic,' she said in a hard, bright voice. 'Your favourite.'

Two

The following evening, Elisabeth was entertaining. 'Supper,' she had said on the telephone. 'Nothing fancy. Just us.'

By 'us' she meant Bella and Daisy, her two closest friends. They would gather early, share a bottle of wine and catch up on the week's news before the men arrived. 'Woman's Hour', Charles called it. Once, that would have amused Elisabeth but just lately her smile had become strained at the inevitability of the phrase. Meeting for drinks was a sort of ritual, had been going on for years, usually at Elisabeth's house because it was the biggest of the three. Daisy's flat was tiny and Bella's house, well – nobody went there except Bella and Tom. 'Too bloody dreary,' was how Bella put it. I bloody hate it, was what she meant.

And now Bella, who was always the first to arrive, sat slumped at Elisabeth's kitchen table, her long bony face white with exhaustion. 'What have you been up to?' she asked, gratefully gulping down a glass of wine.

'Nothing,' Elisabeth replied truthfully.

Bella leaned back in her chair. Her frizz of black hair stood up in exhausted little clumps around her head and her wool suit was crumpled. 'God, what I'd give to do nothing,' she said. 'No wonder you're so happy.'

'Yes,' Elisabeth said, thinking that nothing must seem like happiness if you never have time for it.

Bella was a polytechnic lecturer, taught fine art – as if such a thing as teaching painting were possible. Bella thought so, anyway. It was what made her so tired. Everything made Bella tired: her husband, her son, life in general. She expected so much of them.

'Actually, I *have* been up to something,' Elisabeth said, flushing faintly as she recounted the story of Lily and the wedding dress.

'You've done what?' Bella exclaimed.

'Oh dear,' Elisabeth said fretfully, 'I knew when I said it that it would sound a bit peculiar –'

'Just a little,' Bella said, but her expression moved down a notch, settled into one of mild curiosity.

'She just looked so – well, so lost, I suppose,' Elisabeth continued, 'that I kept wondering how I could help her. She's just moved to London, doesn't know anybody. Then it came to me, maybe a night out, some amusing people and good food and wine might cheer her up. She's terribly thin,' she added, almost absently.

The doorbell rang. Elisabeth went to answer it. Daisy, late as usual, 'Sorry, sorry, completely forgot the time,' flew past her into the kitchen and went and perched on the edge of a chair, bony ankles neatly crossed. She was thin and pale, with fine blonde hair worn close to her head in a gleaming cap and the sort of skin that looks as if it would bruise easily.

'Good week?' Elisabeth asked, thinking how like pipe-cleaners Daisy's legs looked, encased in opaque black tights.

'Oh, wonderful if you *like* nervous breakdowns,' Daisy said. 'About a million things went wrong . . . a visit from the VAT man who says I owe him an absolute fortune, Alex in a stink about God knows what and a sodding great leak in my flat.'

Daisy was a sculptor, quite a successful one, to her continued astonishment. 'It's just like playing at sand-castles,' she would say to anyone who asked, 'except you do it with huge great lumps of clay.'

13

'That's only three,' Bella said.

'But of such magnitude. . . . The bedroom carpet's sodden and Alex is supposed to be spending the night and you know what he's like about things being just so. Next thing I know, he'll run back to his wife.'

'Don't be silly,' Elisabeth said. 'Charles was picking him up from the office at six.'

'How heavenly, to have such a reliable husband.'

'Do stop talking about him as if he was a Morris Minor. Anyway, he just wants to be sure Alex will turn up. He's sick of paying for unused theatre tickets.'

'Better a Morris Minor than an unreliable Porsche,' Bella said. 'You don't know how lucky you are.'

'Oh, I do, I do,' Elisabeth said, sighing slightly.

'Elisabeth has always led a charmed life,' Daisy said, without malice. The two of them had been friends since school, had met on their very first day, well, night actually, when Daisy had found Elisabeth crouched in the corner of the dormitory, curled up in a ball on the floor, her face stiff with tears and homesickness. They were ten years old – though Daisy seemed older, having been a veteran of boarding schools since she was six. 'It will be all right,' she had said in a kindly voice, lifting Elisabeth off the floor and tucking her into bed, deftly smoothing the starchy cotton sheets around her and poking a teddy bear, her own, by Elisabeth's side. 'The first night's always the worst.'

When Elisabeth wondered aloud about the first year, and how she would get through that, Daisy laughed and said, with the wisdom of small children who have to endure a life that they are powerless to change, that it would all soon seem like the most normal thing in the world. As indeed it did, so normal that eight years later when the time came for them to leave, Elisabeth clung to Daisy and sobbed again. Daisy, who was off to art school and whose head glittered with the dazzling luxury of

14

freedom, laughed again and promised her that nothing would change, that they would see each other just as much as they always had.

They didn't, of course.

Somehow the weeks slid by until Elisabeth – it was always Elisabeth – would telephone and invite Daisy round to her small, cosy flat in South Kensington, sensibly close to the secretarial college she attended. Daisy would arrive, looking thin and exotic in a strange but alluring assortment of clothes ('Oh, everybody dresses like this') and clutching a bottle. They would drink a couple of glasses of wine while Elisabeth, wearing a sensible jumper and skirt, sneaked covert but dazzled glances at her bright, unfamiliar friend. After a while, the alcohol would begin its work and Daisy would lose some of her brittleness and Elisabeth some of her sensible caution and they would stretch out on her pretty chintz sofa and slip back into the old, familiar ways. Then Elisabeth would stagger to her feet and produce supper, a proper meal of the sort their mothers would have made and whose completeness always took Daisy – whose idea of preparing a cauliflower cheese was to dump some raw cauliflower and a packet of cream cheese dip on the table – by surprise.

Daisy, slouching at the table in thin, unsuitable clothes, flicking ash over a plate of half-eaten food, would sometimes gaze at Elisabeth's glossy, brushed hair, velvet hairband and pearl earrings and wonder why they were still friends but some part of her was charmed by the tidy order of Elisabeth's life, by the comforting routine of familiarity.

Then, one night, Daisy appeared with a new friend in tow, a thin, tall girl called Bella whose angular plainness was made handsome by the layers of richly coloured velvets and silks in which she was draped, by the rough beads that hung about her scrawny neck and the black kohl daubed like soot around her dark eyes. The two of them settled in Elisabeth's pastel-coloured sitting-room, chattering like exotic birds, while Elisabeth looked on and tried not to feel frightened of this new friend of Daisy's, this fierce, tense creature, with her frizz of foaming curls and clever, flashing eyes. And because she loved Daisy, she tried to love Bella and eventually came to succeed, particularly once Tom appeared on the scene and smoothed down some of the raw, abrasive edges. Even so, she never quite lost her fear of her, not that is until Tom's shocking, unexpected affair when Elisabeth saw a new Bella – stripped of her glittering, protective layer as effectively as if she had been whipped, her outer skin flayed off in jagged strips to reveal the soft, vulnerable creature beneath. It was only then that Elisabeth found herself truly able to like her.

And here they were, twenty years later, at Elisabeth's table, preparing to eat Elisabeth's food, a proper supper of course, but these days it was what the others expected too.

'Have you told Daisy yet?' Bella asked, her gaze sliding from Elisabeth to Daisy and settling in a small, cool smile.

'Told me what?'

'Elisabeth's made a new friend, a poor little orphan girl.'

'Bella –' Elisabeth said, with a pained look.

'A lost and lonely creature with a wedding dress to sell,' Bella continued.

'A wedding dress?' Daisy questioned, with a look of such pure astonishment that Elisabeth felt compelled to tell the whole story, starting with her reading the paper at the table right there – she ran her hand across the smooth, ancient wood as if to reassure herself of the truth of the tale – and ending with the invitation to dinner.

When she had finished, the white, translucent lids of Daisy's eyes momentarily veiled her pale blue gaze and then she lifted her eyes and murmured, 'Well, I'm sure she'll be very grateful.'

'I knew you'd understand,' Elisabeth said, unable to

resist a triumphant look in Bella's direction. 'I just couldn't bear the idea of somebody selling their wedding dress –'

'She's probably skint,' Bella said.

'But – *unworn*.'

'Indeed,' Daisy said, thinking of the pale pink suit hanging in her wardrobe, bought in a burst of frantic happiness when Alex had promised to leave Celia, his wife. Daisy only ever wore black, so the suit wasn't much use to her. Even she, so loudly disdainful of convention, would not have worn black to her own wedding. Would gladly have gone to her own wedding, had she been asked. Alex didn't know about the suit. It was zipped away in a navy nylon bag. Like a body bag, Daisy thought, with a faint shudder.

'No point hanging on to a dress you don't need,' Bella said, but then Bella had no room in her life for sentiment. No good being sentimental when your life's going down the drain. Had very nearly gone, in fact. If she'd had a wedding dress, she would have sold it willingly if she thought it would bring them in any spare cash. But she had never had one. She and Tom had got married in jeans and jumpers with holes in the elbows, their only finery their reckless, endless happiness.

She kept her holey jumper, hidden away in a drawer in her bedroom. She had told Tom she'd chucked it out, but that was during the awful year when she'd wanted to destroy everything he'd ever touched, including herself. Especially herself.

She got it out sometimes, when the present seemed too much to bear, lay on the bed with it clutched to her face. It smelled of fabric conditioner, Spring Fresh. Spring, bottled in a yellow plastic bottle with a lurid pink top and turquoise lettering. Absurd. She wished now that she hadn't washed it, wanted the scent of her memories – roll-ups, beer and languid, stretchy sex in the afternoon.

Tom still wore his when there was some really dirty job

to do in the garden. She tried not to mind but she did, had taken to hiding it from him. She couldn't bear to see him in it now.

She remembered their wedding day so clearly: his hot, bony hand in hers, a grin cracking his thin face as they stood in the windowless, grey registry office in Euston Road, their faces luminous with fear and excitement under the yellow neon light. Those who had had the fortune or, depending how they subsequently looked on marriage, the misfortune to visit it said it was the ugliest building in London. Bella and Tom hadn't minded; had laughed over the sad, dusty, plastic flowers, the glare of the pompous, red-faced registrar as they giggled through the ceremony. They hadn't minded anything then, their marriage and their future before them, a thin, bright ribbon unfurling endlessly into tomorrow.

It was their last day at art school. 'The first day of the rest of our lives,' Tom promised, kissing her as he slid the cheap gold band onto her finger. Bella, usually so sharply critical, hadn't minded the cliché; it seemed tinged with glory.

They'd all met for drinks in the pub afterwards. Elisabeth and Daisy were there, of course. Charles too, although he and Elisabeth weren't married then; Charles said he wouldn't consider it until he was qualified and could support them both. Bella and Tom had laughed about it secretly, just as they had giggled about the idea of dear, pompous Charles having sex. 'I don't think they've ever done it. Maybe he's saving himself,' Bella said, rolling on top of Tom, his sharp pelvic bones bruising her thin thighs. Not so funny any more, Bella thought, gazing at Elisabeth's large, serene, *rich* kitchen. And Charles. Dear, faithful, dogged Charles – who really had saved himself for his wife.

Unlike Tom.

'What if she spends the entire evening weeping into her food?' Daisy said.

'I don't think she's the crying sort,' Elisabeth said, plucking a fragment of Marks & Spencer prawn-flavoured crisp from the grey cashmere sweater straining across her breasts. Her hips, snug in black gabardine trousers, pulled at their casing; the metallic glint of a zip was visible at the waistband where the fabric was stretched tight. Elisabeth always bought clothes a size too small, the size she used to be. She couldn't bear to go up another size, said it would be like giving her body permission to expand.

'Everybody's the crying sort,' Bella said, thinking of the long, hopeless hours she had spent lying on her bed, scrunched up under the duvet, ignoring the telephone and the doorbell, even ignoring Ben as he clattered in from school. Ignoring everything except the pain that made breathing, living, so hard. Remembering the day Ben, aged twelve, had brought her a cup of tea. The clatter as he placed it on the table by the bed, small hands carefully steadying it. She'd heard his voice, asking her if she was all right but she couldn't speak, not even to reassure him, could only hold her breath and wish him, fiercely, away. And then hearing him leave; the slow, bewildered drag of his feet.

He'd never forgiven her for that, not even now when he was a tall, skinny seventeen-year-old who cut through life with an assurance that she found baffling. He had a particular expression he seemed to keep only for her, a sort of hurt contempt – if he even bothered to look at her, which he didn't often these days. He knew nothing about Tom's affair, saw only her harsh, brittle way with him. He took it personally, thought it included him too. Mothers aren't allowed pain. At least, not their own.

'Do stop being so dismal, you two. She's had a rough time. What harm can giving her a nice dinner do?' Elisabeth exclaimed.

'She might nick the silver, case the joint for a burglary, turn out to be a child molester – anything.'

'Don't be silly. She's not like that.'

'Well, what is she like?'

'Young and lonely. She doesn't know a soul in London.'

'Even so –' Bella said uncertainly.

'Say you'll come,' Elisabeth pleaded.

'Do I have a choice?'

'No.'

Bella shrugged. 'Well, when is the great event?' She dreaded explaining it to Tom, knew he would disapprove, sneer at them playing Lady Bountiful, snug in their privileged lives. Not so snug, she thought. Not any more.

'Next Thursday, and Tom had better be there too,' Elisabeth said, yawning. She felt flat suddenly, deflated by their lack of enthusiasm. There was, after all, still food to be cooked, life to be dealt with. She looked at her watch. 'They're late. Supper will be ruined.'

'They said it might go on a bit,' Bella said. 'You know what local theatre's like.'

'A grand title for a bunch of poseurs,' Daisy said languidly, stretching thin white arms. 'Thank goodness they didn't make us go with them this time.'

'Hardly. Not after you laughed all the way through the last one.'

'It was funny.'

'It was supposed to be a tragedy.'

'Well, it was. Tragic, I mean.'

Elisabeth retrieved some crisp, golden parcels of salmon *en croûte* from the oven and peered at them worriedly. 'These are beginning to burn. Well, perhaps they might stand a few minutes longer. What shall we have with them? Green beans or spinach?'

'Beans.'

'Spinach.'

'We'd better have both, then.' She pulled a cellophane

bag of pre-washed spinach out of the fridge and started to top and tail beans with ruthless efficiency. 'Will Alex be eating with us?'

'He'd better,' Daisy said darkly.

Elisabeth dumped spinach in a large pan and salted it well, then gathered up knives and forks and put them on the table in front of Daisy.

'Distribute those, will you?'

The sound of a door slamming echoed faintly through the house. They all started slightly, gazing at each other warily.

'Have you told Charles?' Daisy said.

'Sort of –' Elisabeth replied, pouring boiling water over the beans. 'He doesn't mind.'

'What don't I mind?' Charles asked, walking into the kitchen and bending to kiss Bella and Daisy. Elisabeth smiled, offered him a flushed, distracted cheek. 'Nothing, darling. How was the play?'

He shrugged, fished a stray bean off the chopping board and chewed on it contemplatively.

'It was hell,' Tom said, flinging his long, skinny body into a chair next to Bella. He lifted her hand and kissed it absently. 'Hello, wife.' She smiled but did not move to return the caress.

Daisy squinted at the men myopically through large, unfocused blue eyes. 'Is he here?'

'Having a pee.' Charles extracted three glasses from a cupboard.

Tom yawned hugely and stretched. 'God, it went on and on. We kept thinking it was about to end so we'd start shifting to our feet when some other poor soul would erupt onto the stage and beat their breast for a while.'

'It was torment,' Charles murmured, pouring large glasses of wine.

'Purgatory,' Tom agreed, grimacing.

'Well, he knows all about that,' Bella said, to no one in particular. 'Our lovely, purgatorial marriage.'

Tom cast an opaque look at his wife. The others glanced away, with small, half-embarrassed smiles. They were used to Bella's jokes about her marriage. Nobody found them funny.

'There were infinite stretches of time when nothing happened,' Tom said, yawning. 'Nothing at all.'

'Poor you.' Bella patted his hand, addressed the assembled company. 'And don't we all know how good he is at keeping still?'

Daisy stood up and wandered to the door. 'I'm just going to –' she said, gesturing vaguely and disappearing into the corridor.

'Just going to roger him rigid in the loo,' Tom said, grinning.

'They wouldn't!' Elisabeth turned from the stove, her face flushed pink with steam.

'They would,' Bella said laconically, 'but probably not in your house, Elisabeth.'

'What's different about our house?' Charles demanded.

'The wallpaper costs fifty quid a roll.'

'Does it?' Charles looked at his wife. 'Does it really?'

'Don't be silly, darling. He's pulling your leg.'

'God, that was dull,' Alex said, erupting into the kitchen, bringing a gust of expensive cologne. 'Wasn't that astonishingly dull?' He leaned against the fridge, his sleek, dark seal's head lolling, arms held in a crucifixion pose.

Daisy, who was behind him, slithered quietly under one of his arms, nestling against him. 'A waste of two useful hours,' she said, pouting up at him.

Elisabeth poked at the beans. 'These are done. Shall we eat?'

Alex glanced surreptitiously at his watch. 'Yes, let's. I'm starved.'

Daisy, who caught the slight gesture, looked at him

reproachfully. 'I thought you'd told her you were in Paris tonight.'

'Change of plans.'

'What's that?' Charles said, looking up from the newspaper he had picked up and was immersed in. 'You're going to Paris?'

'Beans,' Elisabeth said, giving her husband a meaningful stare. He looked at her, perplexed.

'Drain the beans,' she said in loud, deliberate tones. He shrugged and wandered over to the sink where he proceeded to empty the pan straight into the sink, ignoring the colander, and then picked the steaming green shoots out one by one, placing them carefully in a dish.

Elisabeth, watching him, rolled her eyes. 'You'd think I'd have him house-trained after seventeen years.'

Bella laughed. 'If you can't, no one can.'

'Lost cause,' Alex said cheerfully.

Charles looked at them all in puzzlement, then grinned.

Daisy walked over to the table and sat down with a loud clatter. 'It's not much to ask,' she said.

Alex kissed the slender stalk of her neck. 'I'll get the weekend off,' he promised.

She gave him a pale, disbelieving smile. 'Of course you will.'

'Salmon *en croûte*.' Tom looked hopeful. 'I suppose it's home-made?'

'Well, of course,' Elisabeth said, contriving to look both smug and indignant.

'I don't know how you do it,' Bella sighed, meaning, I don't know why you bother.

'Yes, you do,' Elisabeth said shortly. My life is not too short to stuff a mushroom, she thought. I have so much time, I could stuff hundreds of them daily. 'Bella, will you serve, while I finish this lot off? If Charles does it, it'll be salmon in bits.'

'I'm not that bad.'

'You are,' they said, laughing and settling down to eat. There was silence as they handed bowls around and refilled glasses.

Daisy nibbled delicately on a bean. 'Elisabeth's found a new lost cause. It's coming to dinner next Thursday.'

'This is news, darling,' Charles said mildly, with a slight smile at his wife.

'It wouldn't be, darling,' Elisabeth said, with a smile that failed to hide the irritation edging her voice, 'if you'd only bother to listen to a word I say –'

'Well, I hope that she's decorative, at least,' Alex said, cutting in quickly.

Elisabeth shrugged. 'She's very pretty.'

Alex frowned. 'And where did you find her, this pretty lost cause?'

'She was in the local paper,' Elisabeth said, watching him with a small embarrassed smile.

'In the Pet Seeks Good Home section?' Charles laughed uproariously at his own joke.

Elisabeth waited patiently for his laughter to subside. 'She was selling her wedding dress. Never worn, the ad said.'

'Oh, God, then she'll be a pale little thing with damp eyes,' Alex said mournfully.

'Is it really a good idea?' Tom asked.

'Probably not.' Elisabeth sensed their disapproval. 'But it's done now.' She passed a bowl of beans around the table. 'Come on, these need eating up. Alex? Bella? Oh, somebody finish them. Anyway, I've asked Lily to come to dinner next Thursday. I thought she might like to get to know some new people.'

'We'd better invite a spare man then,' Daisy said, with a glance towards Alex who was carefully extracting a bone from his salmon. She looked at the others. 'Do we know any?'

'Lots,' Bella said. 'But they're all spare for a reason.'

'It'll be fun,' Elisabeth said firmly.

'Either that, or it'll be a complete disaster,' somebody said but Elisabeth, when she had reason to recall that phrase a year later, could not remember who. Tom, probably, although for some reason it was always Charles's voice she heard.

Three

Lily sat on her bed, painting her toenails. Her long, dark hair was smothered in thick, waxy conditioner and wound around her head like a turban. Usually, she could sit on it. When she wore it loose, people described it in poetic terms. Lily liked 'silk curtain' best. She wriggled her toes, lifting her legs to admire the freshly painted nails. They were dark red and shiny, like cherries. Her grey tracksuit trousers fell back in lumpy folds, revealing thin, white ankles.

Yawning, she swung her legs off the bed and walked across the shabby carpet, toes stiffened to stop the nails from smudging. She yawned again and the face-pack cracked; flecks of white drifted dangerously around her toes. She did a little dance to stop them sticking to the lacquer, then filled the kettle, switched it on and spooned instant coffee and powdered milk into a mug that bore the message 'A Present for a Good Girl'.

While she waited for the kettle to boil, she sat on the floor munching on handfuls of popcorn, out of a packet. The carpet was covered with stains; dim reminders of other people's lives. Prodding at a large, rusty spot with a lazy finger, she considered the people who had made it. It was the colour of dried blood; a murder, perhaps, or a couple having a good time with a bottle of red wine.

It looked like the stain she had made on the carpet in her old house. No, not old, new; so new that it still smelt of plaster and paint. Jim had bought it for the two of them as soon as they got engaged. She'd gone and spilled a glass of red wine the very first week they'd lived there, practising being a wife. She had made a nice dinner – chicken with grapes and wine sauce, the recipe from an old *Woman's Own* magazine of her mum's – laid the table with proper napkins and candles and opened a bottle of red wine. Jim didn't like white wine, he said it was too acidic. The French, as he pointed out, always drank red wine by preference, because it was better for the digestion. Lily, who preferred white, had tried to learn to love red. Jim said it was just a question of re-educating the palate. When Jim had got home from work and found the mark, he'd been furious, had gone slamming out the door. When he'd come back, a little later, with a shiny new can of 1001 aerosol mousse carpet cleaner, she'd wondered if they were right for each other.

'You should have put salt on it straight away,' he said, scrubbing at it furiously, his face the same colour as the stain. Then he got the Dustbuster out and sucked up the crumbs in the corners of the room, the places where nobody looked.

She forgave him. It was a new carpet.

Jim was a nice man. Everybody said so. He did all the cleaning and the cooking, as well as paying the bills. Lily worked mornings, to earn what Jim called her pocket money, for an import and export company in the high street. She liked her boss, Mr Williams. He was a large, jovial man with a red face that described a perfect circle.

Lily typed, did the filing and made coffee when clients came for meetings. There were hardly any clients so this didn't happen very often. When it did, Mr Williams liked to make an occasion of it. She would serve the coffee on a little silver tray, with biscuits. 'My personal assistant,' he would announce, his round, red cheeks inflating with pride. It was true, in a way. Lily was the only other person in the office. Times were hard and Mr Williams couldn't afford to pay her for more hours. He said he'd make it up to her, one day. She didn't mind. He paid her above the going rate and was kind. She had quite a bit of pocket money stashed away.

Every Thursday, Jim came home early from work to collect Lily and drive her to the supermarket. It was late-night shopping on Thursdays. Jim preferred to shop then because it was quieter than Saturday mornings and you got the end of the day mark-downs. He was a patient man and spent quite a long time comparing prices and relative weights. Lily would wait quietly by his side, dreaming over the shopping trolley, as he concentrated on the cereals or the instant coffee. If she had been by herself she would have grabbed the first packet that took her fancy. Luckily, or so Jim said, she never was.

Lily's mum said she was spoiled, but when she said it, she looked proud. She didn't have to lift a finger, unless she wanted to. Jim even brushed her hair for her, a hundred strokes every night and double on Saturdays.

The kettle switched off with a pop.

Lily made a cup of coffee and clambered back into bed with a fresh packet of popcorn. She'd read in the newspaper about this girl who ate nothing but popcorn for two years and was very healthy. 'Cheap and nutritious,' said the doctor who offered his expert opinion. Lily knew it would be cheaper if she made the popcorn herself out of those exploding little golden pips instead of buying it in expensive packets from the newsagent's. She'd burned the pan trying. It was still soaking in the sink.

Her scalp itched with the wax on it. She scratched it cautiously, then wiped the mess on her fingers onto the sheets. At least she'd get a decent meal tonight. She had money, that Elisabeth woman. It was the first thing she'd noticed about her, the way her skin and hair shone, like it was polished. It was only money that brought that shiny look to a person. She'd been a bit surprised at first, a woman like that answering an ad in the local paper. What did she want with a wedding dress – her, who could afford a really posh one and not even blink at the price tag? And she hadn't fallen for that line about looking for a dress for her daughter, neither. It was something else she was after, something that peeked out of those big blue eyes of hers, then scurried away and hid, like a rabbit down a burrow. Well, what did it matter anyway, what she was up to? She'd fallen for that line easy enough, the poor-little-me-lost-in-big-lonely-old-London act. Those daft eyes of hers had filled with tears until even she, Lily, was impressed. Right little actress I am, she thought, contemplating her cherry toes in admiration. It wasn't difficult, after that, to push her that bit further. Well, it wasn't that she wanted much, a bit of excitement was all she was after, a look into a different sort of life. And she thought that Elisabeth was just the person to give it to her.

Anyway, she could do with a night out and a decent meal. If she hated it, she'd just get up and walk right out the door, never see them again. Better than being cooped up in this hovel night after night, with not even a television for company. Not that she minded, not really. She liked having a bit of space about her person after all those months stuck in that house with Jim following her round like he was surgically attached. Mind you, she missed him a bit, missed having someone to do everything for her. Daft he was, if she'd let him he'd even have packed her bags for her when she left. Not that she would have let him, couldn't have borne to see that look on his face: soft, like a beaten dog.

She'd never been to a proper dinner party before. Not a posh one, anyway. She and Jim had entertained, as he called it, but she never felt his heart was really in it. She'd come to dread those evenings: Jim slamming around the kitchen, the Dustbuster whirring, the jumbo peanuts and green olives with red stuffing sticking out of them like tongues arranged in little glass bowls on the marble-topped table in the lounge. Jim never seemed to enjoy the dinner parties much either. 'Thank God that's over,' he said as they left. She didn't see why he wanted to spend the evening with the same people he'd been with all day. He said that's what business was.

She sold the dress, in the end. She got two hundred for it, which wasn't bad, although it cost four in the first place. That was business, too. She'd gone out and spent some of the money on an outfit for the dinner party. 'Supper,' Elisabeth had called it, 'nothing grand.' Silly mare. As if she'd mind how grand it was. Grander the better, that was her view. More so, since she'd bought something special. A skirt and top it was, made of a dark green silky stuff, and she looked very nice in it.

She thought about the evening ahead, wondering how many people would be there. Jim always said that six was a good number. Cutlery sets came in sixes. She didn't feel nervous. She felt mysterious. She'd wear her hair loose, brush it a hundred times to make it shine and paint her lips a deep, ruby red. Jim didn't like her to wear make-up; he said she should save it for later, when she was old and would need it.

She glanced at the travelling clock that sat in its green leather case, on the chair by the bed. Jim had bought it for her, when they first met and before they lived together, because he said she was always late. The clock said that it was time for the conditioner to be washed out of her hair so she gathered up her towel and washbag and went down the hallway.

Mrs Flower was just coming out of the bathroom, her fat pink cheeks shiny with steam, her grey curls squashed under a frilled, pink nylon shower cap. She was humming gently to herself but when she saw Lily the hum changed to a little shriek, then subsided, like a kettle coming off the boil. 'Sorry, dearie,' she said, 'thought you were a ghost.' Lily had forgotten all about the white clay face-pack. Mrs

Flower peered curiously at her head. 'Didn't recognise you with your lovely hair all plastered down like that.'

'It's conditioner,' Lily said, 'to make it shine. It's a special sort. You have to leave it on for an hour.' She found it difficult to talk. The face-pack had stiffened her lips.

'As if you need it!' Mrs Flower smiled, tightening a salmon-pink dressing-gown over comfortable breasts. A puff of talcum powder escaped, settled on its woolly surface. 'Beautifying yourself for something special, are you?'

'Going to a party. It takes four hours to dry,' Lily mumbled, pointing at her head.

Mrs Flower patted at the pink nylon hat and sighed. 'Hard to believe, but in my youth, I had a glorious head of hair.'

Lily smiled politely. A faint yelping could be heard from the other end of the landing. Mrs Flower cocked her head to one side. 'Better be off, lovely,' she said nervously. 'That's my Charlie calling.' It was strictly forbidden to have pets in the house. Mrs Flower lived in fear that Charlie, a Yorkshire terrier, would be discovered. Happily, he was small and fitted easily into the tartan plastic shopping trolley that Mrs Flower kept with her at all times.

Lily suddenly realised why Mrs Flower looked so nakedly vulnerable: it was the first time she had seen her separated from the trolley or the dog. Charlie went everywhere with her; he even, according to Mrs Flower, slept in the same bed. Lily thought it was a miracle he hadn't been squashed.

'Coming, your lordship,' Mrs Flower called.

The barking stopped. Lily stepped aside and waited politely for her to pass. Mrs Flower heaved her huge bulk out of the doorway and swayed down the hallway, opening the door on a volley of excited yelps.

When there was silence, Lily slipped into the bathroom and carefully locked the door. Mrs Flower, whose room was on the same landing, was the only person she had spoken to in the six weeks that she had lived in the house. All she'd seen of the other residents were shadowy shapes, slipping in and out of doorways. She was pleased not to be spoken to. She found the anonymity comforting.

When she had finished her bath, she went back to her room, slipped on a thin cotton dressing-gown and pulled the lumpy armchair, which was covered in a faded but still scratchy green nylon, over to the dusty windowsill. Sitting in the weak sunshine, a towel over her shoulders to catch the drips from her hair, she soaked up the warmth and stretched occasionally, like a cat.

Lily was good at doing nothing. Her mum said that it was one of her talents. She did not have many others – apart from looking decorative. She could type, but she wasn't sure that could honestly be called a talent, and she was good at making people like her.

Yawning languorously, she settled herself more comfortably against the bobbly nylon. She would have to get a job, eventually. Still, the room was cheap and she didn't eat much, the money from the dress would see her through for a few weeks yet. Then there was the ring still to sell. She held up a lazy hand. The sapphire, surrounded by diamonds, twinkled gently in the sunshine. Luckily, Jim had insisted on the best; said that good jewellery was an investment.

Letting her hand fall to her side, Lily closed her eyes and slept.

Four

Daisy was the first to arrive, looking shiny in a new black dress.

'Am I mad, do you think?' Elisabeth said, eyeing the dress and Daisy's thin arms regretfully.

'There are worse signs of dementia. More alarming ones, anyway,' Daisy said, draping herself across a pale marble counter and looking at a handsome silver sea bass suspiciously. Fronds of emerald parsley and crescents of lemon protruded from its slit belly. 'I hope you're not going to ask me to help.' Daisy did not cook, said that what small charm she was blessed with shrivelled in the heat of an oven.

'It's all done, just needs wrapping in silver foil. Cold starters and tiramisu for pudding. You might take a couple of plates of eats through, though.' Elisabeth pushed her hair off her hot forehead with a fish-scented hand. It stuck up unbecomingly. 'We're having drinks in the sitting-room.'

Daisy reluctantly unwound herself from the cool marble and tapped through to the sitting-room, balancing carefully on spindly heels, a tray of smoked salmon rolls in each hand. She found Charles bent over a newspaper. How middle-aged he looks, she thought, noticing for the first time a patch of pale skin glimmering faintly at the crown of his thatch of dark hair. In repose, his face sagged slightly and the unyielding three-piece City suit he wore gave him the look of an ageing clerk. Yet they were the same age, or thereabouts.

Surely not, she thought, accepting the glass he offered. 'Champagne! How lovely.'

'And so are you,' Charles said with stolid charm, toasting her.

'I'll drink to that,' she said, laughing up at him. 'And to this evening. It should be fun.'

His face darkened in bemusement, as he sought to find an expression to match her eagerness. 'Elisabeth's dinners are always – amusing,' he brought out at last.

'God, yes, and this one certainly promises that,' she said, lapsing into her usual weariness. 'What was she thinking of?'

'Elisabeth's always threatening to do some charity work but I hardly thought she'd take it literally and start at home.'

'What will this creature be like, do you think?'

'Underdressed and overwhelmed,' Charles said, with one of his rare flashes of humour.

The doorbell rang. Charles, wearing the resigned look of a man whose peace is about to be disrupted, disappeared to answer it.

'Isn't this exciting?' Bella said, coming into the room and embracing Daisy swiftly.

'You're in a good mood tonight,' Daisy said, sounding faintly offended.

Bella glanced at her sharply. 'He had to take her,' she said, 'it was her birthday.'

Daisy smoothed down her new black dress with restless hands. 'So he said.' The dress had cost a fortune, money she couldn't afford, but she was dressed for battle. *Hors de combat*, as she had murmured to herself in the changing room at Harvey Nichols, thinking of Alex tucked up snugly in some smart little hotel in the country with his wife. Celia was Alex's second wife, had been his mistress first. It made her a different sort of wife, somehow.

'After three days away with her, he'll be crazy for you.'

Bella widened her eyes, mimicked mad longing. 'Absence makes the heart and all that. . . .'

'Out of sight, out of mind, is the other,' Daisy reminded her.

'Have faith, my child,' Bella said, prowling the room in search of salmon rolls and champagne.

Daisy located the bottle, poured generous glasses for the two of them. 'This *is* Alex we're talking about.'

'So it is,' Bella said, flinging her long, rangy body down onto a sofa and drinking champagne greedily. She didn't get her hands on it much these days. She was wearing a loose, flapping jacket of wine-coloured cut velvet, under which was a long, inky, silk shift. Her neck was wound with heavy silver beads and her dark frizz of hair sprang like a halo around her head.

'You're looking good,' Daisy said, settling down next to her on the sofa.

Bella flapped an awkward arm. 'Ancient. From my better days. I suppose she'll turn up?'

Daisy, who harboured similar doubts, said that she expected she would. As she spoke, the doorbell rang. Daisy got to her feet and peered into the hallway to discover Alex, complaining spiritedly to Charles about taxi-drivers. 'Bloody man went round the houses and then had the cheek to charge me full fare. Hello, darling,' he said, catching sight of Daisy. Good humour rolled off him. Daisy's heart sank. She knew the signs of recent and successful sex. Pasting on her face the smile of a good mistress, she went forward to kiss him.

He wrapped an arm around her, enveloping her in cologne and cigar fumes, drew her into the sitting-room where they sat talking with Charles, waiting for the others to appear.

'Tom here?' Daisy said carefully.

Bella pulled a face. 'In the kitchen with Elisabeth, discussing the merits of balsamic vinegar.' Tom was the one who knew about food in their house. Bella just prepared most of the meals.

Tom appeared suddenly in the doorway. 'Elisabeth's in need of moral support. *Female* support,' he said peevishly, helping himself to a glass of champagne and collapsing in a chair. 'I am dismissed.'

'Ah, the secret society of women.' Alex grinned complacently as Daisy draped herself across him.

'To which you're no more privy than the rest of us, though you like to think you are,' Tom said.

Bella sighed, 'Ignore him, Alex. He's pissed off because he's feeling excluded. Tom thinks that girls' talk is the key to unlocking the female mind.'

'Ah,' said Charles, 'one of the great unsolved mysteries of the universe.'

Daisy laughed. 'Or the great black hole.'

Bella got reluctantly to her feet. 'I'll go.'

She found Elisabeth hovering uncertainly over a large fish.

'Thank God,' Elisabeth said, offering a damp cheek. 'We have the makings of a disaster on our hands.'

'It will be a triumph, as usual. Shall I do something useful?'

'You can start by telling me that we haven't made the most ghastly mistake.' Elisabeth squinted as she poured olive oil carefully into a jug. 'How much of this do you need?'

'More than you think. Shall I do it?'

'Oh, would you? It's usually Charles's department.' Bella, who knew that Elisabeth made an excellent vinaigrette but maintained the fiction that she was helpless in that area so that Charles would feel – as she put it – *involved*, accepted the bottle silently.

As Bella measured oil, lemon juice and salt, Elisabeth arranged the cheeses on a wicker tray, decorated with leaves from the garden.

'Rather good, isn't it?' She stepped back to admire her handiwork. 'I got the idea from a magazine.'

'Ingenious,' Bella murmured, scarcely glancing at it, intent on adding more salt to the mixture.

'I've told Charles to come and get me, the minute she arrives,' Elisabeth said, abandoning the Bacchanalian cheeses and producing a crumpled piece of paper, scattered with crossings-out. 'I can't get this table plan right.' She sank down on a chair and stared at it worriedly. 'What do you think? Me here, you between Charles and Peter and Lily between Tom and Charles. At least we can rely on them to look after her. Might be a bit obvious to plonk her next to an available man.'

Bella dipped a finger in the vinaigrette, licked it thoughtfully. 'Peter? He's that bore from down the road, isn't he? The one that comes for drinks at Christmas and won't go home?'

'He's all right. A bit slow but terribly sweet.'

'Like I said, a bore.'

'Oh dear, well if you don't think you can manage him. . . .'

'I'll be fine.' Bella gave the vinaigrette a final whisk and put it on the table, then propped herself against a counter and chewed absently at a fingernail. 'I just hope this Lily creature doesn't think Tom's fair game,' she said after a while, keeping her voice deliberately casual.

'Well, if you're worried. . . .'

'I don't believe I used the word *worried* –'

'Of course not,' Elisabeth said quickly, knowing how sensitive Bella still was about Tom's affair even though it was, what, five years ago? She had been distraught, of course, although Elisabeth remembered the wild glamour that distress had lent plain Bella – how her eyes had glittered and a glow had fired her thin, pale cheeks. She knew it was absurd but she could not help envying her the excitement. How dull her life seemed by comparison. And how thin adultery seemed to make people.

She wondered how she'd react if Charles had an affair. He would tell her about it, of course, assuming that harassed, slightly self-satisfied expression he always wore when he had something to tell her. She swelled her chest pompously, imagined him standing by the tray of drinks, pouring her something strong, like a whisky. Then he'd go over and stand in front of the fireplace, slowly rearranging the ornaments and invitations on the mantelpiece while she waited in an agony of impatience and irritation. She hated that way he had of fiddling with the things on the mantelpiece. Finally, he'd clear his throat a few times and say – well, what would he say? She couldn't imagine. Then again, she couldn't imagine Charles ever having an affair. He was always too tired.

Bella said, 'It's just that she might naturally assume that we've stuck her next to an eligible man.'

Elisabeth wrenched her mind back to the table plan. 'Oh, dear, perhaps you're right. Well, how about Alex next to her and –'

'Not if you still want her in one piece by the end of the evening.' Daisy appeared in the doorway, her cheeks flushed, eyes shining.

'I see that absence does make the heart grow fonder,' Bella said, watching her with a small smile.

'And the part grow longer,' Daisy drawled, with the lift of an eyebrow.

'Has Peter arrived?' Elisabeth asked.

'He's in the sitting-room.' Daisy took the paper from Elisabeth's hand. 'Why don't I have a go? I'm marvellously good at coupling.'

'Incorrigible,' Elisabeth said, handing over the paper and busying herself with putting a decorative finish on the top of the pudding. The three worked in silence for a while,

Bella washing radicchio and Elisabeth concocting an elaborate design with a stencil and grated chocolate.

Finally, Daisy flung down the chewed stub of pencil in triumph. 'There. Perfection. Pure symmetry.'

The others crowded round her to look. 'But it's exactly the same as Elisabeth's,' Bella said.

'Is it really?' Daisy said in astonishment. 'What a leveller life is.'

The doorbell sounded. The three women glanced at each other in alarm. 'My God,' Daisy exclaimed, 'she's actually turned up.'

'Quick, in the sitting-room,' Elisabeth shepherded them out of the kitchen and along the corridor. 'And look relaxed,' she hissed, as she swept past them towards the front door. Daisy briskly saluted her retreating back, then followed Bella into the sitting-room, laughing at some aside Bella flung over her shoulder.

Stopping by the oak tallboy in the hall, Elisabeth smoothed nervous hands over her hair and then, taking a deep breath, marched purposefully to the front door and flung it open.

'Well, hello!' she exclaimed, her voice ringing out, loud and bright, in the quiet night air. 'I'm so glad you came.'

Lily stared at her with large, expressionless eyes. 'All right?' she said, her gaze flickering past Elisabeth to take in the expanse of the high-ceilinged hallway. 'It was nice of you to invite me,' she added, her tone dutiful.

'It was a pleasure,' Elisabeth said, firmly ushering her into the hallway and holding her arm out for the thin wool coat, her eyes quickly noting Lily's shapeless two-piece made of cheap silky fabric, her bare feet thrust into cheap spike-heeled shoes that looked a size too large. A pink plaster was stuck over the scabbed blister on Lily's heel. The sight of it provoked a sudden tenderness in Elisabeth and she hugged the bald wool of Lily's coat protectively, fussing over it as she carefully hung it on the coat stand.

Lily stood motionless, gazing about her at the ornate Victorian tiled floor, stained-glass windows and festoons of chintz.

'Good journey?' Elisabeth said brightly.

Lily's blank gaze swung on her. 'No, not really.'

'Oh dear. Well, never mind, you're here now.' Elisabeth smiled eagerly but Lily said nothing in reply, stood like a doll whose limbs have been clumsily nailed together, large hands swinging by her side, dark, heavy-lidded eyes blinking slowly.

Elisabeth continued, 'I've been thinking about you ever since we met, how brave it was of you to come up to London, knowing nobody, to sell your wedding –' Her voice tailed off under Lily's strangely unfocused stare; only her own eager smile shone in the dim hallway. A sudden stab of panic punctured the protectiveness she felt for this strange, awkward girl. She thought of her friends, waiting expectantly in the sitting-room, imagined curious stares and ill-concealed amusement. Oh Lord, she thought, what have I gone and done?

Eventually, Lily spoke. 'Have you?' she said flatly.

'Yes I have,' Elisabeth said, in the tone she used most often when she was trying to convince her children of something that she, herself, did not feel, 'I thought it wonderful of you. And I'm determined that you are going to relax and really enjoy yourself.'

A glimmer of a smile slowly appeared on Lily's pale face. 'All right then,' she said, her reply almost drowned out by a sudden burst of laughter from the sitting-room. Her eyes flickered towards the room. 'I suppose I must be late,' she added languidly.

'Not at all. We were just having a drink.'

'It was the bus, you see. Always come in twos and threes they do, like they've got together somewhere for a nice cup

40

of tea, then remembered that perhaps they ought to shove off and pick up a few passengers.'

'Oh, yes, they do, don't they?' Elisabeth exclaimed, relief making her voice shrill.

Lily nodded but did not seem inclined to add anything else so Elisabeth said, her voice slightly awkward, 'Well, shall we go in and meet everybody?'

'All right.'

Elisabeth took her firmly by the arm and led her into the sitting-room.

'Lily,' she announced, suddenly conscious of the girl's thin shoulders sprouting like fragile wings through the flimsy dress and of the silence in the room as they all turned to stare.

Feeling a sudden surge of protectiveness, Elisabeth hurried forward as if to shield Lily from their curious eyes but Lily, apparently unperturbed, stood motionless, as if offering herself up for inspection. In her green dress, her neck emerging like a pale stalk from its neat collar, she looked like a flower basking in the sun, her wide, pale face with its dense, waxy skin lifted towards the focus of their eyes.

'Watcha,' she said in her flat, toneless voice. 'Sorry I'm late. It was the bus.'

'You'll never remember everyone's names,' Elisabeth said quickly, conscious of amused glances. A bus? To a dinner party? 'But I'll tell them to you all the same. Over there is Charles, my husband,' her voice took on a slightly hectoring tone, 'who is just about to get you a drink....' Charles, who had been gazing at Lily with the stunned expression of a man who has just witnessed a religious conversion, leapt to his feet and busied himself with glasses and bottles. Lily watched him, a slow smile spreading across her lovely, wan face as he fumbled with a glass and nearly dropped it.

'And that,' Elisabeth was saying, 'is Tom. Then there's

Peter, Bella –' she paused, her eyes flickering warningly at them, in mute appeal '– and Alex. Oh, here comes your drink. Thank you, darling. Now, Lily, why don't you sit here and get comfortable? Oh, and here's Daisy,' she added as Daisy obediently presented herself for duty. 'We were at school together so she's the perfect person to fill you in on all our dreadful secrets –'

Tom stood apart from the rest, arms folded protectively across his thin body. As he watched them gather around Lily, it seemed to him that she was like a person asleep – the slow blink of her dark eyes, the curtain of hair sliding like silk over her shoulders and back as she sank into a chair, her pale arm moving as if in slow motion to accept a glass from Charles who moved away quickly, out of her orbit, as if the heat she gave off was too great. He watched Elisabeth bend over her, her plump, expressive face flickering between indulgence and alarm. Out of the corner of his eye he saw Alex prowl over to the sofa, grinning his Cheshire cat smile.

Elisabeth looked up gratefully. 'Here's a man you *may* talk to,' she said, in a bright, artificial, hostess voice, 'because you're *not* sitting next to him at dinner.'

Glancing over at the others, Elisabeth suddenly caught a glimpse of Bella's set, white face. What's all that about, she thought, with a glimmer of exasperation. Really, Bella could be so difficult sometimes. She turned back to Lily, patting her on the hand, much as one might calm a nervous child. 'Now is everybody happy? Good, because I must just pop through to the kitchen and do a few last-minute things.'

Wearing a bright, fixed smile, she moved away quickly, only hesitating when she reached the door. 'Bella,' she called, 'would you . . . ?'

'Why didn't you say that she was a child?' Bella exclaimed,

hurrying after her. 'She must be about the same age as my students.'

'Don't be silly. She's in her twenties, at least.'

'That,' Bella said, with sarcastic emphasis, 'is precisely what I mean. Elisabeth, whatever were you thinking of?'

Elisabeth, who was feeling foolish and rather ashamed – that poor girl, she thought – bridled slightly at Bella's hectoring tone. 'I was merely thinking of giving a lonely girl a pleasant evening among friends.'

'Even so,' Bella muttered gracelessly, 'you could at least have warned us.'

Elisabeth, who felt tempted to ask Bella exactly what her problem was even though she knew perfectly well that it was Tom, said with determined brightness, 'But I did.'

'But she's –' Bella said, shrugging helplessly. She turned away, began clattering plates onto a tray.

Elisabeth watched her curiously. 'She's what?'

'Never mind.'

It was then that Elisabeth realised. Lily reminded Bella of Amy, the woman with whom Tom had had an affair. Not that Elisabeth had ever met Amy, but she'd spent so many hours with Bella, talking about her, analysing her character (what sort of girl would . . . ?) and examining minutely the photograph she had found in Tom's wallet of lovely, twenty-three-year-old Amy that she felt she knew her intimately. Amy of the dark eyes and golden hair, Amy of the flashing smile and endless legs, Amy of the dubious morals and skin the thickness of a rhinoceros's hide. Amy who had turned up on Bella's doorstep, cloaked in the inviolable armour of beauty and youth, determined to have things out between them. Lovely Amy who had broken Bella's heart.

Feeling a pang of conscience – why had she not thought of it before? why must people be so difficult and messy? – Elisabeth picked up the table plan and inspected it minutely. 'Perhaps Peter would be better next to Lily after all,' she murmured. 'And Tom next to Daisy.'

'It's perfectly all right,' Bella said stiffly, 'I shall play my part. I just hope she will too.'

'I'm sure she will,' Elisabeth said soothingly. 'Now, if you'll just carry those, I'll bring this lot.'

She gave a swift last glance around the room and swept off down the corridor. Bella picked up the jug of vinaigrette and followed.

In the sitting-room, Lily sat motionless, her pale face tilted to Daisy's inconsequential chatter, her eyes flitting restlessly across the room, settling every now and then on Charles, as he moved among his guests.

'Where's Elisabeth's daughter?' Lily asked. 'Is she here?'

'She's at school, I imagine.'

'Is there another daughter, then? Older?'

'No, only James who's fifteen. One boy, one girl. The perfect nuclear family.'

'Funny, when she came about the dress she said –' Lily gave a tiny shrug, her eyes flickering to Charles. 'My mistake. So how long have they been married, then?'

'Oh, sixteen, maybe seventeen years,' Daisy said, looking over at Charles fondly, 'although it seems like forever, they're so settled.'

'He looks nice.'

'He is, heavenly. Mad about Elisabeth, of course. Adores her.'

'She mad about him too?'

The question caught Daisy off guard, and she paused fractionally. 'Why, yes,' she laughed, uncertainly, 'of course.'

A spark of curiosity flared in Lily's eyes, then dimmed. As they settled back to their customary blankness, a smile curved across her pale face.

'That's nice,' she said.

In the dining-room, Elisabeth and Bella surveyed the table in silence. It was set with Elisabeth's best china, with heavy, white linen napkins and crystal glasses and a centre-piece of flowers, picked by Elisabeth from the garden that afternoon and arranged into a heart pierced at its core by thick, cream candles. Elisabeth moved forward to change the place names.

'Oh, it doesn't matter. Leave them as they are. I just hope you know what you're doing,' Bella said, but the edge had left her voice.

'I don't think any of us know that. Do you?' Elisabeth said calmly, arranging a basket of bread, a crystal dish of butter and a bowl of salad on the table.

Bella, remembering her words years later, pondered how much any of them had known. Except, perhaps, Lily.

'I thought it went very well,' said Charles, as he undressed.

He stood for a moment, lost in thought, dressed only in a crumpled shirt and striped boxer shorts. How foolish men's legs look, Elisabeth thought, catching a glimpse of them in the mirror.

'All things considered –' She started briskly smearing cream across her face and wiping it off vigorously with a tissue. Paused, she stared at her greasy reflection. 'I thought, when I first met her, that she might be more amusing. She seemed so – well, plucky, I suppose, living in that ghastly little room –'

'It's hardly her fault,' Charles said mildly, his voice ebbing as he wandered into the bathroom that adjoined their bedroom, 'and I thought she coped very well. A dinner party with strangers isn't easy.'

Elisabeth walked over to the bed, plumped her pillow efficiently and settled against it, reaching automatically for her glasses and a book. 'Of course, it's not, darling,' she said loudly, so he would hear. 'But there's no point *pretending*, is there? That doesn't help anybody. It was a good idea and it didn't work.' She gave a dismissive sigh, then adjusted her glasses purposefully on her nose and extracted a silver page marker from her book.

'If the idea was that she should enjoy herself,' Charles said, emerging with a toothbrush in his hand, 'then it worked very well.'

'Yes, but she didn't even try –' Elisabeth looked up from her book and her voice took on a bright, dismissive tone. 'Never mind. I think we can safely say we've done our bit, don't you?'

Charles looked at her silently for a moment, then put his toothbrush in his mouth and ambled back into the bathroom.

'Well, we did give her a jolly nice dinner,' Elisabeth said, when he emerged, 'which is what we promised. We can't do much more than that.'

He did not look at her. 'I suppose not.'

'It wasn't as if she made much effort to get to know everybody. She scarcely spoke.'

Charles fastened the last button on his pyjama jacket and flipped back the duvet. 'She spoke a little to me and was perfectly charming. Although, of course, I think she was a bit overawed,' he said, climbing into the bed.

'I suppose so,' Elisabeth sighed, sinking her fingers firmly into the duvet as Charles lay down and turned over, rearranging the bedclothes to make himself more comfortable. He always took more than his fair share. She yanked the duvet irritably, stared down at her book unseeingly. It had seemed such a good idea and she had imagined – Oh, she didn't really know what she had imagined, but now she felt, in some curious way, utterly let down.

She looked at Charles. His eyes were shut. She glanced back down at her book, wondering if she could face reading it. Everybody said it was marvellous but she found it opaque and difficult. She settled down with a sigh.

Charles said sleepily, 'What happened to the fiancé?'

'I forgot to ask. I was hoping you'd found out, over dinner.'

'Hardly a subject for light conversation.'

Elisabeth sighed irritably. 'I know that, darling, but sometimes these things do come up.'

Charles said nothing.

'I suppose you think I shouldn't have invited her in the first place.'

Charles was silent but she could tell, by the stillness, that he was listening.

'Well, do you?'

He fumbled a hand out from under the covers, reached out and squeezed her hand. 'Not at all. Good-night, darling.'

Elisabeth waited until Charles's breathing flattened to a loud, easy rhythm. Then she placed her glasses and book side by side on the bedside table, switched off the light and lay down, careful to keep to her side of the bed.

Five

Lily slept late as usual. It was past ten when she woke. Sunlight streamed through the limp curtains in her shabby room, picking out the pattern of orange and brown lozenges, throwing them into relief against the pink, flowered wallpaper.

Very little disturbed Lily's dreams. She fell asleep the moment her head touched the pillow and woke with a similar lack of fuss, cheerful and bright-eyed. The sleep of the innocent, her mum said fondly. It was true but in a way that her mother, stunned by love, did not see. Lily was not like other people; she had no conscience to bother her.

She rolled over and stared longingly at the kettle. Jim always brought her a cup of tea in the morning. She yawned lazily. It was the one thing she missed about him.

Eventually she got up and padded across the room to turn on the kettle, then sat cross-legged on the thin, stained carpet. As she waited for it to boil, she wondered how her mum was. Same as usual, probably. She'd be a bit peeved that she'd run off like that, without a word, but she'd come round soon enough when Lily phoned. She should have done it already, let her know that she was all right. Oh well, she thought, sloshing boiling water over a tea bag, she'd get round to it one day.

As Lily made herself tea in her Good Girl mug, Elisabeth was already on her way to the post office carrying a carefully sealed brown-paper parcel containing Lucy's hairbrush – which, as usual, she'd forgotten when she came home from school the previous weekend. She was not thinking about her daughter (strange, these days, how rarely she did actually think about her) but was busy with plans for supper.

It was Friday and the others were congregating at the house as usual that evening. Bella had suggested that they all meet at her house – Daisy's flat was a bit of a squeeze – but Elisabeth passed the suggestion off with a gay little laugh, almost as if it had not been made.

'It's no bother,' she said. 'It's not as if I have anything else to do.'

Bella knew better than to press her. The one, the *only* time they had spent Friday evening at her and Tom's place, Elisabeth had spent the evening being so conspicuously helpful and enthusiastic about the disgusting takeaway they'd got from the local Chinese that by the end of the evening Bella was itching to slap her.

'I suppose I'm being unfair,' Bella said to Tom later.

He shrugged. 'A bit. Her intentions are good.'

'That's precisely what I mean,' Bella said, clattering plates furiously into the dishwasher. 'She even denies us the luxury of ill-feeling.'

It was not, anyway, as if there was any use reasoning with Elisabeth. She would never admit that something *was* a problem, would far rather add that to all the other problems she was juggling at one time until they built into a great sandstorm of fuss with Elisabeth at its centre, smiling patiently in the eye of the storm.

Elisabeth was, if the truth be told, a bit of a martyr and, like most martyrs, liked to be at the centre of attention.

Elisabeth cut down an alley-way and emerged onto the high street. She was thinking how sweet it was of Bella to have offered to have them all at her place. Just as she was thinking how considerate it was of herself to have refused. Well, she knew how much Bella hated that poky little house that she and Tom had been forced to move into after all that business with his architectural practice going bankrupt. Well, not bankrupt exactly but nobody could deny that these days it was very far from the success it had once been. Not that Bella ever complained, no matter how ghastly it must have been, having to sell that marvellous house they used to live in when times were good. Not to mention that glorious garden – Bella's pride and joy. She'd been so brave about it too, even down to pretending that the old place was too big to cope with when anyone with eyes in their head could see that she'd been mad about it, missed it bitterly. A much more sensible size, she said about the new house, just the right size for the three of us.

Mind you, she never mentioned gardening either these days – Bella, who used to spend every spare hour she had out in her garden, pruning and propagating, cherishing each single leaf and flower. She'd not so much as dug up a weed in the new place, not that it was much of a garden, more a patch of dusty earth. Wouldn't even discuss gardening, not even when Elisabeth went to her for advice over a weigela that started, unaccountably, to sicken. She'd felt rather hurt about that, and about Bella's rather sharp refusal to join her for a day at Sissinghurst. And she'd been so careful to stress that she'd pay for both their entrance fees so Bella wouldn't be embarrassed about money. Bella's manner on the subject of her garden was as if a much-loved friend had died – a friend whose name nobody dared mention. And then, of course, there was Tom; so prickly and abrasive. He'd been such *fun* too, in the old days. Couldn't be much fun living with him now.

Elisabeth walked to the pedestrian crossing, pressed the button and stood waiting for the lights to change. Anyway, she thought, what sort of trouble is it to throw a meal together for friends, although it was not – as her friends well knew – as if Elisabeth ever *threw* anything together. She crossed the road and stopped outside the delicatessen.

A basket of fresh stuffed tortelloni, nicely decorated with hoops and curves of dried pasta, black with squid ink and green with spinach, was arranged in the window. Pasta for supper perhaps, or maybe some sugar ham, carved off the bone, accompanied by a potato salad made with proper mayonnaise – not that insipid shop-bought stuff. Or maybe some of her special grilled peppers, scorched and fragrant with garlic. Anyway, something easy. For pudding they could have ice-cream or fruit.

As Elizabeth contemplated the pleasant evening ahead, Charles, who had already been in the office for hours, was involved in a particularly tricky telephone conversation with a client whose husband had left her for a woman young enough to be his granddaughter. As he talked, he ran his hands distractedly through his hair until it stood on end, like a badly clipped hedge. Angela, his secretary, bustled into his office with a cup of coffee and stood for a moment gazing tenderly at Charles's sticking-up hair, longing to run her stubby, nail-bitten fingers through it. He smiled up at her, thanking her silently for the coffee, and her heart did a little double flip.

He was gorgeous, especially when he smiled and then there was his mind. Angela so admired his mind. She positively glowed with pride when she overheard people talking about him; one of the cleverest men in his field, they said. Sighing, she closed the door gently behind her and sat down to get on with some typing.

A few streets away, in a smooth, glossy eyrie perched high above the City's ancient tangle of streets, Alex was talking animatedly on the telephone, his hair sleeked to his smooth head with an expensive hair oil he had specially made up in a Jermyn Street chemist. His secretary, a thin, scornful blonde called Annabelle – an Oxford graduate who felt she deserved better things – was grudgingly serving up coffee. She clattered the cup and saucer onto the desk and flounced, as much as her thin rump would allow, out of the door.

Alex did not look up. He was negotiating a merger with a Swedish bank that would – although they did not yet know this as they worked silently and competently in their cool, ash-blond offices in Oslo – cause forty people to lose their jobs. Five of those would then lose their homes, and three of those, their families. Alex, who *did* know this, (although not the part about the houses and families) was smiling.

Daisy was also smiling as she happily gouged damp, grey ribbons out of a lump of clay in her studio in Camden Town but Tom, up the road in a once lovely but now crumbling square in Kentish Town, was slamming around the tiny box that his architectural practice now occupied. His thoughts were not happy. He was wishing his wife, together with Amy, the woman he'd once fucked in an idle moment – well, an idle three months – and women in general a painful eternity. As for the business – well, what business? he thought, slamming shut the drawer of a rickety filing cabinet and eliciting a sharp look from his partner, Harry, who was on the telephone conducting what was obviously a difficult conversation.

Tom threw himself down into a chair, put his feet on a desk and waited. After an interminable length of time, punctuated only by Harry's sweetly reasonable tones, 'Yes, of course I do understand but don't you think –' and 'Surely, there's something that can be –' he put down the telephone and looked over at Tom with a tight smile.

'The budget's been frozen.'

Tom looked at him questioningly. 'Meaning?'

Harry shrugged. 'Meaning, thank you and fuck off.'

Tom smiled bleakly, raised his eyes to the heavens. 'Haven't you had enough yet?' he shouted.

As for Bella, she was sipping at her third cappuccino of the day and trying not to think about cigarettes. A pack of ten wouldn't do any harm, surely? She could keep them in her bag, smoke one a day. Well, maybe two. Two hardly counted.

It had been a particularly difficult morning, starting with a row with Tom, and now one of the students was slouched on the chair in front of her desk refusing to do what he knew perfectly well was part of his course work; had known for three years, in fact.

'I still don't see the point,' he said, flicking corn-yellow hair out of his eyes. A sapphire stud gleamed in his nose.

'The point, Duncan,' Bella said patiently, 'is that if you don't do the written paper, you fail the whole deal. End of story.'

Duncan picked up a strand of hair and plastered it delicately across his forehead. 'I'm an artist,' he mumbled. 'I speak with my hands.'

'You write with your hands too.' Bella said, in exasperation.

'It's only a pissy thesis. It doesn't matter.'

'It does matter,' she said, thinking of her son, Ben, who had announced the day before that he couldn't be bothered with A-levels. Actually, couldn't be fucked, were the words he'd used.

'Nobody outside this building's going to care about a dumb piece of paper,' Duncan said scornfully. 'They want to know what I can do with my hands, not what I think about Leonardo da Vinci's cartoons.'

'They may not care,' Bella said patiently. 'But they might be impressed.'

'Yeah, sure.' He slouched over to the door of her office, holding his thin body like a comma. 'See ya.'

'Duncan,' she said as he slid out of the door, 'what about your thesis?'

He looked back at her, his face lit by a sweet smile. 'Bollocks to that.'

Something about his smile reminded Bella of Tom. She

leaned back against the uncomfortable, institution-grey plastic chair and thought unwillingly about her husband.

She'd woken in a sour mood, a hangover pressing over her right eye, groping her way upright to see Tom, sopping wet from the shower, blundering towards her, hands outstretched. The mattress hollowed beneath him, jolting her to one side as he sat heavily on the bed and groped under it for a towel.

'Bloody thing's damp. Who left this on the floor?'

'You did, of course. Oh, must you?' Bella said, rolling over to escape the water that dripped off him, soaking into the duvet.

She opened her eyes again, stared morosely at the old, stained T-shirt that served as her nightdress. Very romantic, she thought. Well done, Bella. No wonder Tom never wants sex these days. She stared balefully at his back.

'I feel like shit.'

He glanced down at her, saw her expression, burst out laughing. 'You do look a bit rough.'

She rolled over, hid herself from his ghastly morning cheerfulness. It was the one thing she'd hated about him when they first married. She could scarcely speak before downing two cups of tea. She wrinkled her eyes shut. Was there really only one thing she used to hate? Awful how the petty irritations mounted by the year to a daily catechism of woe. Like the way he discarded tea bags all over the house (she'd even found one on top of the television the other day), or the way he always let the petrol gauge in the car dwindle to empty and would have to fill up when they were in a hurry to get somewhere. When she'd say, irritable as they sat in a queue at a garage, couldn't he just anticipate occasionally? he'd give her that opaque look, then amble off slowly to fill the car.

She sighed.

Like the way he fucked other women.

Tom shook his head vigorously, letting loose a fine

spray of water. Cold drops landed on her warm, bare skin. She jerked her legs away with a sharp intake of breath.

'Tom, for God's sake.'

'Sorry,' he said, leaning forward to drop a kiss on her bare leg. She flinched, conscious of the scattering of sharp, black stubble across her shins.

He grinned. 'Married legs.'

'Shut up.'

Still grinning, he ducked under the towel, rubbed vigorously at his wet hair. As she watched the bones of his ribs moving smoothly under the skin, she felt a sudden pang of longing. She loved him terribly. She smiled blankly at the stupid appropriateness of the expression. She was terrible at loving him. She, who had loved him so well. Her voice shook. 'You fancy her.'

The rubbing stopped.

'Not again,' he said, his head, crowned with a stiff halo of dark spikes, emerging from the towel. 'I thought we'd been through all that.'

'You were drunk.'

He chucked the towel on the floor, stood up. 'So were you.'

'Is that why you didn't want to do it?'

His back stiffened, then he shrugged, walked away from her.

She rolled over again, buried her face in a pillow, hating him for turning her into this – this what? Harridan, nag, shrew. It was him who'd ruined everything, not her. Unfair. *Unfair*. Anger made her restless; she flung over, sat up and punched the pillows to make them more comfortable and picked at her fingernails in silence, wishing she still smoked.

The bed sagged as, dressed now, in a grey T-shirt, blue checked shirt, faded jeans, Tom dropped down beside her, buried his face in her lap.

'I don't fancy her,' he said, his voice muffled by her thighs.

She raked his damp hair with her fingers, longed to bury herself in him, couldn't.

'You talked to her all evening. Couldn't take your eyes off her.'

He rolled off her lap and stared up at her, his face upside-down so that she fancied she could see his chin as a nose. She remembered being a little girl lying in bed, her father's face looming over her as he read her a bedtime story, his chin wrinkling like a nose. She had found it comforting then.

'I felt sorry for her. She didn't know anybody.' He grimaced and his chin became a snout. 'Can't have been easy, being dumped in the middle of us lot.'

She looked away. 'Bet you wouldn't have been so attentive if she'd been fifty with a hairy chin.'

Stop it, she thought. Stop this now. But she knew that she couldn't. Or, perhaps, wouldn't.

He let out an exasperated sigh, scrabbled around on the floor and pulled on a pair of sneakers. 'Of course I wouldn't.' He was doubled up, tying his shoelaces. His voice emerged in slow grunts.

'So you did fancy her,' she said, resisting an impulse to place her hand on his back and push him to the floor.

He twisted around to face her. 'All right, I fancied her. It would be inhuman not to.'

'And we all know you're human.'

'What's that supposed to mean?'

She dropped her eyes, her expression sulky. 'Nothing.'

He watched her for a while, but she didn't look up.

'I'd better go. I'm late,' he said, jumping up from the bed and striding around the bedroom in search of wallet and car keys. 'Where are the bloody things?'

He stared around in exasperation. She knew his impatience included her and resentment stabbed at her. Unfair.

'Anyway, it was you lot who should have been looking after her instead of scoring points, showing off in front of her. It was like watching something out of the Conservative Women's Association.'

He clasped his hands together, stuck sharp elbows out and cocked his head to one side. 'And would you like some nice sun-dried tomato bread, dear. It's utterly delicious and only costs two thousand pounds a loaf. Don't suppose you see much of it, down your way.'

'Shut up.'

'Not a pretty sight.' He pulled a jacket off the back of a chair and searched its pockets. 'Shit, shit and shit again,' he said, abandoning it, staring wildly at the floor as if the missing items might suddenly unfurl themselves from its depths.

'They're in your black jacket, the one you wore last night.'

He dived into the wardrobe, emerged triumphant, wallet and keys in hand. 'Where would I be without you?'

An absurd schoolboy grin cracked open the thin triangle of his face. She felt the familiar heaviness scratching at her throat.

'Shouldn't Ben be up by now? He'll be late.'

'Revision day,' she reminded him.

'God, then he'll surface some time this afternoon, I suppose.'

'It doesn't matter,' she said irritably. 'Don't go on at him.'

'It does matter. His exams are in two months' time. He needs to get some work done.'

'It only makes him worse.'

He ran a hand through his hair, stared at her helplessly. 'I just don't want him to –'

'To fail.'

'No, not that. It's not a question of success or failure.

Anyway, it's not as if his father's exactly setting him a great example, is it?'

He grinned, but she could see how much it hurt, failing his son. Failing himself.

'I don't want him to – not to have the chance, I suppose. He's so apathetic. He doesn't seem to care about anything.'

'What's there to care about? There aren't any jobs anyway. Sex and drugs kill you. Politicians are useless. Even the music stinks, or so he says.'

'And his dear old Dad going bust is another cause for apathy, I suppose?' he said, suddenly angry.

'I didn't say that.'

'You didn't have to.'

She watched him silently. No good saying anything; it wasn't as if there was anything to be done about it. Nobody wanted architects any more, however brilliant. Nobody had the money. Not like the eighties when the money seemed to pour through the letter-box in a constant stream. Now it had dried to a trickle. The house had gone, Ben's school had gone. Everything gone. Nobody's fault.

'Oh, God,' she said, yawning, trying to sound normal. 'Better get up.'

'Christ, you really do look rough.'

She clambered off the bed and stalked across the room feeling disembodied, her head light, her limbs unattached to her body. 'Oh, shut up.'

He stood by the mirror dabbing on gel in a futile attempt to subdue the spikes of hair that whirled out of his crown. She stopped, stared at him. He was beautiful to her.

'You won't do it again, will you?' Her voice broke suddenly. 'I don't think I can bear it.'

He moved towards her, wrapped his arms around her. 'Stop it,' he murmured, his mouth against her hair. She relaxed against him, rubbed her cheek against the familiar bony ridges of his chest.

'Sorry,' she said. 'It's weird but I feel frightened. As if something terrible's going to happen.'

He stroked her hair back from her face, his fingers knotting in the tangle of frizzy curls. 'It already has.'

'Yes,' she sighed, pressing her mouth against his chest. They stood like that for a while. 'Sorry about last night.'

'Don't mention it.'

She searched for something to say to make amends. 'Lily was all right, I suppose,' she brought out. 'Quite sweet, really, although I've always found that particular brand of sweetness disturbing, like sugar coating on a pill to take the bitterness away.'

He hugged her affectionately. 'Never let anyone get away with anything, do you?'

'I suppose you think I'm being unfair?'

'I was teasing.'

She could hear the exasperation in his voice and wriggled out of his embrace. 'Don't indulge me.'

'I'm not.'

'Yes, you are. You're wearing your let's-humour-Bel voice.'

'If you say so.'

'See? You've done it again.'

Impatience flickered in his face. 'Sorry.'

So it was pity he felt for her now. 'I knew you fancied her,' she said, her voice scratchy.

'Who?'

'Who? What do you mean, who? Lily, of course.' Her voice climbed. 'Or have you been chatting up somebody else recently?'

His black eyes dwindled to pinpoints and she looked away as he raised a hand, ticked off the fingers. She hated it when he did that, thrusting his fingers at her as if she were an errant schoolgirl. Who was errant? Him. *Him!*

'So far this week I've been accused of chatting up three different women, and it's only Friday. First of all it was the girl behind the deli counter. Then it was the woman in the supermarket. Now it's some sweet, stupid creature at a dinner party. God knows what I'll get up to at the weekend. . . .'

'Oh, why don't you just admit it?' she snapped, picking up a hairbrush and tugging angrily at the curls clumped around her head. Christ, she looked a mess. No wonder he didn't fancy her. But he'd promised, hadn't he? For better or for worse, she thought. For better or for worse. She glanced over at him out of the corner of her eye. He was standing in the middle of the room, his hands hanging limply by his sides, watching her sorrowfully.

'She's not my type.'

It was the way he said it, that same patient resignation he'd used after the affair. 'It happened,' he'd said. Not, 'I'm sorry.' Just, 'It happened,' as if it had had nothing to do with him.

She wheeled on him, cheeks flaming. 'So you fancy someone else?'

He dropped his head, beaten. 'Bel, stop this.'

'No, you stop it. You started it.'

'Bel, for Christ's sake, that was five years ago.'

'So? Five years or five minutes. You did it. You can do it again.'

'It was an affair. It happened. It finished. End of story.'

'But it's not the end, is it? It goes on and on, round and round in my head.'

'Please, Bel, don't. You're going to drive yourself insane.'

'You broke my heart,' she said bitterly. 'Picked it up and smashed it.'

He was adrift in her anger. She stared at him longingly.

'We were so – we were perfect,' she said, her voice breaking on the word.

He took a step towards her. 'We were in love.'

'Oh, so it's past tense now.'

'We *are* in love.'

'You said, were –'

He reached for her, took her by the shoulders, shook her gently. 'Stop it. Will you please stop this?'

She let out a sigh, her face crumpling. 'Oh God, Tom. What happened? What happened to us?'

He pulled her towards him so that her head fitted into the crook of his neck as it had fitted, so perfectly, for eighteen years. 'Life happened. We were only twenty-one when we married, for God's sake. We grew up, we changed, we had Ben, the business went bust. Shit happened.'

'I didn't want it to change,' she mourned, her mouth against the rough skin of his neck. 'Why can't it be the same?'

He shrugged, turned away, leaving her arms empty. 'I'm here. You're here. We're still married.'

His coldness froze her. 'Is that all it is, then?' she said listlessly.

He looked at her, exasperated. 'Is that all what is?'

'Marriage. Is that all marriage means, that we're both still here?'

'It means that we both want still to be here.'

'Yes.' Bella sighed heavily. 'Well, I suppose that's as good as it gets.'

'Now who's talking sentimental crap?' he said, striding towards the door. 'Look, I'm sorry, I've got to go to work. Well, what's left of it.'

Her mouth worked sourly. 'And I haven't?'

He stopped, looked back at her. 'I can't take much more of this, Bel.'

She stared at the blank space where he had been. Unfair, she thought. Unfair.

Six

Two weeks had gone by; weeks during which Elisabeth had succeeded in shoving the residual guilt she felt about Lily and the dinner party to the back of her mind. Lily, however, had not forgotten. Far from it. She was merely biding her time; on that particular evening was sitting cross-legged on her narrow bed eating her tea – a bag of popcorn and a can of Diet Coke – squinting at the walls, diverting herself by making patterns out of the orange and brown lozenge wallpaper. After a while she gave up, wondering whether it was worth blowing some of the wedding dress money on a portable television. Everybody else in the house had one; she'd seen the tell-tale blue light leaking out from under dark, closed doors; tinny disembodied voices followed her down the dim corridor to the bathroom.

There was a knock at the door. She clambered off the bed, jiggled the rusty old Yale lock and wrenched the door open.

Mrs Flower's ample shape filled the doorway, an old dented cake tin balanced in her hands, surprisingly white, dainty hands for so large a woman. On her head was a hat of brown felt, trimmed with yellow crocheted wool flowers.

'I wondered if you fancied a slice of cake, dear. Homemade. My daughter sent it. I've just put the kettle on.'

'Oh,' Lily said, in astonishment. She had not imagined Mrs Flower with a daughter, had thought somehow that she had simply taken root in the house, expanding contentedly in her anonymous room.

Mrs Flower smiled encouragingly.

'Um – that would be nice.'

'When you're ready,' Mrs Flower said, sailing off up the dark, narrow corridor that smelled faintly, but eternally, of burnt toast and Indian take-aways.

Five minutes later, Lily tapped on Mrs Flower's door.

It was a large room, much bigger than hers, but seemed smaller on account of the quantities of furniture it contained. A huge oak sideboard with carved legs squatted heavily on one side while the other was dominated by a massive mahogany wardrobe. Crushed between those were a bed, covered with a canary-yellow candlewick cover and bright, crochet cushions, three armchairs and a tiny table, against which was pushed a single chair.

'I like to eat my meals sitting up,' Mrs Flower said, patting the chair proudly. 'Can't abide that modern habit of eating in front of the television with a tray on your lap.'

Lily stared around her. She could see no television until Mrs Flower heaved forward, panting slightly at the exertion, and tugged at a pair of flowery curtains in the corner. They slid back to reveal one of the biggest televisions that Lily had ever seen.

'My daughter bought it for me,' Mrs Flower said proudly. 'Made the curtains too. Nice bit of stuff, that.'

Lily agreed that it was.

Mrs Flower edged the cake out of its tin, slid it onto a flowered plate. 'Couldn't be doing with staying on in the flat,' she continued, 'not after my Reg died. Rattling around like a lone pea in a pod, I was. So I thought, why not a nice little room in a house? Bit of company too, when I fancy it.'

'Yes,' Lily said doubtfully, thinking of the shadowy shapes she had seen slipping through the corridors of the house.

'Keep themselves to themselves,' Mrs Flower said, 'but they're a nice enough crowd, for all that. Slice of cake, lovely? Pot's brewed nicely by now.'

Mrs Flower poured tea in two pretty, flowered Royal Doulton cups ('Anniversary present from my Reg, bless him') and cut two large slices of cake.

'Sit there, lovely. You'll be nice and cosy by the fire.'

Lily looked apprehensively at the gleaming red electric bars. It was already suffocatingly hot in the room, not that Mrs Flower seemed to take much mind. Her cardigan was buttoned firmly to the chin and fastened with a pretty cameo brooch; her felt hat pulled down uncompromisingly over her grey curls. It gave her a curiously rakish look as she lowered herself heavily into the chair opposite and took a mouthful of cake.

'Makes a good cake, my Sheena.' Her huge bulk jiggled with laughter. 'Told her she'll have to stop soon else I'll be getting fat. The doctor says me weight's affecting my heart, keeps trying to put me on a diet, but I said to him, this is the size nature intended and there's no earthly use in changing that, except to make me miserable. My heart's just a bit weak, what with husbands and old age, and there's no diet on earth can cure that.'

'How long were you married then?' Lily asked.

Mrs Flower settled back into the deep recesses of her chair and arranged Charlie comfortably on her lap. 'How long? Thirty years, off and on, lovely.' She had a curious way of sitting, elbows planted squarely on the arms of the chair, hands held high. 'So the blood doesn't gather,' she explained, to Lily's enquiring glance. 'Stops that mottled, veiny look that old hands get.' A low, protesting growl issued forth from the depths of her capacious lap. 'Oooh, sorry your lordship,' she said, peering down at the dog.

'Did you like it?'

'I should say so. Three times, I done it. Cock-eyed

optimist, that's what I am. Lost one, left one and got to bury the last, bless his heart.'

Lily smiled, sipped thoughtfully at her steaming, sweet tea.

'Funny lot, men,' Mrs Flower said, shifting to get more comfortable. Charlie rose to his feet and circled her lap, eventually flopping down on one of her fat thighs. 'Sorry, your highness. Disturbed you again, did I?'

She sighed heavily. 'Take a bit of getting used to, they do. Don't want to go rushing into it, lovely. Not till you're sure. That's what I did. Scuttled in, eyes tight shut. That's why it took me two goes to find my Reg.'

'What was he like?'

'Oooh, not much to look at. First time I took him home to see my old mum, she takes one look and says, "That the best you can do?"' She looked wistful. 'Funnily enough, he was the best, not that she could see it. She didn't live with him, see.'

She wagged an admonishing finger at Lily. 'It's what goes on behind closed doors that matters, not what the world sees. More cake, lovely?' she said, cutting two hefty slices.

Lily shook her head so Mrs Flower settled back with hers, breaking fragments from the slice and raising them to her mouth, little finger cocked.

'He may have been no painting, my Reg,' she said, her mouth full of cake, 'but he was beautiful inside.'

She smiled at Lily. 'You ever think about getting married, lovely?'

Lily nodded. 'Nearly did but –' She ducked her head, gazed into the electric bars of the fire. 'He left me standing at the altar,' she said in a low voice. 'It was awful, everybody dressed to the nines and me in my dress. All the presents had to go back. My gran said she'd never get over it.'

Mrs Flower shifted sympathetically.

'Did a runner, he did.' Lily raised her left hand, on which the sapphire and diamond ring sparkled. 'All he left me was this,' she said, with a gentle sigh, 'and my memories.'

Mrs Flower looked down at the diamonds, her eyes sparkling shrewdly. 'Well, a nice ring like that's a comfort, at any rate.'

Lily smiled.

'Now, dearie, tell me about this party you were beautifying yourself for,' Mrs Flower said, her eyes growing misty. 'Only thing I miss, being on my own, is a bit of glamour. Reg and me used to go dancing, every Wednesday night.'

'Oh, it was lovely,' Lily said, clasping her hands and holding them beneath her chin, 'great big house in a place called Hampstead.'

Mrs Flower nodded approvingly. 'Very nice.'

'All the men were in suits and the ladies in beautiful dresses,' Lily said, laying it on a bit thick for Mrs Flower's benefit. 'There was champagne and a whole fish, silver like it had just jumped right out of the sea and strawberries for dessert and everyone looked so warm and happy.'

'And whose house was this?' Mrs Flower asked, thinking, champagne indeed!

'Just some friends,' Lily said airily. 'Charles and Elisabeth. He's a solicitor and they're rich, so she doesn't have to work.'

'Not work,' Mrs Flower said wistfully, easing her bunions in their cruel plastic cages. She worked as an office cleaner, did the early morning shift. It was murder on the feet, and the hands. She was vain about her hands; slathered them with cream and wore white cotton gloves to bed and would no more have dreamed of going to work without her heavy-duty rubber gloves than she would of leaving the house without a hat.

'My mum nursed Elisabeth's mother, through her dying days. Awful, it was.'

'Must have been,' said Mrs Flower, who was old enough to realise the awfulness of dying days.

'Well, Elisabeth was so grateful, said she'd look after me when I came up to London. And Charles says he's going to get me a job in his office, so he can keep an eye on me. He's kind like that,' Lily said dreamily.

'You'll be off there again soon, then?'

Lily smiled. 'Course I will.'

'It was a disaster,' Elisabeth said.

They were sitting in Daisy's tiny flat, clustered around the steel and glass table placed in the centre of the sitting-room. Elisabeth eased her legs slightly, gazing at the table's sharp corners warily. It's all very well, this modern stuff, she thought, but why must it be so uncomfortable? Daisy came through from the kitchen carrying an open bottle of wine, three glasses and a bowl of pistachios. Feeling unable to talk freely in front of their menfolk (*'Pas devant les hommes'* as Elisabeth said, putting a finger to her lips), they had not yet had a chance to discuss the Lily fiasco.

'Well, not actually a *disaster*, but not one of your more glittering successes,' Daisy said, filling the glasses liberally.

'Tom was foul about it,' Bella said. 'According to him we behaved like a meeting of the Conservative Women's Association.'

Elisabeth flushed hotly at this assault on her carefully nurtured but far from instinctive liberal sensibilities. 'That's not fair.'

Daisy laughed, picked up a nut, cracked it open with delicate fingers. 'I've always rather fancied myself with a blue rinse and stout leather shoes.'

'The really awful thing about that,' Bella said, giving her a hard look, 'is that it's probably true.'

'Some of those tweed suits are really rather fetching,' Daisy said cheerfully. 'Anyway, the girl seemed to enjoy herself, which was surely the point. It's just she didn't *enthuse.'*

'Enthuse? She hardly said a word all evening.'

'Except about the fish. She couldn't get over seeing the head appearing at table.'

'Most fish these days is square and comes wrapped in cellophane with its own sauce,' said Elisabeth absently. 'Hence the decline of the wet fishmonger.' She idly polished a smudge on the table's glass surface. 'Maybe she's like those children who think milk comes from a bottle rather than a cow.'

'A carton,' Bella corrected. 'You hardly ever see a bottle these days.'

'Oh, I don't think she's *deprived,'* Daisy said. 'She hasn't got rickets or anything.'

'You don't have to have rickets to be deprived.' Elisabeth shook her head. 'Not these days.'

'No, you just don't own a dishwasher.'

'Do stop it, Daisy. You know perfectly well that everyone's deprived compared to us lot,' Bella said.

'I suppose they are.' Elisabeth looked stricken.

Daisy glanced at her. 'Oh, God. Hair shirts for days.'

'I just happen to care about being more fortunate than other people,' Elisabeth said stiffly.

'Don't we all?' Bella said. She was silent for a while. 'Not that I notice us doing much about it.'

Daisy yawned. 'Oh, I don't know. I give all my old clothes to the local charity shop.'

'I'm not sure how much use black evening dresses are.'

'Even poor people like to look nice in the evening.'

'Daisy!'

'What?'

'*Poor* people.'

'Very well,' Daisy said, with a sigh. 'Financially challenged. Anyway, just because they've no money doesn't mean all their poor little hearts desire is sad jumpers and torn jeans. I bet Lily would be as pleased as the next girl to get her hands on a posh frock.'

'I think she thought she had,' Elisabeth said. 'That dark green thing she was wearing.'

'Poor lamb,' Daisy said. 'Ah well, I expect that's the last we'll see of her.'

'It was such a good idea,' murmured Elisabeth.

'No, it wasn't,' Bella said crisply. 'It was a rotten idea and she had a rotten time. The whole point was to cheer her up.'

'Her eyes looked quite cheerful,' Elisabeth said doubtfully.

'Her *eyes*?'

'Yes, the way she kept staring at everything.'

'That's because she thought we were all barking,' Daisy said, laughing. 'Eating a fish with its head still on and then strawberries for pudding doused with vinegar.'

'Balsamic, and it was *lightly* sprinkled,' Elisabeth protested.

'It might have a posh name but it's still the stuff that girls like that put on their fish and chips.'

Elisabeth sat back, looking pained.

'Did anybody find out about the errant groom?' Daisy continued.

'No. I made Charles promise but you know how hopeless men are at that sort of thing. Mind you, he seemed quite smitten. Said he didn't think girls like that still existed.'

Daisy looked interested. 'Girls like what?'

'Biddable,' said Bella.

The telephone rang. Daisy disappeared into the bedroom to answer it.

'It'll be Alex cancelling,' Bella said, after Daisy had gone. They were all meeting up for dinner later, at a new Italian restaurant that had just opened up the road.

'Why must he always do that?' Elisabeth mourned.

'Because he's a selfish sod. Talking of which, Tom and I aren't speaking.'

'What about?'

'About – Oh, fuck knows. The demons that drive us, I suppose.'

'Oh,' said Elisabeth, imagining her demons as monsters in a child's story book. They'd be purple with orange spots, perhaps. Bella's, she knew, were green. But as for Tom, what colour was failure? Navy blue, perhaps, or brown. Failed lives always have a brown tinge to them, a vaguely muddy overtone.

Daisy returned, her eyes bright. 'Sod,' she said, sloshing wine into her glass and gulping it back. 'Sodding selfish bastard.'

'Poor you,' Elisabeth said, without much conviction. Odd, she thought, how difficult it is to imagine other people's pain.

'May as well get drunk then,' Bella resolved, imagining it all too well.

'Yes. Cheers.' Daisy raised her glass and braved an unsuccessful smile. She sat down suddenly, making the black leather chair squeak protestingly. 'Actually, I think he's having an affair. Or, at least, he's thinking of having an affair.'

'He's already having an affair,' Bella pointed out. 'With you.'

'I don't count. Well, not in that way, anyway. We've been together for three years which, in Alex's mind anyway, makes us as good as married.'

'And makes him a bigamist,' Elisabeth added.

Daisy scrabbled around in her bag for a cigarette. 'A natural polygamist, I'm afraid,' she said, head bowed.

'Why put up with it?' Bella asked, thinking of Tom.

Daisy lit up, inhaled sharply. 'You know why.' The words emerged on a faint gasp.

'Well, do something about it.'

'I'm not sure there's much to be done, other than neutering him.' She squashed a drop of wine onto the glass surface of the table, drew a flower in the spreading stain. 'In the end I decided that if I love him, which I do, then it must be that I approve of adultery because infidelity is so much a part of his character.'

'What crap,' Bella said, staring longingly at Daisy's cigarette.

'I know,' Daisy flipped the packet across the table to her, 'a discredit to my sex.'

'A man would never put up with it,' Elisabeth said, although she wasn't entirely sure that was right. Some men, surely, had put up with it, were putting up with it even now.

'Perhaps not,' Daisy said thoughtfully, 'but that's because they're more sentimental than women.'

'Sentimental?' Bella said sharply, but her scorn seemed directed at the unlit cigarette threaded between her fingers.

Daisy shrugged. 'I think Alex is a romantic in the purest sense, which leads him on a constant search for Miss Right. That's why he's fixated on the chase, the serenade from the base of the pedestal. Once he gets up close, the frailties become all too visible. The tragedy for Alex, of course, is that Miss Right simply doesn't exist.'

Bella stared thoughtfully at the cigarette. 'But doesn't it become your tragedy too?' she asked.

'Only if I choose to allow it to,' Daisy replied, with a laugh that said that she had already revealed too much.

'But do we have any choice?' murmured Elisabeth, who still secretly, shamefully, dreamed of Mr Right. She knew it was not Charles, had known it since that sunny June afternoon when she had stood next to him wreathed in peerless white in the mediaeval church in her parents' tiny village and had noticed, with sudden horrible clarity, the bubbles of sweat beading his nose, the coarse black hair speckling his fingers, and had shrunk from the stolid corporeality of him.

Even as she promised herself to him, had tilted her mouth up for a kiss, his fleshy lips sent tiny prickles of shock running the length of her spine and she had to remind herself that this was Charles, her Charles, about whom she had spent so many nights dreaming, tucked up in her narrow, virginal bed. Yet in her dreams his body had been yielding and gentle, his mouth sweet and tender. In her dreams their bodies had melded like vaporous smoke.

He was the second man who had ever kissed her, the only man who had made love to her. She had not known that a tongue could be so fleshy and yet so *hard*. She remembered it the first time, squirming in her mouth like a fat, blind grub.

'Ah, you mean *true* love,' Daisy was saying. 'The sort that makes people leave their husbands, abandon their children, face social opprobrium and bankruptcy.'

'Yes.'

'Doesn't exist.'

'You read about it in the papers every day,' Elisabeth said.

'Poor lost souls with a story to sell.'

'And in literature?' Elisabeth cried.

'Ah, literature,' Daisy said. 'Just dreams on paper.'

'Cynic.'

'A mere student of life.'

'Do stop it,' Elisabeth begged. 'I don't believe you mean any of it. You're just tetchy because Alex can't come tonight.'

'Perhaps,' Daisy said, with a small smile. 'But better a cynic than a romantic.'

'Oh, I don't know.' Elisabeth was rather proud of her romantic nature.

Daisy said, 'I always think of romance as the old Chinese curse.'

'What Chinese curse?'

'May all your dreams come true.'

The next day, late Saturday afternoon, Bella was sitting slouched in a chair in the kitchen, flicking through a copy of *Hello!* and wiggling a toe through a hole in one of her socks. She had just forced it through entirely and was examining it – pale and vaguely affronted against the black wool of the sock – when she heard the front door slam violently. She leaned forward, yanked the sock back over her foot and patted ineffectually at her hair which, somehow, she hadn't got round to brushing that day. Ben slouched into the kitchen, his long, thin body held in a concave curve.

'Hello, darling!' Bella exclaimed, immediately regretting the eager falseness of her tone.

''Lo.'

She knew better than to try to kiss him. He hunched his shoulders against her gaze, slid over to the tatty Formica counter and started fiddling with the salt and pepper pots.

'Where's Dad?' he said, without turning round.

The knobs of his spine were clearly visible through his thin T-shirt. She longed to reach out and touch them one by one, the way she used to when he was a small child. It had made him laugh, then.

He turned and looked at her enquiringly. 'I *said*, where's Dad?'

'At a meeting. He'll be back later, about ten. Did you want to talk to him about something?'

'No.'

'Perhaps I could help?'

He shot her a withering look, turned back to the salt and pepper pots which he proceeded to empty in small heaps on the counter. 'Doesn't matter,' he said eventually.

Bella, who knew better than to confront him outright, picked up the copy of *Hello!* and flicked through it carelessly.

'What's he doing out again?' he asked, shifting restlessly from one foot to another. The salt and pepper pots were almost empty. He swept the small piles onto the kitchen floor.

'Must you?' she said, automatically.

'Doesn't matter.' It was what he had always said as a small boy, whenever he had done something wrong.

'It does if you have to clean it up.'

He shrugged, scuffed the brown and white grains across the floor with a grubby trainer. 'That's the third time he's been out this week.'

Bella, who knew – to the precise minute – how many hours Tom had been out late that week, bit down hard on her lip. 'Is it?' she said brightly.

He looked over at her. 'You don't even notice,' he said scornfully.

'He's trying to find work. It's the only time most people can meet up.'

'It's *Saturday*.'

'So he has to work when other people don't. He's gone over to some house in Notting Hill to see some people who are doing up an old place.'

'You mean, kitchen units. Pissy little domestic conversions.'

'At least he's trying,' Bella said wearily. She rose clumsily from her chair, conscious of her stained tracksuit trousers and old jumper, and padded across the kitchen in stockinged feet.

'And I'm not, I suppose?'

She peered into the fridge, pulled out a bottle of wine. 'I didn't say that.'

'It's what you meant.'

Her patience snapped suddenly, as it had always done,

74

even when he was a small child. 'How the hell do you know what I mean?' she shouted. 'You never stop long enough to listen.'

She regretted her outburst immediately, saw the flicker of fear shadowing his face and felt guilt, like nausea, settle in the pit of her stomach. He had always been unnerved by her unpredictability, had, even, been slightly frightened of her. She saw for a moment the sweet, painfully sensitive boy he used to be. They had been so close. Unnaturally so, according to Tom. She remembered the first year of his life, the blinding joy of him and the terror that shrouded her days and nights; the softness of his tiny body so vulnerable to all the sharp corners of the world. And then as he grew, the notes scattered across the house, tucked under her pillow or left in the pocket of her coat: 'I love you.' She thought of his round, childish hand, felt tears rise. She poured herself a glass of wine, took a large swallow. 'I'm sorry,' she said quietly. 'I didn't mean to shout.'

'Does Dad know that?'

She looked bewildered. 'Does he know what?'

'That you don't *mean* to shout,' he said, drawing out the word.

Bella took a deep breath. 'Would you like something to eat?'

He kicked his foot against a cupboard with a slow, repetitive movement. The sound was driving her mad but she didn't dare ask him to stop. 'I'm going out later. I'll get a pizza.'

'Have you finished revising?'

'For what?'

'For Monday. A tiny little thing called interim exams.'

'Leave it out, Mum. I'm not one of your students.'

'No, you're my son.'

'Worse luck,' he muttered under his breath.

'What did you say?'

'Nothing.'

'Have you done the work?'

'Some.'

'So, do some more.'

He looked so outraged, she almost laughed. 'It's Saturday night.'

'And your A-levels are in two months' time.'

'I know.' He smiled unpleasantly. 'Some little birdie told me.'

She gazed at him, stricken. She had not heard the expression for years; it was one she had always used for him when he was a child. He saw the look on her face, dropped his head, started kicking his foot again. 'Like, people tell me that every day,' he said sullenly.

She stared at the top of his head, wanting to rumple his fine, dark hair; remembering how it used to stand up on end, how he hated it and was forever wetting it to make it lie flat. These days he laboured for hours to get it to stand up, spiking it with gel. 'I know it's tough at the moment but once they're done you'll be off to university.' She heard her voice, false and bright. 'You'll have such a great –'

'Oh, yeah, totally great,' he sneered. 'Bunch of adolescents sitting in the library wanking over Nietzsche and picking their spots.'

She looked away, took deep breaths. 'I thought we might go over and see Elisabeth and Charles tomorrow for lunch. James and Lucy are home for the weekend and –'

'Kids,' Ben said contemptuously.

'– And you haven't seen them for a while,' Bella continued, ignoring him.

Ben was silent.

She watched his shoulders hunch. 'You used to like them.'

'That was before,' he said, still kicking rhythmically at the bottom of the kitchen unit. Flakes of rotten wood powdered the old lino.

76

'Before?' she said, although she knew what he meant; before he left Westminster and went to the local state school.

She looked at him fearfully. 'It's a good school.' It was a fiction they all maintained.

'A first-class education in how to keep your back covered.' He smiled sarcastically, but she could see fear sharpening his features. 'What would you like me to talk to James about? Rugger? Oxbridge entrance? Or would you rather I showed him a little knife control?'

Bella's hands shook slightly as she lifted her glass to her mouth. 'I didn't realise it was so bad,' she said, after a while.

He sighed. 'It's not so bad, just different. I'm different.'

'I'm sorry.'

He looked away. 'Yeah. You said.'

'Is there anything I can do?' she asked quietly.

'No!' he said, almost shouting the word. He knew her nature; her tendency to go barging in, eyes blazing, to sort out whatever problem he had. 'I can cope.' He hunched his shoulders in a shrug. 'Most of the time it's fine.'

She sighed. 'OK.'

He looked up warily. 'Promise you won't?'

She nodded. 'Promise.'

He flushed, stuffed his hands into his pockets and hunched his shoulders defensively. She could see the dark hollows made by his sharp collar-bone.

'You treat me like a child,' he said sullenly. 'It's like you're frightened to let me grow up and be separate from you.'

It was true that sometimes she mourned the loss of her child, resented the almost-man who stood in his place, but she gave him as much freedom as her furious love would allow. More.

She turned away from him, moved slowly across to the

77

table and sat down. 'I'm sorry if you think that,' she said wearily.

'You think I'm like Dad, don't you? You're terrified to let me be separate from you, frightened that if you give me an inch of freedom, I'll do something daft.'

She looked at him intently. 'What's that supposed to mean?'

'Nothing,' he mumbled, flushing under her gaze.

'Has Dad said something to you?'

'I said, it didn't mean nothing.'

'Anything,' she corrected, automatically.

He was silent, his head sunk low on his chest. A memory came back to her suddenly; her mother at the kitchen table, her teenage self standing under the harsh neon light, the walls of the house crowding in on her. He's put up with so much, she thought, and without a word of complaint. Suddenly, she felt ashamed. It was more than could be said for her.

'Oh, go on,' she said. 'Go out and have a good time.'

His face lit up and he swooped down on her suddenly, gathered her in his arms and pressed her against his chest. She held her breath at the unexpected embrace, felt the hard knobs of his rib bones pressed against her cheek, breathed in the musty, boy smell of him. 'Thanks, Mum.'

'And don't –'

'Yeah, yeah, I know. Don't be late, don't get drunk, don't do drugs, don't speak to strange men, don't get beaten up, don't get Aids.'

He let her go, flashed a crooked grin, spun on his heel and was gone.

The front door was yanked open and she heard it slam, then his whoop of joy as he leapt the six steps to the pavement and freedom.

She braced herself against the fear. It never seemed to go away, however old he got.

'Just don't –' she said quietly.

78

Seven

The days lengthened. Spring came like the switching on of a light. One day was dim and grey, the next awash with colour and light, which only made Elisabeth's not-happiness feel worse.

Driving home after doing the weekly shop at Sainsbury's, she manoeuvred the heavy Volvo estate into her road, ignoring the cherry trees tripping prettily down the hill, swishing their fluffy pink petticoats like five-year-olds off to a party. She tapped impatient fingers as she searched for somewhere to park. As usual, there were no spaces outside the house so she dumped the car in the middle of the road and began dragging the heavy bags of groceries out of the boot.

No sooner had she unloaded the first bags than a horn blared impatiently. Peering over the boot of the car, Elisabeth saw a man leaning out of a white transit van, the tendons of his neck a snarl of thick white rope. 'Think you own the bloody road?' he shouted. 'Bloody Volvo drivers.'

Elisabeth ducked back down to the boot, resisting a wild impulse to climb into it. 'Bully,' she muttered, fumbling nervously with the bags and banging them painfully against her legs. The transit's engine was revved impatiently. She piled the bags on the pavement and gazed despairingly up the long pathway to her house. It would take her at least five minutes to drag them all up there.

He saw her glance, leaned heavily on the horn yelling, 'Don't even fucking think about it.'

A gaggle of Japanese tourists, fresh from a brief circuit

of the local museum, stopped to stare, the men's black eyes impenetrable, the women's hands raised to their faces to muffle their shrill giggling.

Abandoning the shopping in the middle of the pavement, Elisabeth climbed back into the driver's seat, her hands shaking as she turned the ignition key and clumsily took off the handbrake. The car shuddered slowly down the road until she found somewhere to pull over. 'Bloody women drivers,' the man yelled, as he roared by.

Elisabeth sat in her car, tears dripping slowly down her cheeks. I am crying, she thought stupidly, making no move to stop the tears. After a while, the Japanese tourists walked by, chattering excitedly, a few of them stopping to peer into the car as they passed.

One of them, a woman, lingered longer than the others, her black gaze trained on Elisabeth. Finally, Elisabeth turned, mouthed obscenities at the impassive face. The woman smiled gently, shrugged her shoulders in a universal sign of sympathy and with a quick, polite bow, was gone.

When she got back to her front gate, Elisabeth discovered that the shopping bags had gone. She stood, staring wildly up and down the street but could see no sign of them anywhere. With a sigh, she turned and trudged up the garden path. There, lined up in front of the door in orderly Japanese rows, were the bags of shopping.

Defeated by the unexpected act of kindness, she sank down on the step among the bags of shopping and buried her face in her hands. I have no right, she told herself sternly. I have my blessings, after all. But whose blessing am I? Charles has his work, the children, their lives; even the house has Elsa, who cares for it a good deal more efficiently than I can. I have no rights, no rights at all.

She carried the bags into the house; into her lovely, bright, spacious kitchen where she sat upright in one of the uncomfortable but expensive hard-backed designer chairs and cried furiously. She cried as people cry only when they are alone; with a sort of painful pleasure, gasping like a stranded fish, mouth hanging open, tears and snot running down her face, dripping unheeded from her chin.

After a while her sobs broke into pleasurable, winded hiccups, the skin tightening on her face as the tears dried. When she was calmer, she thought perhaps a cup of tea might make her feel better.

A packet of Lemon Slices peeked seductively from a plastic carrier. She pulled a crumpled tissue from her pocket and scrubbed her face, gazing longingly at the packet. A nice Slice on a plate and a cup of tea with proper milk, not that horrible skimmed stuff.

No. She was fat enough already.

Even so, her hand sneaked towards the package. Why bother to starve, she thought, when everybody knew that dieting made you fat? Just lately she'd been considering trying the food-combining diet. 'Clears the head,' said a friend, tapping her forehead vigorously. Then she'd read the book about the diet, or plan as it was prissily called. She'd found it so hard to keep track of what was starch and what protein, and whether an avocado was neutral, protein or just plain fat ('You *ate* an avocado?' a professional dieting friend asked in horror) that she'd decided that the only thing it cleared from her head was her brain. She'd read all the books. Even her lunch came from a book, a *Hip and Thigh* sandwich; reduced starch bread, reduced portion salad, reduced fat dressing.

I am reduced, she thought mournfully.

Perhaps she should ring Daisy. You couldn't be depressed around Daisy. She wouldn't let you be. Daisy never moped. At least, not as far as anybody knew. Was busy in that studio of hers all day long, happy as a lark. Or so she said. Daisy was famously secretive about her work – 'It's just me messing around. It's not worth seeing; not yet anyway' – which made her studio seem all the more exotic, a tent of white sheets draped over mysterious, soaring edifices, the curves and planes tantalisingly visible beneath the cloth, clay dust covering every surface with a fine white powder, curious sharp tools with worn wooden handles.

It hardly seemed real, yet there were exhibitions of her work; astonishing, monolithic pieces, sombre and brooding and somehow far too serious to have emerged from somebody as fragile and flippant as Daisy.

The mystery of that process always made Elisabeth feel out of place, standing stiffly in her smart clothes while Daisy flitted around dressed in dusty blue overalls, a colourful, clay-spattered scarf over her bright hair, her movements brisk, confident, unfamiliar.

Elisabeth rarely telephoned her there; always felt that she would be intruding. Then again, Daisy hardly ever rang her either, at least, not during the day.

'Oh, you're always so busy,' Daisy said.

'Am I?'

'God, yes,' Daisy laughed. 'Wife and mother, the busiest job in the world.'

Elisabeth sat at her lovely antique oak refectory table, feeling the old wood, like satin, beneath her hands. Drops of water from her tears flecked the shining surface. She drew them into tiny circles with the delicate tip of a finger.

Wife and mother, she thought, smudging them into the wood and watching a small, dark stain spread. Yes, I am a wife. But a wife isn't a whole person; just a bit of one. She wondered idly which bit. The arms, perhaps, ready to comfort, to prepare food, to carry laundry, to soothe and fuss and tidy. No, surely the arms were the mother. Was there any difference? Wife and mother, interchangeable roles, both bits of a woman, except that she'd chosen to make the bits, with Charles's encouragement, her whole person.

No, not even a mother; not since the children both went

off to boarding school – just a sort of part-time carer. A caretaker perhaps. James and Lucy were so independent nowadays, so wrapped up in their own triumphs and disasters that they no longer seemed to need her – hadn't needed her for years, when she thought about it. Not the way they'd needed her when they were very young; their faces lighting up when they saw her waiting patiently at the school gates, their pleasure at the little treats she'd concoct for them for their supper, arranging funny faces out of fish cakes – peas for eyes, chips for ears and a silly, squiggly mouth painted on with tomato ketchup.

These days they told her not to fuss, the eternal adolescent cry ringing in her ears, 'Oh, *Mu-u-m*!' as they snatched a sandwich and ran out of the door. When they were home for the holidays, she organised outings for them, trips to the cinema, to art galleries and museums. They were nice children, obedient and loving, but she could feel impatience fizzing through their long, awkward limbs, understood their longing to be free of her and out with their friends or hunched in darkened rooms over their computers.

How she hated those computers, how old and useless they made her feel with their strange, electronic voices and flimsy, flat keyboards; so unlike the solid, comforting machines of her day. The first time, the only time, she had sat down at one of the children's computers, she had smiled to feel the keys so familiar beneath her fingers, had smiled until the screen thrust into life, admonishing her with strange spiked symbols and urgent, strangled phrases.

'Use the mouse, use the mouse!' Lucy exclaimed, sounding cross, while James rolled his eyes scornfully in the background, 'Oh, *Mu-u-um*!' They had all laughed, giggling together over Mum's incompetence; she loudest of all, to hide how much she cared.

She felt keenly the corrosive power of her children's

scorn, like the Australian spider she'd read about in a newspaper whose offspring repay the care and protection they get from the mother spider by eating her. They start by sucking blood from her leg joints and then, when she is paralysed, gobble her up completely. The article, which was written by a man, protested that this process, known as matriphagy, was rather an eccentric form of maternal care. Elisabeth couldn't see anything eccentric about it at all.

She had worked, of course, before the children had been born, had been private secretary to a rather well-known lawyer. She'd been good at her job, had even thought she might go back to it, or something like it, one day but nowadays there seemed little demand for a woman with impeccable telephone manners and smudge-free carbon copies. Without word-processing skills she was, as the woman at the employment agency said, rather tartly, virtually unemployable.

Well it was not, Charles said, as if they needed the money. And as Elisabeth pointed out – as if reassuring him rather than herself – there were always the holidays. Ah, yes, the holidays. The children might not want her there, but she had to *be* there – like an iceberg, ninety per cent submerged, only her head bobbing, reassuringly, on the surface of their lives. Or perhaps her body wasn't there at all, had been nibbled away until only her head remained. *Matriphagy*.

She had put the idea of working to one side, thinking vaguely that she might one day apply to do a course in word-processing. She never had, of course. The whole business made her feel so useless.

Well, what could she do? It seemed absurd, not being able to do anything. She was only thirty-nine. Well, nearly forty. But forty was young these days. All the women that she knew worked; were separated from her by a smug cocoon of suits and timetables. Whereas she was a housewife or – what was the modern expression? – homemaker. Oh, horrible. *Horrible.* She pictured herself in a gingham apron, a stiff feather duster in one hand, a casserole in the other. What do you do? Why, I make homes.

What was a home after all but an assortment of bricks and mortar, of curtains and carpets and furniture all shrieking to be cleaned and scrubbed and polished? Then, of course, there was the ceaseless cycle of food, lovingly prepared, carelessly swallowed; the tide of socks and vests and shirts seeping across bedroom floors, retreating daily under her brisk hands into cupboards and drawers, only to return with stealthy, relentless inevitability.

She stared around at the gleaming kitchen, felt the walls press down on her, suffocating her beneath their clean, reproachless surfaces; imagined other kitchens in other houses, each containing a solitary tiny, doll-like figure, millions of them crushed beneath the weight of their universe on this sunny afternoon.

Other women seemed to manage – held down jobs, raised families, kept their homes clean. How? Perhaps they handed their children over to nannies and child-minders. She could have done that, she supposed, but it hadn't seemed right, not at the time.

And, as Charles pointed out, using words placed as carefully as stepping-stones across treacherous ground, it was her choice. I know it's my choice, she wanted to say, but a choice is not always the inevitable by-product of free will. Not where women are concerned, anyway. But she'd loved being at home with her kids, not having to go out and work simply in order to make ends meet. Of course she had, knew how privileged she was, although there is no 'of course' about loving a two-year-old determined not to get dressed or a four-year-old intent on suicide on a climbing frame.

She'd been at a dinner party only the other week when

one young couple had explained that they hadn't left the house the entire weekend because their three-year-old refused to put his boots on. The other – childless – couples had stared at them, appalled. Elisabeth had laughed loudly.

And the women who had stayed home like her, the ones she'd been friends with when James and Lucy were small, where were they now? Working, she supposed, or moved away.

Bella suggested that she might consider charity work. 'Is that all I'm good for?' Elisabeth had asked with a smile, although she knew that Bella was only trying to be helpful. Bella had said nothing, but Elisabeth had seen a tiny flicker of irritation, heard a sigh echoing through the silence.

I am bored, she thought. God, but I'm bored.

The doorbell rang. She stared towards the front door suspiciously. Nobody, or at least nobody that she knew, dropped by unannounced. She stared round at the mess, dithering a little over the frozen chicken livers, which looked close to thawing. She knew she should have done the food shopping *after* she went to the post office. There was always such a queue on a Wednesday afternoon.

The bell sounded again.

Who would be that persistent, she wondered, unconsciously squaring her shoulders. Perhaps that lot from Jehovah's Witnesses or some charity do-gooder with pale, watering eyes, determined to make the people in the big houses feel guilty.

As if she didn't feel guilty enough already. Even the supermarket made her embarrassed. She grew hot under the unforgiving lights, flinching under the gimlet eyes of the women around her, their baskets stacked with baked beans and cheap sausages, her trolley piled high with steak, salad and wine.

She'd even felt embarrassed on the Tube the other day flicking through a luridly coloured holiday brochure, had sped past the lyrical descriptions of Tuscany to the package deals in Gran Canaria, not that she had any intention of ever visiting the place. She felt a little resentful of her guilt, but did not seem able to do anything about it.

She tried discussing it with Daisy, but Daisy had just laughed. 'It's not guilt,' she said, 'it's resentment at not being allowed to enjoy what you have. Think of it as the malaise of the decade; you feel resentful if you don't have it and resentful if you do. It's what the Americans call a no-win situation.'

Very helpful, Elisabeth thought crossly as she marched towards the front door and put a suspicious head around it, a polite 'no thank you' already forming on her lips.

Lily stood there, clumsily thrusting a bunch of flowers.

Elisabeth felt guilt prick at her impatiently and almost snatched at the limp stems in their crackling cellophane. Dirty water trickled out of them, staining her sleeve. She rubbed at it surreptitiously, hoping Lily wouldn't notice and glanced down at the flowers, a cheap mixed bouquet of ageing chrysanthemums, faded iris, a sprig of yellowing maidenhair fern, of the sort sold on garage forecourts.

'How lovely,' she said gaily.

Lily's opaque eyes flickered across Elisabeth's face. 'Is this a bad time?' she said in her flat, toneless voice.

'Not at all,' Elisabeth said untruthfully. 'Do come in.'

She led the way into the kitchen. A thin trickle of bloody water leaked from the frozen liver.

'Sorry. It's a frightful mess in here. I've just got back from the supermarket.'

'Wasn't sure what was the best time,' Lily said, standing awkwardly among the shopping bags. She gestured vaguely at the flowers. 'I just wanted to say thank you for a nice evening. I had a lovely time.' She sounded like a child, reciting a rehearsed speech.

Elisabeth glanced sharply at the girl's white face. The dinner party had been weeks ago. Had she been waiting, scuffing her blistered heels in that bleak, lonely room, for a phone call? She felt tears rising again and turned away, guilt and pity making her brisk. 'I'll put the kettle on. Sit here. No, there. You'll be more comfortable. I'll have all this put away in a minute, make us a cup of tea. We can have a good chat.'

'If you've got time,' Lily said, sinking slowly into a chair. Her eyes settled mournfully on the bulging carrier bags. '*We* always did our shop in the evening; late-night closing.'

'Much more sensible,' Elisabeth agreed, methodically sorting fillet steaks, wild salmon, expensive cheeses, organic eggs, jars of pesto sauce, bottles of wine, freshly squeezed orange juice and mineral water; all the careless luxuries that seemed, so overwhelmingly, to surround them. Conscious of Lily's cheap, thin coat, of her dark, mournful gaze, she thrust everything quickly away and hurried to make tea.

'I've been meaning to call,' she said, untruthfully. 'But you know how –' She gestured helplessly, her hands regretting the passage of time.

Lily took this in, blinking slowly. 'I was going to write a proper thank-you letter but I didn't know the postcode and I – well I wanted to see you again.' Her eyes slid over to Elisabeth. 'Don't mind, do you?' There was something vaguely hostile in her tone.

'Of course not,' Elisabeth exclaimed, too forcibly. 'It's lovely to see you. As I say, I've been meaning to . . . Did you enjoy yourself at the dinner party? We all thought . . . well, I felt it was a *great* success. Charles enjoyed himself very much, said he was vastly entertained by you.' Oh, God, was entertained quite the right word or would Lily think she was being patronised? 'I mean, he said you were terribly amusing.'

Lily stared around the room. 'I've never been to a dinner party like that before.'

'Haven't you!' Elisabeth exclaimed, conscious of false-ness, then sought refuge in making tea, warming the pot, measuring out the fragrant leaves, setting out teacups and saucers. As she clattered silver spoons next to the cups she wondered, suddenly, if Lily wouldn't prefer tea in a mug. She hovered uncertainly over the pot. At dinner the differences between them had been softened under the flickering glamour of candlelight, the glow of wine and good food, but seeing Lily here, in the sharp, merciless light of a spring afternoon, with only the nearly empty shopping bags from Sainsbury's gathered limply between them, Elisabeth felt at a loss to know how to treat her.

The faintest glimmer of a smile touched Lily's face.

'Proper tea,' she said. 'Haven't had that in ages, not since I was last at my mum's. She won't use them bags; says they're full of the sweepings from the floor.'

'I expect she's right. Would you like some cake? I bought some at the supermarket,' Elisabeth said, casting around among the packages. 'Ah, here they are.' She fished the lemon-coloured box out from under a pile, arranged the cakes on a pretty plate strewn with violets. 'Lemon Slices. Do you like them?'

'They're all right.'

'Or perhaps you'd rather have some toast? Won't take a minute. Now, where did I put that bread . . .'

'That cake'll do.'

Now that she was here, Lily wasn't quite sure what to do with herself. Elisabeth didn't seem too pleased to see her. She'd seen that look she gave the flowers. Well, they weren't much, but it was like her mum said – it was the thought that counted. She wished Elisabeth would come and sit down, stop jumping around like that. Maybe this was the way people like her behaved; all that money made them restless. Still, she was pleased she'd come. It was a nice house, even nicer than that night at dinner. Mind you, she'd been concentrating so hard on using the proper cutlery, she hadn't taken much in. Always go from the outside in; that's what Jim said. Then you can't go wrong.

She chewed her lips thoughtfully, wondering why it was that Elisabeth seemed different, nervous almost, trying to hide all that lovely food away so she wouldn't notice that she had so much more than she ever had. Or ever would, she thought. And she'd been crying too. She wondered what she had to cry about. Maybe it was that husband of hers, that Charles. Adores her, that's what that Daisy said. Gives her everything, too, Lily thought, gazing around. She'd like to have a man like Charles adore her, had been thinking about it a lot recently, feeling the tingle of it in her bones. He liked her well enough; more than enough, she thought, feeling a flush of power. She could tell that from the look on his face, sort of sharp and scared, all at the same time. She'd been hoping he might be here today but she supposed he must be out at work. Something he'd said that night at dinner about his work had given her an idea. He was the boss, he'd said, so if he was the boss, he could get her a job at his place. Stood to reason. Then she'd be near him every day. Not that she'd mentioned it to him, of course; just came out with some sob story about having no money and work being hard to find. That had set the seed nicely. Now she'd work on Elisabeth. She was soft enough to fall for a line like that.

Lily looked up at Elisabeth, still rebounding across the kitchen like a yo-yo. God, women were daft sometimes. Didn't know when they were well off. She'd seen the way Elisabeth looked at Charles; irritable, like he was an ornament waiting to be dusted, a chore needed doing. 'Are you going to sit down?' she said.

Elisabeth flushed. 'Oh! Yes, of course.'

It was then that Lily realised it was her that was making Elisabeth feel nervous. *Her!* That made her feel good so she smiled and said, 'A scalded cat, that's what my mum would have called you.'

'Sorry,' Elisabeth said, and the way she said it, apologising to her as if she, Lily, really meant something, made her smile even harder. 'I've never been much good at keeping still.'

Keeping still was one thing that Lily knew all about.

'I am,' she said, 'I'm brilliant. Got it down to a fine art, that's what my mum says.'

'Well, you must teach me how,' Elisabeth said, pouring tea.

'Don't know about that. I've been good at it since I was a baby, my mum says. Not like my brother. He squirms like an eel, even when he's supposed to be still, watching telly and the like. Mum thinks keeping still's something you're born with, like blue eyes.'

Elisabeth laughed, was conscious that she was enjoying herself. 'I'm glad you came. I was feeling a bit depressed.'

'Daft, you are,' Lily said. 'I wouldn't be depressed. Not in a place like this. Not with that husband of yours.'

'Charles?'

'He's dead handsome – in a sort of *old* way.'

Lily sounded so young and earnest, that Elisabeth smiled. 'Yes, I suppose he is,' she said fondly. 'One forgets, after seventeen years.'

'Shouldn't do that,' Lily said. 'Forget, I mean.'

Eight

Daisy's studio was part of an old warehouse in Camden Town. It overlooked the railway so rents were cheap and nobody really noticed the noise, once they'd got used to it. And, as the residents were fond of pointing out, it was only five minutes from Regent's Park if you walked fast.

There were four of them in the building; all artists of sorts. Jeff and Chris, who were photographers, shared the top floor which they'd made look quite flash with shiny white walls, polished wood floors and makeshift dressing-rooms of melamine panels with mirrors screwed into the wall, edged with light bulbs. Fashion, they said, although Daisy suspected from the look of the models who clattered wearily up the concrete stairs that there was only a modicum of clothing involved. Then there was Annie, an illustrator, tucked neatly away in a tiny, cluttered corner to the side of the building. She had clouds of soft brown hair and small, blinking eyes. She ventured out very rarely and, when she did, scuttled back in again as if alarmed by the daylight.

Daisy had the ground floor. She'd chosen it for the big double wooden doors that led onto the street, useful for shifting the massive pieces she made and for lugging in bags of clay and the bits of scrap iron she sometimes used. A row of large windows covered in opaque glass let in enough light to work by and she'd painted the walls with whitewash and chucked some old carpets over the cold, grey concrete floor. A sofa stood in one corner next to an old industrial heater that belched out hot air all day, even in summer. In another corner there was a cracked sink, a kettle, and a gleaming new fridge which Alex insisted on keeping stocked up with wine. He'd also installed a telephone although Daisy rarely answered it so he'd bought an answering machine to go with it. She was up a ladder, hatching precise vertical lines on a cliff of grey clay when the telephone rang. She stopped, knife poised in her hand, to listen. The machine clicked and whirred, then static buzzed through it like an infuriated bluebottle trapped behind glass.

'I'm on my way,' Alex said. He was on the car phone, his voice ebbing and flowing as he zigzagged through a built-up area north of the Euston Road. 'Be with you in five minutes.'

Daisy pulled back the wrist of one of the Marigold gloves she wore to protect her hands and peered at her watch, then turned back to the sheet of clay and finished her work. Just as she was scrabbling down the ladder, Alex flung open the heavy wooden doors and vaulted over one of the rusty trailers that she used to lug sacks of clay around.

'Stop showing off,' she said severely. 'You'll give yourself a heart attack.'

He laughed, pleased with himself. '*You* are my heart attack.'

She glanced at him, suspicious of his good humour, and gathered up a bundle of dust-sheets to cloak the damp clay. She could see, from his look, that he had been misbehaving.

'Not even a hello kiss?' he said, catching her to him.

She kissed him briefly on the mouth. 'I'm filthy.'

A faint smell of cigarettes and scent lingered on his clothes, curling around the edge of the expensive cologne he'd splashed on in the car on his way over. Perhaps a harmless flirtation, a wine bar after work, a snatched kiss in some dark, velvet corner. She knew he was not to be trusted. She knew, also, not to show it.

But she could make him suffer, just a little; she was not yet ready to be won over. She ducked out of his embrace, began slowly to clean her chisels and the tiny, pointed trowels she used.

He sighed faintly, watching her. She was in one of her distant moods, half of her attention still focused on the work of the day. Better tread carefully then. 'How's it going?' he asked, nodding at the shrouded figures.

'Badly,' she said, with the faint sneer she reserved for such questions.

He smiled indulgently. 'I know. I shouldn't ask.'

'Then don't,' she said briskly. 'You know I hate it.'

'My sweet, surly artist,' he said fondly. He liked it when she was severe with him, the separateness of her in her studio made his blood pound.

'I can see you've had a good day,' she said, her voice faintly accusing.

His squirmed under her gaze. 'It was okay.'

She paused fractionally, and he saw by the slight stiffness of her movements that she was suspicious. Her eyes stayed on him for a moment longer, her gaze thoughtful, and then she moved away. 'I'll get ready,' she said briefly.

'No rush.' He breathed a sigh of relief as he watched her, seduced as always to see her emerge like a butterfly from the chrysalis of her dusty blue overall. She slid into a black dress, ducked down to pull off heavy boots and thick socks, revealing sheer black tights. Feeling his eyes on her, she looked up to see him advancing slowly, a greedy smile plastered across his face. 'Behave,' she implored, half-laughing, because this, so many times, had been the prelude to sex; long, slow, careful love on the old sofa, its rusty springs chafing their bare backs. 'We haven't the time.'

'No,' he said regretfully, flinging himself down and watching as she unwound the scarf from her head and brushed out her fine hair. As her hands flashed above her head, revealing slender arms, he half-regretted the woman he'd been kissing an hour earlier.

'You'll get dusty,' she said, nodding at his navy blue suit.

'Ah, but it'll be your dust.'

She looked at him through narrowed eyes, a lipstick poised in her hand. 'You're up to something.'

'Taking my mistress out for dinner. That's certainly something.'

She bared her teeth so her lips stretched out like pink rubber bands, applied lipstick to the smooth surface. 'How's Celia?' she asked, pressing down hard on her top lip.

He shrugged, relieved that she hadn't guessed that his good humour was down to a different woman; a solicitor dealing with one of his clients' cases. A meeting last week, a casual phone call – just a point that needed clearing up – a drink to settle the problem. She was brisk, efficient, no nonsense, wanted to take him to bed. Who was he to refuse? What was her name? Ah, Suzanne. Dark hair, wiry body, long, muscular legs from a daily work-out at the gym. He imagined those legs, wrapped around his waist. Ah, ah, ah, Suzanne.

'Celia is –' he sighed gently, indicating the burden of his marriage. 'Celia is Celia.'

'Fucked her recently?' she said coolly, sliding gold rings through tiny, pierced holes in her ears.

He winced slightly, watching metal penetrate flesh. 'I told you, we didn't.'

'And you expect me to believe that?'

Alex was telling the truth. He had not slept with his wife. Well, slept with her but not made love, although not from any lack of effort on his part. He enjoyed fucking his

95

wife. Celia knew that. She also knew that, to her husband, resistance was the most potent aphrodisiac.

'Angel,' he said imploringly.

She looked at him; desire and exasperation mingled in her glance. 'Yes, sweetiepops.' He knew that she hated what she called empty endearments, said that they were signposts to an empty heart but God damn it, he was doing his best. Must she talk to him like that? He lounged on the sofa, sulking.

Sighing lightly, she moved over to him, dropped a kiss on the top of his head. 'Sorry, darling. Rotten day.'

He caught her by the hand. 'We don't have to go. Not if you don't want to. I'll take you somewhere, just the two of us.'

'You mean, we'll stay here and have a take-away?'

'No, a restaurant. You choose.'

She smiled slightly, her expression watchful and he wondered, again, what she was thinking. 'You know we can't cancel, not now,' she said eventually. 'It's too late. Tell you what, why don't you open a bottle of wine, get us in the mood?'

Alex strolled across to the fridge, squatting down to sort the jumble of bottles crammed into its gleaming white innards. As he bent forward, the yellow light from the door struck his handsome, fleshy face on which traces of his earlier petulance still lingered. Daisy slipped on a pair of fragile, high-heeled shoes, watching him thoughtfully as she fiddled with the thin straps. They were due to have dinner, in a restaurant, with mutual friends. It was the only way they could dine out in public. Should Celia, or a friend of Alex's, appear, they could always protest that Daisy was just one of the party; a friend brought along for the evening. It was Tom who had once said that to Alex, a wife without a mistress was like meat without salt. Daisy denied it, although she knew it to be true. What she no longer knew was whether she wanted to be his wife. Not that Celia would be easy to prise off him, for she knew his weaknesses, knew the tender parts of him, the places to hook him to her. Daisy suddenly felt tired of it all, wanted to be out, among normal people, among couples enjoying themselves without games or subterfuge. After three years with him, the excitement of sex and take-aways in her studio had begun to pall. She wondered if he noticed. Wondered if he felt it too. She waited for the sharp stab of pain that always accompanied such thoughts. She felt nothing. Waited again. Still nothing. She gazed at him with widened eyes. He looked so familiar, so dear to her, that slightly sulky expression darkening his handsome face as he wrestled with the bottle. She loved him still, she knew. But she was growing immune to his infidelities. Each one shaved another edge off her love. She wondered idly how many it would take to blunt it entirely.

He walked back over to her, carrying two glasses. 'I can make an excuse. I've missed you,' he said, reproach tingeing his voice.

'I know,' she said, taking a glass. She did know. He did miss her, loved her in his way. The other women were mirages, illusions that promised to succour his quenched soul. He could not do without them, although they bored him once he had them. She also knew that, were she to turn away from him, he would stumble off in a different direction, find someone else. Even go back to Celia, for a while, until he found a replacement. She knew that she was not done with him, not yet.

Smiling, she lifted her mouth to his. 'We could be a bit late,' she said, but his hands were already on her skirt, lifting it higher. As she lay on the sofa, pinioned between the rusty springs and her lover, Daisy wondered whether there was still a spare set of tights in her bag. She lifted her hips, felt him slide into her, tilted her pelvis to rock him gently. If they hurried there was probably still time to stop at the all-night chemist.

As her husband rocked between Daisy's slim thighs, Celia slowly stirred a pan of scrambled eggs. A white plate set with pink strips of smoked salmon waited on a tray, a brioche warmed in the oven, a glass of wine stood by her side.

She took a sip of the wine.

Nice.

Alex had bought her a case of it. He was useful in such small husbandly ways. *Husband.* Even after so long – was it really twelve years? – she still found it difficult to think of him as her husband. Or perhaps she found it difficult to think of herself as a wife. She thought she was better suited to being a mistress but liked the status of married life, knew that she could not have one thing as well as the other. Celia was not a woman who could exist without a man. The thought did not please her as she thought independence admirable, but she knew her own nature.

Just as she knew her husband's.

Now in her mid-forties, her long auburn hair neither as luxuriant as it once had been, nor her beauty so abundant, Celia was still a handsome woman. She had class, which was something that Alex wanted. And Alex had money, which was something Celia wanted. It was a marriage made, if not in heaven, then at least in the calm, still air of reason.

Celia, however, had a secret. She had married for love. Not that she ever burdened Alex with it, had known even as she married him that he would not be faithful to her. Just as she knew, even as he slid the thin gold band onto her finger, that although she minded very much indeed, he would never know quite how much.

She indulged him, accommodated his urgent, impatient thrusting with her cool, white body, careful to measure herself in small but concentrated doses; enough to satisfy, never enough to satiate. He loved her reserve, despite claiming that it drove him crazy, burrowing into her in an attempt to find the closed, private core of her. He never did. It was what kept him there, by her side.

Scooping a mound of creamy, perfect scrambled eggs onto a plate, Celia picked up the tray and carried it into the sitting-room. It was a cool, elegant room, much like Celia herself who had commanded every last detail, decorated in shades of cream and white with bold punctuation points of colour – a painting here, a primitive African wood carving over there – and was perched high in a celebrated but anonymous thirties modernist apartment block overlooking St James's Park. It had cost a small fortune, but then Alex had a small fortune, so why not spend it? Not that he ever flashed his money around; that was one lesson he had learned well at Celia's elegant white breast. A financial genius, Alex Carlton slid through the City's cold, hard landscape with silent, deadly precision, setting up deals, slithering through the leviathan coils of massive mergers and takeovers, wriggling through loopholes and around blind alleys with a careless, luxuriant flick of his tail. He never asked why or even whether, was as happy in the sewer as he was in the boardroom, covered his tracks as lightly as the wind rakes clean the desert.

The rest he left to his wife, for in every other way, Alex was a simple, if not a foolish, man. Not like Celia; clever, complicated Celia who was born to a good but impoverished Anglo-Irish family, bred to face the usual deprivations of a girl of her class – lousy education, low expectations and limited funds. After a desultory schooling Celia left the cold, shambling house just outside Dublin where she had spent her life so far and flew to London, economy class. She had, it is true, a small private income – some money from a trust fund – which was not as much as she would have liked, but was more than the salary usually paid to girls of her background; nice, capable, well-bred girls who worked as assistants in estate agents' offices or cooks, preparing directors' lunches. She'd done the season, of course, had gone to the dances, endured the clumsy embraces and sat drinking tea with the mothers and their sweet, plump, dim daughters. It wasn't, she found, the women she minded but the men; boys really, with dull minds and eager eyes. In the end she'd got bored, found herself a job in a gallery in Mayfair. Not that she worked for the money, or even the work itself. She had worked in order to meet men. The right sort of men. Rich, indulgent, *spoiling* men. Men without money did not interest her. She saw no point in them. She'd done all right. Had a ball, in fact. But somehow, none of them had wanted to marry her. In the end, what they all wanted was a sweet, plump, dim girl and not beautiful, dangerous, red-headed Celia with her sharp smile and even sharper tongue.

She'd been thirty-five when she met Alex, had astonished herself by promptly falling in love with him. She had made it a rule not to fall in love with married men but discovered, past her mid-twenties, that they were increasingly hard to avoid. Alex Carlton was loud, vulgar, flashy and possessed of a vitality that Celia found enchanting. The enchantment held, the rest faded like the mist under the glare of Celia's critical, searching gaze. Alex Carlton's background – 'East End boy done good' he boasted, although Celia knew the truth was centred in one of the bleak, windy suburbs that fringe the outer reaches of South London – slowly dropped away, shed like a second skin, together with Tracy, Alex's childhood sweetheart and first wife. Curiously, it was to Tracy that Celia owed the success of her marriage for it was Tracy who had taught her the only truth worth knowing about Alex; to love him with tender but careless grace. Sadly, it was a lesson the teacher never did learn, for meek, sentimental, loving Tracy had clung like a vine, kept her husband on a rein so tight he had eventually – under Celia's careful tutoring – been forced to sever it, packing her off to a big, mock-

Tudor house near her mum in Streatham with a nice little clutch of nest eggs invested in her name. She'd gone quietly enough, perhaps because she'd never truly believed Alex was hers to keep in the first place, and found herself a nice, decent, reliable man called Robert whom she had married. Tracy's single act of rebellion was to refuse Alex access to his children. Not that she made a fuss about it; just quietly spirited them away whenever Alex was due to go and see them. He visited every two weeks for a year, then gave up. He never mentioned his kids, but he pined for them bitterly.

On the same two days every year Alex disappeared, then came home violently but silently drunk. At first she had been bewildered, but Celia was a sensible woman and had taken herself off to the Office for National Statistics where she discovered what she had been suspecting: that those two days were the children's birthdays. After that, she simply undressed Alex carefully and tucked him up in bed with a soothing, tender kiss. He never referred to it in the morning, and nor did she.

Celia knew about Daisy too, of course, had monitored the progress of the affair through the services of the woman who cleaned Alex's offices, just as she had kept an eye on all his mistresses over the years. It had been easy enough to organise: an early morning visit to Alex's offices on the pretext of collecting a forgotten briefcase, a swift word in the ear, a postal order mailed monthly in a plain brown envelope. 'Not spying,' Celia assured her, 'just watching over him, like a guardian angel.'

Mrs Flower was an unlikely angel – on the wrong side of fifty, fatly cheerful and safely anonymous in her floral sack dress and old coat. Her constant accessory was a shabby tartan shopping trolley with an absurd dog perched among the groceries. Amazing what one could discover shifting pieces of paper around desks, flicking dusters over diaries – and if they happened to be open, then who was to mind if she looked? 'He uses little codes, bless him,' she told Celia, laughing comfortably. 'Like a schoolboy playing a game.' And if her duster occasionally strayed across Alex's private answer machine, dislodging the playback button, well, what harm was there in that? She always carried a spare set of tapes in her bag, for replacement and copies.

She was getting on a bit now, but still had a precise ear and eye for detail. 'Women's intuition,' Mrs Flower called it. 'Good old common sense.' Even so, she knew her worth; 'We girls must look after each other,' she said cosily.

Smiling, Celia surveyed her elegant cream sitting-room and settled down on one of the large, linen-covered sofas to watch a medical drama on television. She forked a lump of egg into her mouth and watched in fascination as a man in green overalls with what looked suspiciously like washing-up gloves on his hands, sawed off the top of a man's head. Scooping salmon and eggs into her mouth, Celia decided that she had grown quite fond of Daisy, who loved Alex sufficiently to be kind to him, but not quite enough to want to take him from his wife – even if she thought she did. In fact, Celia thought, watching the brain flutter delicately in its bone shell, if Alex had to have a mistress, which he most certainly did, for the idea of Alex on the loose was worrying indeed, then Daisy was as close to perfect as a mistress could be.

Daisy and Alex found Elisabeth and Charles sitting in the restaurant, hands entwined.

'This is nice. We had no idea you'd be here,' Daisy said, leaning over to kiss Elisabeth.

'It was very last minute. Richard rang this morning and I thought – well, why not? We haven't been out in ages.' She glanced sidelong at her husband. 'Charles, of course, started muttering about work and how exhausting midweek dinners are so I simply told him that I wouldn't take no for an answer.'

'*Thrillingly* stern,' Daisy murmured, sliding into the seat next to her. She glanced across at Charles who was now deep in conversation with Alex. 'Well, it certainly seems to have done the trick. You two were looking very cosy.'

Elisabeth looked faintly embarrassed. 'Something Lily said, about not taking him for granted.'

'That creature with the wedding dress? I didn't know you'd seen her again.'

'She turned up a couple of weeks ago out of the blue, with a bunch of flowers.'

'Does daylight improve her?'

'Don't be unkind. I think she was just rather overawed, that first night at dinner. She's a sweet little thing, really.'

'Not the very first word that springs to mind.'

'Actually, I rather liked her. She cheered me up.'

'Do you *need* cheering up?' Daisy said disapprovingly.

'Matriphagy.'

'Matri-what?'

'Feeling useless, eaten up. It's a sort of incestuous cannibalism.'

'Sounds revolting. What *you* need is to find yourself something to do.'

Elisabeth sighed faintly. Why was it, she thought, that when people stated the obvious, they always assumed the same, slightly hectoring tone. She longed to widen her eyes and exclaim, 'You don't say!' but it was not in her nature to be provocative and so she lowered her eyes and looked slightly hurt.

Daisy glanced at her sharply, then extracted a tiny gold brick of a lighter from her bag. 'Cigarette?'

Elisabeth gazed at the cigarette longingly but shook her head. 'You know Charles disapproves. I'll sneak a drag of yours when he's not looking.' She sipped at her wine instead and said contemplatively, 'How I long to be old. I shall smoke twenty cigarettes a day, stay up all night eating cream-centred chocolates and reading unsuitable books and in the morning be as crabby and irritable as I like.'

'In that case you may as well start while you're still young enough to have the strength to enjoy it.'

Elisabeth smiled faintly. 'Anyway, what can I do? There's no market for redundant mothers.'

'Don't be absurd. Mothers are never redundant, except mine but that was hardly her fault, poor darling. She should never have had children; had motherhood thrust upon her like so many in her generation.'

Elisabeth sneaked a drag of Daisy's cigarette while Charles wasn't looking, and felt the room swirl around her head. 'Do you ever see her?' Their mothers had been friends since their daughters' schooldays, but after her own mother died, Elisabeth had lost touch.

'Oh, she floats into my life occasionally and mutters at me about wearing a vest and getting married – which is about the limit of her understanding of the maternal role,' Daisy said laughing, 'then she flutters off out again with some ghastly new man in tow.' She retrieved her cigarette from Elisabeth. 'As a matter of fact, I may have just the job for you.'

Elisabeth looked at her in astonishment. 'You?'

Daisy smiled. 'Must you look so amazed?'

'Sorry.'

'Sam Howard is looking for somebody. You know, he's the chap who owns Howard's, the art gallery on the high street. Anyway, I had lunch with him yesterday and he begged me to find him somebody to go in and sort him out. He lives in a state of perpetual chaos.'

'Could I do that?' Elisabeth wondered.

'Nothing to it. It wouldn't be full-time; just a few mornings a week and the pay won't be much. . . .' She shrugged. 'You might like it.'

'I know nothing about art,' Elisabeth said dubiously.

Daisy laughed. 'Well, who does? Anyway, you don't have to *know* anything. You can type, can't you? And file? Marvellous. You're just the person he needs.'

'You make it sound so easy.'

'That's because it is.' Daisy scribbled a number down on the back of an old receipt. 'Here's the number. I'll tell Sam you'll call.' She took a gulp of wine, smiled triumphantly. 'He'll love me for ever.'

'I do hope you're right.'

'I am only ever wrong,' Daisy said, 'in matters of the heart.' She looked over at Alex. 'About which I am famously incompetent.'

Elisabeth, who was feeling expansive said, 'Oh, you're not so bad, you've had your moments,' and looked faintly hurt when Daisy laughed.

Nine

Charles, who was slow in the morning, struggled through the ordinary tasks of brushing his teeth and getting dressed like a man underwater. His slowness made Elisabeth brisk.

That particular morning she was feeling brisker than usual. It had taken her a few days to screw up the courage to call Sam Howard about the job and when, finally, she had woken that morning thinking that if she didn't do it that very day, then she wouldn't do it at all, she was impatient to get Charles out of the house and have the place to herself.

Glancing up from buttoning her blouse, she found him still dressed – as he had been a full five minutes earlier – in socks, underpants and a white shirt, and wearing the plucked expression that half-naked men always seem to assume. His hands hovered vaguely at his neck. 'The top button's come off this shirt,' he said, gazing helplessly across the smooth white expanse of the bed.

Elisabeth bent forward, gave the bedcover a final, curt tug and picked up a pile of washing. 'There are plenty more in the wardrobe. Leave that on the chair and I'll do the button later,' she said, hurrying out of the bedroom without a backward glance.

He gazed at the empty doorway reproachfully. She used not to be so dismissive, he thought, as he unbuttoned the shirt and went to get another out of the wardrobe. There were five clean white shirts hanging there, just as she had said. To the untutored eye, they all looked exactly the same but the one missing its button was his favourite. She knew that. Once, she would have sewn the button on while he waited.

He slipped his arms into the crisp cotton, feeling obscurely hurt. She had once loved this house, had been happy working in it, had been happy – the thought caused him a sharp pang – to be his wife. It was, after all, Elisabeth who used to say, 'We both work to create our life. You do your work and I do mine and both are equally valid.' Charles knew that his idea of marriage was considered conventional, old-fashioned even, just as he knew that their friends laughed about him and teased Elisabeth about their middle-aged ways but he was indifferent to their laughter, found secret comfort in the picture of Elisabeth safe in their house, her hands busy just as his head was busy, bent over a desk, both of them secure in the understanding that they were working in different parts of London but to a mutual end. Or so he had believed. He thought she had too, but these days he was not so certain.

The changes were small – a button left unsewn, a patina of dust dulling the china ornaments on the mantelpiece – but the shift in her mood was marked by a slight tightening of her mouth, an impatient shifting of lips to cheek for the evening kiss, a brisk carelessness over the breakfast table. When, he thought, had it all changed? When had their life, the house, the children, even himself become irritating demands to be dealt with briskly and efficiently but without care? He saw how her gaze had swung, like a searchlight, from the focus of their lives to some distant shore. Sometimes, when she was especially brisk, he felt as though he was simply one more chore to be dealt with.

He knew – through myth rather than experience – that housework was dull, tedious and repetitive. But so was all work, in its way; the same daily grind to produce the bread that would succour them, that gave them the strength to struggle on to that place called happiness. Although where that was, nobody knew. Certainly not him. He sighed faintly. When he had tried to articulate this in his fumbling way to Elisabeth she had accused him of being patronising.

He wrenched at his shirt collar, wrestling to make it lie flat and thinking resentfully that he had always been so careful to make her feel that her contribution was as valid as his, her work equal. Certainly, she had no financial worries; not like Bella, he thought with a grimace. Or Daisy for that matter, for he saw how Daisy's crisp humour hid a fear of growing old, solitary and uncherished.

He knew that Elisabeth thought he was boring, the way he checked their investments and pensions daily and saved every spare penny towards their old age, and he felt deeply, sometimes savagely, hurt when she joked with friends about his 'little obsession'.

He had tried to help, to give advice, for he saw how much it hurt her not to be out in the world making a contribution. Admittedly, he had drawn the line at the part-time job in the Gap clothes shop in the high street. Not that he'd have minded her working in a shop but he could picture James's and Lucy's faces, stiff with mortification at their mother working in a clothes shop where they and their friends hung out during the holidays. He knew the sort of remarks they'd have to put up with; was surprised that Elisabeth didn't know them too but she was so determined to go out and work that all sense seemed to have been swept out of her head. He remembered her expression when she had announced the Gap job, her face flushed and glowing with triumph – and her silence for the two weeks after he had said his bit.

Foolishly, he had suggested that if it was making a contribution that she was after, charity work might be a consideration. Foolishly because she now thought, unfairly, that he considered her only good enough for charity. 'I do my bit already,' she had said stiffly and she did, he knew, do a great deal in small, unremarked ways. All he had meant was that she might focus all that diverse energy in one project. But it was no use talking to her at the moment.

She would not be helped, must muddle through and find her identity as best she could. All he could do was stand on the sidelines, arms held out, and catch her if she fell. When she fell.

He pulled on his jacket, stared mournfully at his reflection in the mirror. He saw how his youth had unravelled; saw the boy he used to be blurred by age, all his smooth surfaces fraying at the edges. How sure I was then, he thought, how certain of destiny. Odd how uncertainty increases rather than diminishes with age.

He smelt coffee, heard Elisabeth's impatient call and made his way slowly downstairs through the silent house, bitterly missing the noise and clamour of his children, their smooth limbs and bursting, youthful energy. He walked into the kitchen, sat at his usual place at the table and unfolded the square of *The Times*. She had even tried to change the newspaper, suggested switching to the *Guardian*, which she went out and bought sometimes, left lying around as a silent symbol of revolt, of her separateness from him. 'Nobody reads *The Times* any more,' she said, wrinkling her nose.

'Well, I do,' he had replied, trying to make a joke out of it, but she had turned from him in silence, presenting him with her contemptuous back. He watched her snapping briskly around the kitchen, busy with some mysterious process that seemed to involve a great deal of energy to no obvious result. 'That,' she had once said, when he commented on this phenomenon, 'is precisely what housework is.' She had laughed as she said it.

He drank coffee and munched his way through a piece of toast, one eye on the newspaper, the other focused warily on her. As he picked up the last square from his plate, she whisked it away.

'I can see you're trying to get rid of me,' he said good-naturedly. 'Something important on today?'

'Oh, just a million things to do,' she said brightly. 'Life to be got through . . .'

'Ah, yes. Life,' he said, kissing her and going off to collect his briefcase from the hallway, in the corner where he always left it.

'Lily's coming to supper,' she reminded him as he went to kiss her goodbye.

He frowned. 'Lily?' he said, feeling a quickening in his blood and a vague, unfocused excitement. He remembered the way she had looked at him at dinner, her open, admiring gaze. It seemed so long since anyone had looked at him like that. Good old Charles, he thought, nice, stolid, reliable Charles, and was surprised by the sudden savagery of his thoughts.

'Do you *ever* listen to a word I say?' she said, and he could sense the tension beneath her smile. 'You're supposed to be asking about the job. For Lily.'

He stared at her blankly. What job? Ah, yes, he remembered Elisabeth mentioning it, had ascribed it to one of her sudden whims and forgotten about it almost immediately. Or perhaps, he thought, he had forgotten because he did not want the girl working there, a hot distraction in that cool, dry place where emotions were filed away neatly under the impervious assessments of the legal system.

'You promised,' she cried. 'Apparently you even mentioned it to her at dinner that first night.'

Charles looked perplexed. 'Did I? I don't remember.'

'Well, you did,' she said impatiently. 'She recounted the conversation in some detail. Anyway, if Simon's secretary is about to go off on maternity leave, there'll be a job going, won't there?'

He nodded.

'So ask.'

'Yes, yes,' he said hurriedly. 'I hadn't forgotten.'

She gave him a sharp, disbelieving glance, then relented and offered her face up for a kiss. 'If it's good news we can tell her tonight.'

'I'll remember,' he said, feeling the yielding softness of his wife's cheek under his mouth and thinking of Lily's cool, dense, pale skin.

Once Charles had left, Elisabeth hurriedly cleared away the breakfast cups and stacked them in the dishwasher. Slamming the machine shut, she straightened up. 'There,' she said brightly, sneaking a glance at the wall clock.

Five past eight. Silence buzzed in her ears.

She turned on the radio, to the *Today* show. A politician – she'd missed which one but she could tell it was a politician from the loud, assured tone – was being questioned. 'As I've already stated –' he said, cutting off the interviewer. 'As I have *just* pointed out –' Elisabeth, shrinking from the hectoring voices, sprang forward and switched off the radio. The sudden silence made her dizzy. Remembering that she hadn't eaten any breakfast, she forced down a square of toast, then drank three cups of coffee for courage.

Feeling even dizzier from the caffeine, she clambered up the stairs to their bedroom and stood motionless in front of her open wardrobe. I am ridiculous, she thought, calmly surveying the contents. Ridiculous to get dressed up simply to make a telephone call. But she knew she couldn't make the call to Sam Howard and put herself into that other life without the armour of clothes and make-up and so she went on flicking through her wardrobe.

The blue, she thought. Or perhaps the red? No, a dress

wouldn't do. Too frivolous. A suit, then. The grey one, perhaps – not too formal but just smart enough. She laid it out on the bed, pleased with her decisiveness, and hurried to the bathroom where she laboriously cleaned her face and applied a thin coat of expensive moisturiser. Apply sparingly, it said on the label – which made her think of the job and of ringing Sam. Apply sparingly, she thought, or eagerly? No, not eager. People find eagerness off-putting. It was a trait she had had to learn to curb in herself. Firm but casual, that was the way.

She cleared her throat, settled her face in a friendly but slightly distant expression. 'Hello,' she said, in carefully modulated tones. 'My name's Elisabeth Delaware. I'm a friend of Daisy's. . . .' Did that sound quite right? Her reflection, shiny with expensive moisturiser, smiled eagerly back at her.

Too eager.

She drooped her eyelids, affected a cool, disinterested tone. 'Elisabeth Delaware here. I believe Daisy Ashton may have mentioned. . . .'

Going back into the bedroom, she sat at her dressing-table and damped down her pink cheeks with powder. Her face stared back, pale and set. 'I understand you're looking for a receptionist . . .' she said, lifting her chin haughtily, then peered in the mirror, alarmed. Pink cracks were forming on her mouth. She bared her teeth. Pale flecks dropped from her powdered lips. Reaching for a lipstick, she drew in a mouth. As she did so a memory of her mother jumped unbidden into her mind, sitting ramrod straight at her dressing-table smoothing Max Factor's String Pink across her thin lips. 'A woman's weapon against the world,' she said, briskly smacking her lips together. Then, noticing her small daughter staring anxiously at the gold tube, as if it might explode, added, 'Small but highly effective if properly used.'

At nine thirty precisely, Elisabeth, wearing a grey suit

and three coats of pink lipstick, walked downstairs, marched over to the telephone and briskly dialled Sam's number. She felt cool, efficient. The telephone was answered after three rings. 'Yes?' a voice barked without preamble. Elisabeth's coolness fled, she heard her voice squeaky with nerves, stammering that she'd like to speak to Sam Howard.

The voice grew louder, more impatient. 'You are.'

A friend of Daisy's, Elisabeth gabbled, no experience of art galleries ... hopeless really ... spent the last fifteen years bringing up two children ... quite good at sums; she'd done the household accounts for years ... she wasn't sure that actually counted ... no experience with the public ... well, *experience* of them but not in any formal sense. ...

Her voice tailed off, swallowed up in the black hole of the mouthpiece. She pressed the telephone to her ear, could hear only an aloof, impenetrable silence.

'Hello?' she said. 'Hello, are you still there?'

Sam said, his voice amused but distant, 'Are you finished now?'

'Yes,' Elisabeth said faintly.

'Friday, then. One o'clock.'

The line went dead.

She stood for a moment by the telephone, gazing vacantly out of the window at the sodden garden. That hosta needs dividing, she thought, putting down the phone and slowly making her way to the kitchen. She dragged a pale, fat chicken out of the fridge and swiftly plunged a knife into the pink, yielding flesh. As she sliced off the legs and wings, she tried to picture Sam; thought, obscurely, that he had a beard. She seemed to remember that Daisy had once had an affair with him, or perhaps that was another Sam. Did Daisy like beards? She didn't know. One more thing she didn't know about Daisy. Amazing, she thought, how opaque our friends are to us.

As she laid the table, slowly polishing knives and forks, dusting glasses, Elisabeth vaguely regretted inviting Lily to supper. What would the three of them find to talk about? Although she had seen Lily quite a few times since the afternoon when she had appeared, bringing flowers, she did not feel at ease with her.

She imagined Charles, who was not communicative at the best of times, sitting at his place at the head of the table, sending the girl vague but baffled smiles. As for Lily, there was no telling whether she would slip out of that placid – although receptive – stupor that was her way. Underneath, she seemed an obliging, even eager creature, although Elisabeth could never quite rid herself of the feeling that she obliged only when it suited her. There was a toughness to Lily too, no shades of grey, no shadows in which to linger. She was composed, sharply, in black and white. Strangely, Elisabeth, who conscientiously tried to see every point of view and dithered somewhere between them all, found her unyielding dogmatism soothing.

When Lily did eventually speak, it was in brief but hectic sprints of talk that left her winded and withdrawn, as if she was gathering her strength for some distant marathon. On one occasion, she had finally told Elisabeth her reasons for selling the wedding dress; a pathetic, dispiriting little tale of broken dreams, dried-up bridge rolls and a weeping mother that had left Elisabeth silent, depressed by the trudging predictability of its telling. 'Better to find out now than later,' she had said, the banality depressing her still further.

She finished laying the table and began to prepare a recipe she'd found in the *Evening Standard*. As she chopped garlic and scraped the zest off three lemons, she pondered on the evening ahead.

She felt uneasy about supper, worrying that it might put their relationship on too formal a footing. The charm of her relationship with Lily lay in its unexpectedness; in the differences of age and background and the way that Lily would suddenly appear, hovering palely outside the front door.

'Can I come back?' she had asked that day.

And Elisabeth, who was unsure – because, after all, what had they in common? – had flashed a warm if non-committal smile and said, of course, whenever she liked. Lily said nothing, turned away and wandered off down the path, trailing an idle hand across the lavender hedge. Elisabeth watched her go, a farewell smile prepared on her lips, but Lily had not looked back, had floated up the road, her face set against the evening sun. Funny little thing, Elisabeth had thought, surprised by a sudden rush of warmth.

Two days later, Lily turned up again, clutching another bunch of bedraggled flowers. Elisabeth was in the front garden, a long narrow patch that swooped down to a green picket fence, pitched low over the pavement.

'Hello!' she called, seeing Lily's pale, moon face rise above the gate, her thick fingers fumbling with the clasp. 'You'll have to push. It's a bit stiff.'

'Forgotten you'd got so many flowers,' Lily said, staring down at Elisabeth, who was kneeling amid a tangle of greenery. She tossed the bunch of flowers among the weeds that lay in the wooden trug by Elisabeth's side.

'No such thing as too many,' Elisabeth said, retrieving the flowers and clambering to her feet.

She led the way into the house. The kitchen felt dim and cool after the bright sunlight outside. She swirled water into a vase, clipped the stalks carefully and arranged the flowers on the table. Lily stood in the middle of the room, watching her impassively. She looked like a mechanical doll, awaiting instructions. 'Do sit down,' Elisabeth said, conscious that her voice had taken on a bullying, imperious tone and wondering, again, what it was that drew her to this silent, awkward girl. Lily moved obediently to a chair, sat down, folded her big, spade-like hands in her lap and looked at Elisabeth expectantly.

Something in the tilt of her head, the mute appeal in her dark eyes, made Elisabeth glow quietly under her gaze and she thought, suddenly, how pleasurable it would be to give Lily some of the things she had so obviously been deprived of, to introduce her to some of the pleasures of music and painting, as well as good food and wine. The idea excited her and she went quickly over to the sink and began to scrub the mud from the garden off her hands. There was really something quite touching about the girl; the eyes, perhaps, focused on her with quiet, dark admiration. And she'd come on in leaps and bounds since that first night at dinner.

'I'm so glad you came. It's such a lovely afternoon that I was thinking of going to the Serpentine,' she called above the noise of the running water. 'There's a good exhibition on at the gallery there and then I thought perhaps a walk in the park.' She glanced over her shoulder. 'Would you like to come with me?'

'All right,' Lily said, although an expression of vague bewilderment crept across her face.

Elisabeth dried her hands vigorously on a towel. 'That is, if you like going to exhibitions?'

Lily shrugged. 'Dunno.'

'Some people don't, of course. I suspect I may be one of them. I mean, I go, because I always think that looking at art is one of those things you have to keep doing to be any good at it. A bit like driving.'

Lily stared at her impassively.

'I wonder if there's such a thing as colour deaf? Like tone deaf but with paintings?' Elisabeth said, pleased by the analogy. Quite clever, she thought.

The cleverness was lost on Lily, who blinked silently.

'Well, it's a thought anyway,' Elisabeth said gaily.

Lily nodded blankly. After all, Elisabeth thought, what

could she know of such things? Not her fault, she's probably never even been to an exhibition, probably knows less than Lucy who's only thirteen. The thought of her daughter, her cool, indifferent gaze, caused Elisabeth a tremor of alarm and she said, encouragingly, 'It's an exhibition of watercolours. The reviews have been quite good.'

She was rewarded with a sudden flicker of amusement. 'I went to the Victoria and Albert Museum once. When I was at school.'

Lily's face cleared, the memory seemed to animate her. 'It was rubbish.'

Lily sat motionless in the car, her face turned towards the pavement, her eyes slowly sliding over the changing pattern of the streets.

'Do you like London?' Elisabeth asked tentatively.

Lily's head moved slowly to look at her. ''S'all right.'

'Charles keeps on threatening to buy a house in the country but I'm not sure that I would be quite happy there. I think I'd miss London rather.' She glanced across at Lily, encountered an attentive, expectant gaze. Odd how the girl sometimes watched her, she thought, as if she was memorising her words. 'Well, I suppose you get used to anything after a while,' she finished.

'You don't want to be letting him do that,' Lily said in a low voice.

'Oh?'

'It's too small, the country. Makes people nosy. Always after minding somebody else's business.'

Elisabeth looked at her enquiringly, but Lily's face was blank. Eventually she turned her head and stared out of the window.

The gallery was virtually empty so they moved slowly

across the great open spaces, Lily gliding obediently in Elisabeth's wake.

'Did you enjoy it?' Elisabeth asked, as they ventured out into the sunshine.

Lily blinked in the brightness of the afternoon. 'Yes,' she said, 'it was soothing. Like being underwater.'

And so it was, Elisabeth thought with a sharp jolt of surprise, remembering the swirling blues and greens of the paintings. She felt happy, suddenly, strolling along in the warm, pleasant afternoon, pleased with the idea that her instincts about the girl had been right. All she needed was a little encouragement, someone to lead her gently by the hand. She suggested tea and was again rewarded with a flicker of a smile, so they walked slowly through the park, cutting down to Kensington High Street. They found a café and ordered tea and cakes.

'My treat,' Elisabeth said.

Lily pointed a greedy finger at a chocolate éclair and a raspberry *millefeuille*. 'Must be nice, being rich,' she said, as the waitress set the laden plate in front of her.

'We're not rich, not really,' Elisabeth said, embarrassed.

Lily looked at her. 'Course you are.'

'Yes, we are, of course we are,' Elisabeth agreed quickly. 'But we're not Lottery rich, not millionaires.' She flushed slightly, realising that to a girl like Lily, who had nothing, the difference was meaningless.

Lily licked cream off her fingers with greedy relish. 'Peculiar, that's what you are.' But she unfolded one of her slow smiles, to show it did not matter. 'Most people mind about having too little. You mind about having too much.'

'It seems so unfair,' Elisabeth murmured.

'So give it all away then.'

Elisabeth was silent. 'Well, I do try to do my bit –' she began haltingly.

'You're what my mum calls a bleeding-hearted liberal,'

Lily said, forking jam and pastry into her mouth, 'the sort who thinks two wrongs make a right.'

'I don't quite follow,' Elisabeth said faintly.

'Well, if I'm poor and you're poor then everything's all right.'

'It's more a question of an equal distribution of wealth . . .'

'What difference is it going to make to the girl in the high-rise with three snotty brats whether you're rich or poor?'

'But maybe if she had half of what I have then she –'

'Bollocks. You think a bit of money's going to change a girl who's daft enough to get herself knocked up when she's sixteen and then hangs around some bloke who beats the shit out of her every Friday night?'

'Maybe it's not her fault,' Elisabeth began earnestly. 'Maybe if she'd had a decent –'

'Course it's her fault,' Lily said contemptuously. 'Everything is always our fault. We've got a choice. It's what makes us different from animals.' She licked the last smear of cream off her fork and added, as if as an afterthought, 'And thinking any different is what turns people into patronising cows.'

There was no malice in her tone, but Elisabeth was silenced. Is that really what she thinks of me? she wondered, covering her discomfort under the bustle of paying the bill and gathering together her glasses and purse and bag. Still, she felt a creeping admiration for the girl, for her courage and blunt truthfulness, and resolved, as they left the café and walked down Kensington High Street, to help her. Her rudeness was not her fault; simply the way she'd been brought up.

'I fancy looking in some shops,' Lily said suddenly.

Elisabeth was about to say that she did too, that she'd join her, when Lily whirled on her heel.

'Goodbye,' she called over her shoulder.

Elisabeth stared after her, watching her plunge into the crowd and give herself up to it, bobbing and ducking through the sea of heads, then made her way slowly back to the car.

'Am I a patronising cow?' Elisabeth asked Charles, as they sat down to supper that night.

'Sorry?'

'Lily says I'm a patronising cow.'

Charles was about to laugh when he noticed a faint flush of pink mottling her neck. He put down his knife and fork. 'I'm sure she didn't mean it like that,' he said gently.

Elisabeth looked at him, her gaze strangely hostile. As the seconds lengthened into minutes he began to wonder what she was seeing. Him? The wall above his left shoulder? Or perhaps some inner place? He was beginning to feel uncomfortable when she grimaced suddenly.

'She's right of course,' she said.

They ate in silence.

Ten

Lily was wearing her best dress. Jim had bought it for her. She didn't like it much, but it had cost a fortune so she wore it anyway. No sense letting good money go to waste. It was bright pink, with large gold buttons and contrast white piping and was made for somebody twenty years older. Consequently Lily and the dress managed to look quite separate, which gave her an air of faintly pained surprise. She had tried to bridge the chasm between the dress and her face with a hairband, in a matching shade of pink.

'Oh,' Elisabeth said, quickly moving forward to hide her astonishment, 'how – glamorous you look. I'm afraid Charles and I shan't be nearly smart enough.'

'It's my best. Cost a lot of money.'

'I can see that,' said Elisabeth, trying not to stare at the cheap, vulgar buttons. For some reason, they made her want to cry.

She shifted her gaze away and said brightly, 'Well, since you're looking so marvellous, we should make a real evening of it. Let's start with a drink. What will you have?'

Lily hesitated, her large, dark eyes blinking nervously. Sensing that she did not know what to ask for, Elisabeth decided that something safe, like a sherry, was best under the circumstances. 'I've got just the thing,' she said, smiling and led the way into the sitting-room where she moved over to a trolley, on which were arranged various bottles.

'One sherry,' she said, offering Lily a tiny crystal glass.

'Aren't you having one?' Lily took the glass awkwardly.

'Never touch the stuff,' Elisabeth said, laughing. 'Makes me drunk in a second. I'll get myself a white wine, in the kitchen.'

'Oh.'

Elisabeth looked at her, marooned awkwardly in the middle of the sitting-room in her best pink dress. 'Why don't you relax for a minute,' she suggested, arranging cushions more comfortably in a chair, 'while I just finish making the supper? I won't be long. There's a pile of magazines over there, if you feel like something to read.'

After Elisabeth had gone, Lily sat down obediently and sipped at the sherry. She screwed up her face. Her mum drank sherry and sometimes Jim gave her some too, but the stuff he bought was dark and sweet, like syrup. She stared around the room, feeling unsettled. When she was with Elisabeth, she sometimes felt as though she'd landed in a foreign country. She took a few more sips of the pale liquid and felt a warm glow in the pit of the stomach. Perhaps this stuff wasn't so bad, after all. By the time she'd downed half a glass, her limbs felt heavy and she began to feel curiously happy.

She sagged back into an armchair and gazed around her. It was a nice room. The cushions were soft behind her back and a huge vase of flowers filled the air with scent. The curtains were made of shiny cream stuff decorated with big, fat pink flowers and twining green stalks and the furniture was made of wood that looked very old and dark and shiny. She'd not been able to take it in, that first night at dinner, which was the only time she'd been in this room. Whenever she'd been to visit Elisabeth after that, they'd sat in the kitchen, like her mum always did. Maybe rich people weren't so different after all. They hardly ever used the lounge at home either, except when there was something good on the telly that they all wanted to watch, when they'd cram onto the settee in front of the huge colour screen. The rest of the time, they'd watch the little black and white set in the kitchen. It was on all hours of the day, from breakfast right through and though her mum was always swearing at it and saying she was going to get a decent colour set, she never did, just kept peering at the fuzzy black and white picture. Never had the time, she said, what with the job and the house and all of them to look after. Mind you, she hadn't done anything about it either, even after Dad had died and Lily had moved out to live with Jim so her mum had more time to herself. Her mum would love this room. Jim too. He always insisted they sat in the lounge, not that they had much option really; you couldn't swing a cat in the kitchen in that house of theirs. Flash it was, and modern, filled with every sort of appliance and shiny, patterned tiles but she'd never liked it much; it wasn't cosy like kitchens should be. Even Elisabeth's kitchen, though it was huge and beautiful and had every sort of flash appliance – except the funny old-fashioned cooker which had a funny strangled name like an ah-ga or something that Elisabeth seemed so proud of – even with all that, it was cosy.

Lily had seen rooms like this in magazines, of course, but she hadn't imagined from the cold, glossy surface of the paper that it would feel so lovely to be inside one. She imagined herself the owner of such a house. She'd wear a long dress, like a sort of floaty white nightie, and drift through the rooms trailing her fingertips across the shiny surfaces and eating chocolates. In her mind, she put Jim in the room, sitting in that chair over there by the fire, but the picture wouldn't come right, so she put Charles there instead, smiling in that lovely way he had that made his eyes crinkle at the corners. She'd float by in her long dress and he'd say, 'all right, darling?' and catch her hand as she passed, just like he'd done to Elisabeth that night at dinner.

She'd know how to make him smile, make him look at her the way he had when she'd sat next to him. Not like

Elisabeth, who hadn't even stopped when he'd put out his hand, just pulled her fingers away with an impatient sigh and got on with serving the vegetables. He was the best of the bunch, was Charles. Not like that Alex with his cold eyes and hot fingers, after every bit of skirt around, but only so long as he couldn't have them. She knew about men like him, only after one thing and bored the minute they'd got it. Still, least he'd be easy enough to play, should she put her mind to it.

Tom, too. A right mummy's boy, that one; bit of love and attention and he'd be waiting at her front door, wagging his tail. Well, he couldn't get much from that cold fish he was married to. Jealous type too; she'd seen the look that one gave her when she walked into the dinner party, her face all white and stiff like a statue.

No, Charles was the difficult one, the challenge. Loves his wife, Daisy said, adores her. Doesn't know she doesn't love him back. Not yet, anyway, Lily thought, feeling a sudden surge of power. It gave her a glow, that and the sherry, and she settled back in her chair, dreaming a little, wondering how it would be to have all those people, those clever, important people, pay attention to her, treat her as if she was someone special. Like Elisabeth, fetching and carrying for her, cooking her a meal, taking her out to look at paintings. Lily liked it when people like that paid attention to her, gave her some respect.

She thought about Elisabeth for a while. Where would she be in this picture?

Nowhere, she thought. That's where. Not after she'd got what she needed from her.

Smiling, Lily closed her eyes. Imagined a blank, where Elisabeth would be.

Elisabeth looked up expectantly when Charles walked into the kitchen.

'Hello, darling,' she said, offering him a cheek. 'Nice day?'

'Uneventful,' he said, dropping her a kiss as he struggled out of his coat.

'Any news about the job?'

'Well, they'll see her, at least. Has she arrived?'

Elisabeth nodded her head in the direction of the sitting-room. 'She's having a drink. Why don't you go and join her? I'll come through when I've finished this lot.'

She glanced over at him. Charles had a habit of pushing his fingers through his hair while he was working.

'And do something about your hair, darling. You look as though you've had a fright.'

'A fright?'

'It's all sticking up.'

'Oh, that.' His hand up went to his head. 'Better?' he said, patting clumsily.

Elisabeth smiled. 'A bit. Oh, and darling,' she said, her voice dropping to a loud, conspiratorial whisper, 'she's got her best dress on. Be nice about it, will you?'

He nodded, mystified.

'Dinner smells good,' he said vaguely, wandering out of the room.

Under his usual, placid exterior, Charles was gripped by fright at the prospect of seeing Lily again. His terror was mixed with a sort of yearning pleasure which he identified as a simultaneous ache in his groin and his chest; an ache he had not felt since he was an adolescent boy. He moved towards the sitting-room, feeling a curious, doomed inevitability, and loitered for a while in front of the long brass mirror in the hallway, running a clumsy, furtive hand through his hair. Then, with a half-sigh, he turned and strode to the sitting-room door.

'Well, hello,' he said, his voice sounding loud and forced in the dim half-light of the room, 'and how are you?'

Lily looked up, her eyes swimming into focus, and he

saw both that she had been asleep and that there was something different about her, something in the flicker of her eyes and the slow, wide curve of her smile. She gazed up at him, blinking until her gaze cleared. 'All right?' she said, in her usual way of greeting.

Charles nodded. 'All right,' he echoed, noticing how she sat, motionless, with her hands clasped in her lap. The dress that Elisabeth had mentioned was stiff and pink with huge gold buttons, quite unlike anything that Elisabeth would wear, or any of the women he knew, for that matter. He liked it, just as he liked her long hair, which was held back by an Alice band, made of the same pink fabric as the dress, spilling down over her shoulders – like a curtain of silk, he thought. She held her knees together, her thin, white legs splayed like a child's, shooting out from the depths of the fat, overstuffed armchair.

He stood over her awkwardly, then stuffed his hands in his trouser pockets. 'Are you all right in that chair?'

She looked up at him and he saw how her eyelashes threw shadows over the translucent curve of her cheek. 'Shouldn't I be?' she asked, in her flat, toneless voice. He found the sound of it curiously exciting, felt a sudden sharp longing to play it until it vibrated with lust and yearning.

'The springs have gone,' he said, his voice reverberating in the twilight peace of the room. 'People have been known to disappear into its floral depths for ever.' He gave a sudden snort of laughter, startling himself.

She smiled slowly. 'Good thing you told me,' she said, extending a long, pale arm. He noticed how large her hands were, square and capable with blunt, spatulate fingers. He took a hand, felt the fingers rough under his own. She let hers lie in his for a moment. 'Help me up then,' she said, at last.

He pulled and she rose slowly, unbending until she stood upright, her body a long, pale curve in the dim light.

126

Suddenly she uttered a loud, throaty cry and fell against him, her arms moving up to his shoulders. She rested against his body for a moment, her head turned in to his chest. A warm, spicy fragrance rose from her and he shifted away quickly in alarm.

She smiled up at him. 'Sorry. Must have tripped.' She giggled suddenly, raised her hand to her mouth in a quick, childish gesture. 'It's the sherry. I've never had it before. I usually just have Coca-Cola.'

'It can be rather strong,' he said, smiling awkwardly, indicating with a vague gesture a chair across the room. He sat in a chair opposite, at a safe distance. 'They do say it gets you drunk more quickly than anything else. Well, other than cider which is extraordinarily potent.'

'Fancy that,' she said, subsiding into the chair, her hips moving in a slow voluptuous curve as she settled her body back into the cushions. Charles glanced away quickly but she went on watching him, a smile on her red lips. He looked back at her, wondering if her lips were naturally that colour or whether she used lipstick. Seeing that she was watching him, he gave a quick, embarrassed grimace. 'But for my money, cheap sherry's the strongest of the lot. That's why the winos drink it.'

'Is that right?' she said, eventually. 'My mum loves it. Says she likes the sweetness. Medicine, she calls it.'

'I didn't mean –'

She smiled at him. 'Course you didn't.'

She raised her glass, looked thoughtfully at the pale, straw-coloured liquid. 'This don't taste too sweet, though.'

'It's rather a delicious amontillado,' he said. 'That one's from the North of Spain. It's rather dry, because of the wine-making process. There's less sun up there so the grapes don't have the same sweetness.'

Her red lips were poised in a small, amused curve. He felt absurdly pompous.

'There are lots of different sorts,' he finished, lamely.

127

'But this is a good one, this amontillado?' she said, stumbling over the word but then repeating it again with slow, deliberate care. To his ears, it sounded like a caress.

'Yes.'

She nodded, pleased.

'That job I mentioned,' he said quickly, 'are you still interested?'

She looked startled, and then a smile spread across her face, warming it. 'That's nice of you,' she said. 'To remember.'

'It's only temporary,' he said abruptly. He saw how her face closed in on itself and he hastened to bring the smile back again. 'Well, it's six months. A maternity leave replacement.'

'Six months is a long time. Anything could happen.'

He gave an awkward half-laugh. 'Yes. I suppose it could.'

'Anything,' she repeated, her voice sounding warm and lazy. 'Anything at all.'

He glanced away, fumbled in his pocket and extracted a crumpled piece of paper. 'Here's the number,' he said abruptly. 'Alice Drake. She's our personnel officer. I told her about you. She's expecting your call.'

She nodded, took the paper. He felt the rough warmth of her hand. 'I'll go and see her next week,' she said, not looking at him, the dark curtain of her hair falling forward to hide her face, her square, fleshy fingers smoothing the paper flat against her pale thighs. He watched the slow, rhythmic movement, his eyes travelling to the dark shadow between her legs. She felt his eyes, raised her face to them. 'I'll call her tomorrow, if that's all right.'

He nodded. 'I'll –' He swallowed hard, cleared his throat. 'I'll let Alice know,' he said.

In the half-light, her eyes were enormous dark pools. Her red lips gleamed. 'Will we be working together?' she said.

128

He shrugged. 'We'll be in the same offices. On the same floor,' he amended.

'We'll see each other every day then,' she said softly. 'I'd like that.'

A light snapped on, making them both start slightly.

'You're sitting in the dark,' Elisabeth said gaily. 'Funny how it creeps up on you. I never realise I'm doing it either, until I go into the kitchen to make a cup of coffee.'

She walked around briskly switching on lamps, closing curtains, until the room was bright and cosy. They watched her, blinking slightly, hearing the faint squeak of her skirt slithering against the crisp chintz of the chairs as she squeezed past them.

Charles stole a glance at Lily. She looked as though she was emerging from a dream, her eyes slightly unfocused. He saw how her red lips were parted slightly, their shape soft and heavy.

'Is your drink all right, Lily?' Elisabeth asked, glancing at her empty glass. 'I'm afraid Charles can be a bit vague sometimes. He goes off into a world of his own. Don't you, darling?' she said, bending to drop a kiss on his cheek.

Charles felt the familiarity of his wife's mouth against his skin and then a swift tremor of release as Lily's lips tightened into a smile. 'Wouldn't mind another,' she said. 'It's rather a delicious amontillado.'

Charles started slightly as he realised that she had used exactly his words, even putting a slight stress on the same syllables.

'Is that what it is?' Elisabeth said, with a startled glance. 'How clever of you to know. I never drink the stuff. One glass of sherry tastes much the same to me as another.'

'Cooking sherry probably don't,' Lily said.

'Well, no. Ghastly sweet stuff. Cheap sherry tastes like cough mixture. Can't think why anybody bothers to drink it.'

Charles flushed, felt a wave of protectiveness towards

Lily. 'Perhaps because they like it,' he said, in mild remonstrance. 'The cheap stuff can be quite good.'

Elisabeth looked at him in surprise. 'I thought you always said –' He returned her look, and she detected a faint gleam in his eye. 'Oh, well –' She sat down, raised her glass. 'Here's to the expensive stuff then,' she said with a slight laugh.

Lily turned her lovely, blank smile on them. 'I'll drink to that.'

Eleven

Lily called Delsey & Delaware about the job the next morning, expecting them to say to come down straight away. She'd laid out a skirt and a jumper on the bed, sponging them down carefully with a J-cloth to get rid of the worst of the marks. But they didn't; they told her to come for an interview at the end of the week.

'Oh!' Lily said, then repeated carefully, 'Thursday. Two thirty. Report to Personnel.'

After she'd put the phone down, she hung the skirt and jumper on a wire hanger on the back of the door, then wandered around her room, J-cloth in hand, aimlessly flicking the dust from one place to another. She felt a brief hankering for Jim's Dustbuster. Thinking of Jim made her think about her mum, which made her think of Mrs Flower, so she went and tapped on her door, hoping for a cup of tea and a bit of company. There was no reply, so she wandered back to her room and moved a bit more dust around until boredom got the better of her. Pulling on a thin coat, she went out of the house, crossed the road and stood waiting for a bus to take her to Oxford Street.

She often went down there, content to wander in the gaping anonymity of the wide, busy street; enjoying the press of bodies and the hoarse cries of street traders hawking counterfeit scent and trashy watches out of battered black vinyl cases perched on picnic stools. That morning she was floating along, caught in the swirl and eddy of the crowd, when a stray current picked her up, swept her past a knot of people and deposited her in front of a shop. She lingered for a while, gazing doubtfully at a display of clothes, black and severe, stretched tautly on dummies with white, attenuated limbs and frozen, super-cilious smiles. One had a finger raised, as if in admonish-ment at the cheap, shabby clothes passing under its haughty nose.

The mannequin reminded Lily of Daisy – the same weary blue gaze and thin, sharp face. She remembered how Daisy's eyes had swept across her new green dress and dismissed it in the blink of an eye and how she had stopped liking it right there and then.

She looked down at herself; registering limp, stained tracksuit trousers and a jumper scattered with bobbles of matted wool, like burrs. Won't do at all, she thought, thinking of the job interview and the drab jumper and skirt hanging on the back of her door. She needed something smart, maybe black and plain – like the dress Daisy had been wearing that night at dinner. She looked more closely at the dresses in the window. They were black all right, but somehow none of them looked quite right. Jim always said that black was ageing.

Sod Jim, Lily thought, plunging into the shop.

Once inside, she blinked slightly, accustoming her eyes to the unfamiliar gloom, then flicked through a rail of clothes and found herself fingering a long tube made of some shiny black material. It looked like a stick of liquorice.

'Doesn't look much off,' the assistant said. 'But it would look wonderful on you, with your figure.'

Lily looked up in surprise. 'Would it?'

'Very popular, down the clubs.'

'Oh.' Lily relinquished the shiny stuff regretfully. 'I need something smart.'

'For work?'

Lily nodded. The assistant jerked her head towards the dim interior of the shop. 'There's some nice suits and that.

Just come in. They're towards the back, by the cash register. Lisa there'll help you.'

Elisabeth too had been out shopping, had bought herself a new suit in a navy blue wool with a straight skirt and neat fitted jacket. It had looked so smart in the shop, but now she felt hot and uncomfortable; the suit seemed to spring about her, stiff and starchy with importance. She peered at her reflection in a car window, despairing of the air hostess who gazed back, patting desperately at her neck to damp down the nervous pink flush that threatened to creep up her neck and overwhelm her.

She glanced at her watch.

It was far too early but she couldn't have stayed in the house any longer. She felt disembodied enough after the six cups of coffee she'd drunk that morning and her face was stiff with the unfamiliar sensation of layers of make-up which she'd kept applying and reapplying, pressing powder to her flushed cheeks until they were numb with friction. She pressed her lips together nervously, feeling the unfamiliar slide of the greasy lipstick, then noticed a man watching her intently from a parked car across the street. Flushing, she turned and walked towards a shop window, her legs stiff with self-consciousness. It was a shoe shop, the windows filled with summer sandals with tiny, fragile straps, improbably spindly heels and soles thin as communion wafers. Elisabeth stared at them longingly, imagined them worn by women with thin thighs and high insteps.

She peered down at her watch again. Twelve fifty-three. Time to go.

Stepping confidently up to the door of the gallery, she kept her movements brisk, a smile plastered on top of the layers of make-up. The door seemed to be stuck. She pushed it discreetly. It didn't budge, so she leant heavily against it until it yielded a few inches. Turning, she shuffled in an undignified manner through the crack, emerging into the high, vaulted room sideways, like a crab.

A man was sitting at a desk on a sort of raised dais at the far side of the room. Their eyes met for an instant, then he shifted his gaze away and stared fixedly at a point on the wall. He appeared to be meditating. Sweat prickled at Elisabeth's scalp. Flushing, she turned away to face a wall on which hung a series of large canvases. It can't be Sam Howard, she thought. The owner of a gallery wouldn't be installed in his own space like a piece of sculpture on show. Unless, of course, it was some sort of performance art. It was, after all, a gallery of modern art.

Her eyes came into focus. She found a painting inches from her nose and had a confused impression of thick, textured swirls of blue and grey, all mixed up with the image of the man: soft, faded blue denim shirt, shabby jeans, thick brown hair that needed cutting.

Elisabeth shifted a little, to bring him back into view. He was gazing intently at the ceiling; his eyes an intense, serene blue. He was tall and powerfully built, in his early fifties perhaps, and his stomach sagged slightly over his jeans.

She found the soft bulge of flesh endearing, wondered whether to ask him where Sam was, but he looked so intent that she didn't dare, turned and picked her way self-consciously over to a painting, a tiny miniature, and stood meditatively in front of it. Her back prickled. She felt horribly conscious of the two of them, frozen like statues in the huge, airy space of the room. She arranged her arms in a more interesting composition but they seemed to be wrongly hinged, kept jerking away from her sides. Without turning her head, she swivelled her eyes in their sockets to look at the man. The effort made her eyes ache. He was looking right at her. She revolved slowly, as if on an axis.

'Is Sam here?'

Her voice squeaked slightly but it had an immediate effect, as if it had activated some switch inside him. Hands, arms, eyes and mouth all sprang into action. 'Elisabeth?'

She nodded mutely.

He got up from his chair, walked over to her and took her hand in a warm, strong grip. 'I never dare look directly at anyone who comes in here. Too worried about frightening them away. I just sit as still as I can, hoping they won't notice me.'

Elisabeth thought that improbable, given his size. 'I think perhaps that may be even more frightening,' she said.

'Do you?' he said, looking interested.

'Much. You ought to have some papers spread out on the desk, pretend to be working or reading or something. Then, when they come in, just glance up and say hi, or something casual, and go back to your work. And you ought to get that door fixed,' she said, looking severely at the offending door. 'It's terribly off-putting.'

He gazed at her intently. She saw now that his eyebrows were threaded with wiry grey hairs and the blue of his eyes was faded, not nearly so bright as she had at first imagined and she thought, I could love this man. The thought went through her like a jolt and she blushed furiously, regretting both the sharpness of her tone and the stiff, bossy suit she wore.

The blush seemed to relax him for he laughed suddenly, slung an arm over her shoulders. 'See how I need you?' he said easily, smiling down at her until she felt the blush spreading, the heat of it tingling right through her body, reaching out to the tips of her fingers.

He moved across the gallery, his arm heavy on her shoulders. The soft cotton of his shirt brushed her neck and she felt the warmth of his arm penetrating the harsh

135

fabric of her suit and longed, suddenly, to be dressed in silk or cashmere; something gentle and yielding and not the impenetrable navy serge of her suit. She felt stiff, armoured, like a traffic warden or a policewoman.

She thought, he smells of lemons and cigars.

When he dropped his arm she felt the lack of it around her shoulders but then he took her by the elbow and led her to an open door through which she could glimpse a desk, almost completely submerged. There were papers everywhere, on the floor, in teetering piles on a chair, shoved carelessly under the telephone. His hand warmed her. He touches all the time, she thought. Not like Charles.

'Look at this mess,' he exclaimed. 'This is why I need you.'

'Yes,' she said.

'Could you manage?'

'My children are teenagers,' she said crisply. 'I manage every day.'

He grinned. 'Daisy was right. She said, if anybody could sort me out, then it was you.'

'Did she?' She tried to sound brisk and efficient. He reached behind her, shut the door.

'Let's face that later.' He crooked his arm at the elbow, offering it to her. 'Shall we go?'

'Where?' Elisabeth said, taking his arm.

'Out. I always do business over lunch.' He looked at her intently. 'You do eat lunch, don't you?' he asked. 'Not one of those silly women who's always on a diet?'

'I've never been on a diet in my life.'

Sam nodded with satisfaction. 'Can't stand skinny women. No tits.'

Elisabeth suddenly felt enormously cheerful.

They went to a tiny Italian restaurant, halfway up the High Street, tucked away behind a green door. 'I didn't even know it was here,' she exclaimed as they crowded into the small room. It didn't seem possible that they would fit but suddenly there were a table, two chairs and a carafe of rich, dark red wine.

'What sort of food do you like?' Sam asked.

Elisabeth looked around. There seemed to be no menus. 'Everything,' she said truthfully.

'Good,' he said, grinning over at the owner and indicating with a broad shrug that they would eat whatever was good that day.

And it was. First a plate of tiny, fragrant crespolini stuffed with spinach and ricotta and then a stew of chickpeas and tomatoes with pungent, salted ham and shards of deep green cabbage.

Sam was a messy, voluptuous eater. Elisabeth watched him, charmed by his evident enjoyment, then felt a sudden pang of guilt as she remembered how irritated she had become recently with the way Charles ate. How irritated she had become with him altogether. Not that he had changed. He ate, as he always had, his head bent to his plate while he forked up mouthful after mouthful in greedy, appreciative silence. He loved her cooking, was endlessly, endearingly, grateful for the food she took so much time to plan and prepare. She ought to have been pleased. But she wasn't. Just the evening before, she had looked at the top of his bent head, watching him shovel in the meticulously cooked food and resented him, bitterly.

Charles, sensing her eyes on him, had looked up, a fork poised at his lips. 'You've got gravy on your chin,' she said, to punish him. For what? For being so achingly, irritatingly familiar to her.

He blundered at his face with a napkin, bent his head back to his plate, scraped the rest of his food up to his mouth. She gazed at the top of his head, where the scalp was beginning to gleam white through the thinning hairs. We're getting old, she thought, and the sentiment filled her with such fury that she said, 'Goodness, darling, you're going bald.' She tried to make her tone light, teasing, but could not disguise the splinter of spite embedded deep in it.

She had apologised, of course she had when she saw Charles's expression – horrified and at the same time ashamed – tried to make it up to him by briskly clearing away the plates and giving him an especially large helping of his favourite pudding: poached pears with mascarpone. He'd laughed about it too, made a clumsy mime of hunching over the table like an old man, but as she spooned up the translucent globes of fruit and set them before him, she couldn't help noticing the way that his hand kept straying to the crown of his head and the expression of pained disgust that crept over his face as his fingers encountered the sparse circle of hairs. Eventually, he made an excuse about needing to finish some work and wandered off, abandoning his food. She sat at the table staring at the pears that languished, pale and smoothly reproachful, in a pool of creamy sauce.

From the hallway she heard the whir of the extractor fan start up and the click of a light switch, knew that he had closeted himself in the downstairs cloakroom, was even then craning his neck furiously in an attempt to see the offending patch on the top of his head.

The thought made her suddenly, furiously, want to cry.

'Tell me about yourself, Elisabeth Delaware,' Sam said.

Elisabeth started slightly, let out a nervous laugh. 'Not much to tell,' she began, but Sam gave her such a fierce blue look that she said, 'Married to Charles, who's a solicitor. Two children, James and Lucy, who are both away at boarding school. We live in Keats Grove –'

'Ah,' he said, 'a rich solicitor.'

'Comfortable,' she said primly.

'So you don't actually need the job then?'

She shifted slightly in alarm. Not need it, she thought wildly. Of course she needed it. She would go mad if she didn't have it.

'No,' she said. 'I don't need it. But I *want* it very badly.'

'Good, but tell me why. Most people are dying to give up work.'

'That's because they've been working for years so the idea of being at home is heavenly – except they've forgotten all the bits that aren't heaven about it. Whereas I, who've been at home all these years, think the idea of working is heavenly and I've probably forgotten all the bits about work that aren't.'

He looked thoughtful. 'Heavenly, is it?' he said, reaching for his glass. He lifted it, held it out to her. 'Very well. I appoint you as my guardian angel.'

She looked at him in astonishment. 'Does that mean I have the job?'

'As of this minute. When can you start?'

Elisabeth thought, this is dangerous. I should run away from this man; run as far and as fast as I can.

She smiled. 'Next week.'

Lily lunched on Dairylea triangles and Mother's Pride bread, squishing the creamy triangles to the bread with her fingers because she'd lost the only knife she possessed, then washed her hands and dressed carefully in a grey cardigan that fitted smoothly over her small, high breasts. It had a neat, curved collar and tiny, mother-of-pearl buttons and she wore it with a black wool skirt, shaped like a soft bell, that swung gently around her knees. She pulled on a pair of dense black tights, then slipped on a pair of black shoes with low spiky heels. Lisa, the girl in the shop, had called them kitten heels. 'Everybody's wearing them.' Lily liked the idea of wearing kittens.

She brushed her dark hair a hundred times, then tied it back with a piece of black satin ribbon and slipped some tiny gilt earrings into her ears. She thought of Daisy's face, smooth, sleek, inviolable, and carefully drew in a slick of black eye-liner just above her eyes, coloured her mouth a deep, rich plum. When she was ready, she posed in front of the mirror, pleased by how fine she looked.

The offices of Delsey & Delaware, tucked away on the third floor of an anonymous fifties block on the fringes of Fleet Street, were a bit of a disappointment to Lily. She had imagined somewhere shiny and imposing, with a wide sweeping portico and a smart, uniformed guard at the door. But when she got out of the lift on the third floor she discovered a pair of thick oak doors, a reassuring brass plate engraved Delsey & Delaware and a receptionist with a wide, bright smile. When Lily told her that she'd come about a job, the smile faded to a dusty smirk that made Lily gladder than ever that she'd bothered to go out and buy a particular outfit for the occasion.

She was told to wait and sat on a slippery black leather sofa, flicking through a magazine and admiring her new shoes, until the receptionist told her that Miss Drake was ready to see her. Lily swept past her with her nose in the air to show that she was as good as anyone but once past the heavy swing doors, she slowed her step and tiptoed cautiously along the grey carpet that faded suddenly from thick luxuriance to a thin, scratchy weave. About halfway down the corridor, she found a plain wooden door marked 'Personnel', and knocked carefully.

A brisk voice said, 'Come,' so Lily put her head back and marched quickly into a small grey room, where she found the owner of the voice, Alice Drake – small, efficient and economical with words. When Lily handed over a letter from her old employer, Mr Williams, together with a modest CV – his parting gift had been a smart silver pen and an effusive, if misspelled, letter of reference – she scarcely glanced at it before laying it on the photocopier and despatching it with a swift jab of a finger. As the machine hummed and whirred, she dictated a rapid letter. 'Got that? Good. Typewriter,' she said, with a flick of a pearly, polished nail.

Lily typed the letter.

'Computer literate?'

Lily nodded. Another flick of pearly nail and she was setting up files on an old word processor. Alice Drake checked her work in silence, nodded approvingly, handed her back the letter of reference and CV and looked enquiringly at the door.

'We'll let you know,' she said.

So it was that Lily found herself standing in the empty corridor regretting her new shoes. Suddenly Charles appeared through the swing-doors in front of her.

'Well,' he said, pretending a double take, 'this is a surprise.' He tapped a pile of papers he held against his chest. 'I was just taking these in to Alice.'

'I'd have thought you'd have a secretary to do that for you.'

'Yes, of course, Angela would normally but she's –'

His eyes settled on Lily's mouth. She'd done something to it, coloured it in. It looked like a voluptuous, shiny fruit. For a moment, Charles was unable to think what Angela spent her whole day so busily doing. 'She's typing something – a letter.'

He stared at her mouth longingly, wanting to put his lips against it, to graze at its dark, fragrant curves.

'I've just been doing that,' Lily said pertly. 'Typing, I mean.'

'Yes, I suppose you have,' he said distractedly, and was amazed to hear his voice echo, so loud and blustering in the quiet corridor.

'Did the interview go all right?'

'I think so.' She ducked her head, looked up at him through a thick fringe of lashes. 'Well, you can't tell, really, can you?'

Charles, while struck by the artifice of the pose – which in any other woman he would have found irritating and in his own wife, laughable – found himself drawn to the admiration in Lily's eyes. He felt a movement in his chest – he was not so sentimental as to call it his heart – like a bubble, drawing up, rising to his throat in a sudden, flooding release of tension. He said abruptly, 'I'm sure it was fine.'

He sensed a change in her, as if she had felt it too; she shifted slightly as she held out her hand and said, 'It was nice of you to sort it.' Her tone had become formal, slightly distant.

He took her hand, felt the roughness of her skin against his palm. 'I hope it was of some use,' he said, blustering a little as he felt her hand recede. He gripped it slightly harder. 'Will you – I suppose we'll be seeing you again at the house soon?'

'Elisabeth did mention something,' she murmured, slipping her hand out of his grasp. He felt a flare of regret as her fingers slid from his, recalled the press of her body against his and her legs, white and innocent, under her pink dress and searched for something to say, to keep her there. Remembering that she and Elisabeth had gone to see an art exhibition the week before he asked, 'How were the paintings?'

'Oh, it was fine. We had a marvellous time,' she said, and he noticed how she had slipped into Elisabeth's way of speaking, pictured her soft, heavy lips opening and shutting like an anemone as she lingered over the word amontillado. Feeling a shiver of desire, he glanced quickly at his watch, to distract his emotions back to the meeting for which he was already late.

She noticed the gesture. 'I'd better be off then,' she said, and he looked up, flustered, not wanting her to go. But she had already turned, was walking away from him, the strong, sweet smell of her perfume trailing after her in a thin, bright stream.

Lily moved carefully, conscious that he was watching her.

Her new shoes, with their little perched heels, lent a swing to her hips. She smiled, pleased by the image. Lily in her kitten heels. The thought lent her hips an extra sway, made her skirt dance around her slender thighs.

A lot of men looked at her like that – especially older men. It was her long hair and round face made them come over all funny. Her mum always said that men were idiots about a bit of hair and a sweet face. Like Mr Williams. He'd been silly about her; not that she let on she knew. She used to play a little game instead, press against him as she leaned over his desk to serve the coffee – just to see the beads of sweat pop all over his fat, red face and his hand shake as he lifted the cup from its saucer.

Then there was Dave, a mate of Jim's, who sometimes gave her a lift back from the pub. He was quite good-looking, in an old, crumpled sort of a way. She knew he fancied her even though he didn't do anything about it, except flush a bit. Then one night, when he'd had a few pints, he'd clamped his hand on her leg the minute she got in the car. It was raining and she didn't want to get out and walk, so she'd left it there.

When they got to the house, they'd sat outside for a bit while he fumbled with the buttons on her blouse and licked clumsily at her closed mouth, but his hands were shaking too much to get the buttons undone. In the end, she'd kissed the top of his balding head and hopped out of the car. Later, as she put on her white cotton nightie and brushed her teeth ready for bed, she kept remembering his pleading eyes. The thought of them made her smile.

She smiled again as she marched past the bored receptionist and out into the busy, City street, remembering the unwilling lust that had darkened in Charles's eyes and how he had pretended to run an errand, acting so casual, just so he could bump into her. A man like Charles too. She'd heard the hush that quivered in Alice Drake's voice when she said his name. Thinking of it made Lily feel bold, powerful. Bit of attention was all he needed. Widening her eyes, Lily drew into them an expression of such intense admiration that the man standing next to her in the bus queue trembled slightly, then turned away, blinking in confusion. That night, he went home and startled his wife by making love to her.

Twelve

When Lily turned up on Elisabeth's doorstep the next evening, she found Elisabeth flushed and expansive. Like a big kid, she thought, feeling Elisabeth's hot cheek pressed against her, arms around her shoulders. 'What a lovely surprise,' she exclaimed but Lily could smell the wine on her breath, heard voices and laughter coming from the kitchen. She had wanted to see Charles, to tell him she'd got the job and see that look in his eyes again but she hadn't bargained with there being other people there. 'You've got company,' she said, turning on her heel. 'I'll come back another time.'

'You'll do no such thing,' Elisabeth said firmly, taking her by the arm and leading her into the hall. 'It's only the others. Come in and have a glass of wine and something to eat.'

Lily hung back, her eyes doubtful. There'd be Bella there, then, with her white face and brittle voice, so sharp you could cut yourself on it. So what, she was as good as her now, what with her new job and all. 'Got the job,' she said. 'They rang this afternoon. I just wanted to thank Charles. And you, of course.' She shrank from a sudden burst of laughter. 'Didn't know there'd be anyone else here.'

'Oh, we often get together on a Friday evening,' Elisabeth said gaily, 'relive the horrors of the week over a bottle of wine. Do please come in. Charles will be furious if he finds out you came all this way to see us and I let you go away again.'

'All right then,' Lily said, allowing herself to be led towards the kitchen. If they were all there, then Tom would be inside, and that Alex too. And Daisy. She wouldn't mind getting another look at Daisy, maybe ask her where she got her clothes. She hadn't forgotten the look she'd given that green dress, felt pleased that she'd got her new clothes on, the ones she'd bought for the interview. Swaying a little in her kitten heels, Lily followed Elisabeth into the dim corridor, felt her pause, bend her head confidingly. The smell of wine grew stronger. 'Actually, we're celebrating,' she said, with a funny, half-embarrassed laugh. 'I've got a job too, in an art gallery.'

'That's nice,' said Lily, wondering why Elisabeth wanted a job. Perhaps Charles didn't give her much money. Her mum always said the rich were a bit queer like that.

Elisabeth gave her a look, a funny, secret glance. 'And my new boss is so *handsome*,' she said, giggling.

'Is he now?' Lily watched the shine that spread across Elisabeth's face. So that's the way things are, she thought, smiling. 'Better not go telling Charles that,' she said, keeping her voice teasing, 'no telling what he'll say about a handsome boss.'

Elisabeth giggled again, a high breathless laugh. 'It'll be our secret, won't it?' she exclaimed, slipping her arm through Lily's, leading her down the narrow passageway to the kitchen. 'But when we're both working girls, we'll still make time to go on seeing each other, won't we? Now that we've become such friends.'

'Won't keep me away,' Lily said, walking arm in arm with Elisabeth into the kitchen and smiling as they all turned to stare.

'Look who's here! Alex, Bella, Daisy, Tom – well, you know everybody, don't you?' Tightening her grip protectively on Lily's arm, Elisabeth led her to the table. 'Come and sit down. I'll get you a glass, and some food.'

Charles got to his feet, pulled an extra chair up to the

table. 'Well, this is a nice surprise.' His voice was loud, slightly blustering.

'Lily got the job in Charles's office,' Elisabeth announced to the table in general, 'they rang her this afternoon.'

Their smiles glittered. They had been drinking celebration champagne and then wine, were all now rather drunk.

Elisabeth fetched a glass, laid an extra place.

'So we both have new jobs. Isn't that wonderful?'

She gestured towards Lily who slid silently into the chair by Charles's side and waited obediently while he poured a glass of wine and pushed it gently towards her, his body leaning with the movement. He did not quite right himself afterwards, but rested against the table, his shoulder close to hers. Lily's eyes slid towards him silently and then she ducked her head, sipped slowly at the wine.

'Wonderful,' Bella said drily, observing the look of unfocused longing that had settled on Charles's face.

'What's she to be doing?' Daisy asked, turning towards Elisabeth.

'Secretary,' Elisabeth mouthed across Lily's bent head, tapping her hands in mime on the table's edge.

'To Charles?'

'No, to Simon. He's having a baby,' Elisabeth said loudly, then collapsed, flushed and giggling. 'I mean, his secretary's having a baby.'

'And are we to expect a burgeoning of modern art in this house now that you are to be curator of a gallery?' Alex said, flirting slightly with Elisabeth who was looking flushed and pretty, freed from the defensive look that had pinched her face for the past few months.

Elisabeth smiled. 'Hardly a curator and I don't think discount's one of the perks of the job.'

'Artists don't give discounts,' Daisy said, watching Alex out of the corner of her eye. 'At least, only in kind.'

'Which brings us to an interesting valuation,' Tom said.

'How much in kind would you have to give for, say, a Matisse?'

'When he was alive, a blow-job would probably have secured you a canvas,' Daisy said, smiling. 'But these days. . . .'

'These days,' Bella said, 'a harem at full service would probably get you a square inch.'

'And a Damien Hirst fly?'

There was a general shout of hilarity. 'Pickled or live?'

Under cover of the noise, Lily leaned towards Charles. 'Didn't mean to disturb you. I just popped in to tell you I got the job.'

'Well, I'm delighted,' he said, in a low voice. 'I'm sure you were the best candidate.'

She shook her head. 'Maybe, but I'm grateful.' She paused, lingering over the silence. 'Just thought you ought to know.'

'Good, good –' he brought out awkwardly.

Her eyes slid to his face, fixed on it intently. 'Think the world of you there, they do. Told me so themselves. Well, if it's Mr Delaware who's recommended you, they said, then it's all right by us –'

He smiled briefly, amused and alarmed by her transparency yet unable to resist the weight of her approval. He felt it settle lightly on him, shrouding him in warmth, and drew his shoulders back expansively.

'Doesn't know when she's lucky,' Lily murmured, her eyes flickering to Elisabeth and away, but her voice was so low that Charles was not sure he had heard correctly. He leaned towards her, frowning slightly, but was interrupted by Elisabeth, her voice shrill with wine and excitement. 'Lily, rescue me. They won't accept my verdict on the Serpentine exhibition.' She turned to the others. 'Lily's frightfully good on art. No preconceptions, you see. Calls a spade a spade.'

A silence descended as the others turned to stare at her, their eyes flickering between discomfort and curiosity.

'Elisabeth,' Charles said reprovingly, 'I hardly think it's fair to –' but Lily interrupted him, her blank gaze fixed on Elisabeth's face. 'It was rubbish,' she said calmly, 'clever rubbish.'

Elisabeth shot a look of triumph at Charles. 'You see?' she said, malice briefly spiking her tone.

Bella lifted her glass with an impatient gesture. 'I don't know much about art,' she said, in a contemptuous aside, 'but I know what I like.'

Tom gave her a sharp look but Lily seemed unperturbed, her heavy-lidded gaze focused on Bella. 'That's all right, isn't it,' she said, blinking slowly, 'to know what you like?'

'Yes, of course it is,' Bella said, her voice taking on a vaguely hectoring tone. 'But not if it blinds you to other possibilities.'

'Well, that would be no good, would it?' Lily asked. 'To be blind to *possibilities*.'

Bella glanced at her sharply, braced for sarcasm, but she could find none in Lily's open gaze. On the contrary, she seemed eager for Bella's answer.

'No,' Bella said, looking down, 'no good at all.'

'I don't know what Elisabeth is thinking of, getting her a job in Charles's offices,' Bella said, as they drove home. 'He's *mesmerised* by that creature.'

'Her name is Lily.' Tom clashed gears irritably.

'She's still a creature.'

'And you are being impossibly patronising. All that stuff about not knowing about art. . . .'

'It wasn't me who started it. Elisabeth was treating her like a performing monkey.' She mimicked Elisabeth's voice. 'Lily, do tell us your views on art.'

'She meant no harm. She was trying to draw her in, include her.'

'She's drawing her in too far, then. Doesn't she notice Charles at all? He couldn't take his eyes off that girl all evening and there's his wife, dangling her like a carrot in front of his nose.'

'Maybe she trusts him.'

'Don't *start*.'

He sighed impatiently, stared out through the windscreen at the desolate, empty streets. A headache thrummed at his temples. Bella glanced at his averted face.

'Seriously,' she demanded, 'didn't you see his face? Like a lovesick camel.'

'All I saw,' Tom said slowly, 'was Charles trying to make a guest, a timid girl, feel at ease.'

'I think she's perfectly capable of standing up for herself.'

Tom grinned, remembering Lily's face. 'Well, she certainly stood up to you.'

'She's not what she seems.'

'Nobody,' Tom said, 'is what they seem.'

She was silent for a while, and then she laughed, a short, reluctant laugh. 'Except me,' she said, reaching for him with her spare hand. 'Tetchy, irritable, suspicious and mistrustful.'

It was her way of apologising, her graceless, angry way of flirtation. He remembered the first time, their first argument and how she had come to him, her furious face blazing with the need to apologise, her voice low and angry. 'I'm a bitch,' she had said, 'an angry, jealous, demanding cow.' 'Impossible,' he had said, reaching for her. 'Unreasonable,' she countered, moving into the circle of his arms. As the insults grew more provocative, so their voices grew lower until there was no noise at all but only sensation, his desire growing as it fed off her angry, jealous nature. They were young then. Young and sure. So sure. But tonight he felt uncertain, old even, the weight of the future pressing down on him. He heard her again – 'Impossible,' she murmured softly but he was too tired to reach out to her, could not face the protracted dance, one step forward, two steps back, that Bella these days played with him, pushing him away and then hauling him back, her face blazing with need and desperation. He put his foot down and sped through an amber light, urging the car through the dark, silent streets, desperate to get home, to the house that Bella loathed so much; the tiny, shabby house they could barely afford. He had suggested improvements but she wouldn't countenance them, refused even to let him paint the place white. 'What's the point?' she had said listlessly. 'It'll only look worse, like those ageing starlets who've tried to patch themselves up with make-up.' It was as if the house had become the brooding, ugly symbol of her misery, a constant jagged reminder of his blind arrogance. If he and Harry hadn't invested in property in the late eighties, if he hadn't refused, point blank, to allow Harry to sell when an offer was on the table – a low offer, but an offer nonetheless – if he hadn't been blinkered by his own arrogance, believed in his own press, 'Architecture's golden boy; the magician of the London skyline. . . .'

If, he thought savagely; if, if, if. . . . He hadn't told Bella how bad things really were with the business. Her salary just about covered the mortgage so they wouldn't be homeless, not yet, at least. He glanced at her, saw her face, white and set under the yellow glare of the street lamps, her eyes fixed on the empty road. He knew that they needed to spend some time together, just the two of them, wished he could take some time off from the business but he didn't dare; instead spent every evening touting for business or persuading young couples to practise more adventurous architecture than two-room knock-throughs and Agas in their open-plan kitchens. Then there were the awful days, the silent restless hours spent waiting for projects that never seemed to happen. He felt petrified, as though the air had clogged around him, trapping him like an insect set in resin, its legs frozen in a scuttle of eternal protest. He eased his shoulders back, jerked his legs restlessly to unravel the tension knotted deep in the cord of his spine. The movement dislodged Bella's hand, he felt her offended withdrawal and then a quick, sharp sense of relief as her fingers slid from his leg.

Thirteen

Lily surprised herself by being a good secretary.

She had her own office: a space just off Simon's spacious, wood-panelled room. It was small but had a window, a pot plant with a sign stuck in it that said 'Water Me!' and a swivel chair which spun efficiently across the grey carpet tiles, transporting her from word processor to telephone to filing cabinet. She watered the plant with proprietorial interest once a week and was happy.

She had been there for a month, had discovered that Simon Delsey was a good man to work for, fair in his demands and careful to keep his personal life to himself. 'No dry cleaning, no shopping, no presents for the wife,' said one of the girls from accounts, rolling her eyes.

The floor on which Lily worked was occupied by the firm's partners, two senior (Simon and Charles) and six junior who, intent on the rise to the heady heights of seniority, kept themselves to themselves apart from a distracted 'Is he in?' when problems became too pressing.

Charles's office was across the corridor from Simon's, replicated right down to the antique partner's desk with its dark green leather surface and shining wooden drawers. She saw him rarely, was conscious sometimes of the murmur of his voice floating across the corridor as he stood in the office of his secretary, Angela, explaining some task that needed doing. Lily thought sometimes that he was avoiding her. She didn't mind, was content to bide her time.

Nor had she seen Elisabeth, not since they had both

started working, although they spoke sometimes on the telephone, Elisabeth ringing from the gallery when she had time on her hands – which seemed to Lily to be quite often. She sounded happy, full of the job, careless of boring other people with accounts of its charms. 'Sam says –' she would say, lingeringly, or 'Sam thinks –' or 'the way Sam puts it –'. Lily sat, the telephone pressed to her ear, murmuring vague words of encouragement while she flicked through correspondence or doodled idly on a piece of paper.

One grey, rainy morning, as spring slid seamlessly into the beginnings of what promised to be another wet English summer, Lily had just put the telephone down after a call from Elisabeth when the internal line on her telephone buzzed. It was Simon, asking for some coffee: 'Something to get me through this tedious morning. Would you mind?'

Lily said she would not and wandered down the corridor to a small kitchen, where the coffee machine was kept. It was refilled constantly by the secretaries, each of whom took responsibility for it according to a fixed rota stuck up on the wall. Lily's day was Thursday, although it said Wendy in the square where her name should be because nobody had bothered to change it. Along one wall there was a sink, a cupboard containing china coffee cups and milk jugs, a biscuit tin (strictly partners only) and a small fridge that was filled with milk and, by nine in the morning, an assortment of Lite salads from Marks & Spencer. One or other of the secretaries was always on a diet.

Lily laid a tray with a dark green china cup and saucer edged with gold and placed a plate of Simon's favourite chocolate Hob-Nob biscuits next to it. Just as she had filled the cup with hot coffee, Angela appeared silently at her side.

'Hope you've left some of those,' she said, eyeing the biscuits as she barged big hips past Lily. 'They're Charles's favourites.' She paused, let the silence hang heavy in the air. 'But I expect you know that,' she finished, banging the fridge shut with a triumphant flourish.

She did not like Lily, had not liked her since she saw the way Charles looked at her when he introduced her, that first day.

'He prefers the ones with plain chocolate,' Lily said calmly.

Angela started, her small blue eyes burning with humiliation and jealousy. She had been buying the milk chocolate ones all along. She snatched the packet away. 'No, he doesn't.'

Lily shrugged. 'I'll be across to see you later,' she said, picking up the tray and walking out of the kitchen. 'Simon needs some papers countersigned by Charles.'

Angela put her head around the door, her plump cheeks pink with indignation. 'No,' she cried, 'no, don't you bother. I'll come and get them myself.'

Charles was standing in the doorway of Angela's office, peering up and down the corridor. 'I've lost Angela,' he said apologetically. 'There's a letter that needs typing urgently.'

'She's making coffee.' Lily eased the tray into her office, put it on the desk and reappeared in the doorway, facing him. 'She won't be a minute. But while you're standing there, could you come and sign some papers for Simon?'

He walked across the corridor into her office, stood smiling over her as she searched through the in-tray for the documents.

She placed them before him on the desk and handed him a pen. He stared at it unseeing for a moment, then took it and bent as if to write but stood, unmoving, above her. She glanced up, wondering if he was reading but saw that his eyes were fixed on some point to the left of the papers. 'I'm sorry we haven't seen much of you recently,' he said in a low voice. 'This new job of Elisabeth's takes up so much of her time and in the office I –' He glanced to left and right, then shrugged.

'It's OK,' Lily said, keeping her voice as low as his so they seemed conspirators, bound in some tryst of confidentiality. 'She rings sometimes. She sounds happy.'

'Does she?' He glanced at her, surprised, but whether he was surprised that Elisabeth rang or that she was happy was not clear from his face. He bent towards the papers, the pen hovering above them. 'I wondered if you'd like to have a drink with me, one evening,' he said quickly. She noticed that his hand shook slightly. 'Somewhere –' he searched for the word '– neutral,' he finished.

She did not know what he meant by the word but understood from his tone that it was to be a secret. A small smile curved across her face. 'All right,' she said and added, her voice growing louder, more formal, 'and if you could just sign these then I can get them off this evening.'

He glanced up, startled, met her eyes and looked away quickly but not before she saw the pleasure that flared in them.

A large form loomed over them. 'I said I'd come and get them,' Angela said, snatching up the papers and making off with them, her loose cotton blouse and skirt billowing around her like a set of sails. Charles watched her go, the pen still held in his hand, then glanced down at Lily and shrugged helplessly. 'Sorry about that. She means well enough.'

Lily smiled conspiratorially. 'I don't mind.'

Flushing, Charles turned and walked, stiff-legged, out of the room.

On her first morning at work, Elisabeth took one look at Sam's office and insisted that he move out temporarily to the dais-like desk in the front of the gallery. 'Just while I get it sorted out. And don't scare them away with that Zen look of yours,' she said severely. 'It's frightening enough coming into this place without you spooking them too.'

Very few people came into the gallery; astonishingly few in Elisabeth's eyes who could not see how Sam could possibly make a living, but when she asked him he simply shrugged lazily and said that the real business was done over the telephone. Calls came in to the tiny shop from all over the world. Sometimes the actual objects didn't even change hands, but were exchanged in name only.

Certainly the tiny number of people who stopped by meant that they were left for the most part in peace, which made Elisabeth's job of sorting out Sam's affairs that much easier. Were it not for the fact that he frequently disturbed her, she would have been finished in no time.

He'd given her the keys that first morning, so she could come in and open up which she did every morning at ten. For an hour she opened post, flicked a duster around the place, made a fresh pot of coffee and on Mondays arranged the fresh flowers that she had taken to bringing in every week. Sam usually appeared at around eleven, his shaggy hair unbrushed and the sleep still etched across his face, clutching two cups of cappuccino that he'd made on the machine he kept in his flat upstairs. Elisabeth would stop sorting and come and sit with him, exchanging news about the morning – somebody who had rung or a letter that needed to be dealt with – and then Sam would slope off to his desk in the gallery and sift slowly through the morning's mail, checking the international catalogues and avidly reading the many art magazines to which he subscribed.

After an hour or so he would come and sit in the doorway to the office, long, jeans-clad legs sprawling on the wood floor, his shaggy head leaned back against the frame, and watch her while she worked, all the while complaining that he was lonely out there and couldn't she stop, just for a moment? Or he'd say idly that coffee would be nice at which she'd sigh good-naturedly and abandon what she was doing and go and make them both a cup while he stared after her admiringly with sleepy eyes which sometimes, when they caught the light in a certain way, turned grey. When she looked at them closely, Elisabeth saw golden flecks dancing in the irises.

Sometimes, when the chaos in the office seemed insurmountable, Elisabeth would grumble a little and wonder aloud how his previous receptionist had occupied her days. What she wanted to know was, was she old, was she young, was she pretty? But Sam never mentioned her, would only unfold one of his lazy, engaging smiles and roll his eyes. At one o'clock sharp he'd stretch and get to his feet and say that it was time for lunch. The third time he did this, on the third morning she had been there, Elisabeth protested that she was only paid for four hours' work a day, four days a week (she did not work on Fridays) which meant that she ought to leave at two o'clock (although she never actually did) and that she was costing him her entire salary and more in lunches. Sam just grinned, told her not to be bossy and said that, if she preferred, she could consider her job title as lunching companion. 'I can't bear to eat alone,' he said, ushering her out of the gallery and flicking over the old-fashioned sign that hung behind the door.

Elisabeth became so used to their lunch-time ritual that the first time he announced that he had to meet somebody else for lunch (and was wearing a suit, linen and crumpled but still, somehow, devastatingly sexy) she was mortified to feel tears of disappointment pricking at her eyes and had turned away quickly before he could see them.

Once she had sorted the mess of papers and got the filing system into some sort of order, Sam moved back into his office and Elisabeth went and sat at the high desk in the gallery where she occupied herself with staring unseeingly at a book or flicking listlessly through one of his art magazines, trying to educate herself into the impenetrable world of modern art.

But as there were so few visitors and so many letters to be typed she and Sam spent most of their time in his office, which was so small that they had to sit with their legs almost touching. And if Elisabeth shifted sometimes so that one of his legs was pressed against the length of her thigh for a moment, then he did not move away or even appear to notice but left it there, until it radiated a heat that spread through her thigh and up to the pit of her belly. Even after his leg was once more absent the heat lingered long afterwards.

Elisabeth had even been startled awake by it in the night, waking to find her vagina engorged with warmth and moisture and hurrying, embarrassed, from the bed she shared with Charles, slipping noiselessly into the bathroom where she sat on the lavatory, a warm palm flattened against her pubic hair until the throbbing warmth dwindled to a slow pulse.

The pulse never quite left her; she could feel it quickening between her legs as she walked to work, felt it flutter in anticipation together with the tick of the hands of the clock as they shifted slowly, so slowly, towards eleven o'clock and Sam would shamble sleepily into the room and lasso her heart with a lazy, infectious grin. The pulse between her legs affected quite separate parts of her body too; kept her cheeks flushed a light and becoming pink, polished the sparkle in her blue eyes. It even seemed to her, as she brushed out her thick blonde hair every night, to add a lustre to its weight.

Nor did it diminish when she sat in the office with him, typing busily, her fingers flying over the keys of the old-fashioned electric typewriter while he leaned his head on one hand and paid her extravagant compliments.

'How lovely you are,' he sighed, staring up at her. 'You

159

must have been quite dazzling when you were young; like a ripe peach.'

Elisabeth, too entranced to regret his use of the past tense, simply blushed and scolded him to stop disturbing her if he wanted his letters finished. Then, when his voice was stilled and his blue eyes busy, absorbed in a new art catalogue, she would sneak a glance at him from beneath lowered lids and long for him to talk again and fill her body with words.

She said none of this to Charles, of course.

Fourteen

Soon after Lily moved into the place, Mrs Flower noticed a man, youngish and nicely dressed, loitering on Orchard Road. She noticed him, she thought later, both on account of the fact that Orchard Road, being on the way to nowhere, was not a place to loiter and on account of his suit, which was dark and nicely pressed, and his clean, white shirt.

She said nothing to him, just kept an eye out to memorise him in case the police came calling, but then he disappeared again and she thought no more about him. So she was startled, a few weeks later, to discover him standing over her, offering to haul her heavy shopping trolley, together with Charlie in it, up the steep stone steps to number 59.

'Nice of you,' she said, keeping a wary eye on him.

He carried the trolley to the top of the steps and looked at her enquiringly. 'I was hoping I'd see you,' he said. 'Wanted to ask you about someone living here. Girl by the name of Lily.'

'And what's it to you?' Mrs Flower asked, although her tone was not unpleasant. There was something appealing in his manner and she was curious about Lily, a young girl turning up like that, with only a small suitcase to her name and her claim to having rich friends. Got a job out of them she had, not to mention invitations to smart dinners. Mrs Flower had not forgotten the champagne or the silver fish on the platter. There was something strange about the girl too, a sort of curious hollowness that she couldn't quite put her finger on and which made her uneasy. Mrs Flower made it her business to know about people, so she smiled and said, 'You family, or something?'

The young man hesitated. 'Sort of. I'm her fiancé. Name's Jim.'

Mrs Flower, who prided herself on being a good judge of character, looked him over carefully. 'Well, Jim,' she said eventually, 'if you do me the trouble of carrying this trolley up the stairs to my room for me, I'll make you a nice cup of tea.'

A couple of days later, Celia, who was sometimes overcome by wifely urges, had made Sunday brunch. 'Just to be sure you're getting your money's worth,' she said, putting a plate of eggs Benedict in front of Alex. 'I'd hate you to feel you were being short-changed.'

Alex stuck a fork in the centre of an egg yolk. It emerged dripping, satisfyingly yellow. 'Do I ever complain?'

'No,' she said, pouring him a generous glass of Bloody Mary. She smiled briefly. 'Then again, you are never given cause to.'

Alex eyed her cautiously over a piece of buttery egg, discovered her green eyes glinting expectantly. His wife unnerved him sometimes. He returned her gaze, feeling vaguely hunted.

'Delicious eggs, darling,' he said quickly.

'It's the hollandaise. You must make it *foam*,' she said, with a dismissive shrug. She picked up a cup of pale Lapsang tea, lifted it to her lips. 'Are you going to let me have any of those newspapers,' she said with an amused quirk of an eyebrow, 'or are you keeping them all for yourself?'

'Certainly. Which would you like?'

She held out a pale, manicured hand. '*Telegraph* business, please.'

They sat in companionable silence while Alex applied

himself to his eggs and Celia flicked through the business pages, tossing out the occasional remark about somebody who was of interest to them both. He watched her, amused. She treated the financial section like a gossip column, kept a careful, daily eye on it.

'I hear your friend Charles is up to no good,' Celia said pleasantly, looking up from the paper.

Alex looked up. 'Charles?'

'Charles Delaware, partner in Delsey & Delaware. There's an article here about some big case they're working on which reminded me. He is a friend, isn't he?'

'Yes,' Alex said carefully, unable for a moment to remember whether this was something to be admitted to. Really, his life was so complicated he wondered sometimes if it was worth it.

'Well, Ann, with whom I have lunch occasionally – you know, you met her at the Academy party last June – she's married to Simon Delsey, the other partner at the practice. He seems to think nobody's noticed but according to the office gossip, Charles is ambling around the place like a love-struck calf, mooning after some creature who goes by the name of a flower. I forget which.'

Alex was silent for a while.

'Orchid? Could that be it? No, perhaps Rose.'

'Lily,' Alex said absently.

'Lily. Yes, that's it. Do you know her?'

Alex looked at her, frowning. 'Lily – it's a girl's name that's a flower.'

'So it is,' Celia said brightly. 'And do you know her – this Lily?'

'I've met her,' Alex said briefly before turning back to his newspaper.

Celia looked at his bent head, her expression thoughtful. According to Mrs Flower, there were a couple of messages on Alex's private business line from a woman who called herself Lily. They were innocuous enough, brief references to returning his calls, but Mrs Flower had sounded vaguely flustered when she mentioned them. Celia sighed faintly. If Alex was growing bored of Daisy, then she was going to have to keep a sharper eye on him. She should have recognised the signs. Alex had taken to coming home in the evenings far too often recently, prowling restlessly around the house in search of entertainment, which meant that he was dissatisfied with present arrangements.

Alex, conscious of Celia's gaze, decided that attack was the best defence. 'Why?' he said, his voice loud in the still room.

She looked up in surprise. 'Why what?'

'Why were you asking about Lily?'

She flicked through a newspaper, tossed it on the table. 'No reason really. It was just something to amuse you.' She looked at him thoughtfully but said nothing else so he went back to his reading.

After a while she said, 'It does amuse you, doesn't it?'

He looked up. Her green eyes glinted watchfully. 'Yes,' he said, with a forced laugh. 'Oh, yes, it does.'

That same Sunday afternoon, Lily and Mrs Flower were eating fish paste sandwiches.

'Haven't seen much of you lately, lovely,' Mrs Flower said, through a mouthful of Mother's Pride. 'Busy girl these days.'

'Suppose I am.'

'New friends, new clothes, and now a new job,' Mrs Flower said, head nodding benignly. 'Looks like you've gone and got yourself a whole new life.'

'Looks like it,' Lily said equably.

'Well, I suppose it's in the nature of things when you're young. Not that I can be doing with it; not in my advanced years. Enough to make your head spin.'

'I suppose –' Lily said doubtfully. She was too young to consider change difficult, only exciting.

'Mind you, a new life's not always the most comfortable fit.' Mrs Flower's massive bosom quivered like a moulded jelly. 'Pinches a bit, at times.'

'Not so's I noticed,' Lily said, wondering what Mrs Flower knew about new lives. She was about to ask her when Mrs Flower let out a low, screeching whistle. 'Ooooh, I'll forget my own head next. I meant to tell you, lovely. There's a man been asking after you.'

'A man?'

Mrs Flower cocked her head on one side, smiled cosily. 'Now don't tell me you haven't got admirers, pretty girl like you.'

'What did he look like?'

'Youngish – sandy hair going a bit thin on top, pink skin like it was scrubbed, nice suit,' Mrs Flower said precisely.

'Jim,' Lily murmured. It didn't surprise her. She knew he'd track her down one day. He had the sort of friends who were good at finding people.

'Boyfriend, is he?' she asked casually.

'Sort of.'

'Seemed like a nice young man.'

'Yes,' Lily said. 'He is.'

Mrs Flower cast her a sharp look but Lily, who was suddenly affected by the soporific stupor that is particular to Sunday afternoons and stuffy rooms, had closed her eyes and laid her head back against the soft wool of the crocheted antimacassar with which the head of each chair in the room was carefully protected.

They sat in silence for a while, Lily apparently dozing and Mrs Flower staring dreamily into the bars of the electric fire. Charlie whimpered occasionally and when he did his little paws scrabbled furiously against the thick polyester of Mrs Flower's skirt.

Mrs Flower gazed at the twitching form lovingly. 'He's dreaming of the blue yonder where the rabbits run wild. Instead, he's stuck in a hovel, poor little mite.'

Lily nodded agreeably.

She found it soothing sitting with Mrs Flower. She supposed it was because she reminded her of her mum. She didn't talk much either. Not unless she had something to say. Not like Elisabeth who had to fill every minute with talk, most of it meaningless. She'd asked her once why she talked so much. Elisabeth, who had looked a bit taken aback at first, had started laughing, as if Lily had made a joke. 'I was just making conversation,' she said; and Lily, who thought that conversation was supposed to involve a few long words, not lots of short ones strung together about the weather or a new skirt, had laughed too, but uncertainly.

'How's the job going, lovely?' Mrs Flower said, rousing herself from her stupor.

'It's nice. I work for a man called Simon Delsey who's a senior partner. My friend Charles, he's the Delaware bit.'

Mrs Flower looked interested. 'Is he now?' she said, musingly.

'Do you know them, then?' Lily asked, catching the gleam in Mrs Flower's eye.

Mrs Flower shook her head and poured more tea into thick blue china mugs, sugaring it liberally. They both liked a bit of sweetness. 'Like some Battenberg, dearie? It's home-made. My daughter sent it.'

'Yes, please,' Lily murmured sleepily.

Mrs Flower's eyes twinkled shrewdly. 'The man that came looking for you. He the one you were going to marry, who left you at the altar?'

Lily's eyes opened. 'Yes,' she said carefully.

'He said it was you that changed your mind, had one foot in your wedding dress and then scarpered without telling anyone where you was off to. Says your mum's a bit upset.'

Lily looked startled, but Mrs Flower gazed kindly over at her. 'No need to go getting yourself upset, lovely.

Everyone has their own version of things, specially things as complicated as relationships.' She hugged her breasts comfortably. 'You talk to anybody about their marriage, about their boyfriend or girlfriend and no two stories ever come out the same. Even people who've been married for years, they remember things differently.' She cast a bright eye at Lily. 'You ever notice that, lovely?'

Lily nodded.

'Or perhaps,' Mrs Flower said, a far-away look in her eye, 'it's that they forget things differently. Me, for example. I forgot how much I loved my Reg until after he was dead.' A tear rolled out of her eye, got caught in the powdery down on her soft plump cheeks and hung there, glistening.

Lily watched it in fascination, wondering when it would drop. She didn't know what Mrs Flower was going on about but it was soothing, sitting there listening to her. Remember things? Forget things? Who bloody cared so long as there was somebody there to look after you, keep you warm. Mind you, that was what Jim used to do but that wasn't enough, not after a while. Trouble with Jim was, he had no ambition. His small world was enough for him. Him and his Dustbuster and his flimsy little house with its nylon carpets and fake antiques he was so proud of and his late-night shopping, every Thursday come rain or shine, never mind what was showing at the local cinema even. Elisabeth had a word for people like him. She called them 'suburban'. When she was talking, Lily felt a strange pang, a sort of dull ache for familiar things – but had squashed them severely. No use crying after spilled milk, as her mum would say. 'Oh, not you,' Elisabeth had laughed gaily, seeing Lily's face. 'You might have been suburban once, but now you're resolutely urban. Just like us.'

No, Lily thought, not like them.

Mrs Flower was saying, 'He used to bring me flowers,

every Saturday lunch-time when he came back from the shops. Nothing fancy, mind. Reg didn't go in for things like that. No, just a bunch of daffs or some nice 'mums, when they were in season. And I'd grill us a nice couple of chops or something like that and we'd sit at the table and eat our lunch with them flowers winking over us.' She wiped a tear from her eye. 'One in a million, my Reg.'

Mrs Flower beamed down at her. 'Like I said, lovely, it's a big step, marriage. No point rushing into things.' She nodded sagely. 'Then again, no point running away unless you've got something better to run to.' She cocked her head enquiringly on one side, fixed Lily with a shrewd eye. 'Am I right, lovely?'

There was a sharp knock on the door and a voice could be heard calling that Lily was wanted on the telephone. Lily scrambled to her feet and, hurriedly thanking Mrs Flower for the tea and cake, slipped noiselessly from the room. Mrs Flower rested a meditative eye on Charlie. 'Yes, lovely. I think I might be right.'

Fifteen

Charles appeared in the doorway of Lily's office. 'I thought you might need a lift home.'

She looked up, flustered, from a large pile of papers. 'Is it six o'clock already?' She gave a helpless shrug. 'Still got all this lot to get through and I'm due to meet somebody in half an hour.'

'I see,' he said, trying to keep the disappointment from his voice. He had taken her out for a drink three times; three sweet, short hours that did nothing to ease the ache that lurked somewhere deep in his abdomen, shifting from groin to heart and, even, to his back. Sometimes he wondered if he was sickening for something, if his yearning for Lily was no more than a flutter of indigestion. But then she'd smile that special, secret smile as they passed in the corridor or her hand would press against his as she handed him a document to sign and the ache would be back, pushing hard against his tired, married heart.

He had thought a drink, an hour with her might ease it, reduce her to more human, manageable proportions but she was so cool, so distant with him – although sweet, ah, but she was sweet – that it only made it worse. And because too many drinks might cause office talk (although they were careful always to meet at least fifteen minutes away in a wine bar that no lawyers frequented) he had come up with another reason for being with her, an innocent offer of a lift home, an excuse about needing to drop some papers in to a colleague who lived a few streets away. In the darkened car he found some measure of contentment, her hair grazing his arm, her perfume, mixed with the slight, musky smell of the day's sweat, rising sharply to his nose. And while sometimes he felt an almost unbearable yearning to take her in his arms and press his mouth down on hers, to linger on the curves of her lips and run his tongue down her smooth cheek and bury it in her very centre, he circumvented the urge by concentrating on the traffic and his driving.

Lily gathered up a large pile of papers and hurried over to an open filing cabinet.

Charles looked at her closely. She looked different, her mouth glossy, eyes darkened, as if she had prepared herself for a party and not the humdrum job of filing with which she seemed so preoccupied. She wore a dress, black and very simple, that he had not seen before. He knew enough, from Elisabeth's clothes, that its very plainness meant that it was expensive. It made her look older, more knowing, and he yearned, suddenly, for the old pink dress.

He loitered in the doorway, wishing she would look up at him with that lovely, intimate smile, the one that he felt she kept especially for him. He wondered suddenly if she ever used it on Simon. Was that why she was so intent on sorting those damn papers? He felt a brief surge of jealousy, was careful to keep his tone jocular. 'Anybody nice?' he asked.

Lily, preoccupied with trying to find a missing letter, did not look up. 'Oh, only Alex,' she said, seizing the errant letter and stepping quickly across to a cabinet to slot the green cardboard folders carefully into a brimming drawer.

Charles frowned. 'Alex?'

'Yes,' Lily said, hurrying back for another armful of folders. She smiled up at him as she passed; a stream of the sweet, bright scent she sometimes wore wreathed his shoulders and clung to his nostrils. For some reason he could not fathom, it always made him feel infinitely sad. She fixed on him eyes that were so black they were almost completely opaque. He could read nothing in them. 'He telephoned last night, asked me to meet him. Said he wanted to talk about something.'

'What about?'

She shrugged. 'I don't know. Daisy perhaps?'

'Why would he want to talk to you about Daisy?'

Lily looked up in surprise. 'Well, why not?' she said, and then she ducked her head back to the cabinet but not before he saw a brief, hurt look on her face.

'I'm sorry, I didn't mean –' he said.

'Course you didn't,' she said, rewarding him with a quick smile.

Watching her, he thought how vulnerable she was, and how often he felt wrong-footed, as if he had said something to upset her.

'It's her birthday soon, isn't it?' she said, frowning a little over a couple of pieces of paper she held in her hand. 'Maybe he's trying to think of a surprise.'

'I doubt that very much.' He was unable to contain the jealousy in his voice.

Lily looked up, startled. 'Do you?' she said, looking bewildered. 'Well, it's something else then. He's picking me up at six thirty so I suppose we'll go somewhere. . . .'

'His office is only two hundred yards down the street.'

'I know where his office is. I offered to walk over and meet him at the wine bar but he said he'd rather pick me up in the car.' She turned away from him and he could see, by the set of her shoulders, that she was irritated. 'Don't see it matters.'

Charles knew the wine bar well, a place frequented by lawyers and bankers (many of who would know Celia), knew why Alex would not wish to be seen with her there. What was he up to?

'You know, I suppose, that Alex is not to be trusted,' he said, trying to keep his voice light but unable to stop jealousy striking a harsh, bitter note. He felt his hands beginning to shake, clenched his fists in his pockets to hide it.

She looked back at him with an expression of hurt bewilderment, but he felt incapable of reassuring her; could only stand, speechless, as he felt a spasm of jealousy twist sickeningly at his gut.

And then she laughed.

Flushing, he spun on his heel and stormed out of the room, his briefcase bruising his legs as it banged against them, so furious was his progress down the seemingly interminable corridor to the lift.

After he had gone, Lily crept out of the doorway and stood watching his stiff, retreating back. The barest glimmer of a smile crept slowly across her face and then, after a swift glance at her watch, she let out a little cry and hurried to get her handbag.

Lily hurried along the road, heels tapping loudly in the rapidly emptying street. When she reached the corner, she stood waiting, her dark eyes dreamy. Alex had been calling her for weeks, first at the office, then at home. She was polite with him, but distant; her distance only increasing his eagerness, as she knew it would. She smiled, seeing a sleek black car draw up in front of her. The door swung slowly open. Inside, she could see Alex's face, his smile glimmering in the pale light.

She climbed in and settled back into the seat, running her hands appreciatively over the soft leather upholstery. 'Nice car.'

He shifted gears casually. 'Gets one from A to B.'

'Where are we going?'

'Where would you like to go?'

'Don't mind. Thought you had something to talk to me about.'

'Plenty of time for that.'

The car purred smoothly along the Embankment, nosing

through the traffic. Alex swung the power-steered wheel with one finger and they tilted left, over Tower Bridge.

'Do you like the theatre?'

Lily shrugged. 'Dunno. Haven't been much.'

'I've got some tickets. Daisy couldn't make it. Seems a shame to waste them.'

'What's wrong with her?'

'She's got the flu.'

'Poor thing. I'm ever so ill when I get the flu and you get no sympathy for it.'

'I think she does all right,' Alex said, thinking of the fifty pounds' worth of roses he had asked his secretary to send, just after he had made the call to Lily. He glanced over at her. 'So how about it?'

A glimmer of pleasure flared in her lovely, vacant face. 'All right then.'

'Good. That's settled. We may as well head straight there and have a drink at the bar.'

'You don't have to, you know,' Lily said, as the car moved smoothly through the busy streets.

'I know I don't have to.' Then, unable to resist showing off, he said, 'With tickets at fifty pounds a go, it seems a pity to waste them.'

He was gratified by her sharp intake of breath. 'Blimey. Better not then.'

'Indeed,' Alex said smoothly.

They got out of the car, walked across to the glass and steel foyer that acted as the landing bay for all three theatres, stood momentarily scanning the signs to see where they should be headed. Alex smiled down at her, noting her dress – black and expensive – and the perfume she wore – also expensive – and wondered where a girl like her got the money for such frivolities.

'Went to Harvey Nichols,' she said, seeing his glance. 'Blew a whole month's pay packet on it.'

'And was it worth it?'

'Yes,' she said, remembering Charles's face. 'Yes, it was.'

'What are you up to, Lily?' Alex asked, smiling down at her, his face so close that she could smell the peppermints on his breath.

'Nothing.'

'Oh, yes you are.' He slid a warm hand between her neck and the curtain of hair that streamed down her back, lifted the heavy, silken mass and watched it ripple lazily over his fingers. Lily stood motionless under the caress, her face blank.

He felt both repelled and attracted by her. 'Lovely hair,' he said abruptly, dropping his hand.

She watched him impassively. 'Thank you.'

'Well,' he said, glancing at his watch. 'Shall we?' Placing his hand in the small of her back, he steered her towards the bar, which was almost empty. He noticed how she moved, gliding noiselessly under the pressure of his fingers. He felt again that small shiver of revulsion intermingled with desire and wondered, idly, what it would be like to fuck her.

He ordered white wine, although he did not much like it and drank his quickly, emptying the glass in three swallows. He put his face close to hers. 'Don't you like me, lovely Lily?'

She shrugged. 'Course I do.'

He smiled, baring small, pointed teeth. 'Course you do,' he said, imitating her rough accent. 'You'd eat us all up without even swallowing if you had half a mind to.'

'Don't know what you mean.'

'Don't you?'

'No.' She pulled out a packet of cigarettes and lit one, inhaling with grateful abandon.

He looked at her with interest. 'I didn't know you smoked.'

She shrugged, blew out a thin stream of blue smoke.

'You don't smoke in front of Elisabeth.'

She looked at him scornfully. 'Course not. Don't think she likes it.'

'So you only do what people like?'

She nodded. 'Something like that.'

'Well, I'd like to take you to bed, Lily.'

She said nothing, merely stared at him with those great, dark eyes of her. The indifference in them inflamed him.

'The idea doesn't appeal?' There was an edge to his voice.

She smiled slightly at the petulance that crept across his face. 'Seems like you get enough of that already without adding me to your list. Anyway, I like Daisy.'

His tone was bored. 'What's that got to do with it?'

'You're not supposed to do stuff to people you like.'

'And what about Elisabeth? Don't you like her?'

Lily shrugged. 'Course I do. She's nice.'

'For a patronising middle-class do-gooder.'

'I never said that.'

'But it's what you think.'

'No. It's what you think.' She gave a scornful lift to one thin shoulder. 'She's all right, is Elisabeth.'

'So her patronage is benign?'

She didn't know the word, had to be content with flashing him a contemptuous look. 'Whatever you say.'

'Benign enough to take her husband off her?'

Lily laughed. 'Take her husband off her? What would I do with a bloke like that? He'd look lovely down the pub, wouldn't he? Blend into the paint-work nicely.'

'He's rich. With him around, you wouldn't be going down to the pub.'

'He's not rich. Not once you take the house away.'

'Which Elisabeth presumably would do.'

'Dunno.'

'I see you've thought it all through.'

She glanced at him. 'Doesn't take much thinking, does it?'

'He's still a lot richer than you.'

Lily gave a weary sigh. 'So's most of the world.' Her eyes flickered briefly over Alex. 'You included. Elisabeth said you're worth a packet.'

'You like money, do you?'

Something like a smile formed around her pale lips but she said nothing.

'So who was this man who ditched you?'

'None of your business.'

'There *was* a man, I suppose?'

'No, I just stuck an ad in the classifieds because I knew that Elisabeth would read it and invite me to dinner.' Her expression was scornful. 'What do you think?'

'I think you're not all that you seem.'

Lily gave him a small, self-satisfied smile. 'Think what you like.' She seemed to lose interest in the conversation and began to glance around. 'Shall we go then, see this play? Don't want to waste all that money.' She stood up, drawing her thin cardigan around herself, hitching her bag purposefully onto her shoulder.

'Not yet.'

She waited patiently, teetering slightly on thin heels.

'I suppose you know that Charles is keen on you.'

'That what he says?'

'No. It's the way he looks at you. Surely you've noticed.'

Lily shrugged. 'Can't say I have.'

'Well, everybody else has. Except, of course, Elisabeth.'

She looked at him with interest. 'Why, of course?'

'Elisabeth only sees those things that she wishes to.'

Her face closed up. 'Her and the rest of the world,' she said, shrugging. She moved towards the darkened mouth of the theatre.

He felt deflated as he followed her. 'Elisabeth wants the

world to be nice so she only acknowledges those things that she thinks make it nice.'

Lily laughed. 'Oh, it's nice, is it?' she said in her harsh, flat voice.

'It can be,' he said, moving closer and circling her waist with his arm. She did not draw away and so he adjusted his position slightly, to make it more comfortable. 'It can be anything you want it to be.'

She turned her head so that he felt the warmth of her breath against his ear. 'That depends on who's doing the wanting.'

'What do you want, Lily?' he asked. As they drew further into the crowd at the entrance to the stalls, they were jostled together.

'Same as everybody else, I suppose.'

He felt her hair brush against his cheek. 'I think that different people want quite different things. I imagine most would say that what they want is happiness but for one person happiness might mean money and for another love, for the next independence, for another success. What's happiness mean to you?'

She looked at him for a moment, then shrugged. 'Can't say as I've ever thought about it.'

'You must have.'

She shook her head. 'No.' They moved into the stalls and stood for a moment, looking for their row. 'It's nice here, isn't it?' she said, pleased. 'The seats look dead comfy.'

He glanced at her, amused. She was like a child at times. He was not sure how he felt about her. All he knew was that he wanted her.

Sixteen

It was quiet in the gallery. Elisabeth was idly pushing pieces of paper around her desk, pretending to sort the post and wondering what Sam was up to. He was in his office, with the door shut, but she felt his presence like a patch of sunlight on her back. He had just returned from a trip to Italy to look at a private collection of paintings he was interested in buying. Only for three days but the time had seemed to Elisabeth to stretch, like an elastic band taken to the limits of its tension, until she thought she could bear the waiting for its release no longer. While he was gone she thought that never before had she known silence so dense, absence so tangible.

He had brought her back a scarf, a square of thick silk patterned in brilliant swirls of colour, packed in pale yellow tissue with a narrow envelope of ivory parchment inscribed in gold with the maker's name. 'A little shop I know,' he said easily. 'I thought you would appreciate it.'

Overwhelmed, she had been unable to do more than mutter a graceless 'thank you', flushing painfully as he picked up the square of silk, folded it expertly and knotted it at her neck. She felt his fingers on the tender skin at the base of her throat, the pulse of her blood leaping, and turned away, pretending to search for a letter that had come when he was away, that needed his attention. 'It suits you,' he said briefly, before turning to the letter and carrying it off to his office, lost to her.

She sat motionless, her hand at her throat, feeling the touch of his fingers burning her skin, the heavy silk whispering at her neck. But while her body was still, her mind was elated, accelerating over a cobbled street in Italy in the early summer sunshine, flashing past mellow stone buildings, watching his easy, loping walk, that way he had of holding himself, poised but relaxed, his limbs fluid, at ease with his body. She pictured him in the shop, surrounded by squares of coloured silk, laughing as he picked them up and rubbed the heavy fabric to his face, discarding them one by one, smiling and shaking his head at the tubby black-clad woman who ran the shop, the silk fluttering around him as he searched. Elisabeth paused, her hand still at her neck. She would be tubby, wouldn't she? And old, with round pink cheeks and shrewd brown Italian eyes. And where had he learned to knot a scarf like that, his hands moving so easily through the fabric? She imagined Charles trying, fumbling the mass into a clumsy wedge, abandoning it with a helpless, sheepish grin. No, she thought, Charles wouldn't even try, would hand her something he had picked up in duty-free, still in its stiff plastic bag.

Sighing, Elisabeth turned her attention back to the post. A piece of flimsy orange paper slid out from beneath a VAT return. It must have come through the letter-box with the post that morning. 'Transcendental Meditation', it said, in cheap, fuzzy black print, 'Discover the real you'.

She wondered what Charles would say if he came back from work and found her cross-legged on the carpet in the sitting-room, humming; imagined him stepping over her on his way to get a whisky. 'Nice day, darling?' he'd say, splashing soda into a glass.

Then again, perhaps he wouldn't even notice.

She flicked open a copy of *Marie Claire*. It fell open at a questionnaire: 'Do you and your partner take each other for granted?' Ah, yes, she thought, an equal opportunities magazine. We are all partners now. She got out a biro and considered the questions. 'Does he bring you flowers? a) once a week; b) once a month; c) once a year.' She frowned, trying hard to remember when Charles had last brought her flowers. In the end she gave up, scratched a spidery question mark in the margin.

'Do you bring him flowers?'

She doodled some daisies across the question, remembering a spring day long ago, the first after a long winter. There was a blue sky, a pale sun, a man walking ahead of her, dark hair springing in agitation from the crown of his head. She'd thought at first that it was Charles, had hurried gladly after him only to discover, when he moved in profile, that it was a stranger. She'd turned away in disappointment, her longing for Charles acute. She often felt pierced by those sudden lances of affection for Charles; more often when he was absent than present. It had always been like that. When he was actually there, beside her, she prickled with irritation instead, little stings of it, like a heat rash.

Her disappointment was so acute that she'd bought him some flowers from a stall in the high street. She'd considered them for ages, had bought daffodils in the end because they seemed genderless against the roses or the anemones with their dark, soulful eyes and blowsy skirts. She presented the flowers to Charles when he got home, watched him standing irresolute in the kitchen, the cheap paper growing soggy in his hand.

'What are these for?' he asked, his eyes darting nervously around the room. Looking for what? For clues of a celebration, perhaps? An anniversary? A birthday?

'For – nothing,' she said, smiling although her shoulders sagged with disappointment. 'For spring, I suppose.'

She sensed a movement, turned to see Sam's face looming over her.

'Ah,' he said, glancing down at the magazine. 'A quiz. My favourite. Let's do it over lunch.'

Cheeks burning, she snapped the magazine shut.

'Don't worry. I always lie,' he said cheerfully. 'I assume everyone else does too.'

It had never occurred to Elisabeth to lie.

She slid the magazine into a drawer in her desk, dislodging a tin-foil parcel.

Sam raised an enquiring eyebrow.

'It's sandwiches,' she said, feeling foolish. 'I brought my lunch with me today.' She had seen the demands from the bank, recoiled at the amounts and had decided not to let him spend any more money on her. Bad enough that she took his money for doing what seemed to her like nothing, other than basking in his presence, like a cat before a fire.

Sam's eyebrow shot up even further. 'Sandwiches? What a sensible woman you are,' he said, plucking her coat from a battered old hatstand and holding it out for her.

She gave a pale smile, slid her arms obediently into the limp sleeves.

'Well, I suppose you'd better bring them with you.'

While he flipped the sign on the gallery door to Closed and locked up, she waited patiently on the pavement, the lunch package clutched in her hand.

'I thought we might go and feed those sandwiches to the ducks. No point in letting them go to waste.'

She stared down at the sandwiches, carefully wrapped in their neat tin-foil prison. How stupid he made her feel sometimes; how prissy and housewifely. They started walking towards the heath. The sun shone weakly through a dense grey sky as the summer struggled to meet them, trailing the last cold snap of spring in its wake.

'What's in them?' he asked, glancing at her in amusement.

She looked at him uncertainly, wondering if he was teasing her. 'Salad,' she said, after a while.

'They'd have preferred tuna.'

'Yes, I suppose they would.'

As they crossed the road, he took her arm and she felt his hand, burning her skin through the fabric of her coat. She wondered whether that were humanly possible, and tucked her arm more tightly to her body, trying discreetly to trap his hand to her waist. She was pleased to notice, once they'd navigated the busy crossing, that he left it there.

They stood by the pond, waiting for the ducks to assemble. They came in twos and threes, skimming across the water or swimming placidly, their little curled tails wagging. They reminded Elisabeth of small, eager dogs. Soon, there was quite a crowd of them. Elisabeth glanced sideways at Sam, his long body bundled into a shabby leather jacket and faded jeans, and lifted her hand, stroking the soft silk at her neck as they waited patiently for the stragglers. Sam's expression was thoughtful, the deep laughter lines around his eyes relaxed as he watched the last few ducks appear, webbed orange feet circling furiously through the dark green surface of the pond. She thought, Charles would never have waited, would have chucked lumps of sandwich in the pond while the ducks were still over on the other bank. She stared down at the birds circling expectantly, gazing up at them with round, solemn eyes.

'Is this bread?' Sam said doubtfully.

She stared at the white, spongy stuff in his hands. 'Low calorie.'

'Fit only for human consumption,' he said with disgust. He ripped off a piece, chucked it into the pond and stared at the large houses opposite. 'Mind you, I expect they're used to it, living around here.'

He fed the ducks carefully, aiming scraps at the weaker ones bobbing uncertainly on the fringes of the group. Once the sandwiches were all gone, he bent and wiped his hands on a patch of grass, then produced a small bottle of red wine from his coat pocket. 'Drink?'

She stared at it in astonishment.

'I got it on the plane, last night.'

He took another bottle from his other pocket. 'Like to get my money's worth,' he said with a grin, lighting one of the small cigars he liked to smoke.

They sat on a bench, his arm round her, drinking the wine in companionable silence. She felt the solid warmth of him against her side and breathed deeply, trying to catch the smell of him. Hearing her sigh, he shifted his arm a little to accommodate her and she thought she felt his mouth nudging her hair. Her scalp burned in patches where his lips touched it. Finally, she could bear it no longer and glanced upward only to discover that his mouth was nowhere near her head, had not touched her at all, that his chin was lifted away from her as he sat gazing at the distant horizon. Burning with humiliation, she stared fiercely at the pond.

'Are you hungry?'

She shook her head, unwilling to speak in case she broke the spell and he moved away.

'Good,' he said. 'Neither am I.'

He took her hand, stroked her fingers one by one. She felt the callus where he held his pen, looked down and saw ink mingling with the fine dark hairs that sprouted above his knuckles. Strange, she thought, how unfamiliar yet burningly intimate a hand could be.

She stared unseeingly into the distance, feeling nothing but the hot, almost painful touch of his hand on hers.

After a while, he released her hand. 'Time to go.'

'Yes,' she said, on a small regretful sigh.

They walked slowly back up the hill, talking idly about the Italian trip and a small sculpture that Elisabeth, to her joy, had sold the previous morning.

When they got back, Sam did not go to the gallery entrance as usual but instead turned aside to the door leading up to his flat. She watched him unlock the door and push it open and then followed the movement of his body as he turned to look at her.

She felt his eyes on her but dared not return his look, could scarcely breathe for the hammering of her heart which seemed to have risen to her throat, constricting it. Thoughts poured through her head in a jumble of images and texture; the burning heat of his hand on hers, the rub of his leather jacket against her neck, his face creased in concentration as he carefully distributed bread to the ducks, his long legs splayed to balance him.

The blue gloss of the door, she noticed, was chipped, peeling in places, and the door knocker tarnished to a mottled gleam. Behind it was a deep dent in the brass plate caused by a hundred, perhaps a thousand, hands rapping impatiently. Did they call for him with the same delicious fear and anticipation that thundered in her heart?

The blood rose painfully to her cheeks, settled to a dim roar in her ears and then, as if from a distance, she heard his voice. 'Elisabeth? Are you all right?'

She smiled, nodded weakly, longing for him to put out his hand, take hers and lead her up the stairs. She did not think she could do it alone, felt that her knees would buckle under her. She saw the bed, as she had seen it so many times before in her imagination, big and white with a wooden headboard and an old, faded navy and white quilt; felt it yield to their bodies as they slowly subsided onto it, clinging to each other, his mouth sweet and tender, their bodies melding like vaporous smoke.

'I said, I'm just going to get something from upstairs. Could you open up for me?'

She stared at him uncomprehendingly as he tossed a bunch of keys towards her, watched them curve through the air in a long, slow parabola and land with a jangle at her feet.

He laughed, seeing her fingers clutch helplessly at thin

air. 'Hopeless,' he said, turning and trudging up the staircase.

She bent slowly to pick them up, fumbling blindly through the tears of humiliation that stung her eyes. Her hands were trembling so violently that she could not fit the keys to the heavy locks, almost cried out in frustration and embarrassment, but at last they slid in and she turned them, fumbling with the catch and pushing the heavy door until it yielded. Hurrying to her desk, she threw down the keys, dragged off her coat and half-ran to the dank lavatory in the back of the gallery where she stood, her hands held to her burning cheeks, trembling violently. Stupid, she thought, how stupid I am even to consider that a man like that would want to take me to bed. But she had been so sure – the way he touched her constantly, his eyes following her around the gallery, his extravagant compliments. And then the scarf, that beautiful, frivolous gift, chosen specially for her. Her hands flew to her neck. She had been so sure that he felt the same way she did; so entirely certain. After a while her trembling subsided and she emerged from the lavatory and walked, still slightly shaky, to her desk.

Sam called out to her. 'Are you all right?'

She nodded, managed to get some words out. 'Too much wine on an empty stomach.'

He walked out of his office, came and stood over her desk, smiling down at her. She could not bring herself to look at him, sensed the movement of his head as he bent to look at her, heard him say, 'You are looking a bit pale. Perhaps you should go home, lie down for a while.' He looked at his watch. 'Anyway, it's time you left.'

She nodded, began to gather her things together, pulled her bag close to her body and turned gracelessly towards the door.

She heard his cheerful farewell but could only nod, willing her feeble legs to carry her until she reached the corner of the street where she subsided, trembling, onto a low wall.

As she sat there she thought, Charles, I never once thought about Charles.

When Charles got home that evening he found his wife pale and subdued. She pressed the cool glass of wine he gave her against her temples and murmured something about a headache, so he ascribed her mood to the weather which had shifted suddenly, growing oppressive as the temperature lifted but the cloud still pressed down, cloaking the city like a damp, grey flannel.

Over dinner, her spirits seemed to lift a little; she was solicitous towards him, tender almost, and that night she turned and reached out to him. He responded to her, as much out of surprise as desire, but afterwards he lay on his side, almost happy for the first time in months, comforted by the heavy familiarity of his wife's breasts pressing against his back and the rain, which had at last arrived, drumming softly against their bedroom window.

Earlier that same evening, Tom and Harry were hunched over the table they shared in their small, dusty office, waiting for the telephone to ring. They busied themselves with unnecessary tasks, trying to ignore the machine's brooding, malevolent silence. When at last it did ring, neither moved but instead sat staring at it in rapt fascination.

'You take it,' Tom said eventually.

Harry reached for it with slow deliberation, uttered a brief, formal greeting, then listened in expressionless silence.

'I see,' he said finally. A note of such controlled despair was woven through those short words that Tom knew he need not ask the outcome.

He remembered, years ago, standing on the site of a

proposed building, watching the demolition of an old fifties block of flats. How implacable they had seemed as they towered above him, soaring away into the blue sky. The engineer had turned to him, pointing out a few cubic feet of brick, and said, 'There.' The heavy metal ball had swung towards the spot in a slow, agonising arc and smashed into it. Still nothing seemed to happen other than a loud cracking of metal and brick and then, with a sound as imperceptible as a sigh of wind, the building had seemed to gather its skirts and sink in a curtsy to the earth. All that was left standing were a few jagged stalactites of brick.

'We didn't get it,' Harry said quietly.

Tom, who found himself incapable of speaking, merely nodded.

Harry said gently, 'It went to two kids, right out of college.'

Tom forced his eyes open, stared up at the ceiling. That joist needs replacing, he thought.

'It was between them and us. In the end –'

'Their first break,' Tom said, pleating the skin between his eyes with his fingers until orange spots danced in the darkness that sang inside his head.

Harry smiled, remembering. 'Yeah.'

And our final curtsy, Tom thought, lifting his head to stare round the small, shabby office; all that remained of the glittering, soaring edifice of their business. They had been together, the two of them, for twelve years, ever since finishing architectural school; had landed their first job within a month of leaving. At college they were known as the odd couple, but they were somehow complementary in their differences – Harry so blond, solid and reliable in a suit and tie, soothing clients, balancing figures, negotiating with banks while Tom, dark and angular in ragged jeans and soft, checked shirts, flipped pyrotechnics across the London skyline, dazzling and infuriating people by turn.

They weren't friends as such – never saw each other outside business hours, sensing it was dangerous to push for too much, knowing that they had little or nothing in common other than their work. Yet they were friends, Tom thought, at least if friendship means mutual trust and dependency, respect and admiration. He sighed. 'Without this contract – can we carry on?'

'No.'

'Shit.'

'With it, we'd have just about broken even. Without it –' Harry spread his hands helplessly.

'How about the Atlas job? They'll be inviting tenders within the month.'

Harry said gently, 'Tom, we don't even have the money for the materials we need to make the pitch.'

'We can borrow it.'

'We're up to here.' Harry sliced a hand across his neck. 'The interest on the overdraft is already running at –'

'So run it some more.'

'It would be suicide.'

'It's a risk, I agree –'

'And if we go down, we take the whole pile with us,' Harry said, in an unconscious rendering of Tom's earlier thoughts. He pushed a hand through the fine, blond hair that flopped perpetually over his smooth, pink face. He looked, though hovering on the cusp of forty, like an eager undergraduate. 'I'm not prepared to take that risk on the back of other people's livelihoods.'

Tom stared at him challengingly. It was what he loved about Harry, his solid integrity, although it drove him mad, most of the time.

Harry returned the stare. '*No!*'

Tom raised his hands in resignation. 'OK, OK.'

Harry dropped his eyes, reached down to his briefcase and fished out a copy of *Building* magazine, which he tossed across the desk. 'There are jobs.' He spread his hands. 'Not what we're used to perhaps, but jobs.'

'Municipal car parks, reinforced concrete, ceramic murals,' Tom said savagely.

'It's a living.'

Tom picked up the magazine, flicked through the Situations Vacant, and slumped back, defeated, in his chair. 'I'll get another copy this afternoon.'

'It's yours. I bought two.'

Tom felt his throat constrict. 'Thanks.'

They subsided into silence, each contemplating the future. Tom wondered what Bella would say and then, with increasing despair, how to tell her. Once, it would have been easy. He could see her thin, intense face burning with fury – not against him, but against the world, for its shabby, small-minded ingratitude. 'Fuck them,' she'd say, taking him in her strong, wiry arms. 'Who needs them? Not us.' It always used to be like that, the two of them against the world. And now? And now we are still two, Tom thought, but separate, divided by pain, by regret, by a distance so great he sometimes thought they could never trudge the long weary way home to each other.

He lifted his head, stared around the small shabby room he had always hated. How dear, how comforting, how familiar it seemed to him now. 'So – when shall we fold this lot up?'

'We start today. Now.'

'Now?'

Harry shrugged. 'There's not that much to do. We can divide the work, such as it is, straight down the middle and finish it off in our own time. All that's left is to give a month's notice on the rent and to hand the papers over to the solicitors for them to dissolve the company. If we do it before the end of the month, that leaves us a month paid up front in which to clear out. We're still solvent – just. It's not as if we have to get the receivers in.' He tried a grin. 'No big deal.'

Tom smiled bleakly. 'No,' he said, 'no big deal.'

They glanced quickly away from each other, contemplating the practice they had spent fifteen years building up (or knocking down, Tom thought wryly), wondering how it could go like this, simply sliding away into a damp, grey evening in Kentish Town.

Tom stared at the awards that hung on the wall, thought of the glass block and steel studio in Euston that they had built and designed, that had employed sixty people and now housed an advertising agency. He heard the distant crack of thunder, looked up. The dusty skylight was spattered with raindrops; at first just a few and then a hundred, like wet pennies in the dust, and then thousand upon thousand.

'At least the heavens weep,' he said.

Harry blinked rapidly, then darted forward suddenly, enveloping Tom's hand in a strong grip. He held onto it like a drowning man, all the while pumping it furiously, pretending to be merely observing the masculine convention of affection; the shaking of hands. How warm it feels, Tom thought, gripping the vibrant, living flesh; how solid and reassuring.

'It's been –' Harry said unsteadily, indicating with his other hand the vast potential of the universe.

'It has,' Tom agreed.

'We'll be back.'

'We will,' said Tom, not wanting to let go of the hand.

Neither of them believed it.

Harry released his hand.

'Now let's go out and get slaughtered.'

Tom heard a muttered curse, the thump of feet on stairs, the sound of a door being angrily wrenched open. A light dazzled his eyes. He looked up, blinking. Bella stood in the doorway, her finger still pressed against the light switch. Her face, pale and smudgy with sleep, loomed over him, haloed by a wild frizz of hair. She wore a short, grey T-shirt spattered with stains. He noticed, with curious detachment, that the skin of her thighs was softened, like crepe.

'Where the fuck have you been?'

He opened his mouth to speak, could not find the words and dropped his head.

Bella dashed over to him, dug her fingers into his shoulder, shook him. 'I said, where the fuck have you been?'

He looked up. 'Out. Getting drunk.'

'Who with?'

'With Harry.'

'With Harry? *Harry*, of all people. You expect me to believe that?'

'Yes.'

'Well, forgive me if I don't.'

'Bella, please, I –'

'Come on, Tom. At least do me the courtesy of trying a little harder. When have you ever gone out and got drunk with Harry?'

Tom said nothing.

She wheeled on him, swooping down, her mouth an ugly, distorted oval pressing down towards him. 'You've been with *her*, haven't you?'

Tom stared at her uncomprehendingly. 'With who?'

'With who? With who, he says. With *Amy*, you bastard.'

'I haven't seen Amy in years. Not since –'

'Since you last fucked her?'

He nodded. 'Not since then,' he said quietly.

'Oh God,' she said. 'Oh *God*, then it's someone else.'

'No, it's not. Bella, listen, please. Something's happened. That contract we were holding out for – we lost it.'

'I don't want to know. I don't want to hear what's

happened to you, you weak, spineless bastard. What about what's happened to me? What about Ben? What about the pain you've caused us?'

He closed his eyes.

'Look at you. You're pathetic. One little thing goes wrong and you crawl off to some woman and get her to massage your ego together with your cock. That's what happened last time, isn't it, when the practice started to go downhill? That's when it all started.'

He looked away. He'd known, oh, of course he'd known, how much she'd minded. But he did not understand why that meaningless encounter should fester, like gangrene, inside her. At least, it seemed to him to be meaningless, had felt that way almost before it began. He had met Amy at a party, at the Architectural Association; had noticed her straight away, her bright gold head bobbing among the crowd, her strong white throat tilted back in permanent laughter. She looked so young, so alive and he longed to take some of that vitality, to press his mouth to her throat and drink deep of it. He felt old suddenly; his bones ached and his eyes felt permanently gritty, no matter how much he slept. That month he and Harry had lost two major contracts, jobs they had been certain of but which had gone to another company, a solid, cautious choice made by solid, cautious men who had murmured admiringly over his work but had, in the end, rejected it as being too ambitious. Tom, still fuelled with the arrogance of early success, had lost his temper, had to be bundled from the room by a beseeching Harry, gripping his arm and thrusting him from the room as he tried, over his shoulder, to smooth things over. After that, word had gone round. Tom Sutherland was difficult and these were difficult times; the late eighties, economically precarious, creatively limited – times made for cautious men.

He was just leaving the party when Amy came over to

him, began talking about his work, how much she admired it, her eyes bright, admiring, her breasts high and firm. So he had fucked her. Just a few times, just to put his mouth to her firm body as if by mere contact he could absorb the bright, gilded youth of her. It hadn't worked, of course. Instead, when he left her, he felt old, shabby, depleted. He finished the affair almost before it had begun. Amy's anger had taken him by surprise. Her certainty too, a pure crystal stream that flowed unstoppably from her mouth, on the telephone, outside his office and finally, fatally, at his house. After she had left, he had tried to explain to Bella. It happened, he said. And it had. It had simply happened. And then – it was over. Except, he thought, that these things are never over.

Bella folded her arms, stared down at him. 'When did you find out about the contract?' Her voice was cold, distant.

He closed his eyes. He knew the danger signs. 'This afternoon.'

'So you went after the nearest bit of skirt. Who is she?'

'Bella, it's not like that.'

'Yes, it is,' she screamed. 'Yes, it fucking well is.'

He said nothing. There was nothing to be said when Bella was in one of her rages. Best to leave her to calm down. He was tired, much too tired and drunk to explain.

'And I get the blame. Oh, yes I do. I know the way your mind works. You think, if I was gentler, more sympathetic, you could bring your troubles home to dear little wifey and have her make cocoa and sit on your cock and tell you you're wonderful. Then everything would be all right. And because I won't do that, won't say, there, there, diddums, it will be all right, you're forced to go somewhere else. Then, somehow, it becomes my fault you fuck other women.'

He kept his eyes shut. She used to, he thought. She used to take me in her arms. When had it become so difficult?

'You make me sick. Do you hear me? You disgust me.'

His chin sunk to his chest. He was tired. So tired. 'Yes,' he whispered.

'You're pathetic!' she screamed.

Tom's head drooped lower, until he was almost doubled. She stared at him furiously and then the fight seemed to leave her and she stood in the middle of the room, arms swinging helplessly by her side. 'I'm going to bed,' she said quietly. 'Alone.'

She left the kitchen. He could hear the slow trudge of her footsteps going up the stairs to their room.

Clutching his overcoat around him, Tom stumbled through to the sitting-room, collapsed on the hard, narrow sofa and fell into an exhausted, dreamless sleep.

Seventeen

He had called her beautiful. *Beautiful.* Elisabeth hugged the word to her. It had all been a misunderstanding, a silly, meaningless misunderstanding. She'd seen that much, when she went into the gallery the next morning. He'd been so solicitous, worried about her. He'd even offered to make the coffee himself. They'd sat, sipping at the steaming liquid, which tasted disgusting, although she'd savoured every bitter drop. He'd never been able to master instant coffee, ladled far too much into the mugs, then complained furiously when it tasted foul.

'Don't drink it,' he said, grimacing at the taste, reaching out to take the mug from her. But she held onto it, pressed it protectively against her chest, feeling the steaming warmth spread through her breasts, curl around her heart.

'You looked so pale yesterday,' he said. 'I was worried about you all night.'

All night.

She'd dressed carefully that morning: a new silk blouse in a blue that matched her eyes and a pair of beautifully cut black wool crepe trousers that she'd found in the second-hand designer shop on the hill. They were Italian, made in Rome. 'Roma' said the label. The scarf was at her neck, lifted carefully from her underwear drawer where she had hidden it from Charles the night before. It had given her courage, that smooth, exotic armour, to face him and she had gone, almost gladly, to work.

She thought, as she stretched her legs out next to his in the tiny office, felt the ripple of soft wool against her thighs, the acrid smokiness of coffee in her mouth, that she could imagine the two of them together in Rome, walking hand in hand through that rich, voluptuous city. He'd lead her through the galleries, take her silently through the ancient buildings, his lips pressed to her cheek as he recounted the story of each painting, filling her ears with meaning, her eyes with colour.

After drinking their coffee, they settled down together to sort the post. She typed up a couple of letters that needed doing urgently and then they went out to lunch, as usual, laughing and talking as they wound up through the high street and fell into the tiny, dim restaurant to sit at their usual table in the corner ('Our table' he called it) to eat peppers, rich and slippery with oil, and drink heady red wine.

No reduced calorie sandwiches for her for lunch today, nor tomorrow, nor ever again; not when she could spend the time with him, eating sweet, rich food, drinking strong dark wine. She'd save those poor mournful crusts for other days, when he was not with her; would eat a slimming dinner, pick delicately through her food, refusing this and that because she could not share it with him, because by refusing everything that was special to him, she could hold the memory of him inside her.

He put his arm around her as they walked back down the hill to the gallery, matching his long stride to hers as they sauntered, like lovers, in the sunshine. She didn't care what people thought, cared only that he was here, with her. What business of others was it anyway? Who were they to judge the sweet, innocent pleasure they took in each other?

And if the throbbing between her legs continued, then it bothered her no longer; she felt content to feel that sweet pulse, to while away the languorous days. All that mattered, after the terrible, stumbling journey home yesterday (was it really only yesterday?) when she had thought she had lost him for ever, had thought that she must give up the job, was that he was here.

It was only when she got home the night before that it dawned on her that perhaps Sam hadn't noticed her confusion, had really believed her when she said that she had a headache from too much wine. And of course, she thought, as she prepared for bed, conscious of Charles downstairs, head bent over those interminable papers, a man like Sam would never expect her to make love with him so soon, had known that it was too early for them; would want to wait until the yearning that affected them both dissolved in the sweet melting of their bodies as well as their souls. She'd felt reprieved, cleansed somehow as she lay in bed in her best silk nightie which Charles had bought her in Paris, and which she had worn as a sort of celebration of her and Sam. She'd wanted to share her pleasure, had turned to Charles, innocent in her happiness, had felt a sort of dull astonishment and then a slight, sinking sense of betrayal when he had returned her embrace so eagerly.

Afterwards, she had felt wretched, had got up to make herself a cup of camomile tea. It was only when she was drinking tea, sitting under the harsh neon light in the kitchen, that she found the source of her wretchedness; the sense of betrayal she felt was for Sam, not Charles. And why, she wondered, are kitchens at night the loneliest places in the world?

The next afternoon, she blew Sam a kiss as she left the gallery, felt the embrace of his smile as she floated up the street and turned left down the hill where she stopped to linger longingly outside the window of the deli. She forgot her promise to diet, wanted to buy sharp cheese and velvety pears, melt sweet tomatoes and peppery basil in a fragrant sauce over thin, slippery spinach noodles. She walked into the shop where she hovered over the brimming counters, gloating over the food and the prospect of supper that night, content to share with Charles her deep, voluptuous pleasure in life. How sweet it is, she thought, accepting a morsel of Dolcelatte from the young man behind the counter.

When she got home, she laid out the pears and cheeses on a plate, arranged purple figs, their skin the colour of bruises against a white dish, heaped tomatoes in a gleaming pyramid, topped with a bunch of green basil, then wandered restlessly through the rooms, waiting for Charles to come home. She looked at her watch. Four o'clock. How early it was; how slowly the time seemed to go when she was not with Sam. In the gallery the minutes scurried past, stealing each precious moment from her.

She stepped out into the garden, thinking that she should at least get some weeding done. She yanked out a piece of couch grass, then tidied up a rose, crushing the velvety petals absently in her hand. A radio was playing in a neighbouring garden, the song 'Killing Me Softly' floated to her on the still summer air; a song, Charles said, his face heavy with distaste, that was played at least every minute in every country around the world. They were sitting in Florence airport at the time, delayed by three hours. 'Imagine,' he said, 'from Dakar to Bangladesh, from Ghana to the Galapagos, this bloody stupid song is played every bloody minute of every day.' She had turned her face from him, busying herself with unpacking and repacking an already orderly overnight bag. It was her favourite song. Philistine, she thought, furiously stuffing a dog-eared paperback that still smelt faintly of swimming pool chlorine and sun lotion back into the bag, what does he know about anything? She remembered the moment quite clearly, the book in her hand, the floor sticky with spilled beer under her feet, the song playing tinnily on the airport's intercom system and Charles's face, heavy with anger; remembered thinking, with a horrible blinding clarity, that she and Charles had nothing in common. It had seemed to last for ever, that moment, until the intercom crackled with static and a voice announced that the flight to London was now ready to leave and she had jerked back into her life, moving with a stiff weariness until, at last, they had reached home and the soothing familiarities of the days had rolled the thought aside until she had forgotten it entirely. Until now.

She lay down on the grass in her new silk shirt and trousers and listened to the song, her face pressed against the sharp green shoots, the damp, warm, mysterious scent of the earth in her nostrils. Sam, she thought, pressing her body down into the cool, damp earth; conscious of absurdity but revelling in it; her arms and legs flung wide, spread like a star across the green and pleasant lawn of her manicured garden.

'Elisabeth?'

She froze, raised her head carefully and looked around.

'Elisabeth, are you all right?'

She located the voice, saw her neighbour peering curiously over the fence and scrambled quickly to her feet.

'Audrey!' she said, with a light, breathless laugh. 'I was just –' she waved a vague hand in the direction of the lawn – 'just checking for weeds.'

'I'd get Joe to do that if I was you,' Audrey said, referring to the gardener they shared. After the first curious glance, her expression had reverted to the usual blank, closed gaze of the habitual city-dweller. 'Talking of which, I wanted to warn you that we're having a bit of light building work done next week.' She raised a hand. 'Nothing major, of course, so the noise shouldn't be too tiresome but there will be a little disruption.'

'So there I was,' Elisabeth told Charles over supper, 'lying on the lawn like a stranded starfish when I heard this voice calling my name and I looked up and saw Audrey, of all people, staring at me in that way she has, you know, that benign but slightly disapproving look. Well, you can imagine how I felt.'

Charles smiled vaguely.

'She probably thinks I've picked up some ghastly New Age meditation or something,' Elisabeth said, laughing. 'Next thing we know, they'll be talking all up and down the street, how Charles and Elisabeth have got mysticism or something.'

Charles gave her a perplexed glance. 'But what exactly were you doing with your face pressed into the back lawn?'

Her smile faded. 'Oh, just – Nothing, really. I was just doing nothing.'

He nodded, pushed his plate away.

'Don't you like it?' she asked, seeing the food uneaten on his plate.

He frowned. 'Oh, it's fine. Not your usual pasta sauce, though. Now, if you'll forgive me, I really must go and get on with reading some case papers for tomorrow.'

'But pudding, darling, I bought some special cheese and pears –'

'Not for me, thanks,' he said, dropping a perfunctory kiss on the top of her head. 'I'll have some coffee later.'

She heard his study door closing but remained sitting at the table where he had left her, staring out over the darkening garden and watching the moths rise and fall in the dim light and the pale gleam of the white foxgloves bending gently in the night air, feeling sharply and profoundly misunderstood.

200

Eighteen

Lily lay on her bed, idly watching television. She had finally bought herself one out of her pay packet; she reckoned she deserved it. Things weren't going as well as she had hoped with Charles; she was growing bored of the sweetly patient face she put on, with her make-up, every morning. Still, she sensed that any sharp movement would make him retreat, back into the burrow he'd built with Elisabeth. She sighed slightly. He was a man dug well into his life. Alex, though, was shaping up nicely, useful for dangling in front of Charles, his limbs twitching painfully in response to every tiny movement of the strings.

A smile glimmered briefly on Lily's pale face. Stretching restlessly, she glanced at the green leather alarm clock that stood on the table by her bed. Nearly time to go. Elisabeth had invited her for supper. She sighed. More boring chat, more breathless confidences about Sam. Sam this, Sam that; she was like a kid, waiting for Christmas. Dozy cow. Still, it kept her occupied and you never knew when a thing like that would come in useful.

Yawning, Lily swung her bare feet onto the floor, prowled over to the window and twitched the curtain aside. The street was empty, quiet save for the fizz of the yellow, electric street lights. No Jim, then. A smile glowed briefly on her face. Silly sod, hanging around out there like that. Still, she liked the idea that he was keeping an eye on her, was looking out for her, although Mrs Flower said he hadn't been by lately. She bit her lip thoughtfully. Perhaps she should send him a card, just to show she was thinking of him, keep him interested. There was no knowing how long a man would hang around waiting, even Jim. 'There's love, for you,' was what her mum said, although she wasn't sure, thought it was more like habit, getting used to having a person around. Anyway, even if Jim did piss off, there'd always be somebody else.

Perhaps she should pop home for the day, give her mum a kiss, drop by and see Jim, wind him up a bit so she could watch him running round her in circles, like one of those clockwork toys she'd had as a kid. Then again, maybe not. He'd hang around for a bit longer yet and she wasn't done here; not by a long way. She wasn't ready to settle; not till she'd had some fun.

Bella looked terrible, Elisabeth thought, watching her unwind a silk scarf from her neck, pull it to her lap and pleat and unpleat it with restless fingers.

'You OK?' Elisabeth said, putting a glass of wine in front of her.

Bella smiled briefly. 'Fine,' she said, 'I'm fine,' but a tightness around her mouth, a pulse thrumming gently but visibly in the left temple, told Elisabeth that nothing was fine with Bella.

'Hard week?' she said sympathetically.

'No more than usual. Tom's being –' She flashed a glance at Elisabeth, looked away. 'Well, he's being Tom,' she said harshly, 'so I don't know why I expect him to be otherwise and Ben's gearing up for A-levels.'

'Can it be so soon?' Elisabeth said on a sigh, remembering Ben's chubby figure lurching at Bella's side, arms raised above his head as if imaginary hands still steadied him. And Bella's face, the painful, furious love that blazed across it whenever she looked at her son. Elisabeth glanced up, half-expecting to see it there now, noticed with a dull shock the lines etched deep on Bella's thin face, the restless fingers, still fiddling with the silky material in her lap.

Noticing the look, Bella stared down at her fingers as if willing them to stop, then pushed the scarf away with a quick, impatient gesture and pulled out a pack of cigarettes from her bag.

'Bella –' Elisabeth said in a pained tone.

Bella flashed her a guilty smile, the lighter's flame throwing her thin, bony face into shadow. 'What?'

'It's been two years –'

'It's my body,' Bella said, inhaling sharply.

'Does Tom know?'

'As a matter of fact, Tom doesn't give a fuck,' she said, flicking ash dismissively, 'and I don't give a fuck what he thinks, since you ask.'

'Oh dear,' Elisabeth murmured, turning away and occupying herself with preparations for supper.

Bella grimaced. 'Sorry,' she said, after a while, 'like I said, things aren't great at home at the moment.'

'Anything I can do?' Elisabeth said, her face still averted. The last thing she wanted to hear about was Bella's and Tom's sad, spiny marriage. She wanted no unpleasantness, wanted only to hug the image of Sam to her; the thought of kind, generous, encompassing Sam. A smile hovered at her lips. Sometimes she felt so full of him it was as if she could barely contain it, felt that if she opened her mouth, bubbles of happiness would emerge and lift her with them until she was floating, far away, off into the wild blue future.

'No,' Bella said heavily. Then after a pause she added, 'Thank you.'

'Is he coming later?'

'Who knows?' Bella replied, but in the undercurrent of her voice the careful listener would have heard the dragging pull of miserable desperation. Who knew whether he would come or whether he would go to *her*, this new woman of his, diving into her welcoming body, into the easy comfort of strangeness. How easy it is, Bella thought, the kindness of strangers. Easy to be kind when there is no shared history, none of the sharp, jagged edges of intimacy and everything is fresh, bright and new. But Elisabeth was not, that evening, a careful listener, was too deafened by her own happiness to hear the cry from the underworld.

'Well, we'll have a lovely evening,' she said, and the trite indifference of that phrase pierced Bella's misery and she looked with greater attention at her friend, noticed for the first time the blush that permanently suffused her cheeks, the sparkle in her eyes and the small, secret smile that tugged incessantly at her mouth.

'You're looking well,' she said, a faint note of disapproval threading through her voice. 'Happy,' she said, trying to edge the irritation out of her voice.

'Yes,' Elisabeth said, bubbles of contentment floating to the surface of her voice, 'I feel very well.' She turned, stared meaningfully at Bella. 'In fact, I've never felt better.'

Bella smiled bleakly. 'Good,' she said.

Elisabeth's happiness could be contained no longer. She must share it. 'I've met someone.'

Her eyes, suffused with radiance, were blind to her friend's startled expression. 'Met someone?' Bella repeated slowly.

'Sam Howard,' she said, lingering over the name. Her expression was shy, startled, too rapt with awe to notice Bella, shifting uncomfortably in her chair.

'The man you work with?'

Elisabeth glanced away to hide the smile that kept tugging at her mouth. 'Yes, him. He's – he's an extraordinary man.'

'And does Charles think he's extraordinary too?'

Elisabeth blinked, startled by the hostility in Bella's voice. 'Why, I don't believe he's ever met him.'

'How *could* you?' Bella exclaimed.

And Elisabeth, who had been expecting her friend to

share her happiness, who was in that state of ecstasy that sees no reason and hears no arguments, because she had, truly, never felt that way before and was thus defenceless against its onslaught, stared at Bella in astonishment. 'I don't know what you mean,' she stammered, and an ugly flush swept up from her neck – not the faint pink of sexual excitement but the mottled red of humiliation.

'You're telling me that you're sexually obsessed with a man who's not your husband and you don't know what I mean?'

Elisabeth looked mutinous. 'It's not like that.'

'Not yet, it's not.'

And Elisabeth, who had not thought of the consequences, had never for a moment considered the future but only the here and now of her undiluted happiness, exclaimed, 'But I'm so happy!'

'Oh, you're happy, are you?' Bella said, throwing her head back with a laugh. 'Well, that's all right then, because we all know that the modern gospel of personal happiness is the only true defence for inflicting misery on those who love you most and fuck the consequences,' she said, snatching up her glass and draining it.

Elisabeth shook her head. 'No, I –' she said helplessly. 'I hadn't thought of it as a defence, not like that. Sam, well – it just happened. It wasn't conscious, wasn't aimed at Charles, if that's what you mean.' She turned away, started moving dishes to and fro across the counter in futile repetition.

'These things don't just happen. We allow them to happen. Or not, as the case may be,' Bella said in a defeated voice.

Elisabeth turned to her, her hands fluttering helplessly. 'We haven't –'

'Then don't,' Bella said shortly.

Elisabeth nodded, turned away in silence and began chopping potatoes vigorously.

'I'm sorry,' Bella said after a while, 'I get rather touchy around the subject of adultery.'

Elisabeth nodded mutely.

Bella sighed distantly, lit another cigarette. 'Let's forget it, shall we? Is there any more wine?'

Elisabeth moved across the kitchen and filled her glass, her eyes averted, her body slightly turned away in distaste; though her distaste was not born out of compunction or regret but out of the sharing of her secret with Bella. How could she possibly understand, she thought, when she reduces everything to the small, sordid little affairs her own husband has? And why does he have them, what drives him to other women's arms? Why, because she is so harsh with him, so unkind. What Sam and I have together is different, is warm and wonderful, gloriously important. What does she know of happiness, what does she understand about the way I feel? Nothing, she thought, furiously chopping carrots, slamming her knife through the fibrous orange cores. She understands nothing.

The doorbell rang.

Elisabeth, wearing a faintly pained expression, went to answer it. It was Lily.

'All right?' she said, offering up her face up for a kiss, a practice that she thought daft but had grown used to with Elisabeth.

'Fine,' Elisabeth said. 'Why don't you go through to the kitchen? Bella's in there having a drink. I just want to pop upstairs and get something.' She hesitated, dropped her voice. 'And tread a bit carefully, she's in one of her moods tonight. Something to do with Tom, I imagine.'

Lily nodded, sauntered off in the direction of the kitchen.

'All right?' she said, seeing Bella.

'I didn't know you were coming,' Bella said with a sharp, unpleasant smile.

'Sorry, I'm sure. And I'm fine since you ask,' Lily said, returning the expression. 'You?'

Bella dropped her eyes, lit another cigarette. 'Fine.'

Lily sat down, poured herself a glass of wine. 'Can I have one of them?' she asked, reaching out a hand towards the cigarette packet.

Bella looked at her. 'I didn't know you smoked.'

'Didn't you?' Lily said indifferently, lighting a cigarette.

'Mind you, I expect there's quite a lot we don't know about you.'

'Well, you never know what you're going to get when you pick something out of the small ads, do you?' Lily laughed, settling back comfortably in her chair.

'No, I suppose you don't,' Bella said, examining her contemptuously. 'One can end up with either damaged goods or a bargain. Then again, one never knows what one's bringing into the house, moth or woodworm or some other such nasty infestation.'

Lily's eyes flicked sideways to Bella. 'Tom been messing you around, has he?'

'How bloody dare you!' Bella exclaimed, blushing furiously at the truth.

'Bull's-eye,' Lily murmured, inhaling luxuriously.

Bella stubbed out her own cigarette violently. 'I know what you're after,' she said, banging the stub down in emphasis, 'so don't think I don't. Elisabeth may be blinded by your Little Miss Innocent act, but I'm not.'

'Sorry?'

'Charles,' Bella said angrily, 'you're after Charles.'

Lily sighed. 'What would I be wanting with a bloke like that?'

'I've seen the way he looks at you.'

'And have you seen the way Elisabeth looks at him?' Lily asked, watching her calmly.

'I don't know what you mean.'

'Like he was a piece of the furniture or something. Not

surprising the poor bloke gets excited when someone's a bit nice to him.'

'That depends how nice.'

'Not the sort of nice you mean.'

'You got yourself a job in his office –'

'Elisabeth got me a job in his office. I was skint. I'm grateful.'

'I'll bet you are.'

Elisabeth walked into the kitchen. 'Sorry I was so long. Oh, good, I'm glad you got yourself a drink, Lily. Have you two been having a chat –'

Lily swivelled in her chair, looked up at Elisabeth. 'Sort of. Bella here thinks I'm after your Charles.'

Elisabeth stared at Lily, let out a shrill, uncertain laugh.

Bella shifted uncomfortably in her chair. 'I didn't say –'

'Yes, you did,' Lily said, watching her impassively. 'You said I'd blagged my way into this house and Charles's office so I could get my grubby little mitts on Elisabeth's husband.'

'Bella, really I do think that perhaps –' Elisabeth said wearily.

'Perhaps I should keep my mouth shut about this and everything else,' Bella said, getting to her feet. 'I'm sure you're right, it's really none of my business.' She moved across the kitchen, dropped a kiss on Elisabeth's startled face. 'I really shouldn't have come tonight. I'm not fit company for anyone.' She walked to the door, turned and gave Elisabeth a brief, strained smile. 'Sorry.' With that she walked out of the door.

'Bella?' Elisabeth called, hurrying after her, but the only sound was the banging of the front door. 'Oh dear,' she said, coming back into the kitchen, 'she's not usually like this.' She cast a quick, anxious glance at Lily, wondering if she could trust her, then said placatingly, 'It's just that something dreadful must have happened between her and

Tom. I mean, she's a bit volatile, apt to go off in a rage sometimes but she's a nice woman really –'

Lily stood up. 'Go on, sit down. You look all upset. I'll get you a glass of wine. No, sit. I'll do it. You look done in.'

'Thank you,' Elisabeth said, accepting the glass with a trembling hand. She drank half of it down, then wiped a hand across her eyes. 'About what she said about you and Charles – I'm sorry to put you through all that. She didn't mean it. I don't know if you're aware but years ago, Tom had an affair with somebody and ever since –'

Lily's opaque eyes flickered. 'Poor thing,' she said softly.

'I know,' Elisabeth murmured. 'Well, now it means that she's so sensitive about Tom that she's apt to think the worst about everyone, which is probably why she went off the deep end with you. When she found out about Tom –' She sighed. 'Well, the girl was only twenty or something, half Bella's age, so she sometimes gets a bit –'

'Don't matter a bit,' Lily assured her. 'I'm just sorry if it was me who made her go.' She stared at Elisabeth with dark, sorrowful eyes. 'Should have been me that went, not her.'

'No, no,' Elisabeth exclaimed, waving her hand as if shooing the thought away.

'Stands to reason,' Lily said. 'She's one of your oldest friends and well, I'm just –'

'You're our friend too,' Elisabeth said firmly, 'and if Bella chooses to behave –' She broke off. 'Anyway, I'm sorry about all that. Let's have another glass of wine and talk about something more cheerful while we wait for the others to get here.'

Lily smiled and filled Elizabeth's glass. 'How's Sam then? Still gorgeous, is he?'

Nineteen

It took Tom and Harry a week to clear their work and sort through their papers, a week of meetings with solicitors and accountants, dealing with the painful, difficult business of failed lives. Then, with sudden, awful finality, all that was left to do was to pack their possessions into cardboard boxes and clear out the office. They worked for the most part in silence. Sometimes, Tom was tempted to hold something up and say, 'Remember this?' But he didn't. It was too painful.

By Thursday they were done, sitting on packing cartons waiting for mini-cabs to take them and their stuff back to their respective homes.

'If there's ever anything –' Harry began. 'You know. Just pick up the phone.'

'You too,' Tom said, although they both knew they wouldn't.

He looked at Harry's guileless pink face, his floppy schoolboy's hair and crisp, ironed white shirt and felt a sudden, terrifying sense of panic, as if the ground had shifted to quicksand beneath his feet. He shifted uncomfortably, got up and paced restlessly around the room. Harry sat perfectly still, staring at the shabby carpet.

'Have you sent off any applications?' Tom asked.

'A couple.'

'Me too.'

Harry smiled awkwardly. 'Probably for the same jobs.'

'Yes. Wouldn't that be funny?'

'Hilarious.'

They glanced quickly away from each other, unsmiling.

When the mini-cabs arrived, they were both relieved to be distracted by loading up the cars, issuing orders, manoeuvring boxes into awkward corners until, suddenly, it was done and they stood facing each other on the pavement, shuffling awkwardly. Harry grabbed Tom, hugged him in a solid embrace. 'You take care,' he whispered.

Tom, who could not speak, merely nodded.

They climbed wordlessly into their separate cars and sat stiffly, staring straight ahead until the cars moved slowly away, going in opposite directions from each other. It was only then that Tom screwed himself round in his seat and watched the back of Harry's golden head, shining like a beacon in the gloom of the battered car, until it had quite disappeared.

When Tom got home, he unloaded the boxes into the narrow hallway and went to make a cup of tea, deciding that he would unpack later, when he had the heart. Although when that would be, he didn't know. It was four o'clock. He could hear a lawnmower buzzing in the next street and a dog barking but otherwise, nothing. He sat for an hour, his mug of tea cooling in front of him. After a while, he felt something warm trickling down his face and putting his hand up, discovered that he was crying.

The front door banged and he heard Bella's voice exclaiming, 'Christ, what's all this?'

He dragged his shirtsleeve across his eyes, fixed a smile on his face and looked up to find her poised in the doorway. She took in his presence and then, without a word, walked slowly across the room and filled the kettle. When it was filled and switched on, she turned to face him, her back against the sink, arms crossed.

'What are you doing here?' she said.

He shrugged. 'May as well ask you the same question.'

'It's Thursday, remember. Half day at college.'

He nodded. He didn't remember, wasn't even sure if he'd ever known.

With a sharp sigh she turned back to the sink, began noisily to wash up the breakfast mugs and plates, her back eloquent with displeasure. He watched her, aware that her anger was directed at him and wondering what it was that he had done to cause it when she banged down a plate with an extra flourish and he understood that, of course, he should have done the washing up himself, not sat around doing nothing, whiling away this pleasant, sunny afternoon.

He looked outside. Was the sky really blue? Yes, a glorious, mocking blue, the sun shining cheerfully through the smeared glass of the windows. Could it be June already, he wondered, feeling time swirl giddily beneath his feet. He looked down, saw the garish lozenge-patterned lino pulsing under his shoes, felt a sickening, vertiginous tilt. June, he thought, his mind grappling for facts, for everyday things to anchor him back to the world. Yes, of course. Ben's exams, Bella tense with the effort of trying to get everything done before the end of the academic year. And him? What about him? He heard Bella's voice, coming at him from a long way away, and looked up sharply.

She was frowning, her face hostile with impatience. 'I said – do you want tea?'

They had not spoken much since the most recent quarrel, other than the necessary exchange of information about arrangements; meals and the like. He remembered, with a vague, disconnected sense of disbelief, that she knew nothing of today's events or those of the past week and the final dismantling of the practice.

'Yes, please.'

She poked the tea bags with a spoon, slopped them onto an empty saucer that stood by the kettle and banged a mug on the table in front of him. She chose a chair at the opposite end of the table, as far away from him as it was possible to get and still be in the same room. They sat in silence, avoiding each other's eyes.

Tom kept clearing his throat, wanting to tell her about closing down the practice, about the painful horror of the week, the despair of being parted from Harry – his round, pink face and his calm, sweet nature. Somehow he thought they would never be separated, had not envisaged a time without him. And because he had thought it could not happen, he did not know how to cope now that it had; felt rudderless, adrift in an infinite, changeless horizon. Christ, how he'd miss him. But somehow, he found he could tell her none of this.

After a while she said, 'What are those boxes in the hallway?'

He shrugged. 'Just some stuff.'

'Thinking of moving out?'

He looked over at her. 'Yes.'

It had not, until that moment, occurred to him that he was leaving, but now that he had said it, he could see it was inevitable. The room swirled, objects blurring in a spin of colour. Through it he saw that Bella's mug of tea was halfway to her mouth. She blinked and put it down carefully on the table. 'Sorry?'

He shook his head, trying to dislodge the dizziness. 'Yes, I am thinking of moving out.' His voice sounded strange, disembodied.

She looked bewildered. 'And you've packed already?'

Tom frowned, trying to remember. 'Oh, that. That's the stuff from the office.'

'Stuff? Office?' she repeated slowly. 'What do you mean?'

'We've closed down the business.'

'You've done what?'

'It happened a week ago, after we lost the contract.'

'Last week?' she said, staring at him. Then she closed

her eyes and put her hands to her face. 'Oh, my God,' she said, in a low voice. 'The contract. That's why you and Harry were out getting drunk –'

'Yes.'

She stared at him through the slits in her fingers. 'I'm sorry,' she said, dropping her hands. 'Tom, I'm so terribly sorry.'

'Yes.'

'That's what you were trying to tell me when I –'

'Yes.' He found it was all he could manage; he was frightened that if he opened his mouth, the tears would start and never stop. His face would dissolve in water.

He got heavily to his feet. 'I'm going now.'

She nodded. As he moved to walk past her she said, 'What would it take to make you stay?'

'I just need –' He stared distractedly at the walls of the poky little room, felt the hard surfaces shift, move towards him, trapping him between them. His voice caught in his throat. 'Some kindness, I suppose.' He turned and walked away.

She leaned forward, caught him by the hand. 'Am I unkind?'

He gazed at her tenderly. 'No, not unkind. Unyielding.'

She hung her head, hunched her shoulders as if in defence against the world. He stared at the frizzy tufts of curls, remembering his first sight of her in the painting studio at college, furiously slapping oil on canvas, defiant and graceless, somehow splendid in her fierce isolation. And later, when they left college and got married, the fight she put up trying to sell her work and coming against one closed door after another. Then, the gradual slide into teaching, first one day a week and then two (but still only part-time) and then the final step into the institutionalised world of paperwork and academic meetings. It was the way so many talented painters seemed to end up, handing their talent over to a new generation, hanging on to their own work in snatched evenings and occasional weekends.

And then those, too, had gone, abandoned in despair when his business started to go badly and they'd had to sell up the house and move. He thought, everything she held most dear had seemed to disappear together with that house: her garden, her painting, her fierce, protective love of space. He remembered when they were living in the old house, how he had been in the kitchen and had caught sight of her through the window, standing in the garden one blue, peerless afternoon; a battered straw hat clamped over her frizzy curls, a scowl of concentration on her face, a smear of paint across her forehead where she had wiped her hand. The paintings she did of the garden she loved so much had hung throughout the house. They were not insipid pastels of flowers, or delicate water-colours, but huge, blazing canvases of colour: chrome, vermilion, violet and livid orange. When they moved, she had packed them all away and refused to get them out again. As far as he knew, they were up in the loft, imprisoned in their dark, splintered wood packing cases.

As he had watched her painting out in the garden, he had felt that there was something glorious, even endearing in her isolation, the blazing battle she was engaged in with life. And now the battle seemed lost; only bitterness remained in the staccato rounds of sniper fire that made up the daily round. He looked down at her bent head and knew that he could not cope with her, could not face her any more.

'I feel defeated, vanquished,' he said.

She whispered, 'I'm sorry.'

Her face, blank with pain, looked like a child's. He could not bear the look in her eyes.

'Will you ever come back?'

He was so startled, his limbs jerked involuntarily, as if an electric current surged through them. He had expected rage, anger, china thrown at his head. He had expected to fight her. 'I don't know. Perhaps.'

She dropped her head again, crossed her arms protectively across her breasts, gazed at the lurid patterned lino that they had not had the money to replace. He thought, suddenly, how it must hurt her every day, that ghastly clash of colour.

He leaned forward, dropped a kiss on the top of her head. 'Goodbye.'

She did not move.

'Been out four or five times, judging by the messages,' Mrs Flower said. 'And I found a note for his secretary in the wastepaper bin, asking that roses be sent to Daisy. Said to say,' her voice assumed a high, girlish note, 'Sorry darling. Something's come up at work. Know you'll understand. Love Alex.' Her voice reverted to its usual tone but was sharpened with indignation. 'That's the third bunch in as many weeks. She's a bit fed up, poor dear. Rotten shame, that's what I say.'

'Thank you, Mrs Flower,' Celia said, 'that's most helpful.'

'Think I might know this Lily, as a matter of fact.'

A faint note of disbelief entered Celia's voice. 'You do?'

'From her voice she sounds like a Lily I got living here. Young thing, looks like butter wouldn't melt. Claims to be a friend of some people called Charles and Elisabeth, if that's any help.'

There was silence.

'You still there, Mrs Carlton?'

'Indeed I am.'

'Don't mind me mentioning it, do you? Thought it was as well to say.'

'Yes. Yes thank you, Mrs Flower.'

'Like me to keep an eye on her, would you?'

'That would be kind.'

'No trouble, Mrs Carlton. Call you as usual next week, shall I?'

'Thank you, Mrs Flower.'

Bella was in some sort of a tunnel. It was very dark, but warm and yielding. Up ahead of her was Tom. He didn't say anything but she knew he was there, could hear his loud, anguished breathing. It sounded as if he was in pain and she kept trying to reach him but somehow her arms wouldn't work, were heavy and weighed down under some sort of soft, thick blanketing. It was like moving underwater, except that the water was made of cotton wool. She saw a light at the end of the tunnel, flapped furiously with her trapped arms, struggling to free them and slowly pushed her way towards it.

It grew brighter and brighter and then she felt cool air, came up gasping like a stranded fish and found herself staring up into a face.

'Tom?' she said, blinking.

'It's me, Mum,' Ben said, putting a mug of tea down on the table by the bed. 'You all right?'

She stared around, bewildered. She was in her own bed, her own and Tom's. The duvet was tangled around her arms.

'You were breathing so loud,' he said, and she noticed that his face was screwed up with fear. 'I thought you were dying, or something.'

She freed her arms, reached out a hand, patted him gently on the arm. 'Sorry,' she said, 'I was having a bad dream.' With a sigh, she hauled herself to a sitting position and patted at the bunched frizz of her hair, trying to restore some semblance of normality.

'Dad rang,' he said, his voice thick. 'He said he'd gone away for a bit, to sort things out.'

'The company went bust.'

Ben bowed his head. 'Yeah,' he said, 'I know.' He lifted

his face, stared at her. 'You didn't shout at him, did you?' he asked, and she saw in his eyes how badly he needed to hear the truth.

'Yes,' she said quietly. 'I'm afraid I did, but not about that. On the day Tom – I mean your father – and Harry lost the contract, they went out and got drunk and when your dad came back late I –' She took a deep breath. 'Well, I thought he'd been with somebody else.'

He looked away. 'It's awful when you shout.' His eyes slid sideways, in a quick furtive glance. 'You used to really scare me when I was a kid.'

'Yes,' she said heavily, 'I know. Sorry.'

His thin shoulders bunched in a shrug. 'I think you scare Dad too, sometimes.'

'I don't mean to.'

He looked over at her, eyes blazing. 'Then why do you do it?'

'Because I love him. Because I love you both,' she said, reaching out a hand to him. He shook it off.

'Try to understand,' she pleaded.

'I don't understand why you're so angry all the time.'

'Why are *you*?'

He scowled. 'Because the world's so – difficult.' He lifted a gangling arm, let it fall with a thud to his knees. 'Because my body's so difficult.'

She laughed. 'I know.'

He glanced sideways at her, a sharp incredulous look. 'How?'

'It gets better.'

He looked dubious. 'It didn't, with you.'

She looked away. 'That's different.'

They sat in silence.

'I know Dad went and fucked somebody else,' Ben said eventually, his voice loud in the still room.

She looked at him, eyes wide. 'How do you know that?'

'He told me, ages ago, when you were being really foul.'

He sighed heavily, and her chest constricted sharply with the sound. 'I guess he wanted me to understand,' he said.

'He didn't say he'd told you.'

He bowed his head. 'It hurts a lot, doesn't it?' he said after a while.

'Yes,' she said quietly, watching him. 'Yes, it does.'

He looked over at her. 'I used to think you just used it as some kind of excuse, for getting at me and Dad but then –' He scowled and a flush lit his thin face. 'Then my girlfriend went and slept with somebody else and I felt like –'

Bella sat up straighter. 'Your what?'

Ben laughed. 'Mum! Come on, I'm seventeen.'

'But you didn't say –'

'Oh yeah? I'm going to share my first sexual experience with my mother?' he said. 'Like, sure!'

She smiled, relieved to see him laughing. 'I could have helped, given you some advice or something.'

He stuck his finger in his open mouth, pretended to gag, like he used to do when he was a child. 'Yeuch! Sex tips from Mom,' he said and then added, his face darkening, 'Anyway, it hurt like hell and I thought –' He shrugged, gave her a crooked grin. Just like Tom's, Bella thought with a pang. 'I thought, so this is how Mum feels.'

She closed her eyes.

'Sorry,' he said, after a while. 'Do you need to go back to sleep?'

'No,' she said, opening her eyes, not wanting him to go. 'As a matter of fact, I'm starving. Why don't I get up and we'll call in a pizza.'

He grinned, said with mock incredulity, 'A pizza! My, my, the old lady knows how to live it up.'

'And some wine,' she said severely. 'Let's not forget the wine.'

Twenty

When Lily got back to the office after her lunch hour, she found Jim sitting on her desk, swinging his legs.

'I always liked that suit,' she said, stopping some way away from him. He turned and looked at her, his eyes flicking over her new clothes. She could see he didn't like them. 'You should have let us know where you were,' he said severely. 'Your mum's been very worried.'

Lily shrugged. 'You know where I am. Mrs Flower told me you'd been visiting.' She looked over at him and smiled. 'Anyway, I always knew you'd find me. You've always been clever like that.'

He looked pleased. 'Even so – it wasn't nice.'

'I know. Sorry.'

'Don't think much of that place you're living in –'

She watched him warily. 'It's all right,' she said eventually.

'Horrible, it is.'

'Nobody's asking you to live there,' Lily said, squaring her shoulders.

'Nice woman, though, that Mrs Flower. Had a good chat.' There was something sly in his look as he said it; some private joke. His smile broadened but she was buggered if she was going to ask him what it was so she just ignored it.

'What do you want?'

His smile faded. 'See how you were.' He looked away, his expression pained. 'Find out why you left.'

'And how am I?'

He looked her up and down. 'Different,' he said eventually. 'New clothes, new words. Different.'

She heard respect tingeing his voice and relaxed.

He fiddled with a pile of paper-clips. 'Never thought of you as a career girl somehow.' Disappointment hollowed his voice.

'I know.'

'You coming home soon, then?'

'Maybe.'

'When?'

'When I'm done.'

He looked over at her, his eyes screwed up, as if they hurt. 'What you up to, Lily?'

'Just finding out.'

'Out?'

'About life.'

'That why you left?'

She let her shoulders droop, dropped her eyes. 'Told you I didn't want to get married,' she said truculently. 'Not yet, anyhow. Too soon, I said, but you wouldn't listen, went ahead like you always do.'

'Sorry.'

She looked up, her expression softening. 'Mum too, she was just as bad. Couldn't wait to get those invitations sent out and all that fuss about the flowers and the caterers –' She shook her head.

He nodded, swung his legs off the desk, slouched to the door. 'She's all right now. Better. Says she'll see you when she sees you.' He ducked his head awkwardly, looked over at her, his expression shy. 'Me too.'

She said nothing.

'I'll be off, then,' he said and she looked at him more closely, saw that his suit was shiny from too many outings to the dry cleaner, and his tie crooked. That wasn't like Jim, he was usually so well turned out. Natty, Mum called him.

'How's the house?'

He looked at her thoughtfully. 'Empty.'

She looked away. 'I suppose it would be,' she said, eventually. When she looked back, he was gone.

'Boyfriend, was he?' Angela said later.

'Who?'

'The bloke in your office at lunch-time.'

'No, just a friend,' Lily said, turning away and occupying herself with some filing. She was still unsettled by Jim's visit, wasn't in the mood for Angela's sly little digs.

'They don't like us having friends making visits,' Angela said. 'Nor taking personal calls.' She let the silence hang for a moment. 'But then, I suppose you're different.'

Lily's tone was neutral. 'Am I?'

'Charles's pet,' Angela said, her voice rising.

Lily watched as Angela's colour rose until her plump, round face was pink and shiny. Lily said nothing.

'Don't think I haven't noticed the way you hang around him, gazing up with those –' she searched around for a suitably lacerating expression, gave up '– with those stupid big eyes of yours.'

'You in love with him?'

'None of your business.' It came out on a whisper.

Lily shook her head. 'Poor cow.'

Angela thrust her chin forward. 'And I suppose you're going to tell me you're not?'

Lily shrugged.

'He's married.'

Lily stared at her. Angela smiled, sensing victory. Her voice took on a mocking tone. 'He's a married man.'

'So?'

'So, he's not free.' The frustration, the agony of so many sleepless nights yearning after Charles, emerged in her voice.

A small, amused smile curved across Lily's face.

Angela's eyes widened, her voice rose to a squeal of frustrated outrage. 'You can't just help yourself to what you want.'

'Why not?'

Angela stamped her small, fat, Marks & Spencer sandalled foot in outrage. 'Because you can't.'

Lily turned back to her filing.

'I was hoping you'd still be here.'

'Oh, you know us lonely, childless, career girls. Don't have a home to go to so we spend all the hours God sends working to fill that bleak chasm in our lives.' Daisy pulled off a brightly patterned headscarf, shook out her fine blonde hair. 'At least, that's what the *Daily Mail* says. Coffee?'

'I'd prefer something stronger, if you have it.'

Daisy strode to the fridge, peered into it. 'Australian, Californian, French or Italian. Wine, that is.'

Bella tried an unsuccessful smile. 'Anything.'

'French, then,' Daisy said, pulling out a bottle of wine and uncorking it. She carried the bottle and glasses over to the sofa and patted it with her hand, indicating that Bella should sit down. Once she had the glass in her hand, Daisy considered her in silence for a moment.

'What's happened?' she said eventually.

Bella shrugged. 'Nothing. I'm fine. Just felt like seeing you.'

'No, you're not.'

'No, I'm not,' Bella said, and burst into tears.

Daisy lit a cigarette, handed it to Bella and waited patiently for her to stop crying.

'God, this tastes disgusting,' Bella said, furiously sucking on the cigarette.

'Kills you too.'

'Good.'

'That bad?'

'Worse. Tom's walked out.'

'Oh Bella, I'm so sorry. When did it happen?'

'Yesterday afternoon. He's camping in his office. He called Ben last night to let him know.' Her eyes shifted away until she looked furtive, guilty almost. 'The business went bust a week ago,' she said bleakly. 'He didn't say anything was wrong, just kept coming home drunk.'

'Oh dear.'

'I accused him of having an affair.'

'Oh dear, oh dear.'

They sat in silence for a while, drinking wine and smoking. Bella began to feel calmer, soothed by Daisy's brisk sympathy.

'I think I may have fucked things up good and proper this time.'

'Oh, I shouldn't take all the credit if I was you. I daresay it's his ego that's hurt as much as anything. Men do like to feel useful in this world and take it very hard when they're not. They like to feel valued.'

Bella sighed. 'Don't we all?'

'Well of course we do but they've had more time to grow used to the idea.'

'I just wish there was something I could do.'

'There is. Leave him be for a while. Just drop him a note, let him know that the door is always open.'

'Drop him a note?' Bella exclaimed. 'This is a marriage we're talking about, not a dinner date. I should be with him, by his side. We should fight this together.' She grew suddenly animated, a flush rose to her thin cheeks. 'I know, I could help him with job applications, type out his CV and letters for him.'

'Well, that would be useful but perhaps not yet. Give him time –'

Bella fell silent, contemplating this. 'What if he is having an affair?' she said, after a while.

'What if he's not?'

Charles and Lily were sitting in a subterranean wine bar situated in a tiny alleyway off what was once Fleet Street. It was their meeting place, about ten minutes' walk from the office and chosen by Charles because, as he said, nobody from the office would ever dream of going there.

There was no particular reason why they should. It was just another of dozens of watering holes that had sprung up to cater to the needs of journalists in the days when expenses were high and expectations, at least of good food and comfortable surroundings, were low. And like so many of those places, which had been burrowed out of the bowels of ancient buildings, it was a dank cellar filled with uncomfortable, dark wood benches squatting under rough hewn tables or rickety wood stools clustered around old sherry barrels. A random stab at old-world charm had inflicted on a procession of elderly waitresses the indignity of being trussed up in long, limp brown polyester dresses and wilting white nylon mob caps. They served stringy, overcooked steak, watery vegetables and very good wine.

'You all right?' Lily asked. 'You look done in.'

'I'm fine,' Charles said heavily.

'Don't look it.' She was inclined to sulk if Charles didn't share with her every detail of his life at home, however small. 'It's because you don't trust me,' she'd once complained, 'even though you say we're friends,' at which Charles, mortified by her sad, wounded expression had hastened to reassure her. He did not, of course, discuss with her the more confidential aspects of his work and his thoughts about his marriage – that increasingly sad, dusty affair for which he felt somehow solely responsible and sometimes bitterly ashamed – he kept to himself. But about the small details of his daily life, he found himself talking quite freely.

It was a very long time since anyone had taken an interest in Charles. Like most men who had married young and given up their youth to the demands of small children and large careers, he had found himself with neither the need for close friendships nor the time to spend on the care and nurture that they require. He had nobody to confide in and nobody who confided in him – except his wife, and she seemed scarcely to bother these days, other than to discuss the children. It was not lack of interest in other people that had left him so solitary but lack of time and he discovered as he grew older that there were fewer rather than more opportunities for meeting and making friends. As a young man he had been rather serious, inclined to spend his university days in the library, and had graduated with only one good friend who had almost immediately emigrated to Canada following a job offer. At the time Charles had minded very much but quite soon after had met and married Elisabeth and left the responsibilities of friendship, together with the care of the house and the children, almost entirely in her hands. He thought that, if he had ever had it, he had lost the knack of friendship.

At least, until Lily came along and he discovered that her interest in him and everything to do with his life was a novel, and delightful, experience. He found her inconsequential chatter and pragmatic, almost brutal view of life soothing precisely because it was so different from his own, and listened happily to all the details of her childhood, her family and Jim, her fiancé, to whom Charles had taken an immediate and intense dislike after hearing Lily's colourful account of the way he had dumped her at the altar. 'I don't mind,' she'd said, her small hand creeping across the table. 'Not now, anyway.' He thought he saw the glimmer of tears in her dark eyes but she blinked slowly in that way she had and an expression, both brave and truculent, crept across her face. He smiled, charmed by her courage.

Charles let out a heavy sigh. 'Tom's walked out on Bella,' he said, looking pained. The news, which Elisabeth had delivered the previous night with a relish that he found disturbing, had affected him deeply, although whether that was out of pity or out of envy, he didn't quite know.

Lily's eyes glittered with interest. 'Has he now? What made him do that?'

'Poor sod's gone bust.'

'What's that got to do with Bella?'

Charles hesitated. 'I don't know exactly but things haven't been good between those two for some time and I suppose that the business going bust was the final straw. He's gone off somewhere to lick his wounds.'

'Silly mare should go after him, make sure he's all right. It's when he's going to need her, time like this.'

'Perhaps. But maybe he doesn't want her to.'

'Probably doesn't know what he wants, poor bugger.'

'No, he probably doesn't.'

Lily subsided into silence, sipped at her wine thoughtfully. After a while, she said, 'Where's he gone?'

'Apparently he's living in his old offices.'

'Where's that, then?'

'I don't know. Somewhere in Kentish Town.'

Lily laughed. 'Funny lot, you are. Don't know nothing about your own friends.'

'I suppose we are,' Charles said, with a sudden look of pained surprise, then added defensively, 'Elisabeth will have the number somewhere.'

'Don't want the number, it's the address I'm after so I can send him a card, cheer him up, like.'

'Well, it'll probably be listed in the telephone book. The company's called Alpha, no Omega –' He shook his head. 'Well, it's one of the Greek letters.'

Lily scrabbled in her handbag, emerged clutching a pen and a scrap of paper. 'Write them down, will you?' She watched as Charles carefully spelled out the words. 'There,' she said, looking satisfied, 'you do know something.'

Charles found himself laughing. 'Not entirely useless after all.'

Somehow, when he was with Lily, he didn't doubt it.

Twenty-one

Tom opened the door a crack and peered uncertainly at the figure standing a little way down the stone steps. Silhouetted against the backdrop of the grimy street, she looked fresh and clean in a pink cotton dress and flat, strappy sandals revealing pearly toenails. Her long hair was caught back by a flowered headband.

'Lily?'

She looked up at him, smiled. 'All right?'

Tom nodded mutely.

'I only live round the corner,' she said, gesturing vaguely in the direction of the pub, 'two streets up I am. So I thought I'd drop in on my way home, see how you were.'

She held up a brown paper package. 'Bought you some grapes.'

Tom's thin face cracked in a sardonic smile. 'Am I sick?'

She contemplated this for a bit. 'It's instead of flowers. Didn't think you'd like flowers, being a bloke and all.'

'Come in,' he said, opening the door wide and turning into the dark hall, to lead the way. She followed him, stepping noiselessly across cracked linoleum, up a narrow, shabby flight of stairs and into a small room, bare except for a rolled-up sleeping-bag and a telephone squatting on the dusty floorboards, the thin black snake of its wire curled around a gleaming new electric kettle.

'Blimey,' she said, looking around for somewhere to put the grapes. 'Not exactly the lap of luxury, is it?'

He took the fruit from her, cradling the lumpy brown paper bag awkwardly in his hands. 'It's our office.' He corrected himself. 'Was our office. We've got the lease for another two weeks so I thought I may as well shack up here for a bit –'

'Yeah, I heard about that. Sorry.'

He nodded.

She looked around, pointed at the rolled-up sleeping-bag. 'Can I sit on that?'

'Sure.'

She sat down, the fine fabric of her dress billowing around her like the petals of a flower. 'Well, come on then,' she said, patting the quilted nylon. 'Else you'll be making me feel like the Queen Mum.'

He sat down next to her and watched as she pulled a bottle of wine, a corkscrew and two plastic cups out of her bag.

'Thought you might need cheering up,' she said, handing him the bottle and corkscrew. 'Bought some Hula-Hoops too. Family size.'

They drank in silence, munching on Hula-Hoops and grapes.

'Suppose she's been round already?' Lily said. 'The one-woman mercy mission.'

'Elisabeth?'

Lily nodded. 'Can't resist strays.'

'Is that what you think you are?' he said, watching her curiously.

She shrugged. 'Think it's what she'd like me to be.'

'As a matter of fact, she hasn't been to see me. She pushed a note through the door instead.'

'Silly mare.'

'I expect I've embarrassed her.'

Lily stared at him incredulously. 'You what?'

'Walking out on my life. Running away.'

'Jealous, more like.'

'Elisabeth?'

Lily nodded. 'She's bored rigid, poor cow. Thinks she's

230

missing out on life. And now she's got the hots for that bloke she works for. Sam, he's called.'

'Elisabeth?'

'What are you? A megaphone?'

'Sorry.'

'She's all lit up, like a hundred-watt bulb.'

Tom looked faintly amused. 'Somehow I can't imagine it . . .'

'You should see her. Talks about him like the sun shines out of his bum.'

'Does Charles know?'

'Don't be daft. Anyway, what's to know? She won't do anything about it except sit there squirming in her knickers and worrying about what she calls her responsibilities.'

'Well, I suppose if she feels serious about this Sam person – I mean, there are the children to consider.'

'Sent them away, didn't she?'

'To boarding school.'

Lily shrugged. 'Same difference.'

'You don't sound as though you like her much,' he said, watching her carefully. 'I thought you two were friends.'

'We are. She's nice to me.'

'Is that what friendship is?' he mused. 'People who are nice to you?'

'Well, you don't want to be doing with people who hate your guts.'

'What if hate's the other side of love?'

She looked at him contemptuously. 'Don't be daft. Hate's the other side of thumping the life out of you.'

'Yes,' he said, thinking of Bella. It was how he felt, that she'd thumped the life out of him.

He glanced sideways at her, saw the cool curve of her cheek shining palely in the fading light. Pretty, he thought, with a sudden jolt. He'd scarcely noticed her before.

'Is that what happened to you?' he asked, feeling a

231

sudden curiosity about this girl and her unexpected kindness.

She turned, gazed at him. 'Might be.'

They stared at each other for a while. How dark her eyes are, he thought, almost black. Not like Bella's eyes, sharp and brown, crackling with tiny yellow sparks.

He looked away.

'Would you mind if it had?' she said, her gaze still trained on his averted face.

He nodded. 'Of course.'

She was silent for a while, sipping her wine, gazing at her polished toenails, wiggling them in their fretwork of fine leather straps. They were grubby, from the dusty floor.

'What you going to do now?' she asked. There was no challenge in the question.

He shrugged. 'Don't know. Find a job, I guess.'

She pointed her toes towards the floor, flexing them like a dancer's. 'It's all right, having nothing, leaving all your stuff behind,' she said. 'Well, it is for a while anyway. It's –' She looked at him questioningly. 'What's the word?'

'Liberating,' he suggested.

'Yeah. That's the one,' she said slowly. 'Liberating. No stuff, no people, no bits and pieces around to remind you –' She waved an arm airily in the dimness, its curve taking in the four walls. 'Just an empty room and the future.'

He grinned, feeling cheered. 'I'll drink to that,' he said, saluting the dusty skylight with his paper cup.

She scrambled to her feet, stood looking down at him. 'It is, honest. I didn't just say it to make you feel better.'

He felt her eyes on him. 'I know.'

'Better be off then,' she said, picking up her bag, fixing the strap securely on one shoulder. She pirouetted across the dusty floor, her pink dress floating around her, came to a stop in the middle of the room and stood there balanced on one foot, like a child. 'I could drop round tomorrow, if you like. Same time. After work.'

He looked at her consideringly. 'Yes,' he said slowly. 'I think I'd like that very much.'

Two hours later, Bella turned up, stood on the same spot where Lily had been standing. Taking deep breaths, trying to calm herself, she put her finger tentatively to the doorbell; heard its hesitant ring echo apologetically in the empty hallway.

She had not been home yet that evening, had stayed late at college, working on the endless reams of paper that higher education these days demanded, putting off the journey home, the empty house. Ben was out as he always was these days, despite the revision work he should have been doing. He'd done two sets of exams last week, the week Tom had left, had one more set in a couple of days' time. He said they'd gone OK, scowling, shoulders hunching up to his ears when she'd tried to press him further. They hadn't talked much, not since that first night Tom left; Ben blanked every mention of his name, changing the subject or slamming out of the kitchen and disappearing into his bedroom. Minutes later, music would flood the house but she hadn't the energy to argue with him; hadn't had the energy for anything much since Tom left.

She glanced down at her watch. It was past ten; perhaps Tom was asleep. She hadn't called to say that she was coming; they had only spoken twice in the past week – odd, stilted conversations that made them both feel like strangers. Her breath was coming in short, nervous gasps; she felt light-headed, curiously detached. She had not slept much the past week, couldn't remember when she had last eaten.

It was a long time since she had stood on a doorstep waiting for Tom, twenty years since they were students and she used to visit him in the flat he shared in Mill Hill.

She had trouble breathing then too.

Tom's voice sounded through the intercom.

'It's me,' she said in a thin, high voice. She cleared her throat. 'It's me,' she said again.

There was silence.

She thought, he's got somebody with him, almost turned and ran, but then the intercom squawked and she pushed through the door and heard his voice: 'Up here. In the office.'

When she rounded the curve of the stairway, she found him waiting, dressed in jeans and a soft-checked shirt that bore the unmistakable film of grime from a recent launderette wash. He looked so shockingly familiar that she felt momentarily winded. She clutched the banisters, stood swaying at the top of the landing. They watched each other warily.

'I brought you some clean shirts,' she said at last, handing him a clutch of wire hangers shrouded in a black bin-liner. An odd note crept into her voice. 'I ironed them.'

His face cracked in the habitual lopsided grin. 'Wonders will never cease.' His voice shook slightly.

She smiled uncertainly.

'Come in,' he said, stepping back into the room, holding the door open for her.

She moved through it, stepping to the right just as he moved to the left; the two of them facing each other for a moment as if they were performing some shuffling, awkward dance.

'Coffee?' he asked, moving away with sudden purpose and bending to switch on the kettle.

She nodded, stood on the threshold of the empty room, staring around. There was a sleeping-bag, neatly rolled, in one corner; brand new and made of bright, quilted blue nylon with a jaunty red trim. Its unfamiliarity seemed like a declaration of his separateness from her. She curled her fingers, dug them hard into her palms to stop herself crying.

'You could have taken a sleeping-bag from home,' she said, in a queer breathless voice. 'There are three in the attic, from that camping holiday we went on to Cornwall –'

He shrugged, did not look at her. 'It seemed easier to go out and buy a new one,' he said, busying himself with ladling instant coffee into mugs. She watched his bent head where the fine dark hair threaded into the nape of his neck, feathering up around the collar of his shirt. He needed a haircut.

'I'm sorry about what's happened,' she said in a low voice.

He frowned down at the kettle. Only a brief nod of his head told her that he had heard.

'Ben says –' She tried a smile. 'Well, he's fine. Coping well, really. Me too,' she said, and added, in case he thought she was OK without him, 'considering.'

He looked up, a brief flare of pain distorting his face, but then he turned his head away again, stared down at the kettle as if willing it to come to the boil.

She walked over to the window, peered through the grimy glass at the traffic on the hill. A red car inched through the traffic, music blaring from its open windows. A woman – not young, about her age – sat in the passenger seat, her feet propped on the dashboard, her hand slung easily on the lap of the man who was driving. They were singing and laughing, and Bella was struck suddenly by the arbitrariness of happiness. How can it be, she thought, that life goes on, that people are happy while we, who were once so happy, are standing in this dusty room with nothing to say to each other?

She pressed her face to the glass. 'I miss you,' she said awkwardly. She had never been one to talk about love, had expressed it instead in the fierce grip of her arms and her urgent, critical demands. She remembered once how he'd remonstrated with her, told her to stop bullying him and she'd said blithely, 'I only do it because I care. If I didn't, I wouldn't give a fuck what you did,' and how he'd looked away but not before she saw a shadow flicker across his face.

She heard him move, the sound of his footsteps echoing on the bare floorboards, waited, back rigid, for the touch of his hands on her shoulders.

The footsteps stopped.

'Coffee's ready,' he said.

She turned to look at him, saw him standing awkwardly in the middle of the room holding two mugs, mute appeal scrawled across his face. She knew that look, had seen it so many times before, at parties, in restaurants or when they were both trying to deal with some adolescent difficulty with Ben. Don't be difficult, it said; don't make a scene. They had always been like that together; she attacking, he playing the conciliator.

She sighed, went across to him and took a mug, cradling it in two hands. 'The place looks better like this,' she said, trying to be cheerful, 'bigger.'

'Empty space,' he said, trying to match her brightness, 'architectural nirvana.'

Smiling, she dipped her face to the coffee, the surface scummy with the chalky residue of powdered milk. She swallowed, tasted the familiar burnt bitterness of instant coffee on her tongue.

'Coffee Mate,' he said apologetically, then gestured formally to the rolled-up sleeping-bag. 'Would you like to sit down?'

She moved to the bag, sat down tucking her legs awkwardly under her, watched while he walked across to the far side of the room and squatted on his haunches against the wall.

'There's room,' she said, patting the sleeping-bag, attempting a smile.

He looked away. 'I'm fine.'

They drank their coffee in silence.

Then Bella said, 'Have you applied for any jobs?'

He squirmed irritably against the wall and she saw in the brief movement a flash of Ben; the same shrug of bony shoulders, the same inward irritation at questions of any sort. Neither of them had ever liked questions, hated recounting their days to her, hated the intimacy she tried to insist on. She remembered Ben scowling with the contemptuous hostility that all children seem to reserve exclusively for their mothers. 'It was boring, OK?' Then, turning away from her on a muttered undertone, 'But not as boring as having to tell you.'

She glanced over at Tom. 'I just wondered what the job market was like these days,' she said quickly.

'Depends how low you're prepared to go,' he said, trying unsuccessfully to smile.

They used to talk endlessly, her and Tom, about their future. She supposed it must have stopped when there was no more future to talk about.

'You can always build up again,' she said, wanting to jerk him into some sort of action. Anything was better than seeing him like this, hunched in the corner of this dusty, defeated room.

A sardonic grin cracked his thin face. 'You mean I've sunk so low that the only way is up?' he said.

'No. You know I didn't mean that.'

He sighed. 'Yes. Sorry.'

'The council must have jobs going for architects,' she said, after a while. 'I mean, they're always building stuff. The amount of work going on down on Euston Road –'

'They don't need architects for that stuff,' he said wearily, 'only people who can draw straight lines with a ruler.'

'It's a start. You can always –'

'Bella,' he said, 'stop it.'

She looked bewildered. 'I was only trying to help.'

'That's what I mean. Stop trying to help.'

She picked at a stray thread, hanging off the cheap, quilted nylon. 'Well, if you can't –' she began.

He looked at her strangely. 'But I can. I can manage, if only you'd let me, stop pushing me to do it your way. Let me make my own mistakes.'

The words were out before she could stop them. 'Well, you've certainly done that,' she snapped.

He bowed his head, his thin shoulders hunching up to his ears, the way he always did when she had a go at him; the way Ben did too.

She put her hand to her head. 'Sorry.'

He said nothing, just tilted his head back against the grimy walls, eyes closed.

After a while she got clumsily to her feet, her knees cracking with the strain of levering herself from the floor. She stared down at him longingly but he did not look up.

Next to him, lying on its side on the floor, was an empty bottle of wine, a corkscrew, two paper cups and two empty, crumpled packets of Hula-Hoops. Why two, she thought. Why two? A wave of bile surged up to her throat. Stop it, she thought. Stop this now. It might have been Harry, Charles, Elisabeth – it might have been anyone, bringing him wine and crisps to cheer him up.

'You've been partying,' she said, trying to make her voice light, heard it break on a keen of jealousy.

He squeezed his eyes tighter shut, his face crumpling with the effort of blocking her out.

This is hopeless, she thought. She felt rooted to the ground, marooned in the middle of the empty space.

'Goodbye,' she said awkwardly, willing him to speak, to make some gesture towards her.

He opened his eyes, stared at her for a while. 'Thanks for bringing the shirts.'

She nodded, turned away from him, walked carefully out of the silent room.

Twenty-Two

'Alex can't make it tonight,' Daisy said, landing a perfunctory kiss on Elisabeth's cheek and heading through to the kitchen. 'Celia's got him jumping through hoops at one of her dreary charity evenings.'

She slumped down into a chair, scrabbled through her bag for a cigarette. 'Any chance of a drink? I'm desperate.'

Elisabeth picked up a bottle from the table, poured a glass of wine. 'Bella's on her way. She just called,' she said, handing it over and pouring another for herself. 'So it looks like it's going to be a girls' night tonight. Charles is working late and what with no Tom –'

They glanced at each other, then away.

'I suppose that's why she was in such a foul mood that night,' Elisabeth said, sitting down. 'Did I tell you? She accused Lily of making a play for Charles –' Her voice took on a faint, scornful note. 'As if he would.'

Daisy shrugged, spoke unthinkingly: 'Of course he wouldn't. Then again, she's a pretty girl. Even *Charles* can't be immune –' Oh dear, she thought, that doesn't sound quite right so she added quickly, 'You know perfectly well that Charles is famous for never looking at another woman but –' She gave a little, despairing shrug. 'Well, we also all know what Bella's like these days, ever since Tom had the affair. She probably saw Charles give Lily a look – purely appreciative, of course – and immediately assumed the worst.'

Elisabeth looked thoughtful. 'The really dreadful thing about this whole sorry affair is that Tom adores Bella. At least, he would if only she'd let him. I don't know what's got into her lately.'

'She's terrified.'

'Of what?'

'Of losing Tom.'

'Well, she's certainly going the right way about it.'

'I don't think terror's a rational emotion,' Daisy said, with a sigh.

They were silent for a while, thinking about Tom and Bella, remembering how once they'd envied them their happiness, their passionate absorption in each other. But that, Daisy thought, was a long time ago – a lifetime. She looked at Elisabeth curiously. 'Do you think either of us have ever felt the same heights of happiness, or depths of unhappiness that Bella feels?'

Elisabeth looked away, thinking of Sam and how, sometimes when she was with him, it was as if her skin glowed with faint electrical impulses and she could feel the very particles of the air move around her like warm water. He had been so affectionate with her lately, taking her hand, touching her cheek. There was a sweetness to him, a gentleness that she had never noticed before and she knew that was what made him hold back. That fateful afternoon, thinking that he wanted her to go up to the flat with him had been no more than a misunderstanding on her part, just her desire for him running riot with her imagination. Charles had never made her feel that way; had never inspired that same passionate euphoria. 'Perhaps not,' she said.

'When things were good with Tom,' Daisy said, 'she was all lit up, as if you could warm your hands on her. I've sometimes envied her that, although perhaps not as often as I've feared finding it myself.'

Elisabeth looked at her curiously. 'Why?'

'Oh well,' Daisy said with a slight shrug, 'I suppose because it has the feel of a Faustian pact about it.'

'I know what you mean,' Elisabeth said, although she didn't; would have sold her soul, willingly, for one burning, truly intimate glance from Sam, had lived her life in trembling anticipation of the discovery of her twinned soul. 'The odd thing,' she said, her voice vaguely disgruntled, 'is that however unhappy they *said* they were – and it's not as if Bella made any bones about it – I still never really believed that they could bear to be apart from each other.'

'I think that Tom was literally at the end of his tether.'

'Even so – Ah, well it's done now. Have you been to see him?'

Daisy grimaced. 'No. And I feel horribly guilty about it, but I think that Bella might feel –'

'I know,' Elisabeth said.

'Whatever she says to the contrary,' Daisy said with a sigh, 'and then, of course, there's that awful business about getting dragged in and having to end up taking sides.'

Elisabeth leaned forward, refilled both their glasses. 'I stuck a note through the door of Tom's office, to say he's welcome here any time for a meal – he only has to ring.'

Daisy sipped at her wine. 'He won't, of course. He's always been hopeless about keeping in touch. I doubt we'd have seen him again after college had he not got hitched up with Bella.'

'Well, I shall feel sad about that but I can't help thinking that if he hadn't gone off and had an affair in the first place, this would never have happened.'

Daisy shrugged.

'Well, you must admit,' Elisabeth said, 'it was an idiotic thing to do.' She watched Daisy carefully. 'Or perhaps you don't think so?'

'Seemed more like a cry for help, to me,' Daisy said, lighting a cigarette. She inhaled sharply, blew out a thin stream of blue smoke. 'The affair was over almost before it had begun.'

'Only because Bella found out.'

'Bella only found out because Tom scattered the evidence under her nose. It was his feebleness that made that creature turn up on the doorstep. The way he was behaving, he may just as well have tattooed a sign across his forehead.'

Elisabeth glanced sideways at her. 'So you don't think Tom's to blame?' she said, flushing slightly.

'I think these things are always more complex than that,' Daisy said. 'Tom wanted her to find out. He's not like –' She grimaced. 'Well, he's hardly like my dearly beloved, doesn't need to keep exercising his cock to keep his ego in shape. I imagine he had his reasons.'

Elisabeth was silent.

'I've always thought,' Daisy went on, 'that the really curious thing about marriage is that it's such a public institution but, for the most part, it's carried out in absolute secrecy, between two people, behind closed doors. We're always making judgements about it, or other people's marriages, despite the fact that we aren't privy to its secrets and, by its very nature, nor can we be.'

Elisabeth said, 'Even so, an affair is a forfeit of trust and trust is the whole basis of marriage,' then bent her head quickly to her glass, to hide the guilty flush spreading up her neck.

Daisy, distracted by her own thoughts, was staring out of the window at the garden. 'How pretty it looks,' she said distantly. 'I love gardens in the early summer, before they get that ghastly, dusty August feel to them. Like a love affair that's nearly over,' she added wistfully.

Elisabeth glanced at the garden impatiently. 'So you don't think an affair is necessarily wrong,' she insisted.

Daisy sighed. 'We're back to the romantic notion again. If you take the view instead, which is admittedly an old-fashioned one, that marriage is based on a partnership and not on some never-never land idea of happy ever after then one lousy fuck is just a hiccup rather than a betrayal of the central tenet of romantic love – which is fidelity.'

Elisabeth opened her mouth to speak but Daisy interrupted: 'And before you say anything, I've never met a man I *like* enough to marry but I have met a number I loved romantically – like charming, handsome and utterly unscrupulous Alex.'

Elisabeth looked thoughtful. 'You mean, one marries men one likes but has affairs with men one loves?'

Daisy waved a hand. 'Something like that.'

'What if you do both like and love them?'

Daisy laughed. 'Then, my dear, you've found the promised land.'

'And what if you're married to a man that you like but then you meet a man that you could love?'

Daisy glanced at her sharply, stubbed out her cigarette with an emphatic gesture. 'Then you've found serious trouble.'

The doorbell sounded.

Elisabeth, relieved by the distraction, went hurriedly out, pressing her hands to her flushed cheeks to cool them before flinging open the door, her smile widening in shock. 'Come in,' she said, moving forward to kiss Bella, feeling her shoulders like blades beneath her hands. 'We were just getting stuck into the wine.'

There was nothing glamorous, this time, about Bella's distress. She looked extinguished; her skin had the papery, defeated texture of grief, her eyes, usually so prominent, had withdrawn to lurk sullenly in the shadows of their sockets.

'How are you feeling?' Elisabeth exclaimed, but Bella said nothing, merely followed Elisabeth silently through the dim hallway into the brightly lit kitchen and kissed Daisy absently before flinging herself down at the table to snatch up a glass of wine. She took half of it down in a couple of mouthfuls, then lit a cigarette, sucking down the smoke in eager, hungry gasps. The others watched her, their expressions wavering between alarm and sympathy. Eventually, Daisy leaned forward, stroked her arm soothingly. 'You look fucking awful, friend.'

Bella inhaled sharply on her cigarette, smiled slightly. 'Thanks, friend.'

'If there's anything we can do –' Elisabeth said, hovering ineffectually over her, filling her glass again, emptying the ashtray. 'You'll feel better, really you will, given time. It's a great healer, far more than one realises when one's in the thick of things. I remember, when my mother died –'

Bella shot her a sharp, disbelieving glance. 'I'll feel better when those platitudes cease pouring from your mouth,' she said, trying to keep her voice light, and failing.

Looking affronted, Elisabeth turned away and went to busy herself with some unnecessary task over at the cooker.

'Sorry,' Bella said, glancing over at her. 'Sorry, *sorry*.'

Elisabeth kept her head averted. 'Don't worry about it,' she said in a subdued voice but withdrew slightly from the two of them, just as she always had done, feeling herself the awkward angle in the triangle of their friendship.

'I saw Tom last night –' Bella began, then broke off and stared into the middle distance, silent but for the eloquent droop of her shoulders.

'He needs time to sort things out, that's all,' Daisy said gently. 'Imagine what a ghastly shock it must have been, losing the company like that. I doubt whether he's even –'

'As long as that's all he's sorting out,' Bella cut in. She heaved an exasperated sigh, then fell silent, staring moodily into her glass.

'Bella,' Daisy said warningly, '*don't*.'

'I can't help it,' Bella said, meeting her eyes reproachfully.

'Well, you must try,' Daisy said firmly. 'It's your

jealousy, as much as anything else, that's tearing you two apart.'

'I do try –'

'Then try harder. Tom needs you on his side right now, fighting with him, not against him.'

'There were two paper cups –'

Daisy frowned. 'What?'

Bella glared at her. 'Two papers cups and two empty packets of Hula-Hoops in Tom's office.'

'Maybe he was hungry.'

'Had you been there?' Bella demanded.

Daisy shook her head.

'You?' Bella said, swinging round to look at Elisabeth.

'I haven't actually been to see him –' Elisabeth began apologetically, 'although I did drop him a note asking him to give us a ring if ever he fancied popping over for supper. I didn't think you'd mind –' Her voice tailed off under Bella's penetrating stare. 'Maybe it was Charles?' she said quietly.

'Maybe it was no one,' Daisy said. 'Maybe they were just two paper cups that Tom had used, two packets of crisps that he'd eaten.'

Bella lit a second cigarette with shaking hands. She exhaled the smoke sharply, pressed trembling fingers to her temples and dug them in sharply. 'What am I going to do?' she said in a low voice.

Daisy leant forward, stroked her gently on the arm. 'Nothing.'

Bella stared at her resentfully from beneath lowered eyes. 'Must you say that? Nothing is the hardest thing of all.'

Alex was in his car, hovering next to an empty residents' parking space and glowering at a traffic warden who was leaning dreamily against a lamppost. He glanced impatiently at his watch. Ten past six. Lily was waiting for him in the wine bar opposite, a small, deserted place just off Grosvenor Square. It was close enough to the flat in St James's to be convenient but anonymous too, frequented mainly by travelling executives from the cluster of international companies surrounding it. They'd been meeting regularly, once a week, since that first night at the theatre although it may as well have been once a month, Alex thought furiously, for all the headway he was making. He glared at the pavement opposite, his impatience increasing as he thought of Lily. Bloody girl was playing some silly, childish game with him. But he was a patient man, he'd bide his time until that lovely, expressionless face crumpled with longing, those dark eyes grew black with desire. Not that they showed much sign of it yet. He swore softly. If the warden would only move, he'd risk the car on a single yellow for twenty minutes.

A car behind him hooted. Alex swung round, gesticulating angrily for it to pass. The driver, a woman, made exasperated flapping movements with her hands, indicating that she couldn't manoeuvre her Volvo estate past his car. 'Oh for Christ's sake,' Alex muttered, putting his foot hard down on the accelerator and shooting off round the bend in the square. By the time he had found somewhere to park, it was nearly six twenty-five.

Lily was sitting in a corner of the wine bar, a glass in front of her. 'All right?' she said, looking up at him.

Alex said, 'I'm sorry. I couldn't find anywhere to park.'

Lily's gaze was indifferent. 'It's OK. I got myself a drink.'

She sat lifelessly against the red plush banquette, her large head drooping slightly as if she was exhausted. Her soft, heavy lips hung slackly, like ripe fruit. He wanted to bite into them, to wrap the cords of her thick, silky hair tight around her pliant white neck. What he wanted, he thought, was to fuck her, which made him dislike her even more.

'Have you been here long?' he asked, wondering if it was her passivity that inspired those feelings. He was not, by nature, a violent man.

Lily shrugged. 'Long enough.'

He gave her a tight smile, looked around to find a waitress, beckoned her over. 'Champagne, I think. A bottle.'

Lily stretched languorously. 'We celebrating, then?'

He smoothed a hand over his sleek, seal's head. 'Not unless you're thinking of inviting me to that charming little bedsit of yours.'

Lily giggled suddenly. 'Not likely. They see a bloke like you in there and they'll be handing out spectator seats.'

'Might be rather amusing.'

'Don't be disgusting.'

The champagne arrived. They were silent as it was poured. Alex picked up his glass, sipped at the cold liquid in appreciative silence. He put down the glass and leaned back against the mock-velvet banquette seat, his eyes flickering lazily over her.

'You don't like sex much, do you Lily?'

Only a fractional widening of her eyes told him that he had taken her by surprise.

"S'all right,' she said, her heavy lids shuttering over her eyes.

'What's all right about it?'

She made an impatient clicking sound. 'Oh, you *know*.'

'No, I don't.'

She ignored him, picked up her glass, sipped champagne silently.

'My wife,' he said musingly, 'regards sex rather as if it were a poker game. Never shows her hand until the stakes are high.'

Lily's eyes flickered. 'How high?'

'Throughout her life? Oh, money, clothes, cars, jewellery, flats and finally, me.'

'Do you give her everything she wants?'

'Of course.' He picked up his glass, took a swallow of champagne. 'Sex, as far as Celia is concerned, is simply the contract on which is written a fair exchange of assets.'

'And what about Daisy? Do you give her what she wants too?'

'Naturally. Daisy wants precisely the same things as my wife, only she expresses them with rather more sentimentality.'

'You mean she's a sucker?'

He allowed himself a small smile. 'Less of a businesswoman, perhaps.'

'You going to marry her?'

Alex looked pained. 'I am already married.'

'That don't mean nothing, not these days.'

He shrugged. 'It can mean precisely as much or as little as one wants.' He put his fingers together, formed a temple with which he touched his nose. 'Celia and I understand each other well.'

'And Daisy doesn't?'

He looked over at her. 'What a curious little cat you are.'

She returned his gaze, watching him with indifference.

'How like one you are too,' he murmured, 'loyal to nothing but the main chance.'

Her gaze flickered. 'Is she beautiful, your wife?'

'Of course.'

'Am I beautiful?'

'I would hardly be interested in you if you were not.'

She nodded, satisfied, and a small smile crept across her lovely, blank face.

Alex watched her carefully, wondering whether there was anything behind that façade or whether it was her lack of conscience, her imperviousness to the demands of morality that left her so unblemished by life. He knew that the only morals she understood were embedded deep in her ego. He did not think her immoral; she was not

249

scheming enough to be called that, but he could see that she had no grasp of right or wrong, no judgement on what was good or evil. In that sense, he thought, watching her, she is amoral, even blameless, rather in the way that a very small child is blameless, having no understanding of the effect of its actions upon others; is surprised by pain, interested by grief but, for the most part, entirely untouched by either unless it is its own.

He leaned forward, his sleek smile close to her face.

'And when, lovely Lily, are you going to sleep with me?'

She stifled a yawn. 'Dunno. When I feel like it, I suppose.'

He shifted back, looked at her with a little glimmer of distaste. 'And I wonder when that might be,' he murmured. 'Before or after you've seen which way the wind blows with Charles?'

She opened her mouth to protest, but the glimmer in his eye told her that he knew how it was with her. 'Not much point before, is there?' she said, with a languid shrug.

'Oh, I don't know,' he said. 'Jealousy is a remarkably galvanising emotion.'

She looked at him suspiciously. 'What's galvanising, when it's at home?'

He smiled. 'Something that makes people behave in a way that they would otherwise not.'

Twenty-Three

The next afternoon, Lily looked up to see Charles lounging in the doorway to her office. 'Simon around?' he said loudly. 'I need to check something with him.'

'He's gone to a meeting,' she replied, giving him a brief smile before turning back to some papers she was sorting.

'Well, I'm through for the day,' he said, glancing up and down the corridor, dropping his voice to a conspiratorial whisper. 'I could give you a lift home. Maybe even stop off for a drink on the way.'

She looked up, smiling.

'We could sit outside,' he said, 'drive down to the river, find a nice pub or something.'

'I'm off out tonight.'

'Out?' he said, an echo of longing in his voice.

'A friend,' she said, glancing back down at the piles of papers, 'had a rough time recently.'

What sort of a friend, he wanted to say. What sort of a friend? But he said nothing, only put his hand to his head, pushed it fretfully through his hair.

'There,' she said, looking at the papers with a satisfied smile, hitching her bag on her shoulder, clattering towards him on high heels. She was wearing a skimpy cotton dress, with some sort of ribbon arrangement at the neckline which pulled the thin fabric tight across her small breasts, and he could smell her perfume, see the fine down of hair on her upper lip. As she walked past him, she stopped suddenly, put her hand out to his head. He felt the warm, rough touch of her hand smoothing his hair flat, and closed his eyes, feeling a wave of longing so strong it made him nauseous.

'It was sticking up,' she said.

He opened his eyes. Her smiling mouth was close to his face.

'We could have a drink tomorrow,' she said, 'if you like.'

'Six thirty, the usual place?' His voice was slow with resignation.

She smiled and moved away. He watched her go, her skirt dancing around her pale, smooth thighs.

Tom was waiting, pacing restlessly around the empty room. Sunshine slanted through the grimy windows, turning the dust motes to shimmering gold. He put out a hand to catch them, balling it into an empty fist; distracted himself like that for a while, punching at the air. When at last the doorbell echoed through the hall, he ignored the intercom, took the stairs two at a time, flung open the door.

'All right?' Lily said.

'All right,' he echoed, gripped by a sudden pleasure at seeing her standing there. Then another, darker emotion flickered across his face and he turned abruptly, motioning her to follow him up the stairs.

'Couldn't make it last night,' she said to his retreating back.

He looked over his shoulder at her, waiting for some excuse, a polite lie perhaps, but there was none. He was intrigued by her, had found himself waiting expectantly for her all the evening before, was surprised by his savage disappointment when he realised, finally, that she was not going to turn up.

She clattered into the room in flimsy sandals, stared around for a moment. 'That's new,' she said, glancing at an Anglepoise lamp and depositing a white plastic carrier bag on the bare floorboards, next to the rolled-up sleeping-bag. 'Bought you Chinese. Thought you might not be eating proper.'

'That was nice of you,' he said, touched by her bringing food, by her even bothering to notice that he'd bought a new light. Feeling a sudden wash of tears in his throat, he turned away, aware that the fragile balance of his self-control was too easily tipped by kindness. Alone, he was fine; it was other people who disarmed him. For the past week he had spent his days in the office, holed up, lying on the sleeping-bag staring blankly at the cracked ceiling. He couldn't face going out. It was the world that frightened him, not this shabby, cosy room that had become his retreat, his hot and fusty womb.

Lily seemed to sense his mood, smiled at him gently. 'You might not say that when you taste it,' she said cheerfully. 'It's from that dodgy-looking place down the road, the one on the corner. You hungry?'

The wave of feeling receded. 'Yes,' he said, although he was not. But he wanted to please her, to show her he was grateful. Well, perhaps more than grateful – interested.

She knelt down on the blue nylon sleeping-bag, began lifting rectangular cardboard boxes stained with grease and lidded with foil, small white polystyrene cups, napkins and plastic chopsticks out of the bag. As she worked, her hair slid over her shoulders and she tossed it back impatiently. He thought, with her hair loose, caught back with a velvet headband, she looked like some modern-day milkmaid.

'Look,' she exclaimed, holding up a fistful of tiny, cheap plastic bottles, 'real soy sauce.'

'A feast,' he agreed, staring down at her. There was something endearing in her absorption, her delight at playing house. Crouched down like that on the sleeping-bag, she looked scarcely older than a schoolgirl – the hairband, the thin dress, one pale, bare leg caught awkwardly over the other, the shoe slipping off to reveal

253

the red welt of a blister carved on the heel. Lifting off the last lid, she sat back on her heels, frowning down at the glutinous, dun-coloured contents of the boxes.

'Don't look too good,' she said, wrinkling her nose.

'It will after a glass of this,' Tom said, producing a bottle of red wine. He had bought two, the night before, had drunk one of them waiting for her to turn up. By the time he slid into the sleeping-bag, he found he could not stop thinking about her; had dreamed of her vividly, all night.

He stared around, frowning. 'Well, maybe not a glass,' he said apologetically. 'I seem to have run out of paper cups.' He held the bottle out to her. 'Do you mind drinking out of this?'

'Don't be daft,' she said good-naturedly, putting the bottle to her lips and tilting back her head.

A faint dribble of wine leaked from the sides of her pursed lips, ran down her chin. Without thinking, Tom leaned forward and put out his finger to catch the glistening drop, felt the cool, unfamiliar flesh under his finger and jerked his hand away.

'Thought it might drip on your dress and spoil it,' he said, wiping his hand awkwardly on his jeans.

She sat motionless on her heels, eyes gleaming. He made no movement either, and they sat watching each other until, at last, she flung her head back, tilted the bottle to her lips and drank deeply while he stared at the movement of her white throat, the spill of her hair down her back, the way her breasts pressed against the thin cotton of the dress.

She finished drinking, took the bottle from her mouth and thrust it towards him without bothering to wipe it. 'Here.'

He took it from her, felt the lingering warmth from her lips as he fastened his mouth around the neck of the bottle.

'May as well eat,' she said, picking up a pair of chopsticks, giggling as the greasy meat slithered between them. 'Can't be doing with these,' she said, abandoning the chopsticks, picking up pieces of meat and vegetables with her fingers. He ate slowly, watching her pink tongue darting across her fingers, licking off the grease.

'Next time I come I'll bring some candles,' she said, after a while. 'They make a place nice, romantic.'

He glanced quickly at her but her face was set in an absorbed, earnest frown as she stared around, contemplating the practical considerations of making the best of his small, shabby room. Something about the matter-of-factness of her manner warmed him, in a way that any deliberate seductiveness on her part would not have done, would have made him withdraw into himself, into the effortless existence of solitude.

'It's all right here,' she said, looking around. 'You could make it nice, if you put your mind to it.'

It was such a contrast to Bella, to her look of distaste as she sat, exactly where Lily was now sitting, nose wrinkled at the cheap, ugly poverty of her surroundings. Yet, once, when they were first married, they too had lived in a place like this, had found pleasure in a Chinese take-away and a bottle of cheap red wine. He felt a thickness catch at his throat as he studied Lily's face, glowing in the fading sunlight, remembering Bella's studied indifference to the mean little house they had been forced to move into when the business failed, her refusal to do anything to improve it; her contempt for the cheap bits and pieces – a rug, a lamp, an old desk he painted – that he brought home. She wouldn't relent, even by an inch, but he dared not say anything, had to endure her constant, sour displeasure in her surroundings as his punishment for the affair. She's so fucking righteous sometimes, he thought, remembering the contempt etched across her face the first time he'd taken her to see the house. 'Here?' she had said, staring at him in disbelief. 'You want us to live here?'

He had followed her around the place in helpless

silence, trying to avoid her set, white face, her rigid shoulders and the almost physical bleakness of her despair. They moved in the following week.

Tom glanced over at Lily. 'I have to be out by the end of next week,' he reminded her. 'This place has only got a business lease on it; I shouldn't really be here at all.'

She stared at him thoughtfully. 'Where will you go?'

'Haven't thought about it,' he said, shrugging.

He wondered, suddenly, what he had been thinking about for the past week, through the long, cold hours of solitude but could remember no single thought; not about Bella, not about Ben, a job, the future. Not even, the most pressing problem, about where he was going to live. It had been a curiously peaceful existence and one that he would regret leaving. I shall even regret leaving this dingy little room, he thought, looking around.

'I suppose I ought to do something about it,' he said heavily.

Lily prodded at a piece of cold chicken. 'There's a room going in the house where I live,' she said casually. 'Not exactly a palace but the rent's okay. Fifty-five quid a week.'

Harry had offered him a spare room in his house but Tom's courage failed at the idea of being beholden to his friends. Better, he thought, a cheap bedsit, cash on the nail every Friday night, a pay-phone in the corridor, a pound in the meter for heat and light. No responsibilities and, he thought with a heavy sigh, no worries.

He nodded. 'Seems reasonable.'

She looked up at him, through lowered lashes. 'I could ask, if you like.'

'Bella would have a fit if she found out,' he said hesitantly.

Lily shrugged. 'Don't see how she would. She don't know where I live.'

'She came round the other night, just after you left,' he

said, wondering why he was telling Lily. Perhaps because he wanted to tell somebody how terrible it was, seeing and ignoring the dark, wounded light in Bella's eyes.

Lily's eyes flickered. 'Didn't go well, then?'

He looked away. 'No.'

'Can't have been nice for her, seeing you in a place like this.'

He was silent.

'Not after that posh house you used to live in.'

He looked at her questioningly. 'Who told you about that?'

'Oh –' She let the silence lengthen. 'People like to talk –'

I'll bet they do, he thought savagely. He could just imagine them, gathered around Elisabeth's table in her gleaming white kitchen, discussing poor Tom – and poor Bella, having to put up with that poky little house after the business had failed. After he had failed. He could see their faces, gleaming with false sympathy. Well, of course, one of them would say, he was one of the most promising architects of his generation, but early promise – well, you know how it has a habit of suddenly fizzling out.

He felt a sudden movement, looked up to find Lily's face inches from his own. Her dark eyes gleamed. 'Don't take on so,' she said softly. 'It's their way. Don't know no other, they don't.'

She leaned forward and pressed her mouth to his; he felt her lips, cool and dry, and then the flicker of her tongue, soft and warm, against his teeth. He closed his eyes, felt her withdraw, and opened them again to find her crouched over him, watching him intently.

'Sorry,' she said. 'Don't know why I did that.'

He smiled shakily. 'I liked it.'

She nodded, stood up abruptly. 'I'll be back,' she said, and before he could say anything, she slipped noiselessly from the room, like a cat.

Bella was parked outside, her eyes fixed on the building.

It housed only offices, so few people came and went other than a harassed young man in a suit, clutching a shabby briefcase and a bunch of limp flowers, taking the steps two at a time, glancing repeatedly at his watch. Late for his lovely young wife, Bella thought sourly, watching the flap of his jacket catch in the wind. Then came two stout elderly women, making their grumbling progress up the steps, on their way up to the top-floor offices for the late cleaning shift. A little later, about nine, the door opened and closed and a figure – a girl – slipped out, was momentarily lost between light and shadow, then emerged to pick her way down the steep stone staircase. With a twirl of her heels, she was gone.

Bella blinked in disbelief, wrenched herself round in her seat to stare down the street, watched her walk away, her skirt twinkling in the fading light.

It was Lily.

Bella leaped out of the car, not bothering to lock the door, chased up the street after her and caught her at the corner, her nails digging into the girl's thin arm.

'What were you doing with my husband?' she panted.

Lily turned, stared at her unblinkingly. 'Nothing.'

'And you expect me to believe that?'

Lily reached down, unclasped Bella's fingers from her arm, one by one. Bella gazed at her hand, as if not quite sure it belonged to her.

'Believe what you like,' Lily said. 'It's all the same to me.'

'Everything's the same to you,' Bella said, her voice rising. 'You haven't an ounce of conscience in your body.'

'What? And you have? Letting your husband doss in a horrible old room on a sleeping-bag while you blame him for everything that's wrong with your life?'

'It's not that simple,' Bella said unsteadily.

'Course it is. Everything's that simple in the end.'

'What, like helping yourself to somebody else's husband?'

'Who says I am?'

'Looks bloody like it to me. Why else would you be leaving his room at nine o'clock at night?'

'Nine's not late,' Lily said, her tone truculent. 'Anyway, maybe I just wanted to see if he was all right.'

'Of course he's not bloody well all right.'

Lily crossed her arms, stuck a hip out. 'Oh, I don't know. Looks like he's managing to me,' she said, smiling provocatively.

'You little slut!'

Lily watched her through narrowed eyes. 'You're one to talk. Seen the state of yourself recently?'

'How dare you!'

Lily shook her head reprovingly. 'It's a bad habit you got, shouting at people like that.'

'Are you after my husband?'

'Don't seem like anyone else around here wants him.'

'Of course I want him.'

'Got a funny way of showing it.'

'That's none of your business.'

'You dump him out in the road like he's one of your possessions you don't want no more and then it's my business.'

'I didn't dump him –'

'Don't see what you're suddenly getting so high and mighty about – that's what girls like me are for, isn't it? To be grateful for your cast-offs. You chuck us a few bin-liners full of old clothes you don't want no more and you think you've saved the world.'

'My husband is not a cast-off.'

Lily looked at her implacably. 'Try telling him that.'

'Stay away, do you hear?' Bella said, her voice a thin cry in the grey, empty street. 'Stay away from him –'

But Lily had turned, was walking away, her skirt

flicking to and fro against her thin thighs while Bella stood frozen, gripped by cold terror. She glanced up, fearfully, at Tom's office. A square of yellow light glimmered at the window, was suddenly extinguished, plunging the building into darkness.

Elisabeth looked bewildered. 'First you tell me,' she said, 'that Lily's trying to seduce Charles. Now you say she's after Tom as well. Next, you'll accuse her of going for Alex, too.'

'Wouldn't put it past her.'

Elisabeth looked exasperated. She had tumbled out of bed in alarm at the insistent ringing of the doorbell, was conscious of her face, scrubbed of make-up and shiny with a residue of moisturiser; of her prosaic brushed pink nylon dressing-gown and white cotton nightdress. And all for this – this pathetic, dispirited tale. Really, Bella's imagination did tend to get the better of her sometimes. Irritation crept into her voice. 'Bella, I must say that I find all this very difficult to –'

'I *saw* her. She was at Tom's office, at nine o'clock at night. What would you think?'

Elisabeth sighed faintly, squashed with her finger a few stray sugar crystals that lay scattered on the table. They were drinking tea; skimmed milk for Elisabeth, full milk and plenty of sugar for Bella. The warmth of the tea was slowly returning the colour to Bella's thin cheeks. Elisabeth glanced up at her, chose her words carefully.

'Bel, I know you've been under a great deal of strain recently, what with one thing and another but really I –'

Bella stared mutinously at the table top. 'I'm not making this up. And nor am I imagining things, if that's what you mean.'

'But –' Elisabeth's voice took on a disbelieving note, 'all *three* of them?'

Bella shrugged. 'Well, maybe not Alex but certainly Tom and Charles –'

Elisabeth shook her head. 'I'm sorry, I can't –'

'Aren't you even interested,' Bella said, her voice rising, 'that some little scrubber is after your husband?'

Elisabeth winced, raised a finger to her lips. 'Charles is sleeping,' she reminded her.

'I am not making this up,' Bella repeated, in a low urgent whisper.

Elisabeth's hands moved helplessly. 'But Lily, she's – she's practically a child. Charles wouldn't –'

Bella looked up, eyes blazing. 'But *she* would. And he's infatuated. Anybody can see that.'

A slight, bewildered frown dented Elisabeth's forehead. She stared down at her hands. 'Can they?'

'Yes,' Bella said heavily. 'Yes, they can.'

Elisabeth got to her feet, walked to the sink, picked up a damp cloth and wandered around the kitchen, aimlessly wiping clean surfaces. She felt as if a film of dirt had entered the room with Bella, coating the gleaming surfaces under a faint, hostile layer of grime and wanted the distraction, the soothing dab and swirl of the damp J-cloth, wiping out her embarrassment for Bella's neurotic, jealous imaginings, for her own sudden, wrenching feeling of sadness.

'You don't believe me, do you?' Bella said, watching her with dark, impenetrable eyes.

Elisabeth swiped at the refrigerator's gleaming white surface, turned to her with a helpless shrug. 'It's just that Charles – well, he wouldn't –'

Bella looked away. 'How do you know?' she said coldly.

Elisabeth wanted to say, because, well because he's *Charles*, but she said, 'Maybe I should make us some camomile tea instead.'

'To calm my wild imaginings?'

Elisabeth smiled faintly. 'Something like that.'

'I thought the same about Tom – once,' Bella said, staring out at the dark garden. 'I thought, well, he *wouldn't* –'

'And I think it's time we both got some sleep,' Elisabeth said firmly. 'James's and Lucy's rooms are both empty. Why don't you stay here tonight?'

'And now he's doing it again,' Bella said, covering her face with her hands.

'You don't know that.'

Bella glared at Elisabeth over the tops of her hands. 'Of course I know that. She half-admitted it.'

'You may have misunderstood –'

'It wasn't what she said,' Bella said contemptuously. 'It was the way she looked at me.'

'I'll go and make up the bed.'

'There's something odd about her,' Bella said. 'Something not quite centred.' She looked over at Elisabeth, who was hovering by the door. 'Have you noticed that?'

Elisabeth shook her head.

'It's as if she's impervious to other people's emotions. She reminds me of Ben, when he was tiny and I tried to explain to him that feelings, although we can't see them, are still something that can be hurt, like fingers or knees.' She shook her head, lit a cigarette. 'He looked at me in exactly the same way,' she said thoughtfully, expelling a stream of blue smoke. 'As if I was – not mad exactly – but speaking in an entirely foreign language.'

She looked up at Elisabeth. 'By the way, I hate camomile tea.'

If Bella wasn't so distressed the whole thing would be laughable, Elisabeth thought, vigorously stripping the sheets off Lucy's bed, remaking it with fresh linen and laying out one of her own nighties for Bella. She was just bundling Lucy's assortment of stuffed animals under her arm when Bella appeared in the doorway.

'Thanks,' she said, picking up a stray fluffy rabbit and hugging it absently.

'I've put out a new toothbrush in James's and Lucy's bathroom,' Elisabeth said, dumping the rest of the animals in a chair and briskly drawing curtains.

'What do you think I should do?' Bella asked dully, sinking down onto the bed, the rabbit still tucked in her arms.

'Get undressed. I'll go and make you a hot drink,' Elisabeth said, escaping gratefully to the calm of her kitchen. As she passed their bedroom, she heard Charles snoring faintly, glanced in to see a pyjamaed leg poking out from under the duvet. She stared at it for a moment, noticing the black hairs sprouting on his toes and the yellowed horn of his toenails; badly in need of cutting, she thought. The sight roused in her a conflict of emotions, part disgust and part reassurance. As if, she thought, closing the door gently and going downstairs.

'Here's something to make you sleep,' Elisabeth said, setting a mug down beside Bella. 'And if you can't, I've left you a pile of magazines to amuse yourself with.'

'What's in this?' Bella said, picking up the steaming mug.

'Hot milk, brandy and ground-up calcium tablets.'

Bella took a sip. 'Tastes like liquid chalk.'

'I expect that's because it's essentially what it is.'

The next morning, Elisabeth woke early, went downstairs to make tea, then woke Charles. 'Is it the weekend?' he said, with a groan. During the week, he always got up first and made the morning tea.

'No, I couldn't sleep so I thought I'd treat you.'

'Lovely,' he said, struggling into a sitting position and resting the mug on his chest. He took a sip, eyes still closed.

'Bella's asleep next door,' she said in a whisper, sitting

down on the bed and leaning back against his propped legs.

His eyes opened. He looked at her in bemusement. 'Bella?'

'She turned up late last night, full of some improbable tale about –' About you having an affair with a girl young enough to be your daughter, she thought. She swivelled her head, watched his reaction out of the corner of her eye. 'She's convinced that Tom's having an affair with Lily.'

'With Lily?' he exclaimed, jerking his arm so that a few drops of the hot tea spilled. 'Damn.' He sat up swiftly, dislodging her from the bed, and dabbed ineffectually at his pyjama shirt.

'*Darling*,' she said, in pained tones.

'It was hot,' he said crossly.

She stood over him, staring down at the pale brown stain spreading on the white duvet cover. 'You've got tea on the duvet. You know how it stains –'

He glared up at her. 'I *said* it was hot.'

She moved away with a sigh, sat down at her dressing-table and began brushing her hair.

'Well, do you think it's possible?' she said, watching him in the mirror.

He swung his legs out of bed, was fussing under it with his bare feet searching for his slippers. 'Do I think what's possible?' he asked, his voice muffled.

She stared calmly at her reflection. 'Tom and Lily.'

'How would I know?' he snapped. 'I don't know what the hell Tom's up to. Wouldn't put it past him, given his behaviour in the past few weeks.'

'Behaviour?' she echoed, laying her brush down and arranging it carefully next to the silver-backed mirror and comb that made up the set.

He stared belligerently at the back of her head. 'Well, he's hardly behaving rationally, is he?'

'No,' she said carefully, 'but then, nor is Bella.'

He slid his feet awkwardly into the slippers, shuffled through to the en-suite bathroom. She heard the splash of water as the bath taps were turned on.

'It wasn't Bella who walked out on their marriage,' he shouted above the roar of the water. His head appeared around the corner of the bathroom door, his eyebrows lowered in a dark, mutinous line. She looked at him with surprise. Charles so rarely got angry about anything. 'And it wasn't Bella who had an affair.'

'Well, no,' she admitted, 'but even then it was obvious that things weren't right between those two.'

'You don't solve that by running off and having an affair with a girl who's young enough to be your daughter.'

'She also said something about you and Lily,' Elisabeth said carefully.

'About me?' he repeated.

'And Alex. According to Bella, Lily's got her sights set on all three of you.'

He let out a short bark of laughter, then his head disappeared, followed by a splash of water as he lowered himself into the bath.

Elisabeth started to rearrange the things on her dressing-table; something she did when she was thinking. Rings to the left, in the red Venetian leather box, necklaces hung on the crystal stand Charles had bought her, shaped like a tree, her make-up tidily arranged in the central drawer. In some ways, she thought, Charles was quite priggish. He loathed gossip, what he called small people's talk. 'It diminishes everyone concerned,' he explained once. She admired that in him, although his reticence sometimes seemed prissy, middle-aged. And he was only, what, forty-four next birthday? Charles had always seemed older than he was, even when they were first married, but she had liked it then; his solidity and way of looking at things had made her feel secure as opposed to the thin, nervous young men all her friends seemed to fall in love with.

Sighing, she closed her make-up drawer and contemplated the fine lines around her eyes. They were all getting older but Charles seemed to have become so staid recently; that solidity she so admired had petrified to a sort of complacent pomposity.

Dabbing some moisturiser around her eyes, she walked into the bathroom. Charles was lying in the bath. His eyes were closed. The water gave his white skin a faintly greenish tinge; his semi-erect penis bobbed sluggishly on the surface of the water. She glanced away in distaste.

'You still haven't said – do you think Tom is?'

His eyes opened. 'Is what?'

'Having an affair with Lily,' she said patiently.

He screwed his eyes shut, making him look as if he was in some sort of pain. 'Fuck knows.'

She glanced sharply at him, surprised by the obscenity. Charles so rarely swore.

'I'll go and make the coffee,' she said, 'and take a breakfast tray up to Bella. She's terribly tired. It would do her good to take the day off, stay here in bed.'

Bella's eyes fluttered open and she scrambled up to a sitting position, blinking away the sleep as she stared wildly round the room.

Elisabeth moved closer to the bed. 'It's me, Elisabeth. You stayed here last night, remember?'

Bella frowned, nodded slowly.

'There's a cup of tea by the bed.'

'Thanks. What time is it?'

'Seven thirty.'

'I suppose I should be getting up.'

'It's OK. I called the college, left a message on the machine to say you weren't well and were staying with friends. I gave this number.'

'Thanks,' Bella said, a touch of resentment sharpening her voice. How like Elisabeth it was to try and control everybody else's life. She lay back heavily against her pillow. She could scarcely keep her eyes open. 'Very comfortable, this bed,' she mumbled.

'And Ben's fine,' Elisabeth was saying, 'I spoke to him just now.'

Bella frowned, trying to remember if there was any food in the house. When had she last gone shopping? She couldn't remember. 'I'm amazed he was awake. Has he eaten breakfast?'

'Do stop worrying,' Elisabeth said severely. 'Ben is seventeen. He'll be moving out to live in his own flat soon. He's perfectly capable of looking after himself.'

'Yes,' Bella said sadly.

'He sends you his love. Says to have a good rest.'

'Thank you.'

'I'm going to work soon. I'll be back about four,' Elisabeth said, moving noiselessly towards the door. 'Get some sleep. You still look done in. And if you're hungry, there's plenty of food in the fridge.'

Bella nodded, turned over and was asleep in minutes.

Twenty-four

When Elisabeth got home that afternoon, she discovered a note on the kitchen table in Bella's spiky, erratic handwriting, thanking her for putting her up for the night and assuring her that she would call later. Elisabeth put down the heavy bags of shopping she had bought to prepare supper for the three of them and wandered around her empty kitchen, feeling deflated. She had been looking forward to having a little chat with Bella, was sure that she would have been able to make her see sense. All day she had been rehearsing a speech, a wonderfully persuasive speech briskly discarding all the nonsense about Lily and convincing Bella that she should go to Tom and tell him how much she still loved him. She had thought for a moment of ringing Charles, trying out the idea on him, but she knew she would get little more than a non-committal grunt so she had told Sam instead; wonderful Sam who had immediately thrown himself into the spirit of things, even playing Tom's part although he had an endearing, if slightly infuriating habit of refusing to stick to the script. 'How simple you make it all sound,' he had said, laughing as he gently patted her hand. But it is, she wanted to say, love is simple but she had instead given herself up to the delight of the touch of his hand on hers.

She switched on the kettle to make herself a cup of tea, noticing that Bella had left her mug in the sink; hadn't even bothered to fill it with water to soak, and felt a sudden, sharp stab of resentment. After all the trouble she had gone to as well, she thought, unpacking artichokes and smoked salmon and storing them carefully away in the fridge. If Bella would only talk to her, she knew she'd be able to help sort things out. As she poured boiling water over the tea-leaves in the pot, she imagined Tom's face, weary but grateful, thanking her for her help. 'Nobody else could have brought us back together,' he would say, 'nobody else would have understood.' She smiled complacently as she carried her cup to the table and sat down, staring out over the garden.

A little later, as Elisabeth began making preparations for supper, Charles and Lily met in the wine bar. Charles, who had been brooding all day over Elisabeth's remarks about Lily and Tom, was silent and withdrawn.

'All right?' Lily said after a moment. She peered at him through the gloom. 'You look a bit peaky.'

He smiled faintly. 'A lot on at the office.'

'You should think about getting yourself a decent secretary,' she said, gazing at him with serene brown eyes. 'That Angela's rubbish.'

'She's very efficient,' he protested.

'If you say so,' Lily said, looking away with a shrug.

'Isn't she?' The seed of doubt was growing nicely.

She fiddled with a stalactite of wax suspended precariously from an old wine bottle; began tearing it off in strips. 'Dunno about that,' she said, squashing a strip into a ball and rolling it on the barrel top. 'I'm always clearing up after her, sorting out some mess she's left.' She bent her head, took a sip of wine. 'Anyway, you don't want to be hearing about all that. Just something to think about, ease some of the burden, that's all.'

'I had no idea –'

Lily looked indignant. 'Course you don't. It's up to her to look after you, same as I do Simon, not the other way around.'

Charles, who had been growing irritable with Simon's increasingly effusive praise of Lily, looked thoughtful.

'Don't mind me saying all this, do you?' Lily said, leaning forward, her brow wrinkled with concern.

'No.' But he did mind, very much. One more thing to worry about. 'No, of course not.'

'So how's Elisabeth?' she asked, propping her chin on her clasped hands and looking at him.

'Oh, she's fine. Busy at the gallery.'

'Seems to love it there.'

'Yes, it seems to agree with her rather well,' Charles said absently. He was watching a pulse flicker delicately in the fine white skin above Lily's eyebrow.

'Well, I expect she's meeting all sorts of interesting people. Like, for example, that bloke she works for. Mad about him she is, always going on about him. It's almost like she was in love with him. If I didn't know her better, I'd say she was having an affair with him.'

'Good God.'

'Just teasing, silly. Now, what is his name?' She thought for a moment, her eyes tilted towards the damp ceiling. 'Sam – that's it.'

Charles look astonished. 'She's hardly mentioned him to me.'

'Oh, she talks about him all the time –' She paused, glanced at him slyly as if she might have said too much. 'But you know what women are like, when they get on the phone.'

Charles frowned. 'Do you speak to each other much?' he asked carefully.

'No. She rings sometimes, when she's bored at work and Sam's out,' Lily said, shrugging.

'And has she mentioned anything about –' he paused, fumbled with the stem of his glass '– about Bella?'

Lily shook her head. 'Only that's she's dead upset about Tom going.' She put an olive in her mouth, sucked on it thoughtfully. 'Can't say I blame her.'

'Why not?' he said sharply.

She stared at him in surprise. 'Can't be very nice, having your husband walk out on you in the middle of the night.'

Charles looked away, fiddled with some loose change in his jacket pocket. His words, when they emerged, tumbled out in a rush. 'Lily, have you been to see Tom?'

'Yesterday,' she said cheerfully. 'Told you I was going.'

'No, you didn't,' he said, watching her closely. 'You said you were going to visit a friend who was having a rough time.'

She shrugged. 'Well he is, isn't he? Having a rough time, I mean.'

'Why didn't you say it was Tom?'

Lily dropped her eyes, stared at the stained barrel top. 'I thought I did.'

He struggled to keep his voice level. 'No, you did not.'

'Well then, perhaps I thought you might be angry with me,' she said, eyes downcast.

He watched the curve of her lashes, dark against white cheeks. 'Why would I be angry with you?'

She glanced up at him. 'Because you are now.'

'That's only because you lied to me,' he said with a sigh.

She lifted her chin, stared at him indignantly. 'No, I didn't. I said I was going to see a friend.'

He slumped back in his chair, defeated.

She watched him for a moment, then leaned forward, put her hand over his. He felt the warmth of her skin, the imprint of her fingers on his hand. 'I won't go again if it upsets you,' she said softly. He made an impatient gesture, moved as if to withdraw his hand but her fingers tightened over it. 'I only went because you seemed so worried about him. I was going to tell you all about it, this evening, only you didn't give me a chance.'

'Bella thinks you're having an affair with Tom,' he said in a tight voice.

Lily released his hand with an impatient gesture. 'She's

mad, that one. Had a real go at me. Yelling like a fishwife she was, right in the middle of the street.'

'In fact –' he paused, aware of the absurdity of what he was going to say '– in fact, Bella seems to think that you've got your sights set on all three of us.'

She stared at him in astonishment. 'You what?'

'Me, Tom and Alex,' he said, bringing out the last name heavily. He had been thinking about it all day, imagining Lily's white skin against Alex's smooth, prosperous flesh, Lily's long pale legs wrapped around Tom's skinny back. He heard her giggle, looked up, startled.

'Blimey,' she said, 'Mata Hari or what?'

He laughed reluctantly. 'So you're not . . . ?'

'I went to see Tom, to make sure he was all right and I had a drink with Alex the other week, but you know all about that,' she said patiently.

'Yes,' he said, staring at her longingly.

'I know what all this is about,' she said decisively. 'Bella's got the hump about Tom having an affair that time, whenever it was, right?'

Charles nodded.

'Well, she's gone a bit daft. Stands to reason, doesn't it? She thinks he's done it once, so he's going to do it again. Then she sees me leaving that place where he's staying, puts two and two together and makes five.'

'So you're not after all three of us at all?'

She shook her head.

'Not even one of us, perhaps,' he said, battling to keep the longing from his voice.

She wrinkled her nose, laughed. 'One would be enough. I'm not the greedy type.'

He glanced at her. 'And which one might that be?' he said, trying to keep his voice light.

She heard it, caught the tremor and held it fast. 'You shouldn't be after asking questions like that,' she said teasingly, 'you a married man and all.'

'And if I wasn't?' he said, trying to keep his voice casual.

She shrugged, suddenly impatient. 'What's the point of talk like that? You're married and that's all there is to it.'

He gaped foolishly, wrong-footed by the swiftness of her change of mood. 'I didn't –' he began, but she had turned away from him, was delving in her bag. Her hand emerged, clutching a pile of loose change.

'For the bus,' she said, slipping from her stool. 'Better be off. Promised I'd drop in on Mrs Flower when I got back. She's got a cake in, from her daughter.' She wrinkled her nose. 'Tasteless, they are, but I don't like to disappoint her.'

He caught her arm, felt the warmth of the flesh beneath his hand. 'Give it a miss,' he urged, emboldened by her closeness, by the sweet, heady smell of her perfume in his nose. 'You can see her tomorrow night.'

She moved her arm away. He recoiled at the coldness of the gesture. 'Elisabeth will be waiting,' she said. 'She'll have your dinner ready.' There was a trace of mockery in her tone. Poised for flight, her hair swinging down her back, she looked so young and unencumbered that he felt the daily ritual of married life close around him. The breath tightened in his throat.

'I could telephone. Say I'm held up.'

'*You?*' she said, her eyes round with disbelief.

'I could.' His voice hit a wrong note. 'I could,' he repeated.

Laughing, she turned on her heel, picked her way quickly through the thicket of tables and chairs. He stared after her, his heart lifting as she hesitated, turned to stare at him. She was too far away for him to read her expression but he felt he saw something beseeching in the tilt of her head, the glimmer of her eyes, black pools in the white oval of her face.

He smiled encouragingly, began to stand, to move towards her.

'Thanks for the drink,' she called, and with a wave of her hand was gone.

Charles sat down slowly, aware of the curious eyes of other drinkers on him. He fumbled for the bottle, tilted the remains of it into his glass and subsided into his stool, wrapping his hands around the glass.

After a while, he lifted the glass, drank it down in steady gulps. A waitress materialised silently at his side.

'Anything else I can get you, sir?' she said, smiling, but he noticed how the smile did not reach her eyes. He sighed. They earned a pittance, these women, made their money on tips. 'The same,' he said, indicating the bottle.

'Would that be a bottle or a glass, sir?'

He looked up at her. Her face was blank. He looked away.

'A bottle,' he said heavily.

'You're looking mighty pleased with yourself, lovely,' Mrs Flower said, cutting Lily a hefty slice of fruit cake. 'Got yourself a new boyfriend or something, have you?'

'Maybe,' Lily said, accepting the plate and popping a glacé cherry into her mouth. She was fond of glacé cherries, poked her finger into the cake and winkled out a couple more. 'Lovely cake this.'

But Mrs Flower was not to be distracted. 'Handsome, is he?' she asked with a coy smile, her head tilted to one side. Mrs Carlton had been on the phone that very evening, to see if there was any news. 'Nothing as I can say is definite,' Mrs Flower had told her, adding that there had been a few more messages on Alex's private line and a number of bunches of flowers ordered for Daisy.

'Man called Tom might be moving in,' Lily said, 'friend of mine. Called Mr Matthews I did, this morning, see if that room at the top's going. Said it was fine by him. Mind you, Tom hasn't been to see it yet.'

'Room at the top? Hasn't been nobody in there for two years, not since old Mr Campbell passed on.'

'Die there, did he?'

'Don't be daft, lovely. Died in hospital, surrounded by machines. Not a solitary soul to wave him goodbye but the nurses and they weren't sad to see him go. Not much wrong with him but old age and they needed the room, they did. Took him some grapes, very morning that he died. Often wondered what happened to them grapes. Who's this Tom then?'

'Bloke I know. His wife kicked him out so the poor sod's been dossing in his office.' Lily stared around thoughtfully. 'This isn't the sort of place he's been used to, mind.'

'And what sort's that?' Mrs Flower said, squaring her shoulders indignantly. She was protective of Orchard Road and all its inhabitants.

'Used to live in a big house but he's lost all his money.'

'Sounds like a careless sort of man to me,' Mrs Flower said tartly, still smarting from the remark about the house, 'seeing as he's managed to mislay both his house and his wife.'

Lily grinned. 'He's all right,' she said, taking a bite of cake. 'Needs feeding up a bit though.'

Mrs Flower was struck by a sudden thought. 'What did you say his name was?'

'Tom Sutherland. He's a friend of Charles and Elisabeth. You know, my friends with the posh house, place I went to dinner when I first got here.'

Mrs Flower had not forgotten. 'Is he now?' she said thoughtfully.

When Charles got home, he felt rather drunk.

'I'm rather drunk,' he said, stumbling into the kitchen.

'No you're not,' Elisabeth said, staring at him in astonishment, 'you're very drunk. What on earth have you been doing.'

'Went for a drink with – with somebody from the office,' he said, slumping into a chair.

'Who with?'

He stared at her bemusedly. 'Sorry?'

'Who did you go and have a drink with?' Elisabeth said, enunciating the words carefully.

He shrugged. 'Oh, you know, somebody's birthday – have a drink, have another.'

'You ought to go to bed,' Elisabeth said, getting to her feet and walking across to the oven. She picked up a cloth, removed a plate of food and scraped it into the dustbin. 'Your dinner,' she announced.

'Was my dinner,' he said, staring thoughtfully after it.

She dumped the plate in the sink, turned on the tap and began noisily to wash it.

'How's work?' he asked, gazing at her back.

Elisabeth felt a prickle of alarm. 'What?'

'Your job – how is it?'

'Fine, thank you,' she said, looking at him in bewilderment.

'And your boss. Nice man, is he?'

She snatched up a drying-up cloth, towelled furiously at the wet plate. 'Very nice,' she said, her head bent over the plate.

'Sam somebody or other, isn't it?'

She put the plate down carefully on the side, hung the drying-up cloth on the rail in front of the Aga. 'Charles,' she said, looking pained, 'what's all this about?'

He shrugged. 'Nothing. Just trying to make conversation with my wife, that's all.' He looked at her. 'I am allowed to make conversation with my wife, aren't I?'

She shrugged helplessly. 'Well, of course –'

'Never mind,' he said, turning away from her, slumping over the table. 'I just thought –' he said, his voice muffled. He raised himself up a little, propped his head on his hands. 'I thought, on the way home in the taxi, that I don't know anything about your job, or your boss, this Sam person. Thought I ought to know, that's all. How things were.'

Elisabeth walked over to him, put her hands on his shoulder, bent her head to his. 'Go to bed,' she said, 'you're well past talking.'

He stared up at her, his eyes slightly out of focus. 'We both seem to be well past talking,' he said distantly. 'We've hardly talked at all since the children went off to school.'

He got to his feet, walked wearily to the door. 'Maybe they were all we had left to talk about,' he said, swaying slightly against the door jamb. 'They say it's what happens to married couples, after the children have left home.' He swung an arm in the air, knocked his hand heavily against the door. 'I read it in the newspaper,' he said, sucking on bruised knuckles, 'some woman writing –'

Elisabeth stared at him.

He stood, his head swaying slightly from side to side. 'I miss them,' he said in a thick voice. 'I really miss them.'

Elisabeth took a step towards him but he held up a hand, as if commanding her to stop. 'Doesn't matter,' he said with a vague grin. 'Couldn't matter a bit.' He wagged a reproving finger at her, shook his head. 'In vino veritas and all that.'

'Charles?' she said, but he turned away with a flapping wave of his hand and went stumbling through into the hallway.

She heard the heavy trudge of his feet on the stairs, the rumble of the hot water cistern as he washed his face and then brushed his teeth, the faint thud of the bed subsiding as he fell onto it.

'What on earth was all that about?' she said, addressing the silent dishwasher.

She made a cup of camomile tea, took it over to the table and sat, staring out at the darkened garden, feeling a faint but unmistakable sense of loss.

Twenty-five

'You are bored,' Celia said over breakfast. 'I'd know that look anywhere.'

'What look, darling?' Alex asked, smearing his toast with marmalade.

Celia poured a cup of tea; pale China tea in a fragile porcelain cup, accompanied by a thin crescent of lemon. Alex was drinking coffee; black and fearsomely strong.

'Either that, or you're going through a mid-life crisis,' she said, regarding him over the delicate gilt rim of her cup. 'Or perhaps, both.'

'Have you noticed any particular symptoms?' Alex enquired mildly.

'For one thing, you're under my feet far too much these days to be healthy for either of us.'

He crunched toast between strong white teeth. 'And for another?' he said, his mouth full.

She frowned. 'Must you?'

Alex stood up, dropping a starched white linen napkin on top of the liberally applied toast. Celia's eyebrows inched up her forehead.

'I am, as they say, in limbo,' he said, striding over to drop a kiss on her forehead. 'Betwixt and between –'

Celia, who had been having the most interesting conversation with Mrs Flower, knew that this was a reference to that delicate transitory phase between affairs. 'Bothered and bewildered?' she said, looking up at him. It seemed that Alex had a rival for the lovely Lily's affections, a person by the name of Tom. If her information was correct, which it usually was, and if this Tom really was a friend of Charles's and Elisabeth's then he must also be a friend of Alex's – which would make the situation quite uncomfortably cosy.

He looked at her with surprise. 'Something like that.'

Affecting indifference, she picked up a white peach and began to strip off the velvety skin in delicate ribbons. 'Well, do hurry up and sort it out,' she said languidly, 'your restlessness is horribly contagious.'

'I'm sorry,' he said, offended.

She knew by his tone that she was right about the ending of the affair with Daisy and felt a sudden, sharp sense of alarm. A mistress of three years' standing and one, moreover, who understood the status quo, was one thing; an untried twenty-three-year-old quite another.

'If there's anything I can do –' she said, arranging the ribbons of peach skin on her plate in a pattern like the rays of the sun. She looked up at him, her green eyes the only colour in her naked, morning face. 'You know you only have to ask.'

He lifted her hand, raised it to his lips. 'I don't deserve you,' he said humbly.

'I think we both know that,' she said briskly. 'Now hurry along or you'll be late.'

She looked after his retreating back thoughtfully. The burden of conflicting emotions – both loving and understanding him so well – sometimes exhausted her. Raising the skinned peach to her mouth, she sank her teeth into the opalescent, juicy flesh.

'I'll pick you up at six thirty,' Alex said, 'on the corner.'

'But I –'

'No buts,' he said, and the line went dead.

Lily stuck out her tongue at the telephone. 'Bully.'

'Some sort of problem?' Charles said from the doorway.

'Thinks he owns the sodding universe.' Lily swivelled on her chair to look at him, heels lifted off the ground.

'Who does?'

Her eyes flickered. 'Some bloke who wants a meeting.'

'Something I can help with?'

Lily shrugged, smiled up at him. 'Thanks, but it's sorted now.'

He moved further into the office, bent over her desk. 'I wondered if we could meet tonight,' he said in a low voice, 'there's something I'd like to say to you.'

She shook her head. 'Sorry. Off out tonight.'

He straightened up, looked down on her with narrowed eyes. 'With Tom?'

'With a friend,' she said, turning away, picking up a file of papers.

He stared at her back. 'A friend I know?' he said, unable to stop himself.

She tossed her hair back over her shoulder, swivelled to glare up at him. 'What are you? My sodding mother?'

He dropped his eyes. 'Sorry,' he said, after a while.

Lily watched him for a moment, eyes flickering. Then she put on her sweetest smile and bent forward and patted him on the arm. 'Me too. I'm a bit out of sorts this morning. Didn't sleep too well last night.'

Charles gave a shamefaced grin. 'Me neither. I got drunk and missed dinner.'

'You devil,' Lily said. 'Bet Elisabeth was surprised.'

He searched her face for traces of mockery but finding none said in a low, urgent voice, 'I had a think – about what you said. We must talk. Soon.'

Just then Angela bustled into the room. 'There you are,' she said, looking exasperated. 'I've been searching the building for you.'

Charles moved quickly away from Lily's desk, looked abashed. 'Needed a word with Simon,' he muttered.

'Simon's at the conference in Abbotsbury. Forget your

own head next,' Angela chided, rolling her eyes. She looked expectantly at him, waiting for his answering smile, but Charles looked studiously away. She flushed miserably, the pink of her cheeks clashing with her jumper, moved busily to the door. 'There's a Mr King on the phone. Says it's urgent.'

'Oh – right,' Charles said and hurried away wearing a preoccupied frown.

'Well!' Angela said, staring down at Lily, arms folded across plump breasts.

Lily leaned back in her chair, looked up innocently. 'Well?'

'You've gone and said something to him.'

'I have?'

Angela's small blue eyes darted longingly after Charles. 'He's hardly looked at me all morning.'

'Saving his eyes,' Lily muttered.

'What did you say?'

Lily ignored her.

'You have, haven't you?' Angela's voice rose to a shrill whistle. 'You've said something.'

'Course I did,' Lily said. 'It was last night, when we were at the Ritz, drinking champagne.'

Angela's mouth hung open. 'You what?'

'Dozy cow.' Lily jerked her head in the direction of Charles's office. 'Poor bloke's got a cracking hangover. Must have had a row with the wife last night or something.'

Angela's face settled in a supercilious smile. '*Charles?*' she said. 'I hardly think so.'

Lily turned back to her filing. 'You know best, of course,' she said, extracting a sheaf of papers and peering at them closely. Abandoned because of Lily's indifference, Angela flushed more deeply. 'So you weren't having a drink with him?'

'Like I said, buckets of champagne,' Lily said absently,

her attention focused on the document. 'Will you look at the state of this?'

Angela shifted a little closer, peered over Lily's shoulder.

'Shocking workmanship. Have to be redone of course.'

Angela snatched the papers out of Lily's hands. 'Where did you get those?'

Lily smiled up at her. 'Charles brought them over just now. Asked me if I could tidy them up for him. Dear, dear, not yours, are they?'

'He knows it's only a first draft,' Angela wailed, her fat cheeks shiny with distress. 'It was waiting for his corrections. He always changes his mind at least once with these things.'

She flicked through them, frowning. 'Funny, I could have sworn I locked these away safely in my personal file.'

She looked up, glared at Lily with small, hot blue eyes, then advanced forward, poking a stubby finger in the direction of Lily's face. 'It was you, wasn't it? You got this out of my file, left it lying around so he'd see it.'

'Blimey,' Lily said admiringly, her gaze focused on Angela's bitten nails. She stretched lazily in her chair, crossed her arms behind her head. 'They'll be sending little white men to take you away in a strait-jacket soon.'

Angela's lower lip stuck out like a fat, pink sausage. 'I'll get you one day,' she cried and ran out of the room, hips jiggling.

Lily smiled, swivelled in her chair and picked up the telephone. Tom answered almost at once.

'It's Lily,' she said, in a voice quite different from the one she had used with Angela.

'Well, hello.'

'That room I mentioned. It's still available. I wondered if you were serious about taking it.'

'Ah,' said Tom, who was not in a frame of mind to make a decision about anything.

'I went up and had a look for you. It's on the second floor, above my room. Not exactly what you're used to, but it'll see you over.'

'Over?' Tom echoed.

'Over whatever it is you need to get sorted.'

Tom sighed heavily. 'Only my marriage, my job and my future.'

'You want it or not?' Lily said, rolling her eyes.

'Yes. Sorry. Thanks.'

'Talk a lot, don't you?'

There was silence.

'I'm busy this evening,' Lily said, with a faint sigh, 'so how about you come over tomorrow? Not too early, mind. I like my Saturday lie-in.'

'Um, OK, about eleven thirty –'

'59 Orchard Road. See ya.'

'Alex is out with Celia *again*,' Daisy said.

Elisabeth gazed at her compassionately. 'Poor you.'

'Stupid me, you mean,' Daisy said, ushering her into the sitting-room. A bottle of champagne stood in an ice bucket on the glass table.

'Are we celebrating?' Elisabeth said, lowering herself cautiously into a chrome and leather chair.

'Drowning our sorrows. Or, rather, mine.'

'Lovely,' Elisabeth said absently. She felt she had not a sorrow in the world. Sam had given her a look that afternoon; such a look that she'd floated home, weightless as a cloud.

'I nicked it out of Alex's supplies.' Daisy lit a cigarette, blew out a hissing stream of smoke. 'I felt it was the least he could do. I mean, she's his bloody wife, *she's* the one who's supposed to hang around all evening waiting for him.'

She eased the cork out of the bottle with an expert twist. 'Quick, a glass.'

She was silent for a moment, frowning in concentration as she filled two glasses. 'What is it that's so heavenly about a few bubbles?' she said, taking a sip and then another. She put her glass down with a bang. 'I mean, *I'm* the mistress, for God's sake. I'm the one who's supposed to have forsaken security for the doubtful pleasures of glamour and excitement. So why is it me, sitting at home like the good little woman darning his socks?'

'You don't –' Elisabeth hesitated '– do you?'

'Don't be absurd, I meant it metaphorically – if anything so prosaic as a sock can be metaphorical.' She splashed champagne in her glass so it fizzed up, foamed onto the table. 'Unless, of course, he's seeing someone else, using Celia as a cover.'

Elisabeth fetched a cloth from Daisy's tiny galley kitchen, began mopping up the pale liquid. 'He wouldn't, surely? Even Alex?' And then she remembered Bella saying how Lily was after Alex too, and bent her head a little closer to the table to hide the flush that stained her cheeks. But if Bella was right about Lily and Alex – then might she perhaps be right about Charles? Surely not, surely it was all just the product of Bella's jealous imagining. Charles was hardly the type to go chasing after young girls.

Daisy was saying '– but of course it's novelty that's the most potent aphrodisiac. Nothing so exciting as the unknown, as seeing oneself reflected in the eyes of a loving stranger.'

'No,' Elisabeth sighed, still clutching the cloth, wondering where to put it. Sam, she thought, with longing. *Sam* –

Daisy held out a hand, dumped the cloth in the ice bucket. 'So I think the time has come to bid that faithless bastard farewell.'

'Oh dear,' Elisabeth said absently, floating gently on her little cloud, 'is that a good idea?'

'The best I've had in three years,' Daisy said, emptying her glass with a flourish.

Alex's black Mercedes purred to a stop by Lily. The door swung slowly open. 'Thank you for agreeing to see me,' he said smoothly, leaning forward to kiss her.

'Bloody lucky I could fit you in,' she said, ignoring the kiss, fiddling with her seat-belt.

Alex laughed, out of surprise. He was used to being accommodated by women. The car slid smoothly away from the kerb.

'I thought – the Hilton. Lovely view.'

'If you like,' she said, gazing out of the window.

He glanced at her, perplexed. 'Have I said something?'

'I'm not dressed right.'

'You look charming.'

'Charming,' she said, mimicking him, 'is not the same as right.'

He smiled. She was learning fast, this little matchstick girl. How much more could he teach her? His skin tingled in anticipation. 'Indeed.'

'And anyway,' she said, 'won't somebody see us there?'

'That was rather my intention.'

'Hold up,' she said, turning to him. 'What about *my* intention.'

Alex smiled benevolently. 'I thought it was rather your intention too.'

'Well, you're wrong,' she said, reaching for the door handle. 'Pull over.'

'What?'

'Over there, by that blue van. I'll get the bus.'

'My dear girl, you can't –'

'Don't you "dear girl" me. I can do whatever I please.'

He looked at her admiringly. He had not seen her so animated before, was excited by the change. 'Yes, and I do believe you would.'

'So pull over.'

Alex stopped the car. 'This is getting a little tiresome.'

She turned to him, her hand on the door handle. 'It's not right, the way you're behaving, as if I was some sort of a parcel, being taken somewhere without a yes or a maybe.'

He tilted his head back against the polished leather of the car seat. 'You can have whatever you want, you know.' He did not look at her, kept his eyes trained on the stream of traffic channelling around the car.

She shifted slightly and out of the corner of his eye he saw her hand slip from the door handle. 'What about Daisy?' she said slowly.

He shrugged regretfully.

She was silent.

'Bloody lunatic, that's what you are,' she said, after a while. 'She's the sort of woman you need. You can't be doing with a girl like me. I'm all wrong.'

His eyes slid over to her. 'That,' he said with a tight smile, 'is precisely why I want you.'

Twenty-six

On Saturday morning at eleven thirty sharp, Tom rang the doorbell of 59 Orchard Road. He bent back, gazed up at the top floor, his expert gaze assessing the original proportions. The house formed part of a row of once gracious but now dilapidated Victorian houses; residences for gentlefolk, rich enough to be considered comfortable and to employ two servant girls housed in small rooms at the top of the house where they froze in winter and boiled in summer. But not rich enough, he thought, to have employed a housekeeper – to the undoubted disappointment of those early inhabitants.

Traces of disappointment still lingered in the street, in its cracked paving stones and sickly trees whose leaves had long since succumbed to the fumes belched out by passing lorries, whose trunks were stained with urine from local dogs, itinerant tramps or drunks making their way home from the pub, the Ship, squatting dolefully on the corner next to the grease-spattered windows of the China Kitchen.

A few signs of gentrification were creeping slowly into the street; a builder's skip outside number 5, two stone urns brimming with scarlet geraniums outside number 33. Tom knew, without looking, the precise layout of the done-up houses: the walls of the ground floor knocked through from front to back, doors and window-frames stripped back to bare wood, salvaged tile-edged Victorian fireplaces installed that were at odds with the original period of the house.

He stared up at number 59. From the looks of it, it had been badly chopped around a number of times, settling finally into anonymous bedsits divided by thin, cheap partition walls and faced with ugly aluminium-framed windows in place of the original sashes.

Still no sign of life. Tom pressed the bell again, saw a curtain twitch on the second floor as somebody peered down, perhaps hopefully, perhaps in fearful anticipation, to see if the caller was for them. And then the sound of footsteps, slapping on cheap lino, the squeak of the unoiled hinge as the door creaked open, then Lily, framed in the doorway, smiling doubtfully.

'All right?' she said. She turned, made for him to follow her. 'Weren't sure you'd turn up,' she said over her shoulder as she climbed the once solid but now rickety wooden staircase. The ancient wood protested at every step. The walls were painted a dark green gloss, bisected at hip level with dirty cream. Lily turned, smiled at him encouragingly. 'Two more floors.'

'I'm at the top, then?' he called, and saw, dimly, in the faint light of the stairwell, her nod in reply.

'Number six,' she said, reaching the top with a grateful sigh, padding along the corridor, a key held in front of her. She slid it into the lock, jiggled it a little.

'It's loose,' she explained with a rueful smile, then flung open the door with a mock-heroic bow; 'And here's Buckingham Palace.'

It was a small room, long and thin, and – judging from the cornice which disappeared into the oblivion of the central wall – chopped in two during the conversion. But he was grateful to see that there was a large window at the far end, with a view over the gardens at the back of the house, and a relatively new, if badly stained, carpet.

'Bed,' he said, 'sink, table, wardrobe – not bad.'

'Was a chair to go with the table,' she said, 'but somebody nicked it. And there's a gas ring here.' She moved to the left of the room, pulled back a grubby curtain concealing a recess in the wall. 'Works on those cylinder things.'

'Like camping.'

She looked bored. 'Is it? Never seen the attraction myself. Insects everywhere and damp –'

'Not a romantic then,' he said, smiling slightly, imagining star-studded night skies, the mingling smells of wood smoke and coffee, remembering a holiday in Cornwall with Bella and Ben.

'Romance is for books,' she said, dismissing it with a shrug, staring around at the bare room. 'You could make it nice, if you like. I got a box from the greengrocer's, had oranges in it from Spain once, covered it with some fabric I got down the market –' she explained with a hint of pride at her enterprise. 'Makes a nice cupboard for your coffee and such.' She looked dismissively at the door, her gaze taking in the house and its inhabitants. 'They've all gone and copied it now, ever since Mrs Flower told them about it.'

'Mrs Flower?'

'Her room's up the corridor from me. Down there,' she said, pointing beneath her feet with a cherry-red nail. 'She's all right.'

'And the others?'

'Dunno. Keep themselves to themselves. Suits me.' She moved towards the door. 'What do you think, then?'

Tom stared around. 'How much is it?' he said, at last.

'Fifty quid. They said fifty-five but I told them, it's one of the small rooms, you can't charge him the same as everyone else.'

He smiled at her, watching the curve of her body as she rested against the door-frame, the light from the window shining on the thin, flowered cotton of her dress.

'Thank you,' he said, 'that was nice of you.'

''S'all right,' she shrugged but he could see that she was pleased.

'What shall I tell them then?'

Tom looked around, took a deep breath. It wasn't much, but it was a beginning – somewhere to stay while he got himself sorted out. 'Tell them, yes,' he said, smiling over at her.

Lily didn't return his smile but stood motionless, watching him, dark eyes gleaming. 'All right,' she said after a while and moved out of the doorway. He stepped forward, to call out to her, but she was gone, the only sound the slap of her shoes against the worn lino as she made her way slowly back along the corridor.

'You're leaving *me*?' Alex said. He was standing in the middle of the car park on Hampstead Heath. Daisy felt faintly sorry for him; he had been expecting to take her to lunch, an expensive restaurant, a good bottle of wine, love in the afternoon.

'I know it's hard to believe,' she said, watching him sympathetically, 'but yes, I am.'

She had chosen the car park because she wanted somewhere neutral to meet, somewhere, she thought, where he couldn't take advantage of her, snapping his fingers for a bottle of champagne, bending her back over a bed to make love to her. No, she thought, looking around; there were no diversions here. She looked down at his gleaming black leather shoes; hand-made, £400 a pair. They already wore a fringe of white dust. Alex looked away from her, gazing towards a clump of trees, jostling around the edges of the duck pond. 'May I ask why?'

'Because, my darling, I am no longer getting anything out of this relationship.' She smiled regretfully. 'And I'm not as young as I used to be.'

A group of small children ran, shrieking, down a gentle

grass slope, followed by their mothers, gossiping, watching after them with indulgent eyes. His gaze followed them. 'Is this something to do with the biological clock? You want children, is that it?'

'Actually, no, I don't want children. Never have.'

He turned to look at her, impatient. 'Then what?'

'I'd like to be cherished.'

'*Cherished*?'

'I know,' she said, watching him with a small smile, 'it's a difficult concept to grasp.'

He sighed faintly, fiddled with his gleaming white shirt cuffs until they extended, evenly matched, from each dark wool jacket sleeve. 'Please don't be patronising,' he said quietly.

Daisy fished in her jacket pocket for a pack of cigarettes. She was dressed all in black; jacket, dress, shoes, bag. Mourning black, she thought. Smiling briefly, she said: 'That was not my intention. You, through no fault of your own, are not the cherishing kind.'

He gave a slight, petulant shake of the head and she turned away from him, lighting the cigarette. Her hands shook slightly and she wrapped them round herself, stood with her arms held below her breasts, as if in an embrace. Glancing sideways at him she added, 'I knew that when I met you of course, but it didn't seem to matter then.'

She blew out a stream of smoke, watched it flicker and evaporate in the breeze, turned back to face him.

'Perhaps it's just that I've got older –' she put on a mocking smile '– am now in need of the gentler things in life, or perhaps that irresistible urge of yours to fuck everything in sight has finally rubbed the edges off my love for you completely.'

His mouth puckered slightly with distaste. He disliked women who swore. 'I see.'

'I got over you, Alex. I think I got over you about a year ago, although I didn't realise it at the time. Perhaps it's come from watching Bella and the sort of hell she's going through – I've realised that what we had together was so, well, so insubstantial I suppose, that it has simply vanished as if into thin air.'

He got to his feet, walked heavily to the door of his car, jangling his keys. He slid into the seat, looked up at her. 'Well,' he said, 'I suppose it's for the best. I was going to make a similar speech myself, although perhaps not as long-winded.'

Daisy looked at him for a while. 'Oh, Alex,' she said sadly, 'a gentleman to the last.'

He looked away. 'If you don't mind,' he said, 'I won't drive you home.'

She blew him a mocking kiss, widened her eyes to stop the tears starting. 'That's OK. I thought I'd go for a walk on the Heath anyway. It's such a beautiful morning.'

He put his foot down hard on the accelerator. The Mercedes skidded forward, wheels spinning on the dusty surface. She watched it bump over the uneven ground, stop temporarily at the busy junction leading onto the main road, the tyres squealing in protest as he hurled the car into the traffic.

She turned away, began to walk slowly up the hill, head bowed, arms wrapped protectively around her thin body, and trudged into the heart of the Heath.

As Daisy walked towards Parliament Hill, Lucy walked into her parents' kitchen a short distance away wearing a skimpy, stained Snoopy T-shirt which passed as her nightdress.

'Morning, darling,' Elisabeth said brightly, even though it was nearly afternoon. 'Sleep well?'

Lucy grunted, made for the fridge to grab a carton of orange juice and a tub of low-fat yoghurt. 'Dad around?'

'In his study. Would you like coffee, darling? Eggs perhaps?'

'Cholesterol,' Lucy said contemptuously.

'I could make French toast – just the way you like it,' Elisabeth said, blotting out the remark with a cheerful smile.

Lucy sat down at the table, spooned up a blob of yoghurt, licked the spoon thoughtfully. 'I haven't eaten French toast in *years*. Fat goes straight to the thighs.' She glanced at her mother's ample frame. '*Everybody* knows that.'

'Do they?' Elisabeth said, refusing to rise. She distinctly remembered making piles of French toast last holiday; three months ago. Funny, she thought, how time creeps so slowly when you're fourteen and have so much of it left; how tediously the clock hangs upon the minute, the months stretching as long as years.

Lucy sighed irritably, thrust a spoon into the yoghurt, lifted it out and watched it dribble slowly off the curved metal back of the spoon. Extending a pink tongue, she caught a drip and curled it back into her mouth. Watching her, Elisabeth wondered whether boarding school was such a wonderful idea after all. You send your charming, sweet daughter off, hand over several thousand pounds and in exchange you get back a rude, snarling teenager.

She walked over to the table, sat opposite Lucy. 'Well,' she said, 'what shall we do today?'

Lucy's face acquired a faintly hunted look, her eyes shifted away. 'I'm going round to see Susie.'

'Is she back for the weekend too?'

'Everybody's back for the weekend, Mother. It's the summer holidays.'

'So it is,' Elisabeth said, repressing a faint sigh. Since when did she stop being Mum, become relegated to the distancing, faintly contemptuous *Mother*? Also, the holidays meant no work and no Sam – one long, empty week of no Sam until the kids went off to stay with friends.

'Well, we'll all get together tonight then,' she said, making an effort, 'have a nice family dinner.'

Lucy looked at her. 'What? Like last night?'

'What was wrong with last night?' Elisabeth asked, staring across the table with genuine surprise.

'You and Dad hardly said a word,' Lucy said, flushing, 'and then you kept *looking* at him.'

'Looking?'

'Like everything he did was wrong.'

'You're imagining things,' Elisabeth said briskly, getting up from the table and walking towards the sink to get started on the washing-up before the lunch-time scramble. James had already gone out, eager to see his friends, dumping his egg-crusted plate in the sink.

'I don't think so,' Lucy said. 'I'm not a kid, you know. I can see what's going on.' Her voice was heavy with scorn but something wavered through it, an inarticulate plea that made Elisabeth turn to look at her, her pink rubber gloves dripping water onto the clean floor.

'Whatever you think you saw,' she said gently, 'you were imagining it. Your father and I are perfectly fine.'

Lucy's blue eyes were hostile with fear. 'So you're not going to get a divorce.'

'What on earth are you talking about?'

Lucy slouched over her yoghurt, stabbing into it viciously with the tip of her spoon. 'Susie's mum and dad are getting divorced.' She thrust the spoon into the yoghurt with a loud squelch. 'According to her, silence and *looks* are the first signs.'

Elisabeth stripped off the rubber gloves and walked over to the table. 'Your father and I are perfectly fine,' she said, laying an arm across her daughter's thin shoulders. Lucy didn't flinch – a good sign, Elisabeth thought – just dipped her head abruptly. 'Sure?' she mumbled. Elisabeth gave her a quick hug, which was as much as she dared do these days. Her daughter reminded her of a hedgehog. At the first sign of maternal affection, she rolled into a ball and presented her sharpest corners. 'Quite sure. Now, what would you like for dinner? Let's have something really delicious, a treat.'

'Don't mind.'

'Come on. You can have anything you like. Make up for that awful food you get at school.'

'It's not awful. Boarding schools are different these days, Mum. They're not like when you were a –' She broke off, scowled. 'When you went.'

Odd, thought Elisabeth, how difficult it is for children to imagine their parents as children themselves; how passionately they resent the idea, perhaps because it reminds them of the hideous future in store for them; to turn out as dull, reactionary and generally irritating as they find their parents.

'Anything you like,' Elisabeth repeated.

Lucy picked up a strand of hair, pulled at her split ends. 'That salmon thing you do, the one with raisins and flaky pastry,' she muttered gracelessly.

'Not too much fat content for you?' Elisabeth said lightly.

Lucy shifted in her seat, smiled crookedly. 'You can let yourself go sometimes.' She stared up at her mother earnestly. 'The occasional binge is OK but my friend Tara – who's really skinny – well she says the real secret is everything in moderation,' she said, as if repeating a mantra. She pulled a face. 'Except red meat, of course. That's utter poison. Nobody in their right mind would eat that.'

'Of course,' Elisabeth said, thinking of Sam and the plates of rare roast beef he loved so much. 'Very well. Salmon it is.'

Twenty-seven

July had brought with it a heatwave and now it seemed as if the summer would stretch out for ever, the hot, still days lingering on into damp, oppressive nights. The city took on a bleached, unfamiliar air; its ancient stone buildings, better suited to damp English skies, seemed to shrink under the unforgiving sun, its green parks became streaked with great swathes of brown, the rich earth turned to dust.

It was a hot Saturday and Tom was still in bed, although it was nearly lunch-time. Since he had moved into Orchard Road and had left behind him the final vestiges of his life, even the notion of time eluded him. He fell asleep, if he slept at all, as dawn was breaking and lay in a stupor until noon when the heat woke him, rising commensurately with the trajectory of the sun. It struck the front of the house in the early morning and lingered there awhile, bleaching the pavements and tarmac, before it crawled slowly across the rooftops to bake the already parched gardens, reaching his window by eleven o'clock. There it stayed all afternoon, pressed hard against the smeared glass.

Tom kept the curtains closed but the limp cotton was no defence against the heat. All day the temperature built, cooking the small room until the walls seemed to boil under his fingers and the hot, still air caught in his throat. He felt defenceless against it, lay day after day on the narrow bed, staring at the ceiling, his mind blank. He had nothing to do and no money to do it with. He forced himself out of the house once a day, dragging himself up to the corner shop for bread and cheese or a precooked pie but found the sound of voices irritating; distant, tinny sounds that scratched at his ears and sent him scurrying back quickly to the solitude of his small, hot, dark room. When, finally, the sky dimmed, he lunged for the window, dragged it open and leaned out, taking great gulps of hot air.

The nights, if anything, were worse. He could not sleep, had no money with which to buy books, to purchase that blessed respite in ideas or other people's lives with which to distract his mind. As darkness fell, so his thoughts became more tangled, rearing up from the flat, soporific day. Most nights he lay flat on his back, tears leaking from his eyes although for what or for whom he was crying, he did not know.

He thought that perhaps he was ill. Sometimes it seemed to him that his body had turned to water, every movement happened in slow motion, as if he was encumbered by the weight of fluid sloshing around in him and he dared not speak, in case it gushed from his mouth and eyes. Lily had tried to talk to him, dropping by his room with a Chinese take-away, sitting next to him on the narrow bed, a greasy carton balanced on her knee. He found he could not speak even to her, although her presence was soothing. She had the knack of stillness, like a cat. After a couple of evenings spent in listless silence, the food congealing between them, she did not appear again. He did not blame her.

Even Mrs Flower had tried, hauling her weight up the extra flight of stairs, all the while complaining bitterly, but Tom had stood in the doorway, dumbly shaking his head, until she too had gone away.

Sometimes he thought about Bella and when he did, he pinned her image to his mind like a lodestar, a fixed point in the chaos of his universe, imagining that if he could only see her and feel the touch of her hand on his, then perhaps the warmth of her skin might spring him from this place, connect him back into the past and himself. He had forgotten why he had left, could remember only the blur of that long-ago afternoon, her glittering, hostile eyes and a dull constriction in his throat.

That particular Saturday morning, he woke from a deep, dreamless sleep and his mind felt calm and still, the way it did when he was a kid and woke after a bad case of flu, or the time when he'd had measles and they'd almost hospitalised him, his temperature went so high. He stared at the ceiling for a while, picking out the cracks that he imagined making up Bella's face; the hard planes of her cheekbones and her long jaw, jutting defiantly to the world. He spent a great deal of time making faces out of the cracks. Bella, Ben, Harry, Lily; they were all there in a myriad changing forms. Mostly, they looked angry or disappointed.

Today, though, Bella's anger was focused – as it always used to be – on the world; sheltering him under the carapace of its hard, protective mantle. 'Me and you,' she used to say, 'me and you against the world.' He heard her voice distinctly and then her words came to him, the ones she had spoken as he left. 'Will you ever come back?' she had said. If that was really how she felt, he thought reproachfully, then why hadn't she ever asked again. Why hadn't she come to rescue him from this forgotten place? He lay in bed brooding on that for a while until he remembered, with a sudden start of energy, that Bella didn't know where he was, couldn't get hold of him even if she wanted to.

He stumbled out of bed, snatching up a shirt and a pair of trousers and scrambled down the two flights of stairs to the call-box. His hands shook as he stuffed coins into the rusty slot but it was not the old Bella who answered; it was the new Bella, the one who was so tirelessly, ceaselessly angry with him, the one who blamed him for all that had gone wrong. Even her voice was different, brittle and guarded as though he was a stranger or an insurance salesman cold-calling her number but he forced the words up through his constricted throat, asking if they could meet. Eventually, she agreed.

He felt tired afterwards, exhausted by her hard, bright voice. Going slowly up to his room, he lay on the bed wondering why the Bella in his head sounded nothing like the Bella on the phone. He knew the one in his head was real; he remembered her so clearly.

'How long are you going to keep this up?' Alex said, his handsome face screwed up in a petulant frown. He prodded disgustedly at a lump of damp, sweaty Brie. He hated picnics.

Lily looked over at him lazily. She was lying on a tartan rug, in the shade of a large sycamore tree whose leaves, prematurely, were turning to yellow.

'Keep what up?' she said, waving away a wasp with an idle hand. It shot off into the air, took a sharp left and buzzed loudly in Alex's ears.

'The ice maiden act,' Alex said, who should have known better than to drink in the sun. It always made him disagreeable. He flapped furious hands, feeling hot and slightly drunk.

'It'll sting you if you go on like that,' Lily said, watching him in amusement. 'Stands to reason.'

'Oh shut up.'

Lily looked away. 'Very nice, I'm sure.'

Alex leaped to his feet, hopped from one foot to another, flapping his arms like a chicken. The wasp buzzed around his head. 'Blasted thing won't leave me alone.'

Lily propped herself up on one elbow. She was wearing a blue cotton dress. Alex thought she looked very fetching, and it was contributing to his irritation.

'Keep still and it'll lose interest,' she said watching him with a small smile.

'They don't have brains, you know. They can't *decide*.'

'You're a big girl's blouse, you are,' she said and lay down with a sigh. The wasp flew off.

Alex flung himself down on the rug, next to her. He smelt of wine and cologne. Lily's face was turned away from him. From where he was sitting, he could see the pale curve of her cheek, the tips of her eyelashes glowing gold in the sun as she blinked. 'If you're not interested,' he said sulkily, 'then just say so.'

She rolled her head on the rug, gazed at him with blank eyes. 'That'll get you even more revved up,' she said accurately.

Alex grunted. 'I feel like a sixteen-year-old,' he complained, 'with aching balls.'

Her brow furrowed. 'Why?'

He flung himself onto his back. 'For God's sake –'

She pushed herself up onto her elbows, put her face close to his. 'What's got into you today?'

He watched her steadily. 'If a man wants somebody sexually,' he said slowly, 'and he can't have them, for whatever reason, then his testicles start to hurt through repressed desire.'

Her mouth wrinkled. 'Ugh.'

He sat up abruptly. 'Is that it?' he demanded. 'Is that the level of your sophistication? *Ugh?*'

Lily watched him for a while, her dark eyes blank. Then she laughed.

'Thank you,' Alex said, getting to his feet, 'thank you *very much*.'

Lily looked up at him, squinting slightly with the sun in her eyes. Alex scowled, his face red with heat and wine, his blue and white shirt crumpled where he had lain on the damp cotton.

'Now what's the matter?'

'You,' he said furiously, '*you* are the matter.'

'So shoot me,' she said, lying down again.

Don't think I wouldn't like to, thought Alex savagely, staring down at her, waiting for her to speak, but she kept silent, her eyelashes dark against the dense white skin of her cheeks. She looked cool, remote.

'I'm going for a walk,' he said.

She said nothing.

Alex set off, walking fast despite the heat, as if frustration sent him bowling down the slope. Lily rolled over and watched him until he dwindled to a dot on the distant horizon, then lay back with a satisfied smile and closed her eyes. Her indifference inflamed him, as she knew it would. She wondered idly if she had taken things too far; this game of cat and mouse, two steps forward, one step back. But she liked watching the dumb frustration cloud his eyes, the pulse thrumming in his temple. She put her hand to it sometimes, just to feel it leap beneath her fingers. He thought the movement of her hand a caress, bent his head to it.

Alex could feel his heart thundering, but he walked on, his legs working furiously until he found a bench in the shade. There was a slight breeze, the first he'd felt all day. He felt himself relaxing as the heat drained from his face and he slumped back, eyes on the dome of St Paul's, shimmering in a silver dust of heat in the far distance. His mind was elsewhere, fixed on Lily's firm, high breasts, set off so nicely by the pale blue cotton dress she was wearing and her indifferent, impenetrable eyes.

Impenetrable.

He let out a short bark of laughter, startling an elderly woman inching along the path a little way in front of him.

'Sorry,' he said, raising a benevolent hand. She glanced at him, her small brown face quivering like a mouse, and scurried off.

Celia's eyes, on the other hand, were green, lively, leaping with intelligence. He could almost feel her watching him, see her cool, assessing gaze. My wife understands me, he thought and longed, suddenly, for the touch of her hand on his back. 'Stop fretting,' she'd say briskly, 'there's nothing to be done by it.'

Whether he understood her, he did not question, just as he did not question his behaviour towards Daisy, felt himself to be reproachless in the whole affair. He missed her badly, had been savagely hurt by her abrupt dismissal. His heart leaped in his chest, like a fish. He lay back against the bench, breathless, winded by her treachery. Cherished, she had said. *Cherished.* His heart banged again, furiously; the horizon leaping on its axis with a sudden, sickening vertigo.

He leaned forward, took deep breaths to calm himself, soothed himself by considering the unjustness of that final parting. She knew, when she met him, that he was married; he had never lied to her, had given her everything she asked for. There had been vague talk of marriage, late into the night, and of his leaving Celia, but he had taken it as no more than a gesture of faith given in that close, languorous state of post-coital satisfaction. They had never talked of love, or, at least, he hadn't, believing it to be the worst sort of perfidy, to declare love to one woman when the rest of one's life was bound up with another. He was a moral man, in his own way.

He thought about Lily, was conscious of the absurdity of his situation. There were plenty of women who would come to him eagerly. Too eagerly, he thought. But he'd seen, once or twice, Lily's sudden shift towards desire. Soon, soon he would make the connection, flood her with longing like a switch being thrown.

He thought perhaps that he would go home, take a cold shower and cool off after this damn heat. Let the silly bitch find her own way back. That would teach her a lesson, show her that he was not a man to be trifled with. Maybe he'd even take Celia out for dinner, somewhere expensive with air-conditioning. The thought cheered him until he remembered that Celia was away in Paris for the weekend. What did she care, anyway? She had her own life, bought at his expense; had established the conditions quite firmly when they married. Daisy too had abandoned him, although he had given her everything. His breathing grew shallow again, he felt the air thicken once more inside his head.

He got up from the bench, feeling restless, knowing that he could not bear a night alone, was helpless when thrown back on his own resources. Turning slowly, he made his way back down the hill and started up the opposite curve, deciding as he walked that he would take Lily out for dinner instead. She, at least, rarely refused the chance of a decent meal. As he trudged slowly back up the sharp incline of the hill he saw that she was waiting for him under the green canopy of the sycamore tree, her back against the trunk, head tilted back. He crept up noiselessly and put his hands gently on her bare shoulders. Her eyes opened to stare at him and he thought that any other woman would have jumped, pretending alarm in faint, provocative cries.

'Sorry,' she said, in a low voice. He dropped his gaze, conscious of triumph leaping through his smile, looked down at her breasts, the milky skin edging out of their blue cotton constraint, the dark cleft of shadow between them. When she shifted easily under his hands, he felt the bones move under the dense, cool skin. 'Thought it was a game,' she murmured, 'thought you liked it.'

'I do,' he said, 'but only for a time.'

She watched him lazily. 'So long as you win.'

'Something like that.'

She moved forward. He felt the press of her breasts against his chest, the flicker of her tongue at his mouth.

Victory, which he so often mistook for lust, gathered in his chest; hammered at his heart in a sudden constricting pain. She wants me, he thought. *It was just a game, all along.* His body jerked in response.

'Come on,' he said, snatching up her hand.

'But the picnic things –'

He leaped a tussock of grass, pulling her after him. 'Sod the picnic things.' He felt young, excited; ignored the constriction that tugged at his chest, the erratic thundering of his heart. Sound roared in his ears, anticipation powered his tired legs.

He drove them to the Holiday Inn in Swiss Cottage, his foot jammed hard down on the accelerator, anticipating recklessly the amber lights, roaring through them, his heart beating with fear and excitement. They did not speak or look at each other, not even when they arrived and he dumped the Mercedes on a yellow line; messily, the engine nosing the pavement, the boot jutting into the road. He did not care. He felt reckless, breathless with anticipation. Blood sang in his ears.

He slid a £20 note to the whey-faced man behind the reception desk.

Lily smiled blankly.

Oh yes, he knew how to do things.

He thought he caught admiration in her smile.

Oh, yes.

'Just the *one* night, sir?' the man said, folding the note between fastidious fingers.

'Cheeky sod,' Lily said as they stepped into the lift.

Twenty-eight

'Look,' Elisabeth said, pointing to the shade of a tree, 'somebody's left all their picnic stuff.'

A carrier bag lay sprawled on its side, regurgitating a clumsily wrapped Brie, wadded balls of greaseproof paper, two empty wine bottles. She moved forward, crouching to pick them up. 'What a mess.'

'Better not,' Charles said absently.

She craned round, still crouched to stare out at him. 'Why not?'

'Unattended bags,' he said briefly, 'bombs.'

A flicker of irritation crossed her face. 'Don't be ridiculous.' She poked her foot at a crumpled tartan rug. 'Somebody's just got carried away in the heat of the moment; decided to run off home and forgot all this.'

'Perhaps,' Charles said wistfully, and thought how glorious it would be to picnic in the spreading shade of the tree on a hot summer's day. He thought of Lily, her thin legs jutting out awkwardly from the skirt of her pink dress, a smear of butter on her lip, her face laughing up at him as he gently smoothed it away with a finger.

Elisabeth gave him a sharp look. 'Don't you think we ought to clear it up?'

He shrugged. 'They might come back.'

'And they might not,' she said in exasperation. 'Serve them right, anyway, if they discover their rug's gone.' She picked it up, shook it out briskly and folded it, tucking it neatly under her arm. 'I'll hand it in to one of the park wardens.'

Charles watched her, frowning. 'Why don't you just leave it? Let them sort it out.'

She walked away from him, ducking under the shade of the tree and was suddenly hidden to him by the massive trunk; but her voice floated to him, carried clearly on the hot, still air: 'If we all just left everything, Charles, nothing would ever get done.'

His throat tightened at her derision, the brooding malevolence of her tone. He knew that in some obscure way he disappointed her; had always known it and also that neither of them had the courage to do anything about it. Perhaps that's why he was acting so foolishly over Lily. Oh, he was aware of his own foolishness, watched his behaviour with a dry, emotionless eye. Yet something in him leaped eagerly at her admiration, at the image of himself she gave him back, like a present, its shiny new wrapping fraught with unconsidered possibility. He was conscious too that Lily was biding her time, considering her options with all the careless cruelty that youth possesses. But at least he was in the running, was a man with possibility.

He walked on slowly, saw Elisabeth emerge into the sunshine some fifty yards ahead; the quick turn of her head as she glanced back to find him, the exasperated twitch of her shoulders at his slowness. 'You amble so,' she sometimes complained, 'like an old man.' He responded once, mildly enough, with the fable of the tortoise and the hare but she gave him a look, a look that said, yes, but which one would you rather be? He had said nothing, had known without asking that she would choose the hare over the tortoise any day, and watched her now, marching purposefully down the hill, the rug clutched tightly beneath one arm, her stiff back reproaching him for his slowness, for his changeless, plodding ways. He stared after her regretfully, wondering why she had urged him out of his study, away from his work, if she did not want to be with him. He had agreed only to please her.

'It's such a beautiful day,' she had said, marching into his study and flinging back the shutters even though she knew he liked to keep them shut during the long, hot summer days. He maintained it made the room cooler. She said, what rubbish, it made the room stuffy, that it was no wonder he emerged from his study so cross and crabby. Like an animal coming out of his den, she said. Her back was to him as she gazed out at the garden. 'How can you sit in here and waste the sunshine?' she complained. He watched her warily. 'What do you suggest I do?' he said, his eyes coming back to rest on the pile of papers he had to read through by Monday morning. 'Do?' she echoed. 'Do?' She turned slowly, her face distorted by sudden rage. 'Why don't you go for a picnic on this glorious day, run in the sunshine, lie under a hedge with a bottle of cool wine?' Why, said her voice, don't you ever *do* anything?

'Very well,' he said, suddenly angry. He shoved his chair back, ignoring it as it toppled and fell, thrust papers savagely into piles. 'We will do something. We'll go for a walk.' She moved past him, her skirt snapping at the papers, her face shuttered with anger. 'I'll get a hat. It's hot out there.'

Lily sat on the edge of the bed, hands neatly folded, waiting for the ambulance to arrive. Alex lay next to her, half-dressed, his face pale and sweating. 'How long?' he said, his mouth distorting with fear.

'Any time now,' she said absently. She did not look at him but gazed up at the window, her eyes focused on the block of flats that stood apparently only inches from the glass.

The paramedics bustled in, led by the whey-faced check-in clerk. He did not look at them directly, kept his eyes fixed on the wall above Alex's head.

'Have you sorted in a jiffy,' one of the paramedics said, advancing on Alex cheerfully.

Lily got up from the bed, went to stand by the window, her back to them. She heard a grunt as they shifted Alex onto a stretcher, turned to look at him. His face was grey, distorted by fear.

'Will he be all right?' she said in an idle tone.

The younger paramedic gave her a knowing smile. 'Be home with his wife, soon as you know it.'

'I'll have none of your lip, thank you,' Lily said, turning away.

She heard them move towards the door.

'You coming with him?' shouted the other.

Lily turned to stare at him. 'Whatever for?' she said.

Later that evening, Tom and Bella met in a pub, near the house. 'Neutral ground,' Tom had said on the telephone that morning. His tone was polite, constrained, as if he was ringing out of duty rather than desire.

'I could cook you supper,' Bella protested.

'That won't be necessary. See you at six thirty.'

'*Necessary*?' Bella thought, as she put down the phone. She kicked the wall hard, hurting her toe. 'Necessary is for strangers.'

She spent the day sunbathing on the small patch of balding grass that passed for a garden at the back of the house. The heat had not been kind to the few remaining shrubs that struggled in the arid, narrow borders; their leaves dusty and brittle, jaundiced under the strong, harsh light. She considered watering them but abandoned the thought while it was scarcely formed and went into the kitchen instead to get a magazine. As she idly flicked through a pile she heard a movement, turned to see Ben emerging from the hot, dark cell of his bedroom, crumpled and closed up, like a moth emerging from its pupa. He yawned, stretched, and the miraculous regeneration of youth worked its magic in the unfolding of his long limbs, the smooth planes of his skin. Yanking open the fridge door, he stood staring into its bright mouth, allowing the precious, chilled air to escape while she bit back a reproach. She watched him pull a carton of orange juice out, tip it back to his mouth. His throat moved hungrily in his strong neck. 'Food,' she said, 'eat some breakfast,' and went back out into the garden.

He followed her out, stood blinking in the strong sunlight. 'Talking about food, Mum,' he said, bending to kiss her, circling the top of her arm with strong fingers, indicating her thinness, 'I think it's about time you ate something too.' She felt dried-up beside him. He smelt of toothpaste and oranges. He met her silence with a faint sigh. 'I'll grab a Big Mac breakfast on the way.'

He was going over to Camden to meet some friends. With exams over, and only the results to wait for, he seemed relaxed and optimistic again, enjoying the long, hot summer days, the unaccustomed freedom from school. Bella hadn't seen him so animated in weeks; felt pleased for him but frightened too. The last day of school had seemed like a symbolic marking of the end of childhood. University next, if his results were good enough. She closed her eyes. God knows what he'd get up to there. She knew enough from her students about the availability of drugs, had pulled them out of enough emotional chaos to see vividly the problems Ben would be facing. And Bristol, which was his first choice, was so far away. She knew his eagerness to be gone, to make his own life, knew that it was her own fear that had to be faced. God knows, she worried enough if he was tucked up in the safety of his own bed. Sometimes she crept into his room as she had done when he was a small child, bending her head to breathe in the smell of him, careful not to touch him. Her eyes had become her hands, lingering over his supple skin.

She remembered when that skin was hers to press her face to.

'No drugs,' she said, opening her eyes to stare up at him, catching his hand. She had just been reading the newspapers, recoiling from the story of a boy of seventeen who had snorted some unknown grey powder. It promised, or so the journalist wrote (without apparent irony), the ultimate rush. Within hours, the boy was in hospital, had died soon after. His parents, said the caption under his photograph, handsome, white-teethed, bright-eyed, were 'too distressed to comment'.

'Stop worrying,' Ben said, squeezing her hand. 'And we're going to a club later so I'll be really late.' His voice took on a warning tone. 'Don't wait up.'

'No,' she said, although she knew she would.

Later, she took a bath, lay in the cool water drinking a large glass of cold wine. In the green light of the bathroom her legs looked yellow and stringy, like half-cooked spaghetti. After the bath she applied make-up carefully, pasting concealer over the dark circles around her eyes, brightening the grey pallor of her skin with blusher. It took her ages to dress, disguising her thinness under layers, adding a fine gauzy cotton scarf, dip-dyed in brilliant shades of blue. Tom had bought it for her in a souk in Morocco. She stared at herself critically in the mirror, squinting her eyes in concentration. Jewellery, she thought, and added a pair of gold hoop earrings. When she looked again, she looked fine, almost normal.

Tom was already there when she arrived, hunched over a pint in a dim corner. He was unshaven; she noticed the faint, musty smell of unwashed clothes as she bent to kiss him, felt the sharp sting of bristles against her mouth.

'Hi!' she said brightly, sitting down.

He did not smile. 'Hi,' he said, pushing his chair back, getting quickly to his feet. 'I'll get you a drink.'

She struggled with her jacket; a button had somehow

become entangled with the strap of her bag. He made no move to help her. 'No, don't worry. Sit and talk to me. I'll have something later.'

He gave her an opaque look. 'I'd rather get it now.'

She wrenched at the button. There was a soft tearing sound. 'Fine,' she said, sitting down with a thud, the fabric bunching in a lump around her hips. She scrabbled in her bag for a pack of cigarettes. When she looked up, he was still standing over her, a curious shuttered look in his eyes.

'Well?' he said.

She stared at him.

He said, 'What would you like to drink?' His voice was slow, touched by a maddening patience.

She bent her head, lit a cigarette. What I always have, she wanted to say; what I've drunk in pubs since we were both nineteen. But she forced a smile instead and said, 'A white wine, please.' Her lips felt stiff, unfamiliar.

He nodded, walked over to the bar. She watched him go, the familiar loping action of his walk. His hair was longer now, spiking over his collar in a feathery fringe. It needed a cut, looked better short. She should tell him. But it was no business of hers now. Her throat constricted. She wanted to reach out, warm her hands on him. He turned, looked at her, his face sombre. She smiled but his eyes slid away. She remembered Ben, when he was a few days old, a premature baby boxed up in a glass incubator; how she had pressed her hands and face against the cold surface, trying to reach him. She felt the same way now.

'Here,' Tom said, sitting down.

She lifted the glass. 'Thanks.'

He nodded, stared down into his pint, shoulders hunched.

'Is this some sort of silent torture?' she said, after a while.

He winced, looked up at her, his face shuttered.

She sighed. 'You said we needed to talk.'

'Just wanted to see you were OK,' he mumbled. His shoulders had almost reached his ears.

'And am I?' she said crisply.

Self-pity clung to him, like scent. He nodded. 'Yeah.'

'Ben's fine too,' she said in a hard, bright voice. She stubbed out her cigarette, lit another. 'Seems pretty relaxed about his results although it's hard to tell how he's done. He won't talk to me about them.'

Tom stared at her, expressionless.

Once, she thought, he would have laughed, commiserated with her about teenage sons. *Their* son.

'It's not my fault,' she said, moving sharply to the defensive, even though he said nothing, just sat staring at her with dull, expressionless eyes. She wanted to kick him, to prise some sort of reaction out of him. Why had he asked her to come here if he had nothing left to say to her? Her mouth narrowed to a thin pink line. 'Bad enough that your dad walks out, let alone doing it just before major exams.'

Tom opened his mouth. Nothing came out.

Bella gave him a hard look, sighed.

Two girls at the next table watched them intently, nudging each other and giggling over halves of lager.

'I've moved,' Tom said in a stifled voice.

Bella looked taken aback. 'Well, I suppose you couldn't have stayed there,' she said, with a shrug.

He continued, as if she had not spoken '– to a boarding house.'

Bella looked at him with sorrowful eyes. 'Oh, Tom –'

He looked away. 'It's OK.'

A piercing giggle came from the next table. Bella shot the girls a hard look, then pulled a cheque-book and a stubby, chewed biro out of her bag.

'What's the address?' she said, smoothing down the back of the cheque-book. Its grey cover was curled up, like a dead tongue.

'Kentish Town,' he said in a flat voice.

'So it's somewhere round here.'

He handed her the telephone number, scrawled on a scrap of paper, in case he forgot it.

'Which street?' she said brightly.

He shook his head.

'Tom?'

He sunk into his shoulders, stared down into his pint.

'Well, if you won't tell me –'

Tom clamped his lips shut tightly.

'Really, this is childish,' Bella said, on a sigh. Out of the corner of her eye, she saw one of the girls dig her friend hard in the ribs. Two sets of eyes turned to stare at them.

Something about their eyes reminded her of Lily; the same blank quality, a similar lack of compassion. Bella stared at Tom's set, white face.

'You're living with her,' she exclaimed, 'with Lily. That's why you won't tell me.'

She could see, from his face, that she was right.

'You are, aren't you?' Her voice was brittle, like shards of glass.

Tom stared at her mutely.

'Bastard,' she said in a low voice. She bent to light another cigarette, her hands shaking violently over the match. 'You stupid, weak, pathetic bastard.'

Tom said nothing. Suddenly, Bella ground out her barely smoked cigarette, snatched up her bag and stood. 'I'm going to the loo,' she announced, her voice furious. 'Try and find something to say to me when I get back.'

Tom gazed after her furious progress. She looked just the same, he thought; better even, as though the past few weeks had never happened. A brittle ache bit into his bones. His eyes felt scratchy and he focused them carefully, imagining Bella's hands on the table, moving to her glass, the dull gold of her wedding ring gleaming in the dim light. She had taken off her engagement ring, the diamond solitaire he had bought her with his first big pay packet. He had wanted to ask her where it was, but he hadn't dared speak, had felt again as if his throat had turned to water, that if he opened it, liquid would come gushing out. He wanted her to take him in her arms. Nobody had touched him for weeks; nobody except Lily and that unexpected kiss. Lily's face, pale and yielding, hovered before his eyes. He looked up, blinking, to see Bella standing over him, her expression as cold and unforgiving as steel.

Tom felt tears gather in his eyes, rush down his face. Water gathered at the corners of his mouth; he opened it, to suck it in. He felt like he was drowning.

Bella sat down sharply, her features bunching into circles of surprise. 'Oh Tom –'

The girls were staring at them open-mouthed. One shifted closer to get a better look, her plastic trousers squeaking on the plush banquette.

'Tom, don't –' Bella said. Dimly, he saw her glance at him then away, over to the girl, whose face was open now, greedy with curiosity. Bella wheeled round, the wooden stool tilting with the sudden movement so she seemed to fling herself across the table. 'Can't you see he's in pain?' she snapped. The girl jerked away, her mouth stupid with surprise, as shocked as if a character in a television play had leaned out from the screen and addressed her. 'Sorry,' she mumbled, dropping her eyes.

Tom's mouth and eyes were wide open, stretched and rigid, his face awash with water. He heard Bella say, 'Tom, pull yourself together. Here, take this –' She ripped the scarf from around her neck, handed it to him. He buried his face in it, remembering a dusty afternoon in Marrakesh, Bella kissing him up against the pink walls of the city. The memory of her scent lingered in its folds. He heard a low moaning sound, then Bella saying, 'Stop it, stop it at once.' She grabbed him by the wrist. He felt her nails dig into his flesh, the shards of her bitten nails scratching him painfully.

The girls at the next table got up noisily. 'Christ,' the other one said, looking at him in disgust. One of them kicked the table as she passed.

Tom's face was awash.

'I think they thought we were on television,' Bella said, trying to keep her voice light. She laughed shakily. *'Play for Today* or something.' She bent her head, lit another cigarette, her hands shaking violently. The bones of her wrists shone white, like ping-pong balls. He noticed suddenly how thin she'd grown.

He wiped a sleeve clumsily across his face. 'Sorry.'

She shook her head. 'Been doing that often?' she asked in a quiet voice. Her brightness seemed to have dimmed; she looked darker, blurry now. 'You should see somebody,' she said into his silence, 'deal with it.'

Tom thought of the job applications lying, unposted, on the floor by his bed, the bank demands, unopened, stuffed into his shoes. 'I know.'

She leaned towards him, smoke curling around her neck. He felt her scarf, warm against his skin. 'It'll be all right,' she said. 'You'll see.'

He wanted her to say something else, something to make it all better but she was waiting for his reply, her eyes encouraging, expectant.

'I can't –' he said, then closed his mouth helplessly.

'You can't keep on running away,' she said, her features getting brighter again, light glistening from them in hard, fiery lines.

He felt the brilliance of her contempt, stumbled up from his chair, blundered at the table. I know, he wanted to say. I'm sorry.

'That's right,' she said. 'Go on, run away again.' Her mouth was a sharp line. 'Go to her. See if she can do any better.'

He stood for a moment, staring down at her helplessly, his arms swinging at his side. 'Sorry,' he mumbled.

She looked up at him, her eyes pinpoints of light. 'Go away,' she said, 'go *away*.'

He stumbled away from her, swinging into a table of people, knocking a drink to the ground. 'Watch out!' somebody called, but he didn't stop, kept walking, banging through the swing-doors and out into the night. An elderly man stood up from the table, fist raised in baffled fury. 'Hey?' he shouted. 'Hey!'

Bella looked over at him, saw grey hair, a shiny brown suit, checked shirt, spotted brown tie; just a bloke down at his local for a quiet night out. She walked over to the table, put a ten-pound note down on the beery surface. 'Please,' she said.

The man turned on her. 'He drunk, your boyfriend?'

'Husband,' she said. 'No, he's having an affair.'

The faces at the table turned up to stare at her. There was a still, respectful silence.

'Sorry, love,' muttered the old man. 'Didn't mean no harm.'

'Of course not,' Bella said, and started to cry.

She felt bodies cluster around her, hands pressing down on her shoulders and then she was sitting in a chair and a woman was saying, 'Get her a brandy. Go on, Dave, hurry now.'

'Look,' said another, 'there's this money she put down.'

'It's too much,' Dave protested, 'she didn't have to do that.'

'Just get her the brandy,' the woman snapped.

Bella sat there for half an hour, sipping quietly at the brandy, feeling it burn down her throat as the flow of words and laughter poured over her. She felt a hand, heavy on her shoulders, swivelled her eyes to look at it, saw a wedding ring sunk deep into the flesh of the finger, the brown giraffe blotches of age distorting the skin. The hand patted her shoulder gently; she felt a slow, even rhythm, then a sudden tightening as the owner shouted out some ribald comment, then a sudden pulse as she relaxed again and the hand resumed its slow, soothing beat.

After a while, Bella got up to leave.

The owner of the hand, whose name she knew from the conversation was Gloria, patted her once again on the shoulder and let it drop. 'He'll come round, love, you'll see.'

Bella nodded and slipped away. As she pushed against the swing-door she heard Dave's voice, rising in exasperation. 'She didn't take her change. I told her it was too much. Didn't I say –?'

Lily crept down to the hallway on noiseless feet, shoved ten pence into the pay-phone, dialled a number.

'Daisy Ashworth,' said a voice.

'Thought you ought to know that Alex is in hospital; a suspected heart attack.'

'Who is this?' Daisy's voice was sharp.

'He's at the Royal Free,' Lily said, glancing quickly towards the door, hearing the sound of a key being jiggled in the stiff lock. 'Don't know what ward.'

The door swung open. Lily put down the phone.

Tom stood poised in the doorway, caught unawares. He watched her for a while, frozen to the spot, then pushed the door shut with his foot, his eyes fixed on her. She did not move but her hand, lingering on the receiver, dropped suddenly to her side. Tom moved towards her, slowly, measuring his footsteps like a cat.

'What's happened?' she said as he moved into the light. His face was white, his eyes staring. He did not take them from her face. 'What's the matter?'

'Help,' he said, moving into her arms. 'Help me.'

The following afternoon, Celia materialised silently by Alex's bed, bringing a sliver of colour into the gleaming white hospital cell. She wore a new green dress, sleeveless and beautifully cut, her red hair caught back with a gold barrette.

Alex stared at her. 'I thought you were in Paris.'

She bent to kiss him, her lips cool on his hot cheek. Paris still clung to her, she wore a warm, voluptuous scent that mingled with the dark perfumes of Gitanes and rich, burnt coffee. 'Daisy called me.' He held out his hand to her but she ignored it, moved to the end of the bed and picked up the clipboard of notes that hung there. She read them in silence.

Alex frowned, perplexed. How had Daisy known? Lily, he supposed. And had Celia known about Daisy or was the call a terrible surprise? He imagined them on the telephone, red lips moving, betrayals being shared. His infidelities stretched like trip-wires around the bed.

He glanced at Celia warily, out of the corner of his eye. She did not look surprised, her expression was distant, bored even. She moved easily across the room, gliding to the window where she stood motionless, her eyes fixed on the hot, sleepy Sunday street.

'Daisy and I have just been for lunch. We sat outside, in the sunshine.'

'You and Daisy?' he asked, his voice incredulous. 'Just now?'

She nodded without turning round.

He stared at her back reproachfully. 'You were worried, then.' Daisy too, he thought. Neither of them had even bothered to come and see him.

'There was no immediate danger,' she murmured, lifting a slat of the white Venetian blind, peering down into the dusty gardens.

'Thanks.'

Celia turned green eyes on him. He saw, now, why she

had chosen the dress. 'You have Daisy to thank,' she said. 'I left a message on the answer machine, to say that I was in Paris, but not where I was. It seems she understands you well, knows you're a creature of habit.'

He looked away.

'Or perhaps a man without imagination. Really, Alex, the same hotel.'

His chest itched where they had shaved it to attach the plastic discs to monitor his heart. Wires sprouted from them, trailed over his arms to the grey machine standing by his bed. He wore no shirt, because of the wires and the heat, only a pair of old pyjama trousers the nurse had dug up for him. He had worried all night that he was wearing dead men's clothes. Celia went and sat on a chair, across the room, watched him with that cool, assessing gaze.

He felt vulnerable without his clothes, bent his knees up, like a sitting foetus. The white sheet sprung into a protective tent. Scratching at his chest, he watched a red mark blossom, like jagged petals, around the plastic disc.

'They say I'm not too bad.'

'A panic attack –'

'They're not entirely sure,' he protested.

'I spoke to the consultant this morning.'

She had been here, then, this morning. In the same building, perhaps on the same floor and hadn't even bothered to look in, see that he was all right. He said resentfully, 'Still, they say they're going to keep me here tonight.'

'A precaution.'

'Perhaps.'

'I suppose you take all your mistresses there?' she asked, after a while.

His heart skipped a beat, skittered in his chest. How much did she know? The red light on the machine flashed. Celia watched it silently. He felt exhausted suddenly, leaned his head back against the pillow and closed his eyes.

'Daisy tells me that you have decided to part,' Celia said, in the same distant tone.

He rolled his head wearily. 'It seemed best.'

'And that you have a new interest, a young woman called Lily. It was her you were with when it happened, as I understand it, in a hotel room. It was she who telephoned Daisy, to tell her where you had been taken. She must care about you a great deal, to have allowed you to go in the ambulance alone. Or perhaps she's coming to see you later. Then again, perhaps not. Perhaps, like Daisy, she feels –'

'Please stop,' Alex said, closing his eyes.

'– indifferent,' she continued inexorably.

Alex had been badly frightened by the attack. He was still more frightened by Celia's glacial calm. He did not think it assumed, nor did he believe it to be a hysterical symptom of shock or outrage. It sounded, he thought with a sudden cramp of fear, more like boredom. He heard a faint scuffling noise, the squeak of shoes on a polished linoleum floor and opened his eyes to see Celia moving towards the door. 'Where are you going?'

'Home.'

'Are you coming back?'

'In the morning. I'll pick you up.'

'That would be kind.'

She looked at him, amused. 'Yes. I know.'

'They didn't mean anything, you know,' he said. 'None of them.'

Her lips curved in a small smile. 'No,' she said, 'of course they didn't.'

For a moment, he thought she was laughing at him but she gave him a small, cool wave, a gentle flex of her fingers, and was gone.

'It turned out to be a panic attack.'

'Alex? Panic? Whoever would have thought it –'

'God, how embarrassing. All that fuss –'

'Not half as embarrassing as getting caught with your trousers down in a hotel room.'

'Oh dear.'

'With Lily. At least, I'm sure that's who it was on the telephone.'

'Lily?' Elisabeth said uncertainly.

Bella gave a defeated sigh. 'Lily. Why is it that I'm not surprised to hear that name?'

Twenty-nine

'I thought we might have lunch together. Go somewhere nice.'

Celia glanced up from the paper. 'Sorry, darling, busy today.'

Alex smiled benevolently. 'One of your girlfriends?'

'A new acquaintance. Terrifically good fun.'

'Would I like her?'

'Oh, very much.'

'And am I to be allowed to meet her?'

Celia gave him a cool smile. 'No, I don't think so,' she said, turning back to the newspaper, 'I think she's rather got over men like you.'

Tom was lurking in the hallway, waiting for Ben who had telephoned to say, could he come round to see him?

'Here?' Tom had asked doubtfully. He was on the payphone in the corridor. He stared at the chipped green gloss on the walls, examined minutely the rotting cardboard pin board by the telephone. 'Here?' he said again. Yes, Ben said insistently. I want to see where you live, I want to see you *there*. So in the end Tom had been forced to agree, had arranged to meet at twelve o'clock on Saturday.

He glanced, for the hundredth time, at his watch. It was ten past twelve. He wondered if Lily was awake yet. She'd left his bed, as usual, at about three that morning. It had been the same, ever since that first night they'd spent together. She insisted they use his bed and always left in the early hours, slipping noiselessly through the door in bare feet, padding back to her own narrow bed. 'Don't like sleeping with other people,' she explained, 'they *breathe*.'

They didn't make love much, not since that first night when they'd gone at it like rabbits. They didn't talk much, either; just hugged like children, legs tangled, taking reassurance from each other's bodies. He was confused by her, frustrated by her lack of connection but grateful for the warmth of her skin against his, by her shallow, even breathing. She made him feel better. The sense of drowning had receded, he was able to get out more, found the surfaces of the world less sharp-edged, less shockingly glittering to his eyes and ears.

'Expecting somebody, dearie?' Mrs Flower said, appearing at his side, tartan shopping trolley in tow. A silken flap of ear emerged suddenly from under the canvas cover; she glanced at it nervously, bent forward and tucked it away carefully.

Tom groaned inwardly. Just what he needed to reassure a potentially hostile seventeen-year-old – a welcoming committee. 'Yes,' he said vaguely.

'Makes me nervous too,' Mrs Flower said cheerfully, 'waiting around for people.' Her eyes glinted shrewdly in her plump, red face. 'It'll be fine, you'll see. Always is when you're dreading it.'

Just then, the doorbell rang. Tom glanced at Mrs Flower, then bounded forward and flung open the door. 'Great,' he said in a loud, forced voice. 'You're here.'

Ben scowled, trying to disguise his pleasure. 'Hi, Dad.' He wore jeans, trainers, an old T-shirt with 'Fuck Off' scrawled across it and a new leather jacket. Expensive, Tom thought, wondering where he'd got the money, whether Bella had bought it for him as a bribe, as a making-up-for-his-rotten-father present.

'Nice jacket,' Tom said evenly, ushering him into the dingy hall, watching his son's bony shoulders hunch defensively against the compliment.

They found Mrs Flower bent tactfully over her shopping trolley, fiddling with a strap, a huge, shapeless form in a flowered overall.

Tom glanced down at her, reluctantly slowed his step.

'Mrs Flower,' he said, 'I'd like you to meet my son, Ben.'

Mrs Flower straightened up, panting slightly with the exertion. 'I'd have known you anywhere,' she said, smiling broadly, holding out a surprisingly dainty hand, 'image of your dad, you are.'

Ben flushed slightly.

'Handsome too,' Mrs Flower said admiringly.

Ben scowled, stared down at his trainers.

'Well, I'll be off.' Mrs Flower manoeuvred the trolley towards the door. 'Need to pick up a few things at Spar.' She looked over her shoulder. 'Can I be getting you anything, Tom?'

He smiled, shook his head.

'Well, ta ta,' she said, with a coy little wave.

'She seemed nice,' Ben said, staring after her with a vague look of yearning which made Tom realise how young he was still; young enough to need mothering. We're all young enough to need mothering, he thought, with a sudden hollow sense of isolation.

'Runs the place,' he said, trying to keep his voice bright.

'She the landlady?'

'No,' Tom said, leading the way up the narrow rickety staircase. 'More like the good fairy.'

Behind him, he heard Ben laughing. 'Bit of a fat fairy,' he said.

As they turned into the corridor, Tom saw Lily walking towards him and stiffened slightly.

'All right?' she said. She was wearing a skimpy cotton wrapper, pale green, which showed her small tight breasts and thin white legs.

'Fine,' Tom said, slowing his pace slightly as she

approached, but was relieved to see that she walked straight past them.

'Who was that?' Ben said.

'Who was what?'

'That,' Ben repeated, jerking his head in the direction of the staircase down which Lily had disappeared. '*That*.'

'Oh, that,' Tom said, keeping his voice as casual as he could. 'That was Lily.'

Ben looked at him suspiciously. 'She your girlfriend?'

Tom slipped the key in the lock in his door, which was loose, fiddled with it until it finally turned. 'No. She just lives here.'

'Mum know about that?'

Tom looked at his son with exasperation. 'Yes, she's organised a police line-up of all the residents of the house.'

'*Sarcastic*.'

'Sorry.'

Ben shrugged, slouched over to the bed and sat down. ''S'all right. It's your life.'

Tom glanced at him sharply but Ben's face was averted as he stared around the room. 'Not bad. Quite cool really.'

'Cool?' Tom repeated, staring at the ugly room.

Ben grinned. 'Yeah, no possessions, no resources, living on your wits.'

'Ah,' Tom said, with a grin, 'fuck the capitalist pigs, property is theft, up the underdog.'

Ben looked taken aback. Fathers weren't supposed to say stuff like that. His face closed up. Tom could see he was hoping he wouldn't go all mushy on him; nothing worse than your dad wanting to be your friend or, God forbid, to start spouting stuff from his seventies campus days.

'Yeah,' he said diffidently, 'something like that.'

Tom sat down next to him on the narrow bed. There was nowhere else to sit. I'll buy a chair next week, he thought vaguely.

'Everything going all right?'

'Yeah. Mum's a bit –' He glanced sideways. 'She's a bit calmer now.'

'Sorry,' Tom muttered. 'Sorry, it's all been very bad timing for you.'

Ben flushed furiously. Tom watched the blood flood beneath his thin, white cheeks. 'Can't timetable a divorce, Dad,' he said stiffly.

Tom felt a jolt of shock. 'Divorce?' he repeated. 'Who said anything about divorce?'

Ben shook his head violently, examined the tops of his trainers. 'Kind of thought it was obvious,' he mumbled.

Tom said nothing, stared bleakly at the peeling wallpaper and wondered what Bella thought, whether she thought it was obvious too. And then he wondered what he thought, realised that he had no idea. He'd gone away to think, or at least that's what he'd told himself, to get his life in order and all he'd achieved was – he looked around the bare, shabby room, thought of the job applications, still unposted, sitting in the pocket of his jacket and realised that he had done nothing. Nothing at all. Time, he thought wearily, it will all sort itself out with time.

Ben was watching him, scowling fiercely.

'Early days yet,' Tom said, trying to summon a smile.

'It's your life,' Ben said again, his eyes sliding away but not before Tom saw the quiet desperation in them.

'You'll get your results soon. Then you'll be off to university and free as a bird.'

Ben considered his feet. 'Yeah,' he said, 'sure.'

Tom stared at the nape of his neck; fought an urge to press his fingers to the twin hollows that shadowed the pale, vulnerable skin.

'Shall we go out and get a pizza?' he suggested.

Ben shrugged. 'If you like.'

'Yes, I do like,' Tom said, adopting a cheerfulness he did not feel. 'I'm starving.'

'It's me.'

'Hello, me.'

'I wanted to apologise.'

'For what?'

'Well, I suppose – that thing you said the other day, about not cherishing you enough.'

'Ah.'

'Is that all you've got to say?'

'Yes. Yes, I do believe it is.'

'Daisy, can't we stop all this nonsense? I miss you.'

'Do you?'

'Must you answer everything with a question?'

'Sorry.'

'I thought we might have lunch together, go somewhere nice.'

'Buy me caviar, that sort of thing?'

'Whatever your heart desires.'

'Ah, yes, my heart. Speaking of which, how's yours?'

'OK, I think. They say I should be careful, take things easy.'

'No more sex in the afternoon, then?'

'I can explain all that. Over lunch –'

'Now that might really be worth hearing –'

'Good. Where shall we go?'

' – but I'm afraid I'm having lunch with Celia.'

'With Celia?'

'I know. Infuriating, isn't it? Goodbye.'

'I wondered if you'd like some lunch, darling,' Elisabeth said, standing in the doorway of Charles's study.

'That would be nice.' He looked up from the papers he had been absorbed in.

'We could go out. That nice Italian down the road.'

'Out?'

She felt irritation tighten at her throat. Why did she bother? She'd been sitting in the kitchen, gazing out at the parched garden, watching the clock tick towards one o'clock, a time that inevitably made her think of Sam. If she was with Sam, there would be no question of cheese and a cracker at the kitchen table, or a bowl of tinned tomato soup.

She sighed. But Sam wasn't there, wasn't going to be there for two whole days. Funny, she thought, how it used to be the weeks she dreaded the most. Now it was the weekends, those empty lustreless days when she drifted aimlessly around the house and Charles hid in his study, emerging only to grab something to eat before retreating behind closed doors. Even the kids were away, off to some smart Italian villa with their friends. She had suggested Cornwall this year but hadn't got round to booking anywhere, not after the cool response she got to the idea. She sighed, stared around at the empty kitchen, the pretty, rag-rolled yellow units that had cost a fortune, the bowl of home-grown roses, fat and pink, sitting on the table. It seemed such a waste, having no one to share it with. Then she remembered her resolution, taken only the week before, to be kinder to Charles, to try and include him more and thought that perhaps he too might welcome a diversion on this beautiful day, lunch in a nice restaurant, a bottle of wine, good food. It had been their weekly treat, once, before the children were born.

Now he was staring at her, his mouth slack with bewilderment. It was always like this. Sometimes she thought there were two Charleses; the one in her head – charming, funny, kind, spontaneous even – and this other Charles, the stolid, slow, pompous man who sat gazing at her as if she had just suggested they fly to the moon.

'Is anything wrong?' he asked, seeing her expression.

She shrugged. 'I just felt like getting out.'

Charles smiled suddenly, his expression fond. 'You're missing the children, I expect.'

'I expect –' she said, her voice flat.

She thought, with a flash of bitterness, is that it then, is that the sum of all my parts – *mother*? If my soul is sickening, my spirit restless, is it only my children who feed it?

She looked at him challengingly. 'I thought it was you who was missing them.'

He gestured vaguely, 'Well, of course I do –'

'And it was you who said that we never talk these days.'

Charles frowned and she saw, suddenly, that he'd forgotten his drunken speech, that any regrets he'd voiced had been articulated under the loosening influence of alcohol and were now absorbed back into the daily ebb and flow of their lives.

'Well,' she said, giving him a sharp, bright look, 'here's your chance.'

Watching his bewildered face, she was conscious of a dragging, leaden disappointment. She'd been astonished by his drunken outburst, charmed even, had for a moment glimpsed the inner man and had thought, maybe there is hope for us still. But now, seeing him behind his desk wearing that habitual expression of resignation – what does *he* have to be resigned about, she thought savagely – she thought that she could not bear the bland predictability of the future.

'Never mind –' she said, turning away.

But Charles flung down his pen with an expansive gesture. 'No, it's a good idea; a wonderful idea. What could be nicer,' he said, smiling over at her, 'than a drunken Saturday lunch with my lovely wife.'

For some reason, Elisabeth's heart sank.

The pizza place that Tom and Ben tumbled into, promising home-cooked rustic Italian food – always suspicious, the word *rustic*, Tom thought, peering at the menu – turned out to be run by Chinese whose idea of a pizza was a rubbery base of undercooked dough, topped with a slop of tomato sauce and a scattering of processed cheddar.

'Heinous,' Ben said, pushing his plate away.

Tom stared at the uneaten pizza regretfully. Great father I am, he thought, my son comes to visit me and I can't even get a bloody meal right. He remembered the place they used to go to when Ben was a kid, all knees, elbows, ears and teeth, before he'd grown into his various parts. 'Remember the pizza place we used to go to, the one near the Heath?'

Ben grinned. 'Yeah, on Saturdays,' he said, his voice rising with pleasure, 'after we'd been to fly my kite and then Mum would come and –' He flushed, glanced away.

'We can talk about her,' Tom said, leaning forward and touching him gently on the arm.

Ben moved his arm away. He didn't even snatch it back, Tom thought sadly, just removed it with deliberate, adult care.

'She'll be OK,' he said, keeping his voice even, reassuring.

'How would you bloody well know?' Ben said, glaring at him. He dropped his eyes, sunk down into himself. 'You don't bloody see her at night, wandering the house like a frigging ghost.'

Tom kept silent.

Ben's shoulders hunched higher, his head disappearing onto his chest. 'I have to tell her to go back to bed,' he said, his thin face contorted in a scowl, 'like she was a bloody kid.'

Tom stared at him despairingly. He's still a kid, he thought, even though he wants to be a man. He remembered it well, the fierce, prickly feeling of independence, the terror of getting it. 'And what about you? Are you OK?' he said gently.

'Oh, great!' Ben said, flinging himself out of the chair,

and moving fast across the restaurant. He pushed open the door, stared back at Tom. 'Fucking great, *Dad*.'

Tom watched the door until the swinging had subsided, then dropped his head under the gaze of three pairs of curious Chinese eyes.

'Let me.'

'No, this one's mine,' Celia said, her hand closing over the bill. She produced a small leather folder from her bag, snapped a credit card on the table. 'Or, rather, Alex's. I think that he should pay for this, don't you?'

'What a good idea.'

'I thought so.'

Daisy watched her curiously. 'Did you know about us, all along?'

Celia looked at her in surprise. 'Why, of course. I was his mistress before I became his wife.'

'Does Alex know you know?'

'I've never asked him.'

'And you didn't mind?'

Celia's green eyes flickered. 'Of course I minded. But it's either take Alex as he is or not at all.'

'Will you do anything about Lily?'

Celia's mouth curved in a small, amused smile. 'From the sound of her, I rather think she might do that all by herself.'

'It's Alex.'

'Wotcher. How's the old ticker then?'

'My heart is fine. It was the heat –'

'Thought so. Didn't look too serious. My dad went, from his heart. Terrible colour, he turned. Like a mushroom.'

'I'm sorry.'

'I'm not. He never amounted to much.'

'I thought we might have lunch together, go somewhere nice.'

'Yeah. All right. Haven't anything better to do.'

'Thanks.'

'Don't mention it. You picking me up then?'

There were two tables free: a nice, cosy one in a corner and another, right next to the kitchen, subject to constant battering by the waiters, barging through the swing-doors with trays of food.

They were shown to the one by the kitchen.

Elisabeth hovered over her chair. 'What about that one?' she said, in a loud whisper.

Charles glanced briefly in the direction of the other table. 'I expect it's reserved,' he said, unfolding a napkin placidly.

'There's no sign on it.'

'Maybe they don't use signs.'

'Maybe we should ask,' Elisabeth said, pulling out her chair from the table with a mutinous clatter.

'This is fine.'

'It's in the *doorway*.'

Charles read the menu in silence.

She glared at the top of his head resentfully. 'We may as well be sitting in the kitchen,' she said eventually, but the fight had gone out of her voice. Charles said nothing so she picked up the menu and read it quickly. 'I'll have a green salad, followed by the grilled sole.'

'That was quick,' Charles said, without looking up.

Elisabeth closed the menu with a loud snap. 'Yes,' she said pointedly, 'it was.'

A waiter hovered over them. Elisabeth, after a quick exasperated glance in Charles's direction, gave her order, then stared fixedly at the kitchen door. This wouldn't happen if Sam was here, she thought. Charles, as usual, ended up ordering grilled peppers followed by lamb, then pondered the wine list for some time before ordering a bottle of house red.

I am being uncharitable, she thought, watching him deal with the wine waiter with leaden charm. He's doing his best.

They talked about work for a while – Elisabeth keeping Sam's presence in the gallery to a minimum, Charles scarcely mentioning Lily at all – then about the children and then, when those topics were quite exhausted, about their holiday plans and whether they'd find anywhere at this late date.

'I'm sure we'll get a late booking or a cancellation,' Elisabeth said doubtfully. 'Let's see when the kids get back.'

'We could stay at home,' Charles suggested. 'Enjoy the garden for once.'

'Not such a bad idea,' Elisabeth said, avoiding his eyes.

After that, they lapsed into silence, catching each other's eyes occasionally and, after a brief, guilty smile, filling the silence with a smattering of conversation before lapsing back into their own thoughts. Once they had been served their main courses – Elisabeth picking virtuously at her sole – and had demolished the better part of a bottle of wine, the tension between them began to ease.

'Quite like old times,' Charles said, smiling over a forkful of grilled lamb chop. 'Must make it a regular thing.'

'We used to,' Elisabeth said, a touch wistfully, 'before the kids.'

'That place up the hill that's closed down now,' Charles said, frowning as he struggled to recall the name. 'Villa Bianca, that's it.'

'Villa Maria,' she said.

'Bianca, surely, it was all white inside.'

'Maria, after the woman who owned it. Dumpy little thing in black, used to stand by the front desk glaring at the waiters.'

A trace of unease hovered in the air.

333

They were silent for a while.

'Ah, well,' Charles said, 'don't suppose it matters.'

'No,' Elisabeth said with a strained smile, 'couldn't matter a bit.'

Both, in their different ways, thought that it mattered very much.

Thirty

Lily tipped the dregs from her coffee mug into the wilting pot plant above her desk and wandered across the corridor to Charles's office. Angela was sitting squarely at her desk, eating diet cottage cheese out of a plastic carton.

'He in?'

'He's with someone,' Angela said untruthfully, then blushed. Rubbery flecks of cheese were stuck between her teeth.

'Tell him I need to see him, would you.'

'I'll make an appointment for you, shall I, madam?' Angela said, snatching up the diary angrily. 'And would you like coffee and biscuits served too?'

Lily looked at her wearily. 'Just tell him. It's important.'

'What's important?' Charles said, smiling anxiously.

Lily's eyes flickered across his face. 'You've been looking tired,' she said softly, 'just wanted to see how things were with you.'

Charles was momentarily speechless. It struck him like a ferocious blow that it was a long time since anybody had asked him how things were with him. 'Fine,' he said, on a winded sigh, 'fine.'

'That's good.'

Her voice was so low that he had to lean forward to hear; his hands on the desk, his body crouched over her.

'Too much work,' he said awkwardly, 'the usual thing.'

She glanced sharply at him, then smiled. 'Sure.' He felt clumsy and slow, as he so often did with her, unable to follow the mercurial dance of her emotions. He thought how distant she had been with him recently, abrupt even; noticed how her features had sharpened since he had first met her, as though a film of gloss had settled over them. He remembered the cheap, pink dress with its vulgar gold buttons marching over her small breasts, the pale vulnerability of her naked legs, her dark, admiring eyes. He felt a terrible, wrenching sadness and, for a dreadful moment, thought that he might cry.

'Elisabeth still enjoying her job?' There was a gleam in her eyes.

'She's very busy –' he said in a tight voice '– preoccupied.'

Lily caught a slight movement behind him and looked up to see Angela's pink face looming in the doorway. Her eyes flickered back to Charles, she inched a hand across the desk. 'Looks like you need a bit of looking after.'

Charles felt a dull shock as her hand crept onto his, the spark of her skin against his flesh. Elisabeth had not touched him for weeks. These days, when he kissed her goodbye, he felt a minute recoil under the surface of her skin, a quivering repulse as her soft dry cheek moved under his lips.

'Let's go out, shall we?' Lily said. 'Have a proper talk.'

Her sympathy made him helpless. 'When?' he said, his gaze fixed on her fingers. A curled white flake of Tipp-Ex clung to a pink nail, like a question mark.

Lily glanced back at the doorway. It was empty. 'Soon,' she said, her fingers pressing down on his. 'Soon.'

Elisabeth was drunk.

She and Sam had disposed of a bottle of red wine at lunch, then indulged in two glasses of rich, sticky dessert wine. Elisabeth thought, as the sensation of fruit and honey exploded in her mouth, if you could taste pleasure, then this is how it would be.

336

After lunch they idled down the hill, arm in arm, stopping occasionally to stare into shop windows.

'Mine, I think,' he said, pointing at a lurid lime green and purple shirt.

She laughed. 'Marvellous for that little Caribbean trip, darling.'

Darling. She rolled the word on her tongue, felt her heart turn with it. What was that poem? She searched through her mind, turning the words this way and that. Bliss, what bliss . . . Yes, that was it. What bliss it was in that dawn to be alive. . . . Or something like that. She blinked in the bright sunshine, caught the gleam of blond hairs scattered down Sam's arm. Not that it was dawn, of course, but bliss it was to be alive. She let out a gentle hiccup, giggled slightly.

Sam glanced down at her. 'Private joke, or can anyone share?'

She laughed. 'How does that poem go?' she asked, as they walked lazily towards the gallery. 'The one about bliss and dawn and being alive?'

'Bliss was it in that dawn to be alive,' he threw his head back, 'but to be young was very heaven!'

'Oh, wouldn't it be!' Elisabeth exclaimed. 'Wouldn't it be heaven!'

'Yes,' he said, and the vehemence in his voice startled her, 'yes, it would.'

'Do you mind, very much?' she said gently.

He looked down at her. 'Doesn't everybody?'

'No,' she replied, thinking of Charles subsiding gently into middle age with scarcely a whimper of protest, 'no, I don't believe they do.' Then she exclaimed, 'But I do, I mind very much.'

He laughed. 'Me too.'

They reached the gallery, stood on the doorstep while Sam fumbled in his pocket for the key. It used to bother her, leaving the gallery unattended for so long but as Sam

337

said, the rich don't shop at lunch-time. 'Most of the selling's done at night, when you're safely tucked up with that husband of yours,' he had said, smiling.

'I could help,' she had exclaimed, stung by the allusion to cosy domesticity, 'I could stay late.'

'You do help,' he had said, smiling down at her. 'All your hard work leaves me free to get on with selling, which is the easiest part.'

She had pressed him a little, but his face had closed up and he was almost short with her for a while, so she let the matter drop. Which did not stop her imagining him at work in the evening, picturing herself at his side in some sort of silk evening gown, charming bankers and millionaires and making brilliant sales – for which he, of course, would be eternally grateful.

She stood like that, dreaming a little, the hot August sun warming her shoulders through the thin silk of her blouse, while Sam fiddled with the stiff lock of the gallery door, cursing slightly under his breath. He mumbled something that she did not catch; all of a sudden was retracing his actions, slipping the key back in his pocket, stepping away from the gallery and towards the door leading up to the flat. Feeling the touch of his hand, she looked up to find his face close to hers, his expression quizzical.

'I said, would you like to?'

Elisabeth blinked slightly, in confusion. 'What?'

He gestured with his arm. 'Upstairs.'

She felt shock waves reverberate through her, a tide of heat rolling up to suffuse her neck and face, then her voice saying, distantly, 'Yes. Yes, of course.'

They climbed a set of narrow wooden stairs, emerged into a wide, square room with whitewashed walls and a low ceiling, half of which seemed to be made of glass.

'It moves,' Sam said, pressing a button, indicating the panels drawing back above their heads, revealing a pale blue sky.

'Wonderful,' Elisabeth breathed, blinking at the unreality of it all, the sensation of being in the clouds, the bareness of the room, empty save for a huge bed covered with a white quilt and linen pillows and scores, perhaps hundreds of canvases, stacked against the walls. 'Wonderful,' she said again.

He smiled. 'At least in one area of my life I am disciplined.'

'Yes,' she said, thinking of the chaos downstairs, the tumult in her head. She stood in the middle of the room, yearning after him, waiting for him to come towards her and take her in his arms but he turned from her, moved to the far corner of the room and picked up a small canvas.

'Here it is.' It was an oil painting of a woman sitting on a ladder-back wooden chair. She was naked save for an extravagant red velvet hat – the only colour in the composition, startling against the pallid tones of the flesh, the deep olives and browns of the surrounding ground.

'Isn't it marvellous?' He smiled down at it, his hands running caressingly over the rough oil surface. He looked over at her. 'I saw it last night, at the graduate show at the Slade, but the moment I set eyes on it, I knew.'

'Knew?' Elisabeth echoed.

He lifted the canvas, held it at arm's length, his eyes roaming its surface. 'Talent,' he said, in awe-struck tones, 'real talent.'

He set the canvas down lovingly, turned its face to the wall. 'She's only twenty-three,' he said, shaking his head, 'and last night they were queuing up to take her on. But I've got her,' his voice rose in a triumphant note, 'I've got her.'

Elisabeth was still standing motionless in the middle of the room, her arms hanging limply by her sides, mesmerised by the passion in his voice, yearning for him to direct it at her.

'It sounds stupid, doesn't it?' he said, turning away from the picture, smiling at her. He moved towards her, put his hands on her arms. She felt the flesh burning into hers. 'Getting so worked up over a few inches of paint.'

'No,' Elisabeth whispered, 'passion is never stupid.'

He put his arms around her, enveloped her in a gentle embrace. 'I knew you'd understand,' he said, rocking her slowly, 'I sort of felt you'd feel the same way.'

'Yes,' she whispered, lifting her face to his, offering her mouth up to his lips.

She felt his body tense momentarily, a sudden shift of movement and then the chill of the air where his body had been, a sudden gaping coldness on her breasts. Opening her eyes, she stared at him in confusion. Sam's face was blank with embarrassment.

'Oh, my dear. Elisabeth, you didn't think – ?'

Elisabeth smiled uncertainly.

'You don't mean that you thought you and I – ?' Sam threw his head back and roared with laughter.

A wave of humiliation gathered at her feet, surged up through her body until it towered over her, crashed with a roar about her head.

She heard dimly, through the muffled roaring in her ears, Sam saying, 'That's the sweetest, nicest thing anybody has ever done for me.'

'But I thought you – we –' she whispered. 'You said we had so much in common.' She turned away, tears stinging her eyes. 'You said I was beautiful.'

'And so you are; I meant every word of it –' She heard him hesitate, pick his way delicately through a thread of words. 'You are beautiful. But it's not – we're not – Oh God, Elisabeth, I thought you understood.'

She stared at the buttons on his shirt. 'Understood?'

He looked at her regretfully. 'Oh, dear, we seem to have found ourselves in a bit of a mess.'

She squeezed her eyes shut. 'It doesn't matter.' I am old and fat and ugly and empty and it doesn't matter. Nothing matters, she thought, her mind working wildly, wondering how to extract them both from this – this foolishness she had created.

'Would you mind –' she stammered, forcing her eyes to open, her mouth to smile '– would it be all right if I took the rest of the afternoon off?'

He lifted his hands, let them drop helplessly to his sides. 'Take anything you need,' he said quietly.

'Thank you,' she said, turning from the sympathy in his eyes.

I cannot bear this, she thought, moving stiffly across the room. Her hand grasped the stair banister, she felt cool polished wood slide under her hot flesh, heard him call her name.

'Yes?' she said, not turning.

'When I laughed just now –' he shrugged helplessly '– it was only out of embarrassment – like a nervous reaction.'

She dropped her head, nodded slowly.

'We're good friends,' he said, his voice coming as if from miles away. 'Please don't forget that.'

She managed a small smile. 'Thank you.'

Mrs Flower's bulk loomed in the doorway. She was panting slightly from the strain of climbing the stairs. 'Cup of tea, dearie?' she said. 'My daughter sent me a nice sponge, home-made.'

'Actually,' Tom began, 'I was just –'

'Now, dearie, you take your time while I get the kettle on,' she said, smiling cheerily. With a coy wave of dainty white fingers, she was gone. Her voice floated up the stairs. 'Don't you be long now.'

Tom went and put on a clean shirt. It seemed appropriate somehow. He presented himself at her door five minutes later.

'There you are!' she said, as if he had just journeyed for miles. 'You just sit yourself down and get comfortable while I see to things.'

A small table was set by the gas fire, which was on despite the heat of the day. It bore an ornate lacquer tray, laid with two flowered china cups, a milk jug, a sugar bowl, a tea strainer and the promised sponge cake.

'Needs a light touch, a good Victoria does,' she said, following his gaze. 'I always say to my Sheena, I say, Sheena, you've got air in those fingers. She tells me not to be so daft, says it's all in the beating. Well, I don't know that's true, not strictly. Me, I beat and whisk and sift my heart out and my cakes come out heavy as damp flannel.'

Tom smiled vaguely and headed over to the window, to a chair out of range of the fire.

'No, no,' Mrs Flower said, shooing him back to the vicinity of the fire, 'you take that chair, dearie. Very comfortable it is too. Now you just relax and enjoy yourself.'

The springs protested as Tom sank into the chair. He felt heat press down on his chest, like wet feathers.

Mrs Flower brought the teapot over to the table and lowered herself carefully into the chair opposite. She wore a grey cardigan, buttoned firmly to the neck and pinned with a little silver brooch. She hovered over the teapot like a plump partridge, cooing gently as she plucked off the lid and peered into its depths.

'Settled nicely, that is. Nothing like a cup of tea to set the world to rights. I'll be doing you a cup, then we can have a nice chat. Lily comes down here sometimes, for a bit of cake,' she said, her small, bright eyes flicking over to him, gauging his reaction. 'Says I make as good a cup of tea as her old mum. Well, I said, that's high praise, that is,' she added, handing him a liberally sugared cup of tea and sinking a knife into the pale mass of the cake.

A large slice appeared at Tom's side. Mrs Flower settled herself comfortably, wedging her vast hips further into the chair. Charlie heaved himself up from his basket and waddled over to her, then flopped down with a grunt, his head resting on her slipper, ears spread like a silken fan.

'Nice girl is Lily,' she said, without preamble, 'but delicate.'

'Delicate?' Tom said in astonishment.

Mrs Flower's brown eyes glinted over the flowered rim of her cup. 'Not quite all there, if you get my meaning.'

'Well, she seems bright enough,' Tom said, looking puzzled. 'I mean, if you consider her lack of formal education.'

Mrs Flower looked at him kindly. 'I don't mean her head, dearie. I mean her heart. She's not quite all there in her heart.'

Tom frowned. 'You mean she's damaged in some way?'

It was Mrs Flower's turn to look puzzled. 'Now, did I say anything about damage? All I'm saying is that she's different from you and me so don't you go expecting her –'

Tom wasn't listening, was too intent on marshalling his own confused thoughts about Lily, and the curious vacuum he met in her. He sometimes felt that he could put his hand straight through her and encounter no resistance. 'Some childhood trauma, perhaps,' he said slowly. 'I mean, she never talks about her father. Her mum – well, she features in every other conversation but have you noticed that she never mentions him?'

Mrs Flower considered this for a moment then applied herself to cutting another hefty slice of jam sponge. 'Eat up,' she said, nodding at the slice of cake which lay on his plate, scarcely touched, 'time you put a bit of flesh on those bones.'

Tom began silently to eat, watched with satisfaction by Mrs Flower, her eyes tracking each morsel of cake from his plate to his mouth. 'I can see you're a clever fellow –'

Tom shrugged, his mouth full of sugary crumbs.

'– and you like to find a reason for everything.'

343

He pushed his empty plate to one side. 'There usually is a reason for everything.'

Mrs Flower shook her head. 'No, dearie, there isn't. That's where people get things wrong. Some things just are and that's the hardest thing in the world to accept –'

'Well –'

She held up a dainty, commanding hand. 'Take that man who shot all those little kiddies. Bad enough in itself, but do the papers leave those poor people alone? For weeks there's interviews with this expert and that, stories about his mum and dad, even the colour of the wallpaper in his bedroom. Like a dog chasing its tail, they are. And for what? So they can find a reason.'

'They're only trying to make sense of –'

Mrs Flower shook her head. 'Can't ever be no sense in seventeen dead kiddies.'

Tom thought of Ben, the pale, tender skin of his neck, his large crooked ears trapping the light and the way it shone pink through the thin, pearly cartilage. 'No.'

'There you are then.'

'Surely you're not suggesting that Lily is deranged in some way.'

Her mouth closed with a little pop. 'Not suggesting anything. All I'm saying is, life's not a series of round holes and round pegs. People come in all different shapes and sizes so there's no good trying to squeeze a square peg into a round hole and then asking why it won't fit or why it turned out that way. Just did, that's all.'

'So you mean – well, it's the concept of original sin,' Tom murmured.

Mrs Flower looked at him with kindly exasperation. 'Don't recall mentioning no sin. All I say is that some people are born different and there's no earthly use trying to explain away the difference.'

'She's had a difficult time of it, though, what with

moving to a new city and starting again after that bastard jilted her.'

Mrs Flower shook her head. 'Now did she go telling you that?'

'Yes.' Tom shook his head in bewilderment, thought for a moment. 'Well, now you come to mention it, I don't believe she's talked about him at all.' He shrugged. 'I suppose I just assumed –'.

'I expect she wanted you to,' Mrs Flower said comfortably.

Tom glanced at her sharply, but she was smiling.

'Jim he's called, and a nice lad he is too; pops in to see me occasionally and catch up on Lily.'

'He comes here?'

'Likes to keep a watch over her. It was him put me on to her, sharpened my eyes, you might say.'

Tom watched her attentively but Mrs Flower was fussing over his empty cup. 'More tea, dearie?' she said, holding out the pot.

Tom held out his mug, waited for her to pour tea, add milk and a generous dose of sugar. He disliked sweet drinks but Mrs Flower considered tea without sugar to be undrinkable. She heaped two spoons into his cup.

'So he didn't jilt her?'

'Oh, no, lovely. She scarpered with the frock and the ring, leaving them all behind to pick up the pieces. Jim seems to think she'll be back, when she's good and ready.'

Tom wondered why Lily would lie and then realised, with a jolt, that she hadn't – except by omission. He wondered if the others knew, if Elisabeth had realised that first night and then he remembered her face, presiding over the dinner table, her expression of smug benevolence, Daisy's and Bella's sly, pitying glances and knew that they hadn't; knew that they had all, himself included, misjudged Lily entirely. He remembered Lily turning up at his old offices the day after he left Bella, the faint gleam of malice in her voice when she talked about Elisabeth, the one-woman mercy mission, the nights when she had lain in his arms and he had tried, haltingly, to tell her something of his confusion and found, as his only audience, the blank impenetrability of her gaze. Still, he was grateful to her, was strangely soothed by her unquestioning presence, by her long cool body in the bed beside him.

Mrs Flower's eyes twinkled shrewdly.

'And her fiancé,' he found the word curiously difficult to say, 'this Jim person, he's prepared to accept that?'

Mrs Flower cocked her head on one side, her smile coy. 'Oh, yes, dearie. He's in love with her, see? Warts and all.'

'But you said that she was damaged in some way, unlovable.'

'Me? Said no such thing. All I said was that she's not good at love, passes her by like the number 19 bus when it's full of an evening. Sails right on past, however much you want it to stop.'

'Yes,' Tom said, thinking of Lily in his bed, of her thin back pressed against him, the pearly knobs of her spine moving under his fingers. Her pale limbs made him feel uneasy sometimes, as if he was embracing a child.

Mrs Flower caught his unease. 'I'm only saying all this because I don't like seeing a nice young man like you make a mess of his life.'

Tom grinned ruefully. 'I think I've done that already.'

'Not from where I'm sitting.'

'No?'

'Got a head full of brains, a wife who loves you and that lovely young lad of yours.'

'You think I should go back to Bella?'

'Like I said, lovely, not up to me to pass judgement on others. I says what I see, that's all.'

'There you are!' Lily exclaimed, pushing the door open. 'Telephone for you.' Her voice was flat. 'I think it's Bella.'

'Right,' Tom said, scrambling to his feet.

'It's Ben. I've just had a call from the school.'

Tom felt the air whoosh from his lungs, a black mist wreathe around his eyes. 'Not an accident?' he said, forcing out the words.

'No, nothing like that.' Bella sounded impatient, irritated even. 'He's gone and messed up his A-levels. Badly.'

'Oh.'

'Is that all you can say? *Oh*? This is his future we're talking about.'

Tom was silent. What did exam results matter if Ben was safe?

'The school want to see us but I think we need to talk first, have it out with him too.'

'What exactly has he done?'

Bella let out a short laugh. 'I'll tell you when I see you. Can you come over tomorrow? Six thirty, at home.'

'Home.' The word felt strange in his mouth.

'I'll cook,' she said and put down the phone.

'Up here,' Daisy called. 'No, *here*.'

Elisabeth stared up at the cavernous ceiling, eventually found Daisy silhouetted against a dim wall, clinging to some scaffolding. 'Isn't that dangerous?'

'Yes,' said Daisy, clambering down, stripping off a pair of pink Marigold rubber gloves. Moving towards Elisabeth she bent forward to kiss her, holding her arms wide, like a diver, to save Elisabeth's clothes from the grey dust that coated her overalls.

'This is a nice surprise. What brings you here?'

'Humiliation,' Elisabeth said, turning away and pretending to inspect a lump of clay.

'Oh dear.'

Elisabeth glanced at her, attempted a smile. 'I've made a terrible fool of myself.'

'That seems unlikely,' Daisy said crisply.

'Unlikely or not, I have –'

Elisabeth trailed off into silence, stood contemplating a sheeted statue. Daisy's eyes flickered impatiently from Elisabeth's face to the figure. 'It's not finished. Are you going to tell me or am I going to be forced to play one of those tedious guessing games?'

'You won't laugh?'

'Why is it that whenever anyone says that, I get an uncontrollable urge to do so?'

Elisabeth looked at her fearfully. 'I fell in love with somebody and –' she took a deep breath '– and when I told him, he laughed.' Her mouth wobbled perilously.

'Not funny,' Daisy said, moving forwards, putting thin arms around Elisabeth's shoulders, 'not funny at all.'

They stood like that for a moment, gently swaying. How strong her arms are, Elisabeth thought with surprise. She felt Daisy's muscles, like thin ropes pressing into the soft, fatty flesh of her upper arms and pulled away, dabbing at her eyes. 'I feel like such a fool, and on top of it I've gone and ruined a friendship. At least, I think I have.'

'I doubt that,' Daisy said, giving her an odd look.

Elisabeth knew what – or rather who – the look was for: Charles. 'You're shocked, aren't you?'

Daisy shrugged. 'Not shocked, surprised perhaps. I always thought that you and Charles had –'

'A good marriage,' Elisabeth finished wearily. 'I know.'

'Far be it from me to judge a marriage,' Daisy said cheerily, 'being as I am a girl of such outstanding success and qualifications within the arena of relationships –'

'With Sam,' Elisabeth interrupted.

Daisy's eyes grew round with shock, then her eyes tilted skyward and a small smile skittered across her face. 'Sam?' she said, beginning to laugh. 'You declared undying love for *Sam?*' she sputtered.

Elisabeth flushed. 'Yes.'

Daisy fell about, clutching at her sides. 'Sorry, sorry.'

'I don't see what's so funny,' Elisabeth said stiffly.

348

'Sam's gay, you idiot,' Daisy said, the remnant of a laugh floating on the surface of her voice.

Elisabeth stared at her in horror. 'Gay?'

'Well-known fact.'

'Not to me.' She closed her eyes. 'God, what a fool he must think me.'

'I doubt it,' Daisy said, suddenly sober. She leaned forward and patted Elisabeth gently on the arm. 'I expect he was flattered.'

'Don't,' Elisabeth said, snatching her arm away. 'Just don't.'

Daisy's thin face was bright with pity. 'How about a cup of coffee?' she said, after a while. 'No, a better idea ... Let's have a glass of wine.'

Elisabeth was silent.

'You sit down. I'll get a bottle,' Daisy said, taking her by the shoulders and steering her towards the sofa. 'Just pull off the dust-sheet. It's quite clean underneath although it is a bit tatty. I keep meaning to do something about it.'

She trailed off in the direction of the fridge while Elisabeth dragged off the dust-sheet, rolled it into a ball and dumped it on the floor. Soon Daisy appeared, emerging from the gloom in the far corner of the cavernous studio, carrying a tray.

'How organised you are,' Elisabeth said, staring in astonishment at the crystal wine glasses.

'A present from Alex; a mistress's booty, you might say,' Daisy said, pouring the wine. She handed a glass to Elisabeth, took one herself, raised it to the light. 'To men, God bless their fractured souls.'

'I'm sorry about Alex,' Elisabeth said stiffly. Her voice trailed off. 'I meant to say –'

'Other things on your mind. I quite understand,' Daisy said, not quite repressing a smile. 'Still, good things may yet emerge from the whole sorry business.'

'How is he?'

Daisy thought for a moment. 'Quiet,' she said after a while.

'Does everybody really know about Sam?' Elisabeth asked quietly, not looking at her.

Daisy grimaced. 'I'm afraid so. When he was very young he had a rather public affair with George Lewes.'

'The conductor?'

'The very same.'

'Anyway, it went on for years. It was George who set him up in that gallery, all the money came from him. Sam's never had a bean of his own. He's hopeless at business.'

'Yes,' Elisabeth said wistfully, 'he is.'

'Anyway, when they finally separated, George settled quite a lot of money on him and then, when he died, and his wife found out about the settlement –'

'His wife?'

'When his wife found out, she went mad and started contesting it furiously by which time, of course, it was far too late.'

'I see.'

'The newspapers got hold of it. Sam became rather famous – or perhaps I should say, notorious.'

'No wonder he was astonished,' Elisabeth said, remembering Sam's face – but I thought you understood.

'He was very beautiful in his youth. I've seen photographs. Exquisite.'

They sat for a while in silence, drinking their wine.

'Elisabeth, you haven't – well, you haven't told anybody else about this, have you?'

Elisabeth flushed. 'Bella. And got very short shrift.'

'Ah, yes, well, Bella is not a passionate advocate of adultery. What I meant was – you haven't said anything to Charles?'

Elisabeth turned to look at her in astonishment. 'To Charles? Of course not.'

'It's just that one can get rather – well, impatient, about love.'

'Yes,' Elisabeth said sadly, remembering the sensation of dizzy lightness in her head, the ground moving swiftly beneath her feet. She looked down at her sensible navy court shoes, planted squarely in the grey dust of the studio floor, thought of them lined up neatly in the wardrobe next to Charles's shoes where they had always sat; where they would always sit.

'I suppose I'd better go home,' she said dully.

Charles found the house in darkness. He went into the sitting-room, poured himself a whisky and stood at the window watching the garden settle. He felt a curious pleasure to be alone in the house, freed from the brooding presence of Elisabeth's disapproval. Taking off his shoes, he wiggled his toes, enjoying the sudden sense of freedom, and thought it would not be so bad to live alone.

Later, he went into the kitchen and made himself an omelette, washed it down with another large tumbler of whisky. Elisabeth would not allow him to drink spirits with dinner; something to do with acid on the stomach. He felt the bite of it in his guts. A faint, bitter smile crossed his face. According to his wife, it was the closest he would ever come to having fire in his belly. He disappointed her, he knew, but there was a stubbornness in him that faced her disappointment with neither sadness nor regret, but a sort of rapt indifference. That blankness infuriated her, as he knew it would, and while in the beginning it had been a sort of game, a slow, cumbersome match of wits, it had over the years become so ingrained in him that he had discovered he could present her with no other face. He considered this for a while, wondering if familiarity did this to everyone, if all marriages were the same, causing a similar settling and hardening of the dust of habit until its players were petrified, set in stone. Perhaps that was why he was vulnerable to Lily, to the unexpected delight of finding himself to be a different man, seen through new eyes. He knew very well the game she was playing, the childlike joy in discovering her power, but he did not resent her for it. He was her final target, she would get to him soon enough. He wondered about himself, how he would respond when she did, but considered it with the sort of curious, almost idle detachment that people feel when they imagine themselves facing a crisis – expanded to magnificence or diminished by fear.

The dull slam of the front door echoed through the quiet house and, a few moments later, Elisabeth appeared at the kitchen door. She looked washed out except for two hectic spots of pink anointing her cheeks.

'I've been out,' she said pointlessly. 'To see Daisy.'

'How was she?'

She sat down on a chair, facing him, her body slumped as if in exhaustion. 'Oh, you know,' she said, without looking at him, 'she was Daisy.'

He got clumsily to his feet, knocking the chair with his thighs. She winced slightly at the clattering noise.

'You look done in. Shall I fix you something to eat?'

She looked up at him. '*You*?' she said, and for a moment contemptuous disbelief blazed in her face. 'I'm not hungry,' she said, passing a hand across her eyes, as if to wipe her expression clean. 'I think I'll go up to bed.'

He said nothing.

She walked slowly to the door, then turned and looked back at him. 'I'm sorry,' she said, in a stifled voice. 'I'll be better soon.'

They stared at each other in silence. She was waiting, he knew, for him to say something but he could find nothing to say and so kept his peace. Eventually Elisabeth dropped her gaze. 'Good-night then,' she said, and he heard resentment tingeing the edges of her voice. Turning, she went quietly along the dim corridor and up the stairs to bed.

Thirty-one

The next morning, Elisabeth let herself into the gallery and set to work with brisk efficiency, sorting the post by attaching a Post-It note to each letter. Each was marked 'urgent' or annotated with a question mark, neatly inscribed in a round, childish hand. She laid the letters carefully on Sam's desk, then disposed of the fliers and begging letters.

When the post was dealt with, she picked up a duster and can of Mountain Fresh spray cleaner and set to work, conscious of the echoing emptiness of the vaulted room. As she wiped and polished, she felt the surfaces, cold and lifeless under her hands, wondered at the change in the place, the sudden air of neglect as if some previous occupant had simply abandoned it. She could not, for a moment, put her finger on the change and then she realised, with a sudden start, that it was not the room that was different but herself. Her flat mood infected the room, was absorbed into its very walls, and she thought how strange it was that an exchange of only a few sentences had been enough to alter the very contours of the space around her, and that the emotions of the past few months had been strong enough to colour the atmosphere of the place, lift it to life. When Sam appeared at the usual time of eleven o'clock, she settled a smile on her face that made the corners of her mouth ache. 'The post has arrived,' she exclaimed, as though it was a surprising event. 'I've marked the urgent stuff for you. It's on your desk.'

He put a tray down on her desk. 'I've made coffee.'

'Oh,' Elisabeth said, glancing down. The tray was laid with a clean white linen cloth, a plate of sugary almond croissants, two cappuccinos and a vase of flowers, as if she was ill.

Tears pricked at her eyes. 'You didn't have to.'

'I hope you're going to eat one of these,' he said, offering her the plate, 'they cost a small fortune.'

'They're cheaper at the bakery round the corner,' she said, taking a bite of croissant, 'you should have gone there.' A sliver of almond stuck like a limpet to the roof of her mouth. She worried at it with the tip of her tongue, trying to dislodge it.

'You look like a frog when you do that,' he said.

She started to laugh and found that she was crying.

'I'm sorry,' she wept, 'so sorry.'

He put an awkward arm around her. 'Don't be or I shall have to be sorry too and it's an emotion I particularly dislike.'

Elisabeth was silent, conscious of an unfamiliar coil of tension in the muscles of his arm. Realising that the embrace was one of pity rather than affection, she stiffened and moved away. Sam looked immediately contrite. 'Look,' he said awkwardly, 'I really am most dreadfully sorry if you felt that I'd –' he paused, searched for a delicate phrasing. 'Well, if I caused you to think that I was interested in you in some –'

'Aren't you?' Elisabeth interrupted, her face assuming a stiff, bright look. 'Don't you find me utterly fascinating? Or were all those lunches you took me to just some sort of play-acting?'

'Of course not,' he said quickly, as if eager to ignore the reproach, 'I asked you to have lunch with me because I find you interesting. It's just that –' He paused, spread his hands in an expression of helpless supplication.

His consideration infuriated her suddenly and she turned away, scrabbled in her bag for a tissue and blew her nose. 'You don't behave as if you're gay,' she said, resentfully, 'don't give any sign.'

The corners of his mouth twitched. 'I shall make a placard, wear it around my neck.'

She gave an impatient jerk of her head. 'As a warning to all unhappily married women, I suppose.'

He gave her an odd look. 'I didn't know that you were unhappy.'

'Nor did I,' she said, briskly blowing her nose, 'until recently.' She saw his expression, said quickly, 'Oh, it's nothing like that. Charles wouldn't. He hasn't the imagination.'

She had meant it lightly, as a sort of joke, but saw from the sudden shift in Sam's expression, a sharp embarrassed recoil, that bitterness had leaked through her voice.

Flushing slightly, she said, 'Sorry, just me being silly.' She stood up, tucked the tissue firmly in the cuff of her blouse and began to shuffle paper into neat piles, her smile starchy with self-pity. 'Time we got on with some work.'

When Elisabeth left the gallery at two o'clock, having eaten a sandwich at her desk, she thought she saw relief sharpen in Sam's face. The air was hot and still but the sky had darkened to a pale, milky grey. From time to time, she glanced up uneasily, wondering if a storm was on the way, then toiled on, treading heavily along the dusty pavements. Remembering that there was no food in the house, she stopped outside the deli's windows trying to muster some enthusiasm for supper. In the end she bought a couple of slices of ham and a plastic tub of pale, waxy potato salad, then trudged home through the quiet streets. As she pushed open the door of the house, she stepped on a letter lying on the mat. She took her foot away, saw the grey wedge of her footmark imprinted across the address; 'Mrs Charles Delaware' it said in neat, typed capitals. Inside was a folded sheet of lined paper, torn from a memo pad. Frowning, she opened it carefully. A message was written in pencil, in a coarse, juvenile scattering of letters.

'Your husband is having an affair with a girl in his office,' it read. 'Her name is Lily Clifton.' It was signed 'A friend'.

Elisabeth stared at the letter in disbelief, then crumpled it quickly, wadding it into a tight ball, and hurried through to the kitchen where she shoved it into the pedal bin, using her fingers to push it down among the tea bags and banana skins. Walking quickly to the sink, she filled it with hot water, as hot as she could bear, and scrubbed at her hands with a nail brush until they were red and raw.

'How could he,' she thought, 'how *could* he?'

'How could he?' Bella said, 'how *could* he do something like that?'

'Obviously he's angry.'

'Of course he's angry, but to write "Fuck You" across three sets of exam papers –'

'Have you talked to him?'

Bella shook her head. 'I was waiting for you.' Waiting for you to tell me, she thought. He's sleeping with her, he's sleeping with her. The thought strummed in her head. He looked unbearably familiar, sitting in his usual place at the table, wearing the shabby checked shirt and jeans that she knew so well. She wanted to hit him.

'Has he any idea we know?'

She shook her head. 'The results aren't due in for a week.' Anger pulsed in her head, made her restless. She got to her feet, walked over to the oven, peered inside.

'Smells good.'

'Lasagne,' she said, not looking at him. It used to be his favourite.

'Thank you.'

She shrugged, walked over to a drawer, pulled out some cutlery. 'It's quick and easy.'

'Yes,' he said, knowing it wasn't.

She stood in the middle of the room, her hands full of cheap cutlery. 'The weird thing,' she said with a puzzled frown, 'is that he's seemed so happy recently. You wouldn't know anything was wrong.'

Like you, she thought, like you. You wouldn't know anything was wrong with you.

'There's no mistake? The wrong set of exam papers?'

She moved to the table, began clearing it. 'I've seen them. It's his writing.'

Tom folded a newspaper neatly and added it to the pile that sat by the table, to make space for the cutlery. It always had been too small for them, that table; too small for Bella's lists, for Ben's discarded fliers advertising some new club night or music venue, for the letters and bills that piled up under the old plate they used as a paperweight. A few wizened apples lay in the fruit bowl, covered by a thin layer of dust.

Bella's hands moved across the table, deftly negotiating the familiar obstacles. She looked so permanent, so comfortable, absorbed in that small, domestic task, that he felt a sudden swimming sense of desolation and stared at the pitted wood surface, the scorched mark where he had once carelessly put a hot casserole, the faint white pattern of rings from Ben's habit of washing a glass and not drying it properly and then a new collection of scuffs and burns, collected in his absence.

He looked up to find Bella hovering over him, trying to reach out to lay the knives and forks down, careful not to touch him. 'Would you mind moving that glass?'

He held out an awkward hand. 'Let me do that.'

'Don't worry,' she said, slapping the knives and forks down with deft, proprietorial movements.

Tom stared at the table bleakly; his hands, denied the

comfort of familiarity, moved restlessly across the wooden surface. 'I'm not worried,' he said in a tight voice, 'I'd like to do something useful.'

She glanced over at him and he saw anger flicker across her face as well as a sort of reserve and knew that she didn't want to allow him in; by refusing to let him help, she was refusing him access to her life, to their life.

She thought, he's sleeping with her. I know he's sleeping with her.

He said, 'Please.'

Silently, she turned away from him and fetched mats, side plates, the old, chipped glass salt and pepper pots. She put them on the table, in little neat piles. Her cheeks were flushed, she would not look at him.

'I told Ben to be back at seven thirty,' she said, crouching down to stare unnecessarily into the oven. She twisted around to look at him, still hunched over the oven. Her voice carried a challenge. 'I've told him you'll be here, but not why.'

He stared down at the cutlery, thought how many meals he had eaten with it, how many times the scratched steel had slid between both their lips, stitching them to each other, anchoring them in the small domestic pattern of their days. Her anger pulsed across the room, shutting him off. No point remembering, he thought, laying down the last chipped china plate. Her anger felt solid, like a wall of toughened glass separating them from each other. He felt the bruise of it against his skin and picked up the bottle of wine with trembling hands, poured them both another glass.

He struggled to keep his voice steady, heard it emerge on a bored, flattened note. 'Have you thought how we should approach him?'

Bella caught the tone. 'I thought perhaps you might start.' Her voice was polite, distancing.

'If you think that's best –'

'Yes, yes I do.'

Elisabeth said nothing to Charles when he got home, busied herself with preparations for supper, banging pots down on the stove, chopping vegetables furiously, her back stiff with indignation.

After attempting, unsuccessfully, to land a kiss on her cheek, Charles decided to remove himself to the sitting-room and pour a large drink. Years of experience had taught him not to approach his wife's stiffened back. He said mildly, 'I'll be in the sitting-room.'

A few minutes later, slightly to Charles's surprise, Elisabeth joined him, settling herself in the chair facing his, by the unlit fire. He glanced up cautiously from his newspaper, but she was staring at the fake logs in the fireplace, her arms and legs held awkwardly, stiff with unspoken reproach. He waited for a while, his gaze attentive, but she would not look at him so he glanced back down at the paper. He had learnt, during their marriage, to live with the reproaches; had discovered that they were not aimed at him directly – other than over some minor domestic failing on his part – but at the world in general. Elisabeth was by nature a woman who felt misunderstood. Charles sympathised. On the whole, so did he, although he had discovered it was best not to express it.

Realising that he had been staring at the same page of the newspaper for some time, he turned the page. Elisabeth gave a sharp sigh and, picking up a book, cracked the spine in that infuriating way she had, then settled down to read it.

The minutes ticked peaceably by and Charles was just beginning to relax, to enjoy a story about a politician whose sexual escapades had recently been causing much hilarity in the media when Elisabeth said, her voice sharp, 'Charles, do stop doing that.'

He looked up, mild curiosity blurring his features.

She leaned forward, rapped her knuckles sharply on the table. 'Tapping.'

He stared down at his hand. 'Sorry.'

'It drives me mad.'

'Yes. I'm sorry.'

She raised her book, tried to concentrate on it but found the letters blurring and expanding before her eyes. She put it down with a sharp sigh. Charles looked over at her.

'Is there something the matter?'

She laid down her book and clasped both her hands in her lap, to stop them trembling. 'Yes.'

'Anything I can help with?'

'Yes.'

He looked at her enquiringly. After a moment, her gaze wavered.

'Perhaps a drink,' she said, in a low voice.

'Glass of wine?'

'Whisky.'

He frowned slightly, but got to his feet and walked towards the drinks cabinet. She watched in an agony of irritation as he fiddled around with glasses and bottles. 'A large one.'

He turned to look at her in surprise, the bottle suspended over the glass.

'Very large.'

Turning away, he poured a good two inches into a glass. 'Ice?'

'No, thank you.'

She took the glass with both hands and raised it to her lips. She was trembling so violently that some of the liquid spilled down the front of her silk dress. He hovered above her. 'Shall I get a cloth?'

'No.'

Charles stared at her in bewilderment, then slowly walked back to his chair and eased himself down into it.

She sat in silence, sipping at her drink. He watched her from time to time but said nothing.

'I said, it's driving me mad.'

He frowned. 'What?'

She rapped her fingers on the arm of her chair. 'I *said*. Tapping.'

'Sorry.'

'I can't bear it.'

He looked at her again. 'Are you in some sort of pain?'

'Yes, yes I think I am.'

He hunched forward in his chair, his face flooding with concern. 'Bad?' he said. 'Should I call Dr Wilson?'

She shook her head. 'It's not that sort of pain.'

He stared at her in confusion, waiting for an explanation, but when none was forthcoming he sank back into his chair, keeping a wary eye on her.

'It's Lily,' she said, at last.

The name registered a curious sort of blankness in his face. 'Lily?'

'Are you having an affair with her?'

He looked away, stared at the knuckles of his hand which had begun, of their own volition, to tap out a tune. 'No,' he said, eventually.

'Oh, for God's sake stop doing that.'

'Sorry.'

'And stop saying that you're sorry. What are you sorry for?'

He shrugged. 'I don't know,' he said simply. 'Perhaps you could tell me.'

'You mean, you haven't slept with her?'

'No.'

'Do you want to?'

He looked at her thoughtfully and then fell silent, his head tilted back, the newspaper abandoned on his lap. It was the way that he had sat, that they had sat, in this same room for so many years that she began to imagine the whole Lily affair – Bella's wild accusations, the grubby note, Tom's extraordinary behaviour, even Daisy finishing so suddenly with Alex – had happened only in her imagination.

'Yes.'

The word was so unexpected that Elisabeth's whole body jerked violently in response, spilling the remains of her whisky. She stared at the stain slowly spreading across her breasts and then leaned her head back wearily against her chair. 'Yes,' she repeated dully. 'Well, I suppose it's true then.'

'What's true?' he said, frowning.

'The letter. There was a letter. It came in the post.'

'What did it say?'

'That you're having an affair with Lily.'

'Well, I'm not.'

'So you say.'

They sat in silence for a while.

'Do you still have the letter?' Charles said, after a while.

Elisabeth jerked her head towards the kitchen. 'It's in the bin.'

'What exactly does it say?'

'Does it matter?' Elisabeth said coldly. 'You yourself said you wanted to sleep with her.'

'I also said I hadn't.'

'But you want to.'

'So does every man who claps eyes on her.'

Elisabeth dropped her gaze, stared at her feet. Charles watched her, exasperation mingled with something like tenderness in his face. 'Really Elisabeth, surely you'd realised that.'

She shook her head. 'No,' she said, getting heavily to her feet. 'I suppose that just goes to show what kind of a fool I am.'

She got up, moved slowly towards the door, stopped and stared over at him.

'Does that include Tom and Alex? Do they want to –' she waved a hand helplessly in the air.

'To sleep with her?' Charles said. 'Almost certainly, yes.' His tone was sharply irritable. 'Bella maintains that they already have.'

'But *you* haven't.' The flat contempt in her voice made him wince with shock. Is that how she sees me now? he thought and the idea angered him so greatly that he was tempted to blurt out a scarcely formed thought that simmered somewhere on the edges of his consciousness. It was something Lily had said, about Elisabeth having an affair with that man she worked with, Sam Howard. He wavered slightly, unwilling to pass on idle gossip, then glanced over at her, caught her expression in an unguarded moment, saw the stark hostility in her face and said, his tone icy, 'I believe you also have something to tell me.'

Elisabeth stared at him in confusion. 'Do I?'

'Something about Sam Howard?'

'Sam? No, I –' She stumbled, a guilty flush rising to her cheeks.

He saw then that it was true – if not true in deed, at least true in thought – and felt a sudden sharp stab of pity. Poor, stupid woman, he thought, poor gullible fool, for Charles had long ago realised that his wife's disappointment with their marriage had nothing to do with the realities of their relationship but was coloured by some overblown notion of romance. And I am a poor knight in shining armour, he thought, watching her sadly.

'Nothing's been going on. It's not – I mean, I haven't – Oh, for God's sake, Sam's gay,' she blurted out, tears springing to her eyes, spilling down her cheeks. She stared at Charles and said, her voice rising in anguish, 'Everybody knows that.'

'Everybody, it seems, but you.'

She dropped her gaze, nodded dumbly.

'Poor Elisabeth,' he said gently.

She looked up, caught on his face a look of such compassion that, uttering a strangled cry, she fled from the room.

Ben's key turned in the lock at exactly seven thirty.

'My God,' Bella said, checking her watch. 'He's on time.'

'Don't say anything,' Tom warned, suddenly anxious. He knew how the two of them were together, how alike they were in temperament, the sudden fury of their anger, the suffocating tangle of their intimacy. 'Don't get him upset.'

She glanced at him; a quick, contemptuous look. 'Of course I won't,' she said but then they heard the scuffle of steps on the thin carpet in the hallway and turned away from each other, raising their faces to the door, their expressions composed in calm, expectant smiles.

Ben poked his head around the kitchen door, his face wary with disbelief, but then his eyes lit on his father and he gave a quick, cracked grin. 'Hi, Dad,' he said, scowling with pleasure, darting a thin arm out in a quick, awkward embrace, then withdrawing just as suddenly, moving away quickly to clatter into a chair.

'Good to see you,' Tom said, his voice rough with inarticulate love, but the words were drowned out by the loud scraping of a chair on the cracked lino as Ben shoved himself up from his seat, prowled restlessly across the room before swinging round, heading towards the fridge and pulling out a can of beer. Cracking the flimsy tin tab, he lounged against the fridge staring at them. 'Weird,' he said, swigging beer.

They smiled meekly.

'Go easy on that,' Bella said.

'It's only beer, Mum.'

'I know it's only beer,' she said, suddenly snatching up an oven cloth and pulling the hot dish out of the oven. She

364

slammed it down on the table, looked over at him. 'But it's still alcohol.'

'Which you never touch, I suppose,' Ben said, with a slight sneer.

Her hands shook as she picked up the serving spoon. 'Wine,' she said, 'I have an occasional glass of wine.'

'Occasional?' Ben exclaimed, his eyes flickering guiltily from her to his father, torn between loyalty to both.

Tom's gaze was fixed on the jerking quiver of Bella's hands, the flailing rap of the lasagne-filled spoon on the china plates. 'Bella –' he said warningly.

'You just stay out of this,' she snapped.

Ben looked at the two of them. 'What?' he said. '*What*?'

Bella finished serving out the meal, shoved plates haphazardly on the place mats. 'Let's eat.'

'No,' Ben said, watching her. 'Let's not. Not until you've told me.'

'Told you what?' She was forking lasagne into her mouth in rapid, jerky movements. Bolognese sauce spattered the table.

Ben moved over to the table and stood over his mother, staring down at the dull frizz of her hair.

'What you're both so uptight about.'

'Ben,' Tom began, 'I think –'

Ben wheeled round on him. 'You keep out of this. If she's pissed at me, it's up to her to say why.'

Bella put her fork down quietly, said in an exhausted voice, 'The school rang.'

Tom said, 'Bella, I thought we'd agreed –'

Neither of them looked at him.

'Yeah, and – ?' Ben said, his eyes fixed on Bella's white face.

'And they showed me your exam papers.'

A flush crept across Ben's thin cheeks, his shoulders moved up to his ears.

'Oh, that,' he mumbled.

'Oh, that? Oh, *that*! Is that all you've got to say, all you can manage about the reason for fucking up your future?'

'At least it's my future I'm fucking up. At least I decided how to fuck it up.'

'What about us?'

'Well, what about you?'

'You forget, Ben, you're *our* future.'

'I'm your future? Oh, great. You fuck up –'

'We care about you.'

'– you fuck up and I get to carry the can as *your* future. Well, here I am, the future of your fuck-up.'

Bella looked at him wearily. 'I didn't mean –'

'What? What didn't you mean, Mum? You didn't mean to yell and shout and drive Dad away?' He kicked a foot angrily against a leg of the table. The salt and pepper pots jumped. 'And you,' he said turning to Tom, 'you didn't mean to fuck other women? Is that right?'

Tom closed his eyes. Bella sat rigidly, staring at the table.

'Well, I didn't mean to fuck up my exam papers either. So that's all right, isn't it? None of us fucking *meant it* so it's OK.'

Tom and Bella sat at the table, their heads bowed like penitent children. Ben stared at them for a while, then dragged open the fridge door and pulled out another can of beer. They heard the crack of the tin tab being pulled. 'Fine fucking example you two are,' he said bitterly, crashing out of the door. There was a sudden silence, then the door slammed open again. 'And some fucking surprise that was, Mum.'

The silence reverberated through the kitchen.

Eventually, Tom said, 'He thought you'd arranged supper so we could tell him that we were getting back together, didn't he?'

She stared at the opposite wall, her face white and set. 'Didn't he?'

She looked at him. 'Yes.'

'Jesus. No wonder he looked so happy when he came in.'

She whispered, 'Are you fucking her?'

'What?'

'You heard.'

'What did you say to him?'

'Just that you were coming to supper. Are you fucking her?'

'Yes.'

Bella was silent for a while and then gave a sigh like air being let out of a balloon. She crumpled slightly, pushing away her uneaten plate of food, and said in a low, defeated voice, 'It's just that he wants it so badly, us all together again. That's why he's so angry.'

She looked over at Tom with a deflated smile. 'Do you remember,' she said, 'how when he was little he used to say "my family" as if we were all one person. "Is my family going?" he'd ask or, "Will my family be there?" '

Tom smiled, remembering. 'Yeah.'

They sat at the table in the gathering darkness, hunched over the cooling plates of food.

'I'm sorry,' Tom said, after a while.

Bella frowned. 'Me too.'

Eventually, Charles stood up and put a light on, then went and sat back down in his chair, his eyebrows drawn together in a deep frown.

Presently, Elisabeth appeared, pale but composed, to announce that supper was ready. They ate at the kitchen table, the silence only broken by Elisabeth asking him if he would like some pudding. He refused, just as she refused his offer to help clear up; turning her back on him and stacking the dishwasher with quiet, methodical care. When she had finished, she rinsed out the saucepans, wiped clean all the surfaces, hung the drying-up cloth on the rail in front of the Aga to dry and left the room on noiseless feet.

Once she had gone, Charles went to the pedal bin, plunged his hand into its depths and began to sift through the debris. His face betrayed no emotion, although his white shirt cuff gradually grew stained, dark brown tannin leaching up from discarded tea bags, tomato pips and smears of grease. Once he had found what he was looking for, he carried the crumpled letter to the table, and walked back across the kitchen to tear off a couple of pieces of kitchen paper from the wooden roller by the chopping board. Dabbing his shirt cuff with one piece, he walked back to the table and carefully cleaned the worst of the stains off the letter with the other.

Sitting down, he smoothed the letter flat with both hands and read it carefully a number of times, as if he was memorising it. After a while, he got to his feet, went into the sitting-room and poured himself another large whisky.

Thirty-two

'What's wrong with his lordship this morning?' asked Lily, splashing coffee clumsily into a director's coffee cup. She didn't bother to wipe around the saucer.

'Don't know what you mean,' Angela muttered, her flushed face turned to a plate of biscuits that she was arranging in a careful pattern.

'Charles, you idiot,' Lily said, glancing at the biscuits scornfully. 'And if you're making those pretty for him, you're wasting your time. He won't even notice.'

'He might,' Angela said in a strangled tone.

Lily reached past her for the milk. 'Suit yourself.' She glanced at Angela's flushed, miserable face. 'He said something to you then?'

Angela looked at her fearfully. 'What do you mean?'

'Told you what he's got his knickers in a twist about?'

'No.' Angela's lower lip trembled, her face crumpled like a wad of wet pink tissue and she fled back to her office with the tray of coffee and biscuits.

Lily watched her go, then picked up a director's biscuit, a plain chocolate Hob Nob, and ate it thoughtfully.

Charles didn't eat the biscuits, and he said to Angela, who fussed round him, hovering hopefully over the stacks of post piled at his elbow, that he would attend to it later and would she mind please only putting urgent calls through that day. She dithered all morning about what constituted urgent calls, finally only allowing anybody who threatened life or death to talk to him. At six o'clock, in desperation, she slipped a hand-drawn Smiley card on the desk in front of him.

He scarcely glanced at it.

Angela sat bolt upright on the bus all the way home, her jacket buttoned askew, eyes bright, biting her lip hard to stop the unshed tears from falling.

After the polytechnic term ended, Bella had abandoned the piles of academic papers on the kitchen table where they sat brooding, waiting to be attended to. She gazed at them resentfully. She'd left them for weeks now, far too long, which meant a hard slog of at least three weeks to get through them. Sighing, she sat down with a cup of coffee and leafed through them in a desultory way. Almost immediately, the doorbell rang.

'Bloody typical,' she murmured, going to answer it.

A fat, elderly woman leaned heavily on a shopping trolley, her bright little eyes fixed attentively on Bella's face. At first she thought it was Gloria, from the pub, but then she noticed the hands, white and unblemished, surprisingly dainty for so large a woman.

'Mrs Sutherland?'

Bella nodded.

'And would you be married to Tom Sutherland? Tall young man with a lovely smile?'

'Look, what is all this –' Bella began.

The brown eyes crinkled in a pleased smile. 'Oh, I'm so glad it wasn't a wasted journey, not that it's far, but at my age even a walk to the corner gets to be a trial. I looked you up in the phone book.'

'And you are?'

'Mrs Flower. I've come about your Tom. Oh, don't take on, dearie, it's nothing serious. Just thought it was time somebody came and had a chat with you.'

'Well,' Bella said doubtfully, 'you'd better come in then.'

'Right oh,' Mrs Flower said, heaving the shopping

trolley over the stone step and thrusting it ahead of her so it snapped at Bella's ankles.

'But he's all right, you say?' Bella said, quickening her pace fractionally as she led the way into the kitchen.

Mrs Flower gave her a shrewd look. 'Well, I wouldn't say *right* exactly, would you, dearie?' She stood squarely on the coloured lino, her bag clasped in both hands, her gaze expectant.

'Oh!' Bella said, remembering her manners, 'would you like a cup of tea?'

Mrs Flower smiled gratefully and divested herself of her hat which she laid neatly on the kitchen table, next to her capacious bag. The shopping trolley was parked in a corner, by the door, where she could keep an eye on it. 'Just take the weight off my feet, if you don't mind.' She settled herself in one of the chairs, stretched her legs cautiously. 'It's my ankles. They swell.'

'It's close today,' Bella said, hunting anxiously through a cupboard for a teapot. She felt there was something about Mrs Flower that demanded such ceremony.

Mrs Flower nodded. 'They say it's going to rain. Mind, they've been saying that for weeks now and the sky just seems to press closer and closer to the earth. Some days lately I've felt it might squash us entirely, like ants.'

Bella glanced at her, surprised by the lyrical turn of phrase, but Mrs Flower smiled comfortably. 'Don't go to any trouble on my account,' she said, watching Bella's feverish search.

'I'm afraid it's going to have to be mugs. I did think we had –'

'Tea's tea, however it comes.'

'Well, I think I've got some biscuits somewhere,' Bella said, scrabbling around in an old tin.

'Don't you worry about me,' Mrs Flower said, but Bella couldn't help noticing that when the biscuits finally appeared on a chipped plate, Mrs Flower helped herself to three. 'And two sugars please, dearie. To my mind, tea's a drink that needs a bit of sweetness. Takes the sharpness off.'

Mrs Flower settled herself to her tea and biscuits.

Bella waited expectantly, plucking nervously at a hangnail on her thumb. 'You said something about Tom?' she said, once half the mug was emptied and the biscuits eaten.

'He needs you to come and take him home,' Mrs Flower said calmly, brushing biscuit crumbs from her capacious bosom. 'He's lost, poor lamb, wandering in the wilderness.' She looked at Bella, her brown eyes reproachful. 'And you've gone and let him.'

'Well, I –'

'Not that it's any of my business and it's not my way, as a rule, to interfere. People must lead their own lives, as best they can, but I said to myself this morning, I said, I can't be doing with watching a nice young man like that just throw himself away.'

'How do you know all this?' Bella said slowly. She felt as though she was in the middle of a dream and glanced involuntarily at Mrs Flower's feet, half-expecting to see a pair of glass slippers, but found only a pair of cream, basket-weave sandals, bulging slightly over her bunions.

Mrs Flower's eyes were round with surprise. 'Didn't I say? I live with him, dearie. Have done these four weeks past so I've –'

'With Lily?' Bella said faintly.

'People always say that we have a choice,' Mrs Flower continued, as if Bella had not spoken. 'Well, some of us do but for the most part I'd say that things happen by accident, like. Next thing you know it's a habit which most of us are too idle or frightened or plain bone-weary to break. Then,' she said, helping herself to another biscuit and chewing on it contemplatively, 'next thing you know you're lying on your deathbed and what was an accident turned out to be your life.'

'You mean that Tom might –'

'All I mean is, you should come and fetch him home, where he belongs,' Mrs Flower said firmly, 'else you'll find yourself with nothing left but regret.' She rose slowly to her feet. 'Very indigestible, regret.'

'But what if he doesn't want to come?' asked Bella, following her to the front door.

'Course he wants to come,' Mrs Flower said, manoeuvring her tartan trolley in the narrow hallway, 'he just needs to be told he's wanted.'

'Can it be that simple?'

Mrs Flower's mouth was set in a firm line. 'Simple as you make it. A mountain of pride's not an easy thing to climb, mind.'

'No,' Bella said wretchedly.

Mrs Flower looked at her kindly, then reached out and patted her on the hand. 'Nothing you can't deal with, if you've a mind to. Like I said, what was an accident becomes a habit. Before you know it, it's a life. Nice to meet you, dearie, and thank you for the tea. You must come and call on me one day. My daughter sends me a nice cake, every week, home-made.' She gave a little formal bow of her head. 'You'd be welcome to some, I'm sure.'

'Thank you,' Bella said faintly and stood watching her steer her tartan shopping trolley up the path, her knitted hat bobbing gaily over her vast bulk.

'I'm considering resigning,' Charles said to Elisabeth later that evening. She was standing at the sink, peeling potatoes. '*What?*' she said, her quick fingers growing still. She stared down into the cold eye of a potato, winking dark against the pale, uncovered flesh.

'I'm considering resigning.'

Elisabeth dropped the potato with a splash. 'You said. Over what?' she asked, turning to look at him.

'Over this Lily business.'

'But you said you hadn't done anything.'

'I haven't. Well, nothing dreadfully much but that's not really the point.'

'Would you mind very much getting me a drink?' Elisabeth said, sitting down hard at the kitchen table.

Charles scraped his chair back across the terracotta tiles, which made Elisabeth wince irritably, and got up. When he reappeared, holding a large tumbler of Scotch, she said, 'What do you mean, it's not really the point?'

Charles sat down, stared out at the garden. 'I've taken her out for a drink a few times.'

'How many times?'

He shrugged. 'Six or seven.'

Elisabeth was silent.

'And I've quite often given her a lift home.'

'I still don't see –'

'The letter came from Angela, my secretary.'

Elisabeth's eyes slid over to the white pedal bin. 'Why would she do a thing like that?'

Charles looked vaguely embarrassed. 'She's got some sort of crush on me.'

'Dear God,' Elisabeth said, 'I hadn't realised you were the office Romeo.'

A muscle twitched spasmodically in Charles's cheek. Elisabeth watched him for a moment, then took a large swallow of whisky.

'Even so,' she said after a while, 'I scarcely see that it's a matter for resignation.'

He said tightly, 'Apparently my attentions to Lily have made Angela jealous. Her jealousy impelled her to write the letter –'

'Charles,' Elisabeth interrupted, 'this sounds like a bad schoolgirl romance.'

'That may be so but it's still my fucking future we're talking about.'

'Don't shout, I'm only trying to –'

'And if she's distressed enough to do something that

374

stupid and malicious,' he went on, pausing only to take a large swallow of whisky, 'then God knows what else she's capable of.'

'So fire her.'

'On what grounds?' he said coldly.

'On the grounds of unprofessional behaviour.'

Charles smiled bleakly. 'Whose?'

Elisabeth was silent for only a moment. 'OK, then you'll have to get rid of Lily. Get her out of that office.'

'And how do you suggest I do that?'

'Oh, for God's sake, just tell her to go. Hasn't she caused enough trouble in our lives already?'

'You can't just take people's jobs away, Elisabeth, not without good reason.'

'What's she going to do about it?'

'Take the case to Tribunal. Accuse me of foisting my attentions on her and when she wouldn't cooperate, firing her to shut her up.' He spread his fingers. 'There are any number of variations she could come up with, particularly if there's gossip all round the office already.'

'It's a storm in a teacup,' Elisabeth said impatiently. 'It'll blow itself out. Unless, of course, you intend to continue this ridiculous affair with Lily.'

'I am not having an affair with her.'

'No,' Elisabeth said bitterly, 'just some pathetic school-boy fixation.'

He looked up, startled by the contempt in her voice, then dropped his gaze. 'I'm sorry you see it that way,' he said quietly, getting heavily to his feet. 'I just wanted you to be aware of the gravity of the situation.'

'Oh, for God's sake, stop being so pompous.'

Charles turned to stare at her. 'I wasn't aware I was.'

'No,' Elisabeth said in tones of such quiet savagery that they were both startled, 'you never are.'

Thirty-three

'I think we need to have a little talk,' Charles said.

Angela gazed beseechingly across the desk at him, her plump, earnest face flushed with guilt. Something in her expression reminded him of his daughter, Lucy, when she was young and had been caught out in some misdeed. For a moment he was tempted to apologise, to say that it was he who was wrong but he knew that his future depended on her guilt. He cleared his throat. 'I believe that you may have written my wife a letter.'

She nodded dumbly, her plump face crumpling like paper. 'I don't know what happened,' she wept. 'One minute I was sitting at my desk,' she glanced nervously over her shoulder at the offending desk, 'and the next – I was standing by the post box.'

Charles handed her a tissue, his fingers stiff with distaste. She fumbled at it, clutched it to her face. 'I didn't mean to get you into trouble,' she sobbed, 'I only meant –' Her eyes slid towards the corridor, sent little hot, stabbing glances in the direction of Lily's office.

'And have you –' He paused, stared down at the papers piled on his desk. 'Have you mentioned your feelings to anyone else?'

'Anyone else,' she stumbled, 'what do you mean?'

'In the letter you say that I am having an affair with one of your colleagues –'

She nodded dumbly.

'Well, have you mentioned the same thing to anyone else inside or out of this office?'

Outrage distorted her shiny cheeks. 'No,' she gasped, 'no, I'd never –'

Relief settled like nausea on Charles's stomach. 'Well, in that case,' he said smoothly, 'no harm has been done. If you promise never to repeat those ridiculous rumours then I think we can forget the whole incident.'

Angela's mouth hung open stupidly.

'Do I have your word?' Charles said carefully.

She let out a sob and lunged forward, grabbing his hand in both of hers and showering it with tears and kisses.

'Angela,' he said gently, loathing himself for manipulating the poor stupid girl's feelings, for hating the touch of her mouth on his skin, 'don't, please.'

She let go off his hand and wiped a clumsy sleeve across her face, smearing mascara down her cheeks.

He said carefully, 'Lily is a friend of my wife's. Did you know that?'

She shook her head, eyes round with disbelief.

'Some connection with her family,' Charles said, bile rising in his throat at the outright lie, 'who asked us, when she moved to London, to keep an eye on her. Lily hasn't had an easy life so her parents are, naturally, worried about her.' He paused to allow time for the information to sink in, forced a smile to his face; a caring, concerned sort of a smile. 'So you see that my interest in her is purely paternal.'

'Your wife,' Angela whispered, shame distorting her plump face, 'the family ... Oh, I'm so sorry, I didn't –'

'So I apologise if my feelings have seemed less than impartial,' he said, his voice tight with the effort of repressing the bile that now flooded his throat, 'but I can assure you that –'

Angela was on her feet, backing towards the door. 'Such a fool,' she was whimpering, 'so sorry ... so stupid ... don't know what I was thinking. . . .' She turned suddenly, feeling the door-frame hard against her back, gave him one last mortified glance and fled.

Charles leaned back against his leather chair, closed his eyes in relief. He thought he might vomit.

'I don't think she knows what she's doing.'

Bella's mouth twitched in disbelief. 'Of course she doesn't. She just happened to stumble on Tom when he was homeless, squatting in his office, just happened to find a room for him to rent, just happened to fuck him by accident.' Her voice rose. Elisabeth shot her a warning look as a thin girl in a droopy black dress appeared, slopping two cups of pale milky liquid in front of them.

'Two cappuccinos, sugar's on the table, pay as you leave,' she droned in a breathless, nasal whine.

'Thank you,' Elisabeth said crisply, extracting a tissue from her bag and ostentatiously blotting spilt coffee from the saucer. She wadded the tissue into a ball and dropped it into the ashtray, then stared up at the girl, waiting for her to move out of earshot. The waitress gave a thin, scornful shrug, then moved to the next table, slapping a grey, dripping cloth on its greasy surface.

'I think it's more complicated than that,' Elisabeth said. 'Or perhaps more simple. She's like a child playing a game, but a child who doesn't understand the rules.' She sank a spoon into her coffee and stirred it idly although she was religious about not taking sugar in any form. 'Well, not our rules anyway.'

Bella sighed deeply, wondering whether Elisabeth was being deliberately provocative. Easy enough for her to sit there protesting Lily's innocence; it wasn't *her* husband Lily was fucking. 'And are you going to explain them to her?'

Elisabeth looked hurt. She didn't much like Bella's tone. 'I thought I'd have a word. I'm sure if somebody put it to her reasonably –'

'Oh, *please*,' Bella said, rolling her eyes. 'You think a girl like that –'

'Why not? When she picked up with Tom, he was on his own, after all. It's not as if –'

'No, he wasn't on his own,' Bella said furiously, 'not spiritually anyway. He's married. She knew that perfectly well, just as she knew that he was going through a rough patch, that things would have got better.' She snatched a cigarette out of a packet, snapped a lighter at it. Her hands shook. 'Anyway, what about Charles? This letter you said you received –'

Elisabeth shrugged. 'His secretary. Girlish jealousy. Charles will sort it out.'

A curl of smoke floated up into Bella's eyes, stinging them. She squinted accusingly at the cigarette, stubbed it out violently in the ashtray, mashing it to a pulp of shredded tobacco. Really she thought, Elisabeth's complacency was breathtaking. Serve her right if Charles really was having an affair with the girl.

'I called Lily this morning,' Elisabeth went on, watching as Bella churned the disintegrated cigarette stub. Those nails, she thought, looking at the jagged splinters edging Bella's ink-ingrained fingers. Does she never wash them? 'She's coming over to see me this evening.' Her mouth settled in a firm, pink line. 'I think it's about time somebody made that young lady see reason.'

Bella looked at her uneasily. 'Well, I hope you know what you're doing.'

Elisabeth smiled. 'She's just young, that's all. Naive.'

An accident, Bella thought, staring at the phone. That's what Mrs Flower had said, *an accident that becomes a habit.* She chewed at a hangnail, ripped it with her teeth, then watched the pink, jagged dent slowly darken until it oozed beads of bright red blood. *Then, before you know it, it's a life.* Sucking on her finger, she picked up the telephone.

A man answered, said grudgingly that he'd go and see if Tom was in his room. 'It's three floors,' he said, his voice taking on a malevolent whine. Bella worried at a piece of jagged nail, feeling it prick sharp against her tongue.

'Tom Sutherland.'

She took her finger out of her mouth. 'It's me.'

'Everything all right?'

'Fine.' Well, as fine as everything can be, Bella thought, when your husband's living in a boarding house and fucking a twenty-three-year-old nymphomaniac.

'Ben OK?'

'That's why I called. It's been agreed that he can resit his exams in the New Year.' She paused briefly. 'We went to see the school.'

'Oh, God, sorry darling,' Tom said, remembering. 'I know I said I'd come with you.'

Darling. The word sent up a tiny quiver of shock, lodged itself in Bella's ear. What was that for, she thought, habit? Still, it warmed her; left a flush in her thin cheeks.

'Doesn't matter. They were extremely understanding, once I'd explained things and Ben says – Well, he's sorry.'

'I think we all are.'

'Tom – ?' He heard her voice emerge on a gasp, imagined the vocal cords bunching in her thin neck, tension etched in the white, rigid bone of her jaw. 'You and –' She could not get the name out. 'Is it serious?'

He frowned at the chipped cork noticeboard that hung by the side of the pay-phone, pushed his thumbnail into a large dent. 'No.'

Her voice rose. 'You could come home –'

He dug his nail harder into the cork, felt it crumble beneath the pressure. When he took his finger away, it left a large, gaping hole. 'I can't.'

'Can't or won't?' The warmth had gone from her voice.

Tom put his finger back in the hole, wiggled it round. 'There's something I have to do first.'

'One final fling?' He heard the jagged splinters of her voice, pushed his finger harder into the hole, felt the edges of the cork crack and buckle around it.

'No,' he said, 'not that. First, I have to get a job.' But when he listened for her answer, there was only the voice of the telephone, echoing tinnily in his ear.

Elisabeth led Lily into the kitchen.

'Would you like a cup of tea?' she said pleasantly. Kind but firm, she thought. That's the tone.

'No, ta, I'm swimming in the stuff by the time I leave that place.'

'A drink, perhaps?'

'Glass of wine be nice. You having one?'

Elisabeth nodded, walked briskly over to the fridge, located a chilled bottle of Chardonnay.

'You all right?' Lily said, watching her ease the cork out. 'You look a bit funny.'

'I'm fine,' Elisabeth said, putting the glasses on the table and going to stand behind a chair. Discovering that her hands were trembling, she caught hold of the back of a chair and held it fast for support. 'There's something I have to ask you.'

'Yeah?' Lily watched her trembling hands with lazy interest. There was something so insolent about her indifference that Elisabeth felt momentarily winded.

'Are you –' Elisabeth began. Her voice failed and she glanced away, as if to collect herself. 'Are you,' she said, her voice gaining strength, 'having an affair with my husband?'

Lily stared at her for a moment and then a smile glimmered briefly on the pale oval of her face. 'An affair with *Charles*? Whatever gave you that idea?'

Elisabeth looked away. 'I have my reasons.'

'Oh yeah?' Lily said. 'And what might they be?' Her head was angled in a little, triumphant tilt. Elisabeth suddenly saw, with a faint prickling of unease, that she was enjoying herself. Well, she wouldn't give her the satisfaction, wouldn't even *mention* Tom. Alex neither. 'The way he looks at you.'

'Blimey. Is that all?' Lily said with a sudden peal of laughter.

When she laughed like that her mouth cracked open, splitting the fleshy lips painted a deep purply red, like a bruised plum. Is that what Charles likes, Elisabeth thought uneasily, that hungry mouth? 'I think it's enough,' she said, flushing.

'If that's the way you look at things, every bloke in the world would be at it.'

Elisabeth stiffened. 'That may be the case in your world, but it's certainly not in ours.'

'Like that, is it?' Lily said, after a while.

'I'm sorry,' Elisabeth said quickly. Something in the girl's eyes made her recoil. 'One says stupid things in anger.' Her gaze wavered uncertainly. 'So you're not having an affair with Charles?'

'Asked him yourself, have you?'

Elisabeth looked at her wearily. 'Yes. Yes, of course.'

Lily's mouth curved into a slow, amused smile. 'And what did he have to say for himself?'

'He said –' Elisabeth hesitated, turned the words round carefully in her mind '– there's been some unpleasantness in the office that seems to have upset him rather badly.'

Lily's eyes flickered. 'Unpleasantness?'

'Something about a letter.'

'What sort of a letter?'

'It seems Angela has got things a little confused.'

'Silly mare. She's the one you should be worrying about, drop her knickers soon as look at Charles, that one –'

'So I asked you here,' Elisabeth continued, ignoring her, 'to see whether there wasn't something that could be done to put an end to these ridiculous rumours. You must see that they're not in your best interests either.'

Lily leaned back in her chair, sipped slowly at her wine. 'Aren't they?' she said after a while.

Elisabeth flushed impatiently. 'Well, I hardly think that rumours of an affair with a senior partner, particularly one who's married,' she said, laying careful emphasis on the word, 'are going to do your career much good.'

A slow, mocking smile spread across Lily's face. 'You telling me that anybody gives a toss about the way girls like me behave?'

'Yes, of course they –'

'Oh, leave it out, Elisabeth.'

Elisabeth took a deep breath. 'All I'm asking, Lily, is that you please leave my husband alone.'

'Me!' Lily exclaimed. 'Leave him alone? I never even touched him. Never made a move. It was your precious husband come chasing after me. Like Mary had a little lamb it is, the way he follows me around.'

Elisabeth flinched at this picture of Charles, the cruel accuracy describing his meek, lugubrious face. Idiot, she thought, idiot. 'But you've done nothing to stop him.'

'Why should I?'

'Because he's my husband –' Elisabeth began angrily, but her rage subsided almost as quickly. Because, she thought, he's getting older and his wife pays him no attention so he's vulnerable to girls like you. She sighed heavily. 'You played on his sympathies because you were feeling vulnerable yourself, after being dumped by your fiancé.'

Lily laughed. 'He didn't dump me. I left him. Boring sod.'

Elisabeth stared at her in bewilderment. 'But all those stories you told me, about him leaving you at the altar. The bridesmaids playing catch with the bouquet. Your gran in tears –'

'Oh, that. That was just a laugh.'

Elisabeth stared at her. 'A laugh?' she repeated unsteadily.

'Yes, you know. You said I was here to amuse you.'

'I really don't know what you're talking about. I said no such thing.'

Lily looked at her calmly. 'Yes, you did. Tom told me. He said you invited me to dinner that first time because,' she dropped into a horrible parody of a flat middle-class accent, 'it might be an amusing idea.'

'I did no such thing,' Elisabeth said heavily. 'I invited you because I felt sorry for you, all alone in London. I felt you might be miserable.'

'You? Sorry for me? Blimey, Elisabeth, have you looked at yourself recently?'

Elisabeth averted her eyes, fixed her gaze on the gleaming work surfaces of her kitchen. 'I don't know what you mean.'

'You whinge about your husband, your kids, your house. You even whinge about having too much money.' She laughed contemptuously. 'The original bleedin' heart – except it's bleedin' for yourself. I'm surprised you've even noticed Charles; too busy wringing your hands over that pansy you set your sights on.'

'He is not a pansy,' Elisabeth said in a stifled voice.

'Not what I heard.'

Elisabeth stared at her. Even this slow, stupid girl knew more than she did. She wondered how long she'd known, if she'd said anything to Charles, remembered the girlish confidences she poured down the phone, how she'd giggled and exclaimed, feeling young again. Young, like Lily. Young and firm and unexplored. Uncharted territory, undiscovered lands. Was that what Charles thought? Oh God, she thought, oh God, what have I done? Tears sprang to her eyes.

'Get out,' she said.

Thirty-four

The letter arrived with the early morning post; a flimsy buff envelope addressed in blue biro and a thin, spidery hand. Fuck, Tom thought, I've done it. I've got a job.

Clutching the letter, he ran up the stairs to Lily's room, taking them two at a time, hammered jubilantly on the door.

He heard a muffled exclamation, the creak of floorboards, then she appeared, a thin dressing-gown clasped around her.

'Where's the sodding fire?' she said sleepily.

'I've got a job.'

She yawned. 'That's good.'

'It's not much, but it's a start. It'll give me a steady income and I can start taking on private commissions, maybe even build up a business, go back out on my own again or with Harry.'

'Well, that's good then,' she said again.

Tom felt a flicker of exasperation. He wanted someone to share his pleasure. He thought with a pang of Bella, how her face would have lit up with pride, joy, her thin arms reaching out for him, gripping his shoulders. He stared at Lily, drooping against the door-frame, her head propped against the wood, her face expressionless.

'You don't look very pleased,' he said sullenly.

She shrugged, pushed herself upright and trailed over to the sink, leaving him standing in the doorway. 'Well, it's not me who's got a new job,' she said, switching on the kettle. 'Wouldn't mind one myself, as a matter of fact. Sick of that place, I am.' Sensing his stillness, she glanced over at him. 'What's up with you?'

'You could at least say well done.'

'Well done then.'

'Thanks.'

She saw his expression, burst out laughing. 'It's only a sodding job.'

'No it's not,' he said, shrugging his shoulders, 'it's my –' He was going to say, it's my life, a new beginning. She watched him blankly. What did she know of him, after all? What did she care of his hopes and dreams, his miseries and triumphs? To her, he was just another bloke in another room, a body at night, a face in the morning.

'Never mind,' he said, turning away.

'Don't be like that,' she said, her tone wheedling. 'Come and sit down. I'll make you a cup of coffee.'

He turned reluctantly, wanting to shake her, make her sit up and take notice of him. Moving into the room, he leaned against the peeling wallpaper. 'I don't think this is going to work out.'

She looked over at him. 'What isn't?'

'You and me. Us.'

She said nothing but took two mugs off a pair of hooks screwed into the wall above the kettle, spooned instant coffee into them, poured boiling water. He looked down; the letter was still in his hand. He thrust it into a trouser pocket. 'You don't mind then?' he said, his voice flat.

'If that's what you want.'

'I don't know what I want.'

She looked up at him, surprised. 'Well, why say it then?'

'Because –' he began and then thought, I said it to get a reaction, to feel that I mattered, was connected to another human being in some way, however small, but he could see that her indifference was absolute. 'I was just thinking out loud.'

She carried a steaming mug of coffee over to him

carefully using both hands, then went back to collect hers, picked up a packet of popcorn and took it over to the bed where she settled, cross-legged. The cellophane crackled as she opened the packet, extracted a few puffed white kernels, chewed on them slowly. 'Popcorn?' she said, holding the packet up to him. He shook his head.

Shrugging, she fixed her gaze on the far wall, stared at the shabby wallpaper as if in deep contemplation.

He watched her, wondering if her indifference was feigned, was a game she was playing, carefully calculated to draw him back to her, plundering his need to be needed.

'You don't mind then?' he said again.

She looked up at him and he saw that she had been thinking of something else entirely. She shrugged. 'Course I mind, stupid.'

'But not enough.' He could not keep the bitterness from his voice.

She frowned. He could see that she was trying to make some sense out of him. 'Enough?'

'To make a difference.'

'We like each other, don't we? Make each other happy. . . .' Her voice trailed off, she stared up at him with large, expressionless eyes.

'I don't know what you want,' he said in exasperation.

Lily sighed slightly, crunched on another handful of popcorn. 'You're a nice bloke, Tom, and it's nice being with you but if that's not what you want no more then that's all right too.'

She turned on a smile but he could only stare, over-whelmed by a terrible feeling of desolation. She feels nothing for me, he thought, nothing at all, and then he remembered Mrs Flower and how she had said that Lily was fragile, in her heart, that she was not connected in the same way that other people are and he said, 'Well, let's just leave it as it is then.'

She dived into the bag of popcorn, tossed some of the white blown kernels in her mouth. 'Yeah, all right,' she said, her mouth full, and he wondered again about her. It was as if she was wrapped in some thick, insulating gauze, cut off from the usual electrical circuit of emotion, the jumps and beeps, the positive and negative impulses that spark between strangers, the irresistible currents that plug us to our fellow beings. Or did she live so much in the circle of her own self that other people were mere shadowy shapes, slipping and sliding past her, coming up against her sometimes with a bump, connecting to her for one brief moment before disentangling themselves to slide away again, unnoticed and unremarked?

She said, 'Better get ready for the office then.'

'Yeah, right,' he said, and for a moment he forgot her indifference and felt only a spark of excitement as he remembered that this time next week he'd be back at work, freed from the shadowy, shapeless world of unemployment. Perhaps he'd call Harry, see how he was doing, pick up with some old friends, go out for a drink. He patted the letter in his pocket for reassurance. It was only the local council, but it was something, a start. He wasn't sure he could cope with going back out on his own; this way he could build up slowly, get his confidence back and then, perhaps later –

'Go on then,' she said.

He looked up, startled, but she was gazing blankly at the wall. She didn't hear him go.

Elizabeth wondered why she had never noticed it before, remarking the boneless curve of Sam's wrist as he lifted his cup of cappuccino, the languid drape of his body arranged across the chair. Faggot, she thought savagely, spineless *faggot*, and her face lit with a flush of shame. She could not rid herself of it; these days when he touched her, she felt it coil and uncoil in her belly, her skin rippling with minute shivers of disgust. 'Of course,' she'd say quickly, moving away from him, snatching up the letter he'd asked her to type, turning her eyes from the sadness she saw etched in his face. Or was it pity? Surely not. What did he have to pity *her* for?

Charles too. That same compassion lit his face when he looked at her these days; a sort of clenched sympathy that made her want to hit him, to pummel her fists into the disappointed droop of his shoulders.

She looked down. Her fingers were curled into her palms, the nails digging into the soft flesh. She straightened them slowly, easing the stiffness in them, examined the blameless pink of her pearly nails. It was as if they no longer belonged to her, those crabbed handfuls of resentment. She discovered them like that quite often these days, balled into clumsy fists which had to be smoothed flat before she made the morning coffee, prepared the evening meal, waited for Charles to finish one of his long, interminable sentences. She blamed him, conscious even as she did so of unfairness; blamed him for his diffidence, his lack of spontaneity, for the defeated slope of their life. Had he been a more vital man, she would never have turned to Sam, would have seen him for the faggot he was. Pansy, that's what Lily had said. *Pansy*. Funny, that's what she'd thought when she first saw Lily – that wide, pale face, those bruised dark eyes – thought how strange it was that they'd named her after the wrong flower. Is that what Charles had thought too? She tried to remember him at that first dinner, how he had been with Lily, but all she could recall was the dining-room table, the linen and crystal and silver, her friends' faces in the candlelight, laughing and happy. *Happy*. Strange now, to think it. Tom and Bella separated, him living in that dingy boarding house, Daisy split with Alex, her and Charles – It was all because of Lily, surely even Charles could see that? She refused to take this whole Lily thing seriously. Charles couldn't be serious, wouldn't turn his back on all the things they'd spent so long building up. He adored his children, their house, the life they had together. She felt a surge of tenderness. He was a good man, a kind man. She resolved to be nicer to him in future, quell the irritation that prickled under her skin. All marriages went through bad patches occasionally; everybody knew that. She'd cook him a nice dinner, make him see how good their life could be together. Soon he'd see Lily for the scheming little bitch she was. She felt a prickle of unease. Tom hadn't, but then it was different for Tom, of course, vulnerable after the business going bust and as for Bella, well anybody could see that she was a nightmare to live with. No wonder he'd had some sort of nervous breakdown, at least that's what Bella had said, the last time they spoke. As for Alex. Well, Alex was Alex. No, Charles would see sense.

'Where have you gone?'

Elisabeth started, looked up to see Sam watching her with an amused smile. Only last week it would have made her heart turn, a remark like that. Her eyes settled on his mouth, the petulant droop at its corners.

'Nowhere far,' she said, with a bright dismissive smile, 'just home, that's all.'

'Are you all right, darling?' Celia asked. She was dressed to go out, in a black suit and patent shoes, wearing what she called her luncheon face of glossy lips and cool, powdered cheeks.

'Very smart.'

'Some do at the Royal Academy,' she said dismissively. 'I'll be crushed with boredom by the time I emerge.'

'You love it.'

'Perhaps.' She walked over to him, put a hand lightly on his shoulder. Alex had to quash a sudden, overwhelming urge to grab it, bury his face in it. It was not the way they were with each other. 'Not going in to the office today?

Slacking are we?' Her briskness masked the concern in her voice.

Alex stretched, easing the ache in his shoulders and back, the leaden fatigue that he seemed unable to shake off. 'Thought I'd work at home today, test out all this modern technology I've invested in,' he said, nodding in the direction of the gleaming machines humming in the corner.

'Rather you than me,' she said, dropping a kiss on his forehead and walking briskly to the door.

He watched her admiringly. 'Be good.'

'I'll do my damnedest,' she said, smoothing her crease-less jacket flat with red, glossy nails. A faint frown had appeared on her smooth forehead. 'You're quite sure you're all right?'

'Be gone,' he said with mock severity.

'There's something wrong,' Celia said, later, to Daisy. 'He hasn't been out in weeks.'

'You're complaining because your husband is staying home?'

'Perverse, I know. But you know what he's like.'

'Yes,' Daisy said, after a while.

An odd sort of friendship had sprung up between the two women; odd, Daisy thought, because of Alex, who acted both as a bond between them and a constraint. They liked each other instinctively, had done so since they first met. In any other circumstances, they would have become very good friends.

Men, Daisy thought, more bloody trouble than they're worth; a sentiment she had voiced to Bella just the evening before. Amen to that, Bella said, and promptly burst into tears at which Daisy had told her, somewhat briskly, to stop pissing around and go and get Tom. Drag him out of there by the hair if you have to, she said. They're frail, weak creatures, they need a firm hand; it's what they understand. Bella said with a sigh that she supposed she was probably right.

'He complained the other night of being tired,' Celia said, 'and he's not a complaining man.'

'Only in certain circumstances.'

'I think he's embarrassed by any admission of physical weakness. As if it's a reflection on his virility.'

'I'm sure he's fine. Probably just recharging his batteries. After all, he's had a tiring few months –'

Lily stood in the doorway of Charles's office. It was seven o'clock. Angela, still flushed and nervous with guilt, had left for the day. Charles's head was bent over a pile of papers; a yellow pool of light from the Anglepoise on his desk threw the rest of the room into darkness. His pen scratched across the document he was working on, leaving a trail of black ink. He was drawing up a will. Is that it? he thought. Is that all there is to show for a life? He gazed thoughtfully at the list of bequests until something alerted him; the flicker of a pale face in the shadows, perhaps, or simply the sensation of being watched. He looked up to see a pair of dark eyes gleaming.

'Lily?' he said.

She stepped forward into the light. 'Didn't mean to disturb you.'

He laid down his pen. 'You're not,' he said, running weary hands through his hair. When he took them away, his hair stood up in a crest.

'Working late again?' she said, stepping closer and bending over the desk, her dark hair falling forward across her shoulders and snaking onto the white papers.

Unnerved, he pushed his chair back abruptly. The castors squeaked slightly.

'Should get Angela to oil that,' she said, nodding at the chair.

Charles watched her silently.

She sank into the chair opposite him, folded her hands on her lap, her pale face raised to him expectantly. 'Thought we were going to get together,' she said softly. 'Soon, you said.'

He felt his body clench with helplessness, sat stiffly in his executive swivel chair, his shoulders pressed back against the padded grey wool.

'You've been busy,' he brought out weakly.

Lily's mouth curved in a smile.

'So have you. Hear Angela's been writing letters. Naughty, naughty.'

'Yes, well,' he said, clearing his throat, 'we've had a word about that.'

'Poor little cow. Probably sobbing into her pillow, nights.' She leaned back against her chair, tilted her head on one side. 'How's Elisabeth? Taken it well, has she?'

He saw then how she had been toying with Angela, like a child intent on a game of make-believe, winding her up and setting her down, watching with rapt fascination her dizzy destructive progress across the nursery floor. It was her way of telling Elisabeth, of making sure she knew because she had guessed, probably rightly, that he would never tell her himself. He felt strangely touched by the childish malice of it, by the trouble she had gone to, and all for him. He said carefully, 'She's fine. Thinks it's just a bit of fun, a schoolgirl crush.'

Lily's eyes flickered in the shadows and he was struck again by her stillness, by that way she had of absorbing light, blotting up movement. He thought of Elisabeth, how restless she was these days, flitting between guilt and resentment, her hands clenching and unclenching in futile fury. His wife's jerky unhappiness exhausted him, made him want to pillow his head in Lily's lap, steal some of that blank indifference. He felt again that sudden clench of helplessness and closed his eyes, his back stiff against the chair.

After a while, he heard her flat, toneless voice. 'And is that what you think,' she said, 'that it's just a bit of fun?'

He opened his eyes, said awkwardly, 'She's unhappy, poor girl –'

'I wasn't talking about Angela.'

'No.' The word escaped on a sigh, an exhalation of defeat, and Charles understood, with a drear sinking of the heart, the answer to his question. How would he cope in a crisis? Why, he would do just what he had done throughout his life. Nothing. The pale oblong of Lily's mouth loomed expectantly in the dim room, her eyebrows twisted in question marks. As the silence settled between them, she seemed to gather herself up, like a woman drawing in her skirts, and he saw contempt dawn like understanding in her eyes. Perhaps it's true then, after all, he thought. I am a disappointing man.

Lily stood up, moved slowly towards the door, stood silhouetted in the light from the corridor. He watched her small, high breasts, the long pale lines of her limbs. 'See ya,' she said, and was gone.

Her absence settled on him like dust.

'Are you in love with her?'

Tom stared at Bella, then his eyes moved past her. 'No,' he said, after a while. 'Not at all.'

'Then why?' she exclaimed.

He looked at her with an expression of almost comic surprise. 'Because she suited what I needed. She's like an empty canvas – no talk of love, no talk of need, no talk of rights.' The words came out with a harshness that surprised both of them.

Bella didn't notice his use of the past tense, didn't notice much at all except for the laboured noise of her own breath as she forced it through stiff lips, determined to have her say, to blurt out what she had come to tell him. 'Before I go,' she said, her voice coming in uneven gasps, 'I just want to say something. I love you very much. I have never stopped loving you since the first day I saw you, standing in the doorway of the painting studio.' She frowned, looked away from him. 'But I'm not sure I have loved you very well.'

He opened his mouth to speak, but she stopped him with a quick movement of her hand. 'Please let me finish. In a way I did blame you when everything went wrong and maybe I was too hard on you but I think,' she smiled bitterly, 'I think that in some ways I worshipped you so when –' she faltered slightly, looked away '– when you had the affair and then the business went wrong, I felt not just that you'd let us both down but that you had become a stranger, someone inhabiting the space where my husband used to be.'

'Up on the pedestal?'

She smiled wryly. 'Oh, I'd say much higher. Mount Olympus.'

Tom was silent.

'I was wrong, of course,' she said with a shaky laugh. 'You weren't a stranger at all, just my husband, stepped down from the Mount, visible suddenly but in sharper focus.'

She picked up her bag, hoisted it onto her shoulder and moved silently to the door. Just as she was about to slip through it Tom said, 'Bella?'

'Yes?'

'Thank you.'

She nodded. 'Just thought you ought to know,' she said stiffly, and walked out, leaving the door to bang on its dodgy hinge.

Thirty-five

'What a ghastly day,' Bella said as they made their way across the grass, soaking their thin leather shoes. The rain, which had been threatening for weeks, had finally come, settling on the shoulders of their black suits and making them shine like patent leather.

'Miserable,' Elisabeth agreed, catching hold of Bella's arm. 'How's Daisy taking it?'

'Remarkably well, considering.' She gazed ahead at the group standing around the grave. 'I suppose I ought to have worn a hat.'

'It is usual.'

'I look so daft in them. Which one is Celia?'

'Over there, standing by the vicar.'

'My god, she's a beauty. Whatever was Alex thinking of?'

'What Alex was always thinking of,' Daisy said, appearing at their side and hugging them. 'I'm so glad you both came.' She was paler then ever, almost translucent, and a faint blue vein throbbed in the hollow of her neck. 'Will you be OK if I abandon you? I feel Celia might need propping up when they get to the ashes-to-ashes bit. I'm afraid it hasn't quite sunk in yet.'

'Well, she's got a good turnout,' Elisabeth said. 'Although I'm not sure Charles will make it. He said something about a meeting.'

'He's here somewhere,' Daisy said vaguely, casting anxious eyes in Celia's direction.

'Where?' Elisabeth stood on tiptoe, peering over the

heads of the crowd. 'Oh, there he is. Thank goodness. Look, and Tom too.'

'Tom?' Bella said faintly.

'Standing just behind him.'

'Oh Lord,' Daisy said, 'I'd better go. Celia's looking distinctly wobbly. We're having drinks later, at her and Alex's flat.' She gave them an address card from a clutch held in her hand. 'Mr and Mrs Alex Carlton' it said in stiff black copperplate. 'St James's. Do try and come. There'll be champagne,' malice briefly touched her voice, 'for the serried ranks of mistresses.'

'Can she be serious?' Elisabeth said, clutching Bella's arm in astonishment but Bella had already turned, pulling to make her way towards Charles and Tom.

They stood with their backs to their wives, heads bent in conversation. Tom's hair had been recently cut, his neck marked by a tidal line of pale, tender skin. He'd put on a black leather jacket, a concession to the occasion, and his oldest, favourite pair of jeans. For comfort, he'd thought as he buttoned them that morning, for safety in a precarious world. From the back he looked like a boy which made Bella remember another time they had all been gathered together to mark an occasion, eighteen years ago at her own wedding. 'The first day of the rest of our lives,' Tom had said, kissing her. Fuck it, Bella thought, catching a glimpse of Celia's white, agonised face. Fuck it all. And what had Alex thought, on the last day of his life? What had he thought as he stared at himself in the mirror, his toothbrush in his mouth, his heart stammering to a last full stop? And what did Celia think when she found him on the bathroom floor, Colgate smeared across his cooling cheek? Did she think, why didn't I tell him how much I love him? Did she wonder why they had wasted so much precious time?

Tom turned, his face cracking in a smile.

'Fuck it,' Bella said, pressing her face to the bony plate of his chest, 'just fuck it all.'

They lined the grave like soldiers on parade, shoulders back, legs stiffened as if against the pull of the earth. Bella glanced down nervously into the gaping pit of the grave. She'd never been to a burial before. Tom shifted beside her, she felt the warmth of his body against her arm, his hand in hers and resisted the temptation to pull him away and run home.

'Well, of all the nerve!' Elisabeth exclaimed, staring at a figure some distance away.

Bella peered in the direction of her gaze. 'Who is it?'

'Lily.'

'She wouldn't.'

'Well, she has. I always said that girl had no shame.'

'No, you didn't,' Bella retorted, somewhat sharply. 'You said she was merely naive.'

They watched as Lily moved slowly across the grass, picking her way round the tombstones in teetering, unsuitable shoes. When she got to the fringes of the group, she sidled her way through the press of bodies, emerged opposite them, her needle heels sinking in a furrow of fresh earth. She fixed them with black eyes, her mouth curved in a small, amused smile. Elisabeth felt Charles stiffen at her side, and then he clasped his hands together and bowed his head, as if in prayer. Bella glanced up at Tom, was relieved to discover that he was staring fixedly at the skyline, at a point some way above Lily's head.

Elisabeth peered down the line of bodies that fringed the grave, then nudged Bella. 'Has Daisy seen her?'

'Hope not,' Bella said doubtfully. Lily, who was wearing a large and inappropriate cartwheel hat of black lacquered straw and a simple, black sleeveless dress that looked as though it had cost the earth, was not easy to miss. Elisabeth glared across the grave. 'What does she think she looks like? You'd think she'd have the sense to slink in quietly and hide at the back. God knows what Celia thinks. And as for bare arms at a funeral –'

'Well, I hope she's not coming to the reception.'

'Even she wouldn't, surely?'

But she did, walked in to Celia's mellow cream sitting-room wearing her absurd black hat, helped herself to champagne and asparagus rolls and stood by herself, smiling and aloof, bang in the middle of the room.

'Shameless,' Elisabeth hissed, huddling further into the group as if for protection. None of them looked directly at Lily, their consciousness of her presence mirrored only in the shift and slide of their eyes.

'He was so young,' Elisabeth mourned. 'I feel so guilty now, for laughing about that panic attack. It must have been the real thing, after all; a warning of sorts.'

'I suppose it proves he had a heart,' Bella murmured. 'I often wondered about that.'

'Oh, he wasn't so bad,' Elisabeth said indulgently, 'not really. At least he was honest, wasn't a dissembler.'

'No,' Tom said, 'nobody could call him that.'

'He had spirit too.' Elisabeth's voice rose, two bright spots of colour flamed in her cheeks. Her gaze shifted to Charles and away. 'Nobody could accuse *him* of subsiding feebly into middle age.'

Charles turned on his heel. 'I'm going to get a drink.'

'I mean fifty's not old, is it?' Elisabeth continued, her voice carrying after Charles. 'Not really. It's all in the mind. We're really only as old as we allow ourselves to be. After all, just look at –'

'Elisabeth,' Tom said, 'shut up.'

She jerked back, affronted, and then her shoulders sagged. 'If only I could,' she said wearily.

Charles found Lily in the dining-room, posed like a mannequin against a magnificent fireplace.

'Watcha,' she said, raising her glass.

'You look very becoming.'

'Elisabeth thinks I look like a dog's dinner.'

'A very becoming dog's dinner.'

Lily smiled. 'You all right then?'

Charles dropped his eyes, stared down into his empty glass. 'I'm sorry,' he murmured.

'Least you don't pretend to be something you're not,' Lily said, in her harsh, flat voice. 'Not like the rest of them.'

'They're all right,' he said quietly.

She shrugged. 'If you say so.' Her dark eyes settled on him. 'You staying with her then?'

'I don't know.'

Lily gazed at him. 'Bit your trouble that, isn't it?' she said, but her tone was unusually gentle.

Charles smiled briefly. 'What about you? What are you going to do?'

'Dunno. Won't be coming back to the office, mind.'

'No, I didn't think you would.'

They stood in silence watching the groups of people in the far room shift and re-form, like the patterns in a child's kaleidoscope.

'Well, better be getting back,' Charles said after a while. 'Elisabeth will be wondering where I've got to.'

'Can't have that,' Lily said, turning to the mirror, rearranging the tilt of her hat. Her back was to Charles, who watched her in silence.

'Would you have come away with me?' he asked, after a while.

She did not turn around. 'Now you'll never know.'

A spasm of pain distorted his face and then he turned, made his way across the polished parquet floor, his hands shoved deep in his pockets. As he pushed through the crowd gathered in the main room, a woman happened to glance up, stare full into his face, recoiled slightly at the grim determination she saw mirrored there. Affects us all in different ways, she thought, staring after his retreating back.

Elisabeth drew Daisy to one side. 'What's *she* doing here?'

Daisy followed her gaze, over to Lily. 'Celia invited her.'

'Celia? His own wife!'

Daisy peered at Elisabeth through myopic blue eyes. 'Really, Elisabeth, sometimes you are the most absurdly pompous woman,' she said, and wandered off, plucking a glass of champagne from a tray as she went. Elisabeth stared after her in astonishment, then consoled herself with the thought that grief does strange things to people. 'Beside herself,' she murmured, to no one in particular.

'I'm so very sorry,' Bella said to Celia.

Alex's widow gave a glimmer of a smile. 'Me too.'

Bella shuffled awkwardly. 'Well –' she began and found that she couldn't think of a thing to say. 'Well –' Her voice appeared to be stuck, like a needle in a groove. Lovely champagne, she thought wildly, vintage is it? Beautiful suit, you should wear black more often. She stared around her, frantically searching for inspiration. 'What an amazing number of women,' she exclaimed suddenly, 'hardly any men at all. Mind you, I don't suppose Alex would have known many –' Her voice faltered as she realised what she had just said but Celia was smiling, a wide, genuine smile this time. 'I went through his address book, rounded them all up. He would have been appalled, don't you think? Wouldn't have seen him for dust –' Her voice trailed off and she laughed rather wildly. 'Oh dear, that was most inappropriate. Ghastly, isn't it, the things that come out of one's mouth at funerals? I will keep on saying things like I'm dead tired. I don't even know I'm doing it until I notice everyone around me curling up like dying flowers. Oh, God, I've gone and done it again –'

'What did you think, when you found him?'

Celia stopped, open-mouthed, and then her eyes filled with tears.

'I'm sorry, I should never have asked anything so stupid. Please forgive me, I didn't mean –'

'It's the first sensible question anybody's asked me all day,' Celia said briskly, blinking back tears. 'Actually, my very first thought was how absolutely furious he'd be when he found out he was dead.'

Thirty-six

'You'll be off then,' said Mrs Flower, arms crossed over her capacious bosom.

'Looks like it.'

'Reckon you'll not be needing me to say take care.'

Lily's eyes slid past her. 'Reckon not.'

'Back to your young man, is it?'

'Maybe. Maybe not.'

Mrs Flower plunged a hand into her cardigan, rummaged around in her front, her hand moving under the grey wool like a cat under a blanket. 'Thought for a minute I'd lost it,' she said, withdrawing a thin brown envelope and presenting it to Lily with a flourish. 'Left it for you, he did. Said to give it to you when the time was right.'

Lily took the envelope, peered inside. 'What's this?' she asked, taking out a sheaf of used notes.

'Money for your fare home,' Mrs Flower said, smacking her lips together in a firm line.

Lily shook her head. 'Still thinks I'm a kid.'

'Just looking out for you, that's all. Can't do better than that for a person.'

'Think he's daft, don't you?'

'Not for me to say, lovely,' Mrs Flower said, shaking her head. 'Takes us all in different ways, it does.'

Lily counted the money carefully, snapped it shut in her black bag and picked up a large black straw hat. She handed it to Mrs Flower.

'What's this then?' the old woman said, staring at it in wonder.

'Thought you might like to have it. Won't be much good to me, not where I'm going.'

Mrs Flower's dainty white hand inched forward, fingered the glossy straw caressingly. 'Nor to me,' she said wistfully.

'Could wear it for tea,' Lily said, a smile glimmering briefly in the pale oval of her face.

Mrs Flower chuckled, took the hat and perched it on her head. 'Royal, I feel,' she declared.

'Like a duchess,' Tom said approvingly, descending the rickety staircase and coming to a stop in front of them. A rucksack was hoisted on his back; the three jackets he wore, buttoned each over the other, made him look strangely fat. 'Wouldn't fit in my bag,' he explained, catching their curious glances.

''Bout time you got a bit of flesh on them bones,' Mrs Flower said, heaving herself over to him and planting a kiss on his cheek. 'Mind me hat,' she said, clutching possessively at the brim which tilted precariously under the embrace. Her brown eyes twinkled approvingly. 'You'll be off home, will you?'

'Yes,' he said, awkwardly, glancing over at Lily. Her blank eyes rested on his face for a fleeting moment, then she turned and picked up a large suitcase, so new it still bore the manufacturer's label. 'See ya,' she said, pulling open the front door and slipping noiselessly through it.

Tom stood motionless, staring after her, his long arms hanging at his sides. After a while, Mrs Flower put her dainty white hands to his shoulders and propelled him across the shabby lino. 'Off you go,' she said, opening the door and herding him through it with her large, soft body.

Tom stood on the doorstep, staring up at her. 'What did you say to her?' he asked, after a while.

Mrs Flower tilted her hat rakishly, folded her arms across the pillow of her breasts. 'Go home,' she said firmly.

Thirty-seven

Tom found her in the kitchen, sitting where he had left her three months before, in the same chair, still staring at the lurid lino.

'I thought,' he said, 'that it's about time we got round to replacing that floor.'

Bella looked up. 'Oh, I don't know. I've grown sort of fond of it.'

'You don't mind, then?'

She shook her head, and he noticed how the frizz of curls quivered like a halo around her face, and how much he'd been missing that tiny, shimmering movement.

'I painted the bedroom,' she said, 'put up some shelves.' She paused, looked away. 'I thought you might need some space for all your architectural books. They're still in their boxes, behind the sofa in the sitting-room. I would have sorted them for you, but I wasn't sure how you'd want them arranged; by name or subject.'

He was silent for a while, then he asked, 'What colour are the walls?'

She pulled a face. 'White.'

He sat down at the kitchen table, traced a finger across the ghostly white circles left by a hundred cups of hot coffee. 'Good,' he said, 'then we can hang some of your paintings too.'

She reached her hand across the table, palm up. He laid his on top of it, let it lie there for a moment, then picked up her hand and pressed its coolness against his tired eyes.

Elisabeth heard the sound of rattling keys and walked into the hallway. Charles looked up in astonishment to find her there, then glanced away, his face closing in on itself. Extracting the key from the lock, he turned away from her, placing it carefully on the Georgian side-table.

Elisabeth moved towards him as if to help him take off his raincoat. Ignoring her, he removed it and hung it carefully on the old hatstand.

'Lily's gone,' she said, her voice sounding harsh in the still hallway.

He glanced at her briefly, moved past her in a wide arc, allowing her the sort of space with which one distances a stranger. 'I know.'

She addressed his back. 'Bella called this afternoon. Tom's back at home.' A curious note of pleading entered her voice. 'She sounded so – normal, I suppose. It's almost as if none of it ever happened.'

'A chimera,' he said, 'a fool's paradise.'

'What do you mean?' Her voice rose in panic. '*What*?'

His answer was his retreating back. She stood for a moment, feeling panic rise and clutch at her throat. Now that Lily had gone, everything should be better, shouldn't it. Shouldn't it? Why then did she feel the ground shifting beneath her feet, the abyss snapping at her ankles? Uttering a cry, she ran into the kitchen. Empty. She wheeled around, hurried into the sitting-room where she found him standing motionless, staring out at the grey, rain-sodden garden, a tumbler of whisky in his hand.

'Peculiar summer we've had this year,' he said after a while, 'all that sun and now, this rain.'

She said carefully, panting slightly from her exertion, 'I feel that I've scarcely noticed.'

He looked over his shoulder at her. 'Really?' he said, his voice polite. 'I think that I shall remember it very well.'

'Charles?'

He turned to face her. 'Yes?'

'You're not –' she took a deep breath '– not going after her, are you?'

He stared at her for a while, then shook his head and turned away, looking back to the rain-spattered lawn.

She moved across the room, went up behind him, laid her cheek against his shoulder. 'Can we start again?'

She felt his shoulders twitch impatiently. 'I scarcely think we stopped.'

'Then can we just forget everything that's happened,' she said, 'put it all behind us?'

He said nothing, lifted the glass to his mouth, drank mechanically. Her cheek was still pressed against him, she sensed the creak of muscles and sinews working inside his back, pressed her mouth against the solid reality of him, almost wept at the familiarity of it. 'Do you love me?' she asked impetuously.

He moved away from her, turned to stare. 'Does it make any difference what I feel?'

'Yes,' she cried in astonishment. 'Yes, of course it does.'

His shoulders sagged defeatedly. 'It doesn't seem to have made much difference so far,' he said quietly.

She looked at him uncertainly. 'You don't mean that.'

He looked at her. 'Don't I? For the past five years I feel I have been tolerated.' He shrugged. 'Not loved, not even much liked, just tolerated.'

'That's not true.'

He looked at her, his face serious. 'I bore you, don't I?'

'No.'

'You think I am not –' he paused, stumbling in his mind for the words '– that I'm not a passionate man.'

'No,' she cried, 'no, of course I don't.'

He looked at her sadly. 'Poor Elisabeth, I have always been a disappointment to you.'

'It's not that,' she cried, desperation rising in her voice. 'It's marriage – marriage that's sometimes disappointing.

You can't expect it always to be good, it's the nature of it, those great tracts of boredom.'

'The nature of a good marriage,' he said with quiet emphasis, 'is accepting the boredom, just as one accepts the disappointments with as much equanimity as one celebrates the triumphs.'

'Triumphs?' she echoed.

'Every life has its triumphs, however small.'

'Even Lily's?' she said, with a small flash of malice.

He looked at her with interest. 'Why do you say that?'

'She seemed so –' she shrugged '– so unaffected, I suppose. She moved through us like a force of nature, causing devastation in her wake.'

'I think we may have done that all by ourselves.'

'So she is to bear none of the blame?'

'Can you blame someone who is emotionally absent? I think, because she has no moral centre, that she's like a mirror, reflecting our desires, good and bad, back at ourselves.'

'Of course,' she said bitterly, 'you would take her side.'

He looked at her strangely. 'Side?' he said. 'There are no sides, only the responsibility of our own actions, our own lives.'

'Were you in love with her?'

Charles stared at her and she noticed for the first time how haggard he had become. 'I have no idea,' he said quietly.

'But you must,' Elisabeth cried. 'You must know.'

He looked at her strangely. 'Why must I?' he said quietly. 'Did you, when you married me?'

'Let's not fight,' she said quickly. 'Not when Alex has just died. I kept thinking that it might have been you, like that, without warning.'

'And did you think how easy that would be? How nice and tidy and blameless a solution?'

'Charles!' she said, blushing at the truth.

'No need to look so stricken. It's what we all think, at one time or other. Those little gremlins that leap, unbidden, to our minds and whisper malice. Or, perhaps, truth.' He looked at her kindly. 'It's nothing to be ashamed of.'

She looked away. 'It's nothing to admit to either,' she said in a low voice. 'Why are you saying these things?'

'Alex, I suppose. I've been wondering lately, what there is to keep us here.'

'To keep us?' she echoed incredulously. 'What about our life, this house, the children.'

A spasm of pain distorted his face. 'Yes,' he said heavily, 'the children.' He looked bleak. 'And us? What about us?'

'Us?'

'Yes, Elisabeth,' he said, his voice suddenly harsh. 'Us.'

'But I love you.'

'What does that mean?'

'What are you saying?' she said, her voice rising on a note of panic. 'It means – I love you.'

He shook his head sadly. 'No, you don't. You never have, really. It's only the idea of me you love, the exterior rather than the interior man. The one who goes with the life, the house, the children.'

'That's not true,' she cried, shrinking from him.

He looked at her tenderly. 'I know how hard you've tried.'

Elisabeth felt panic claw at her throat. 'Why did you never say any of this before?'

He looked at her sadly. 'What was there to say?'

She was silent for a while. 'All this is Lily's fault,' she said eventually. 'We were fine before she came. All of us. Perfectly fine.'

He stared at her, his gaze blank.

'Are you going to her?' she cried. 'Is that what you're saying?'

He looked away. 'No. Lily was just a foolish interlude, a

sort of buried yearning after –' He shrugged. 'Anyway, it's passed now.'

'What are you going to do?'

Charles stared out at the sodden garden. 'I don't know.'

Jim looked up. 'You're back, then.'

Lily nodded, put her suitcase down cautiously but kept hold of her coat, clutched in both hands.

He turned away from her, stared at the television. A game show was playing. 'Took your time.'

'Needed to have a bit of a think.'

Jim picked up a can of beer, tipped it to his mouth. She watched his Adam's apple bobbing.

'What happened to your fancy friends?'

'Nothing much. Same as ever, they were, when I left. Same as everybody else.'

Jim drank beer silently.

'Shall I hang my coat in the cupboard?'

He did not look at her. 'If you like,' he said after a while.

Going out to the hallway, a narrow space painted magnolia white, Lily hung her coat neatly above the Dustbuster.